"No, you don't, sister, this is my claim!"

"No, it's mine, you cheap tinhorn!" Lacey glared back at the tall, broad-shouldered man and began to pound her stake in the ground.

"Listen, I've got big plans for this lot."

"So do I, and I'm not about to give it up." She wiped her hands on her dusty dark skirt and glared up at him. She was tall for a woman, but he was taller by more than a head, and some women might think him handsome.

He frowned at her. "What does a gal need a lot for? Your husband not providin' for you?"

A Texas drawl. She might have known. Lacey glared back. "I am not married," she replied with ice in her voice. "Now get off my claim!"

Her accent told him she was a Texan, too. And the most stubborn, annoying female he'd ever met. He had a strong male urge to yank her up and spank her backside, but he knew that to win this fuss, he must hold his temper and use his charm. He smiled at her, took off his hat, and made a sweeping bow.

"I am Blackie O'Neal, lately of Del Rio, and you are—?"

"Don't waste your sleazy charm on me. If you were a gentleman, you'd let me have the claim."

"Well," Blackie grinned and touched the brim of his hat in salute. "I'll see you in Guthrie to register with the land office—if you can find a way to get there."

Lacey watched the Texan saunter away, furious with his confidence. Why, he was like a rooster that thought the sun came up because he crowed. Since he was a man and a Texan, naturally, he thought he'd alrady bested her. Outrageous. Well, she wasn't ready to yell "calf rope" yet.

Also by Georgina Gentry

TO TEMPT
A TEXAN

Georgina Gentry

Kensington Publishing Corp.

http://www.kensingtonbooks.com

ZEBRA BOOKS are published by

Kensington Publishing Corp.
850 Third Avenue
New York, NY 10022

All Kensington titles, imprints and distributed lines are available at special quantity discounts for bulk purchases for sales
promotion, premiums, fund-raising, educational or institutional
use.

Special book excerpts or customized printings can also be created to fit specific needs. For details, write or phone the office
of the Kensington Special Sales Manager: Kensington Publishing Corp., 850 Third Avenue, New York, NY 10022. Attn.
Special Sales Department. Phone: 1-800-221-2647.

First Printing: February 2005
10 9 8 7 6 5 4 3 2 1

Printed in the United States of America

This story is dedicated to the memory of Nanitta Daisey, the feisty lady reporter for the *Dallas Morning News* and the *Fort Worth Gazette*, who actually rode the cowcatcher of a train into the Oklahoma Land Rush and jumped off to stake her claim right here in my hometown of Edmond.

And to the memory of a movie star and *real* man, Clark Gable. Old Rhett Butler would have felt right at home playing my gambler, Blackie O'Neal,

And finally, to the memory of the real Lively, a lazy hound that only moved when someone said "dog biscuit."

Prologue

Lacey Van Schuyler Durango has been reared by her aunt and uncle down in the Texas hill country between Austin and San Antonio. Prim, uptight Lacey is an ambitious newspaper woman who has no time and no use for men and with good reason. She's also the national president of the Ladies' Temperance Association. With her cat, Precious, Lacey is riding a train to the Oklahoma land rush with plans to stake a claim and start her own newspaper. She and her L.T.A. ladies plan to mount a crusade to keep this new town dry, figuring if there're no saloons, the town won't attract disreputable rogues.

Speaking of disreputable rogues, enter Blackie O'Neal. Blackie's a charming Texas rascal who could talk a dog off a meat wagon. This handsome scoundrel has already been run out of half the towns in the Lone Star state. Think Rhett Butler, only more so. On a fine chestnut stallion, followed by his lazy hound dog, Lively, Blackie is galloping into this new settlement with plans to build a fancy saloon and bordello, Blackie's Black Garter. Unfortunately, the lot he's racing to grab is the very same land that our Texas temperance leader is about to claim for her newspaper office. Uh-oh . . . .

Chapter One

Monday afternoon, April 22, 1889, the Unassigned Lands of Indian Territory.

Lacey clung to the cowcatcher of the moving train as the scenery rushed past.

My word! This damn-fool, outrageous stunt was going to get her killed. Worse than that, it was blowing her hair and smudging her perfect white shirtwaist. Lacey Van Schuyler Durango had never done anything so outrageous. Well, maybe twice . . .

She wouldn't think about that now. It was all she could do to hang on and keep from falling under the churning wheels of this racing locomotive. The wind whipped her hair loose and caught her dark blue skirts, making them billow so that her white bloomers showed. So very unladylike!

Would most ladies be clinging to the front of a moving locomotive anyway? Certainly not. And to think she had bribed the engineer to let her ride up here. The fumes from the engine choked her and, beneath her feet, the cross ties raced by as she clung both to the iron cowcatcher and her claim stake and hammer. Lacey was only too aware that if she loosened her grip, she might fall beneath the train. The thought was frightening, thinking of what a mess she would be when they found the body; so undignified and dirty. Instead, Lacey concentrated on looking up ahead as the site of that new, nameless town came into view. It was a hodgepodge huddle of tents, dusty, lopsided shacks, people arriving in wagons with a few riders galloping into town to stake a land claim.

So untidy, but she would change all that. Yes, she would. Emboldened by new resolve, Lacey hung on to the cowcatcher as it chugged along the track. Yes, she would help change this pitiful settlement into a perfect town for the Ladies' Temperance Association to populate. They'd made no mistake when they'd elected her president.

The train was slowing now as it neared the scattering of tents and hurrying people. Up here on the cowcatcher, she'd be first off the crowded train, a distinct advantage in staking a claim to a choice lot for her newspaper, the *Crusader.* She clasped her wooden stake and hammer tightly and searched the horizon, trying to choose a lot before the train chugged to a halt.

Ah, yes, there was a choice corner lot in the center of this nameless settlement. It would be a perfect place to build her newspaper office. Even before the train came to a complete stop, Lacey hiked up her skirts, jumped off the cowcatcher and ran as fast as her long legs could carry her.

Galloping into town on his fine, chestnut stallion, with his bloodhound, Lively, following behind, gambler Blackie O'Neal's dark gaze searched the town site for the perfect location for the big saloon and bordello he planned to build here. Ah, up ahead lay a prize corner lot right downtown. It would be an excellent site for Blackie's Black Garter. Out of the corner of his eye as he rode, Blackie saw a train chugging into town. Great God Almighty, he had to beat that train. It would be full of eager settlers racing to stake claims. He urged his lathered horse to run faster.

What was that ridiculous sight? A woman, yes, it was a

woman clinging to the cowcatcher of that locomotive. Was she loco? All he could see was wildly blowing dark hair, billowing skirts, and white lace bloomers. At that moment, his horse stumbled and fell, throwing Blackie into the dirt. Lively loped up and licked his face.

Cursing, Blackie scrambled to his feet, grabbed up his wooden claim stake, checked to make sure his horse was okay, then began to run. The woman was off the cowcatcher now, holding her skirts high as she ran. What did that crazy female thinking she was doing? Her husband must be loco to put up with a damn fool like that.

Abruptly Blackie realized the woman was running toward the same lot he was. Surely she wasn't going to stake a claim? He realized as he ran that that's exactly what she was planning to do and on *his* lot. He renewed his speed, but he was out of shape and puffing. Cigars and late-night card games did nothing to improve one's athletic ability, and it had been awhile since he'd worked a ranch. But he was a Texan. Surely he could outrun a woman.

They met in the middle of the prize lot at a dead heat, she looking as surprised as he felt.

"No, you don't, sister, this is my claim!"

"No, it's mine, you cheap tinhorn!" Lacey glared back at the tall, broad-shouldered man and began to pound her stake in the ground. After risking her life to get this free land, she wasn't about to be bluffed out of it by some arrogant rascal.

He muttered a curse and began to pound his own stake into the dirt with the butt of his six-shooter. "Listen, sister, I've got big plans for this lot."

"So do I, and I'm not about to give it up." She wiped her hands on her dusty dark skirt and glared up at him. She was tall for a woman, but he was taller by more than a head, and some women might think him handsome. He paused now, put one dirty black boot up on his stake and tipped his Stetson hat back.

He frowned at her, a masculine and suntanned brute

of a man as he lit a cigarillo. "What does a gal need a lot for? Your husband not providin' for you?" A Texas drawl. She might have known.

Lacey glared back. He was a rogue, she was sure of it by the way he dressed. The flat black hat, the string tie, the bright silk vest and a diamond ring on his little finger. "I am not married," she replied with ice in her voice. "Now get off my claim, you cheap tinhorn."

He shook the match out and took a puff. "Listen, sister—"

"I am not your sister, thank God."

He grinned at her with easy charm. She knew his type immediately. *God's gift to women.* Or so he thought. "I tell you what I'll do, sweetheart—"

"I'm not your sweetheart, either." She didn't budge an inch as he grinned and smoked.

"Well, hell, you're certainly no lady, comin' in like that with your skirts blowin' and your underpants showin'—"

"A gentleman would not mention that." My word, she must look a mess, but there was no mirror to check, although she did make a vain effort to push her hair back. "Don't try to sweet-talk me, you rattlesnake."

He grinned in that superior way that made her want to smack him. "Sister, I never claimed to be a gentleman. Now I know it's futile to talk reason with a female, but I reckon the little millinery shop or bakery you're plannin' could just as easily be built on some side street—"

"You arrogant pig, I intend to build a newspaper right here on this land."

"A newspaper? You?" He looked baffled.

She took a deep breath, proud of herself that she didn't hit him with her hammer. It would be so undignified to be arrested right here on Main Street. Okay, so some women might think him attractive, but he wasn't perfect. His ears were a bit too big and he had one slightly crooked front tooth. "My word, you can read, can't you? I'll bet the only reading you ever do is a deck of marked cards."

Blackie felt himself flush and took a deep breath as he holstered his pistol. Her accent told him she was a Texan, too. This dusty, untidy mess of a gal was the most stubborn, annoying female he'd ever met. He had a strong male urge to yank her up and spank her backside, but he knew that to win this fuss, he must hold his temper and use his charm. Women told him he could talk a dog off a meat wagon. Would it work for a Texas bitch?

He smiled at her, thinking she wasn't bad looking for a woman, although it was hard to tell with that dark hair a tangled mop and her face smudged by smoke from the train that was now pulling out. "We've gotten off to a bad start here, Miss." He took off his hat and made a sweeping bow. "I am Blackie O'Neal, lately of Del Rio, and you are?"

"None of your business." The girl snapped back. "Don't waste your sleazy charm on me. If you were a gentleman, you'd let me have the claim."

He started to tell her again that she was no lady, not when she rode into town on the cowcatcher of a train with her skirts billowing and her bloomers showing. Since she was a Texan, that meant she might be as stubborn as he was himself. "Suppose I go look after my horse, Miss, and then I'll buy you some dinner and we'll talk about this."

She shook her head. "I don't think so."

Well, damn. Even though she looked like she'd been ridden hard and put up wet, she still had full, round curves and she might be pretty under all that soot. If he could get a few drinks in her and an hour to sweet-talk her, he'd not only get the land, he'd enjoy an hour's entertainment besides. "Perhaps I could buy your claim from you."

"What if I buy your claim from you?"

"No. I need that land worse than you do." He was out of patience and very hot and tired. This gal was different, and he didn't like it. He was used to getting his way with women. This one was not only savvy, she was too smart. Blackie didn't like smart women, he liked eager ones. "All right, sister, we seem to be in a Mexican standoff. So now what do we do?"

In answer, she hailed a passing settler. "Hey, Mister, how do I legalize this claim?"

"*My* claim," Blackie corrected, but she paid him no heed.

The settler was a worn old farmer. He took off his straw hat and wiped his sweaty brow. "No land office here." He pointed north. "Got to go up to Guthrie to register your claim."

"Guthrie?" The girl said, "how far is that?"

"'Bout five miles."

Blackie grinned as the farmer ambled away. The train had just pulled out in a cloud of smoke and the sooty girl turned and stared after it.

"Well," Blackie grinned and touched the brim of his hat in salute. "I'll see you in Guthrie—if you can find a way to get there."

He turned and sauntered away to where his horse grazed on the grass at the edge of the dirt main street. Lively, the bloodhound, had lain down next to the horse and dropped off to sleep, which was always what Lively did best. This stubborn gal wasn't going to be any problem after all. Just like most women, she couldn't play when the stakes were high, she didn't have the brains or the cunning, even if she was a Texas gal.

Blackie mounted up and turned his stallion north. The chestnut took two halting steps. Immediately, Blackie dismounted, everything else forgotten in his concern for his horse. "What's the matter, boy? Hurt a hoof in that fall?"

After a moment's inspection, he decided the stallion was temporarily lame. What to do? He hailed a passing freckle-faced boy. "Hey, sonny, if I pay you, you reckon you could find my horse some water and some good hay? I need someone to look after him until I get back."

The boy nodded. "Sure thing, Mister."

Blackie wiped his sweating face. He'd like a cold drink himself. "Any place I can rent a horse around here?"

The boy shook his head as he took the chestnut's reins. "My folks came with a team of oxen pullin' our wagon. There ain't a spare horse in the entire camp."

"We'll see about that. I'll be back for my horse later." Blackie loved a challenge. Followed by the lazy hound, Blackie started down the dusty street, stopping to ask about renting a horse. The boy had been right; there wasn't a spare horse or a fresh one in the settlement. Finally a cowboy pointed out a makeshift shack down the road. "I think Clem might have a horse and rig he'd rent out."

"Much obliged." Blackie grinned and started down the road. His luck was running good, as usual. By tonight, he'd be the legal owner of that choice lot and have the new saloon under construction by the time Moose, his bartender, and Flo and her girls arrived.

Lacey watched the Texan saunter away, furious with his confidence. Why, he was like a rooster that thought the sun came up in the morning because he crowed. Since he was a man and a Texan, naturally he thought he'd already bested her. Outrageous. Well, she wasn't ready to yell "calf rope" yet; the Texas term for "surrender." She ran to the temporary depot and saw that Isaac, her printer, was unloading the equipment and the crate with Precious in it. "There's been a hitch," she said to the short, balding man. "I'll take Precious with me because you will be too busy to look after her. You see if you can find a temporary place to set up our offices."

He paused in unloading the boxes and said in his thick foreign accent. "You didn't get a claim, yes?"

Lacey sighed. "Sort of. If I can get to Guthrie in time to file it."

"Whatever I can do to help, Miss Lacey, for you, anything."

"I'm much obliged, Isaac." Her mind was already busy.

Damned if she was going to let that rogue gambler best her, but she'd seen he had a good horse.

She grabbed the cat carrier and the white Persian meowed in protest. "Now, Precious, dear, I know things are hectic, but when we get to Guthrie, I'll get you some food."

How was she going to get to Guthrie? There seemed to be hundreds of people milling about or brushing past her, all intent on their own business. "It might be just dusty shacks now, but it can be a perfect town; and I'll help mold it."

The train had pulled out while she was arguing with that cheap tinhorn. Maybe she could rent a mount instead. Lacey started asking up and down the street. There were no horses available. She couldn't let that gambler claim that prize lot. Why, it was right downtown and a perfect place for her newspaper office. She'd been elected president of the Ladies' Temperance Association because she was so resourceful. Where had the Texas tinhorn gone? She'd lost sight of the rogue. Maybe he was already on his way to Guthrie. Well, she wasn't going to give up without a fight.

As she trudged along carrying her indignant cat, Lacey passed a horse trough and stared down at her reflection. My word. No wonder she hadn't made any impression on that silver-tongued devil, she looked like she'd been dragged around under the porch by hound dogs. Lacey always kept her appearance perfect. Now she couldn't even wash her face. Oh, the horror of being dirty. "First things first, Lacey," she reminded herself. She dipped a palm in the water to give Precious a drink. Still carrying her cat cage, she stopped a passing army sergeant. "Sir, do you know of any way to get to Guthrie?"

He smiled, touched the brim of his hat. "Why, ma'am, there's a train tomorrow."

She felt tears of frustration gather in her dark eyes. "I can't wait until tomorrow, I'm trying to file a claim."

Immediately, his ruddy face turned sympathetic. "Tough for a little lady in this big world, huh?"

She resisted the urge to give him a good kick between the thighs. Instead, she let the tears run down her cheeks. "It certainly is, sir, and a helpless woman like poor little me just doesn't know what to do next."

He chewed his lip then pointed. "See that corral over there with the new barn? It delivers supplies up to Guthrie for the army. Maybe he'd rent you a rig or something."

"Oh, Captain," she sighed and fluttered her eyelashes, "you're so wonderful."

"I'm a sergeant, Ma'am, but being's you're a gal, I don't expect you to know the difference."

It was a good thing she had left the hammer with Isaac. She managed to grit her teeth and thanked him again, then hurried toward the corral, carrying her cat cage. Inside, the white Persian set up a howl. "Do be quiet, Precious, when we get to Guthrie, I'll see if I can buy you some fish."

She found a lean, weathered man loading crates of squawking chickens on a wagon.

"I need to get to Guthrie."

He laughed and paused, wiping his face with a ragged red bandana. "You and about ten thousand other folks, Ma'am. Even my regular driver has run off to get a land claim. Lucky for me, a gambler who said his horse was lame offered to drive this load of chickens up to Guthrie to feed the troops. I can't leave to do it."

A gambler. She tried to look helpless, although it galled her. "A tall Texan with dark hair? Oh, that's my husband." The thought made her shudder.

He nodded. "Why didn't you say so, Ma'am? He went off to get hisself a drink, said he'd be back about the time I got loaded out."

A drink. Of course the rascal was a whiskey-swilling sponge. "You see, there's been a change of plans. My husband told me to drive your wagon up to Guthrie. He'll come later."

The man looked at her and then at the wagonload of squawking chickens. "I don't know, ma'am. You ever drive a wagon before?"

"My word, are you joking? Why, on our farm, I used to drive loads of hay into town all the time."

He nodded. "All right then. You see these chickens get to Captain MacArthur, you hear?"

"I certainly will." She put her cat cage up on the front seat, clambered up beside it, took the reins. "I'll get your wagon back to you as soon as the soldiers get it unloaded. Which way to Guthrie?"

"North. Just follow the road." He smiled, pointed and stepped back.

Lacey slapped the reins on the dozing bay horse and started north on the dusty road.

"Meow!" complained Precious.

"I'm sorry, kitty," Lacey said as she urged the horse to step a little faster, "I can't do anything about you until I get to Guthrie."

"Squawk!" said the chickens, "Squawk! Squawk!"

"Meow! Meow!" yowled Precious.

This was going to be a long trip, Lacey decided, but it was the only way she had. Better than that, she'd beaten that Blackie O'Neal at his own game. It made her smile to think about it. In the meantime, it upset her to look a mess and that she was driving a ridiculous rig with chicken feathers leaving a trail behind her. Lacey always perfectly planned everything and she had come to this. Thank God, nobody from home (especially Homer) was around to see her making a spectacle of herself.

Resolutely, she kept driving. Her cat never stopped howling, nor did the chickens stop squawking. The afternoon was promising to be pure hell. The only thing that kept her going was the prize that awaited her when she got that deed registered. Well, there was something else. She grinned as she imagined the gambler showing up to drive the wagon only to discover he'd been out-smarted and out-maneuvered. If that rascal wanted to get to Guthrie, he'd have to walk and he was wearing boots. "Walk" was a dirty four-letter word to most Texans and in high-heeled cowboy boots, it would be painful. She hoped he got blisters on his blisters.

She'd gone only about a mile when from behind she heard a loping horse, and a man's deep voice yelled, "There she is!" She recognized that Texas drawl without even turning her head and whipped up her horse, but the rider was gaining. She glanced up as Blackie, riding double with some cowboy, galloped up and dismounted, running to grab her reins. "Of all the lowdown, dirty tricks!"

Lacey stood up and slashed at him with her whip. Blackie grabbed it and jerked, Lacey lost her balance. The dog, scampering about and barking, ran behind Blackie, tripped him, and the gambler fell. Lacey tum-bled out of the wagon, landing on top of him. The good-natured bloodhound promptly scampered up and licked her face with a long, wet tongue. The crates of chickens set up an ungodly squawking and feathers drifted. Precious meowed.

The young cowboy leaned on his saddlehorn. "Mister, that's no way to treat your wife."

"His wife?" She lay on Blackie and stared in horror into his grinning face. Now she regretted not keeping the hammer. Lacey managed to sit up and push the dog away. Before she could say anything else, that rascal was getting up, dusting himself off and turning on the charm to the cowboy. "Oh, it's just a mistake. We had a little spat and she went off and left me, but everything's fine now, isn't it, sweetheart?"

"Don't call me sweetheart." Lacey stumbled to her feet, dusting off her skirts. "You lowdown polecat."

"See?" Blackie grinned to the cowboy, "Isn't she a typical Texas gal? Sweetheart, you shouldn't have left me."

The cowboy looked uncertain and Lacey was suddenly afraid for him. If he attempted to interfere, she had no doubt the big Texan could wipe up the dirt with him. Blackie looked like he'd won many a saloon brawl.

"Never mind, cowboy," she said, "we'll work this out ourselves. You can go." As soon as he was out of sight, she intended to grab that whip, beat the Texan senseless, then take off with the wagon.

"If you say so, ma'am." The cowboy touched the brim of his hat with two fingers in a polite gesture, turned his horse and started back toward the nameless town. They both watched him go.

When he was far enough away, Lacey made a sudden dive, grabbed the whip, and ran for the rig. Unfortunately, the good-natured hound galloped with her and she tripped and fell over him, landing sprawling in the dirt. "My word! This is outrageous!" Lacey scrambled to her feet and tried to climb up in the rig.

"Meow!" protested Precious. The hound, discovering the cat, ran about the wagon barking which set both the cat and the chickens off again.

"*Hush, Lively!* No, you don't, sister!" The gambler grabbed at her and came away with a piece of her smudged shirtwaist, leaving her lace camisole showing. "You can't outsmart me."

"You scoundrel!" She whacked at him with the little whip and he grabbed her again. They went to the ground in a tussle of flouncing petticoats and lace bloomers as they wrestled for the whip. The dog gamboled around them, eager to get in on this new game while the chickens squawked and the cat howled.

"You little wildcat!" Blackie came up on top, lying on her full, soft breasts, his face only inches from hers. He was suddenly very aware of her warm flesh and how much of it was showing now. As he stared into her eyes, he realized just how pretty this female was. Well, she might be if her hair wasn't so tangled and her face so smudged. He gave her his most disarming grin. "Now, honey," he crooned, "maybe we can work something out. Maybe we could be partners."

She smiled back. "Oh, I didn't realize how charming you were, and so handsome, too."

He relaxed, the overconfident Texas brute. He stood up and picked up his hat, dusted it off, put it on. Then smiled confidently as he offered her his hand. "Here, sister, let me help you up."

The big dope. She smiled and let him take her hand. As she came up off the ground, she gave him a solid knee to the groin, the way the cowboys had taught her to defend herself at her uncle's ranch. He went down like a felled tree, groaning and thrashing in the dirt.

"You oaf! How stupid can you get?" She made a run for the wagon and tripped over the barking dog, but scrambled up on the wagon seat and lashed the startled horse. The dog must have thought it was a new game because he ran along beside the wagon, barking and wagging his tail. The cat squalled and the chickens set up a bigger racket as she drove away. She glanced behind her, smiling with satisfaction. Men. They were hairy, flawed brutes who seemed to think with what hung between their legs. That was when they weren't guzzling demon rum. Somewhere there must be a perfect, sensitive mate for her, but she sure hadn't found him so far. That made her think of her wedding ceremony which had been so perfect right up until her ideal groom . . . She brushed that humiliating memory aside and concentrated on her driving. A few more miles and she'd be at the land office in Guthrie.

Blackie was in a world of hurt, writhing on the ground. He finally managed to sit up and wiped the drops of sweat from his brow as the pain subsided. "That sneaky little—! She almost deprived a lot of eager women some future pleasure."

Pleasure. It would give him a great deal of pleasure to turn that sassy dame across his knee and paddle her until she was wailing as loud as that damned cat. She had outsmarted him and gotten away with the wagon. He almost had to admire her for her grit, but then Texas gals were always a cut above other women. If this had happened to another hombre, Blackie would have thought it was funny.

For him, it wasn't. It was hot and he was thirsty. He stumbled to his feet and stared up the road. The wagon had disappeared to the north in a cloud of dust and squawking chickens. Even his own dog, the traitor, had gone happily along with the girl.

"Great God Almighty, Blackie, you let her outsmart you. You thought the prim old maid could be charmed and tempted like other women. You should have known better."

Well, he wouldn't make that mistake again. He'd get to Guthrie somehow and contest her claim if she did manage to get it filed. That choice corner lot was too valuable to give up. Besides, he wasn't about to have it breezed around town that Blackie O'Neal had been bested by a woman. He looked up and down the deserted road. Nothing in sight except a few chicken feathers blowing on the warm spring air.

With a sigh, he started walking north. *Walk.* A dirty four-letter word to a Texan, especially in boots. "If man had been meant to walk, God wouldn't have invented horses," he muttered to himself and felt through his pockets for his cigarillos. They'd been all mashed and broken in the tussle. For a moment, he recalled the feel of her curvaceous body under his then remembered she'd outsmarted him. "Damn, my fine Havanas are ruined."

He stuck a broken cigar in his mouth, lit it, and shook out the match. He was nothing if not stubborn, and he'd always been one lucky hombre since he'd managed to escape that shack back in east Texas when he was a hungry, motherless kid. He wasn't licked yet and he wasn't gonna be, not by a lanky gal who was as independent as a hog on ice. Maybe her wagon would break an axle or her damned cat would escape and she'd stop to hunt it down. There were lots of things that could delay her, still giving him a chance to file his claim first. He started limping toward Guthrie. "Sister," he promised through clenched teeth as he stumbled along, "you ain't seen the last of Blackie O'Neal!"

Chapter Two

The town of Guthrie was bigger and more disorganized than the one she'd just left. There must be ten thousand people roaming about the prairie, setting up tents, unloading wagons. The afternoon air rang with shouts and the sound of hammers banging together shabby shacks. Somewhere a dog barked and a baby cried. People pushed past each other in the disarray, and new arrivals clogged the dusty road. She hated the confusion since she liked everything orderly and perfect, but then, this was an unusual and exceptional day. She couldn't even wash her face or comb her hair; she couldn't spare the time. Tomorrow when she got her land claim filed, she'd get her life straight and print the first edition of her newspaper.

Precious had finally stopped yowling but the chickens still squawked and here and there folks turned to grin and stare. She felt very conspicuous and tried not to notice the pointing fingers and the dog still walking alongside her wagon, looking up at her, tongue lolling. The dog must be tired. "Here, hop up, what's your name? Oh, yes, Lively."

When she snapped her fingers, the bloodhound jumped up in the wagon next to her and tried to lick her face. "You're as bad as your master," she complained. "Are you always so familiar with ladies you don't know?"

In answer, the dog settled down next to her and dropped off to sleep.

She thought of the gambler with grim satisfaction. Served him right. He'd probably always had his way with women and had never met one crafty enough to beat him at his own game. She'd get her claim filed and then deliver the chickens to the army. "Hey," she yelled at a young boy who stared at her moving menagerie, "where's the land office?"

He pointed wordlessly and Lacey drove up that street. She found the shack with a board hanging across the front proclaiming "Land Office." There was a long line of men out front, but no women. Even though women were allowed to make the run and claim their own land, most wouldn't have the guts to do it. Around her wagon in the swirling dust, people came and went in mass confusion. There were settlers in canvas-covered wagons, cowboys, soldiers, a few women carrying crying infants. Here and there a dog barked and a mule protested the amount of work along the main street of this raw new town. Ragged tents dotted the landscape as far as the eye could see. It appeared soldiers were attempting to bring a semblance of order, but without much success.

"At least I'm part of history," she said to herself, thinking what a good front page story the land rush would be for the first issue of her paper. She hoped Isaac had managed to get the printing press and supplies unloaded. Lacey smiled. She was hot and tired, but triumphant. She'd get her claim registered and then let Blackie O'Neal howl like a wounded coyote about it.

Lacey tied up her horse at a hitching rail and got down. "Come on, Lively, let's get in line."

The hound's tail thumped as he joined her in the line before the claim office. The line didn't seem to be moving very fast. She felt perspiration running down inside her dusty, torn shirtwaist and her lips felt dry. Oh, what she'd give for a drink of water. She looked around. In the confusion of people coming and going, she didn't see a pump or even any barrels of water. If she stepped out of line, she might not get back in. She did see a horse trough in front of a small store. Lively wandered over and got himself a drink, then came back and dripped water on her shoes. She took the edge of her skirt and gingerly wiped them off. She must look a mess, but she couldn't do anything about that right now without getting out of line. The line inched forward. At this rate, all these people wouldn't get processed tonight and would have to come back tomorrow.

Heads seemed to be turning, looking at her torn blouse and her tangled hair. She tried self-consciously to pull the blouse closed and brush her hair back. She'd always been so persnickety about everything. Lacey liked everything orderly and here she was looking like a rumpled, unmade bed and accompanied by a ridiculous dog with the saddest expression she'd ever seen. Time was too important to waste on her appearance today. "Lively, I hope you're not as unhappy as you look."

The dog's tail thumped and he lay down nearby and promptly dropped off to sleep. Lively. The name must have been a joke. She craned her neck and peered ahead. The untidy line ahead must be at least a half block long and barely inching forward. Her feet hurt and she felt perspiration running down between her breasts. Ladies never perspired, they glowed, she reminded herself. While thirst was her biggest problem, she was getting a little hungry, too. Oh, she hoped owning her own land was going to be worth what she'd been through to get it. In her mind, she saw that Texas rascal rolling in the dirt and groaning. Yep, she grinned, it was worth it. She wondered if he'd limp on in to Guthrie or give up and go back? Five miles was a long way to walk in cowboy boots. She smiled when she thought about it. Served him right for not being a gentleman and ceding the claim to her.

Lacey heard titters and guffaws and turned to see where everyone was looking. Blackie O'Neal came up the street sitting on the back of an army wagon, his long legs dangling down. The wagon was loaded with horse manure and it smelled rank when the breeze blew the scent her way. Blackie himself looked like he'd been dragged through a knothole backward, all rumpled and dusty. His suntanned face appeared dark as a thunder cloud.

Uh-oh. She tried to shrink in line to make herself invisible, but she saw his eyes widen as he seemed to spot her. "Aha! Stop the wagon, driver."

Then he was advancing on her in long, angry strides. "Great God Almighty! Thought you'd lose me, did you?"

"Hey, don't break into line!" Several men yelled.

"I'm not breaking into line," Blackie shouted back as he came up to her. "I'm with her."

"No, he's not!" Lacey protested as the gambler pushed into line beside her.

The little man behind her cleared his throat. "Stranger, the lady says you're not with her."

Blackie grinned at the little man. "Of course we're together, little spat between me and the missus, that's all. See how glad our dog is to see me?"

Indeed, Lively was gamboling around his feet, wagging his tail with delight and licking Blackie's hand.

The other man smiled and nodded. "Me and the wife had a few dust-ups in our lifetime. You been married long?"

"Married?" Lacey protested. "Why—"

"Now, sweetheart," Blackie cooed and took her arm, turning her toward the front of the line, "It just seems like hardly any time at all, don't it?"

"One minute would be way too long," Lacey seethed, "and don't call me the missus—"

"Hush your mouth, sister," he lowered his voice close to her ear so that she felt the warmth of his breath, "or else I'll tell the nice soldiers about you attackin' me and leavin' me on the side of the road. I believe the charge would be assault and battery; maybe attempted murder."

"Murder? All I did was knee you in the—"

"Tsk! Tsk! And you a lady, too."

She took a deep breath to control her temper. "Stop reminding me before I do it again."

"In front of all these people?" He looked around.

She was concerned about what other people would think and anyway, as stubborn as the Irishman was, she didn't think she was able to discourage him.

"Sweetheart, hold my place and I'll get a drink."

"But—" before she could say anything else, Blackie and his fool dog had sauntered away. Damn him, she'd give anything for a drink of water, but he of course, was thinking of whiskey.

The line barely moved and she licked her dry lips. Even demon rum would be almost tempting. Then she remembered the humiliation of her wedding day. No, she'd never be that thirsty again.

In a few minutes, Blackie strolled up with a tall, cool drink in his hand and joined her. She snorted in disgust as she eyed the tumbler. "Where'd you get that?"

He sipped it and sighed. "Ahh! Very refreshing. It's got ice in it, too. Did you notice?"

She looked at the moisture beading on the cold glass and ran her tongue over her dry lips. Of course she'd noticed. "Must have cost a lot to get ice around here."

He nodded and grinned. "A dollar. Want a sip?"

"A dollar? That's outrageous."

"I agree, but that's free enterprise. I reckon they had to haul ice a long way to get it here." He look another sip of the dark liquid and rolled his eyes upward, sighing as he did so. "Delicious. Are you sure you wouldn't like to share, sister?"

Lacey wrinkled her nose. "I'd rather die of thirst."

"Great God Almighty, woman, you are stubborn."

She smiled without humor. "And that's precisely the reason I'm going to end up with that choice lot."

He winked at her and sipped his drink. "Don't count

me out yet, sis, I'm an awfully lucky hombre . . . or was until I tangled with you."

"There were other lots you could have claimed," she hissed at him.

"So could you," he reminded her.

"So this is not even about the land anymore, it's a battle of wills."

He grinned. "If you say so."

She decided to ignore him. He was the most infuriating man she'd ever had the bad luck to cross paths with; not at all like the gentle, sensitive type of ideal male she envisioned. She simply must have some water. Besides that, she was worried about Precious. "I don't suppose you'd be enough of a gentleman to hold my place while I get a drink?"

He grinned down at her. "Would you trust me to be a gentleman and do so?"

"Gentleman? Ha! Any gal who would trust you might end up losing her drawers. I know your type."

"Tsk! Tsk! Such a vulgar comment from a lady."

Oh, he was maddening. She had the most terrible urge to smack that handsome, grinning face even as he took another sip of his devil's brew. "You know, you're almost pretty when you're mad."

She snorted again. "Do idiotic remarks like that cause most women to swoon at your feet, Texan?"

"Sometimes," he conceded.

"Well, this Texas girl isn't buying it." She turned around to face the front of the line, deciding to ignore him. The warm April sun beat down on them as the afternoon lengthened and the line seemed to be only inching along. By now, she was not only thirsty, she was in dire need of an outhouse. Behind her, the Texas rascal kept sipping his drink and shaking the ice around so that she could hear it. Finally she decided she could stand it no longer. "I'll be back in a minute," she flung the remark over her shoulder and hurried away into the crowd. Lacey had to find an outhouse fast before she soaked her bloomers and humiliated herself in front of the whole world.

Lacey found an outhouse and then a snaggle-toothed man selling water. He wanted a dime for a cup.

"Why don't you get a gun and mask?" she complained, "that's highway robbery."

He gave her a grin like a broken white picket fence. "Maybe so, lady, but it's the onliest water around, so take it or leave it."

She took it although it was lukewarm and tasted like an old lake. She thought again with longing of Blackie's tall, ice-chilled glass. But of course she dare not touch demon rum. The last time she had . . . she pushed that embarrassing thought from her mind and went to the wagon to check on her cat. Precious lapped up the last of the water from her cup and meowed in complaint. "I know it's a miserable crowded cage. I'll take you with me."

Lacey gathered up Precious and headed back to the claim line which had moved up a few more feet.

"Hey, lady, no line-breakin'," a gruff man yelled.

She walked up to Blackie who did not acknowledge her. "Tell them, you rogue."

Blackie shook his head as if bewildered. "Have we met?"

"Oh, you rascal. All right, I'll say it. I'm with him," she announced to the crowd.

"Why, sweetie," he tried to put his arm around her, "What took you so long? I missed you while you were gone."

She moved very subtly to grind the heel of her high-button shoe into the tender instep of his expensive, dusty boot. "Unhand me, you villain or I will knee you again."

"For a lady, you never cease to shock and surprise me." He scowled. "I see you brought the cat."

At the word "cat", Lively woke up and barked at the white dust mop.

"Meow!" Precious jumped for a higher, safer position, which just happened to be Blackie's shoulder, then she went to the top of his head, balancing on his mashed hat.

"Great God Almighty!" Blackie flailed his arms. "Get this critter off me!"

"Woof! Woof!" Lively danced around his feet while the cat arched her back, spat, and hissed.

"Call your dog off and I will. He's scaring the poor thing. Hey, kitty. Here, Precious."

Around them, people laughed and tittered. "Wal," said a man farther back in line, I seen a goat ropin' and a circus, but never anything this much fun."

Lacey turned on the man as Blackie struggled to get the enraged cat off his head. "Oh, shut up. Haven't you ever seen a cat before?"

"Not worn as a hat, Ma'am."

The line laughed again and Blackie ordered the dog to desist. Reaching up to pull the protesting feline from his mangled hat, he handed her to Lacey. "Great God Almighty, does it never end, Miss? Miss?"

"Lacey Van Schuyler Durango," she said.

"Ah," he nodded in recognition. "Of *the* Durangos, owners of the famous Triple D ranch?"

"My uncle is Trace Durango," she admitted.

"I think I've played cards with one Ace Durango several years back," Blackie mused.

"My cousin," she admitted. "Ace is quite a rounder, but he's married now."

"Let himself get branded, did he?" Blackie shook his head regretfully. "Won't happen to me. Anyway, with a million acres of Texas ranch land, sister, what are you doin' up here?"

"My uncle owns that, I don't." She stroked her indignant cat. "Besides, I'm an independent woman who wants to make it on her own. When I get the deed to that choice lot, I'm going to build a newspaper."

He snorted and sipped his drink. "A woman runnin' a newspaper?"

"I've had experience as a reporter and my uncle has loaned me enough money to get started."

"Why don't you do yourself a favor, go back to the ranch, get married, and raise a passel of kids?"

She was outraged. "You'd like that, wouldn't you? Give you that lot without a fuss."

"Great place for a saloon and gambling palace." He smiled dreamily. "I can see it now: Blackie's Black Garter."

"In your dreams, you rogue." She was so outraged, smoke seemed to come out of her nostrils. A house of demon rum. She might have known. If he only knew the Ladies' Temperance Association was concentrating its efforts to run demon rum completely out of the Territory. But of course she wouldn't tell him that yet. First, she must keep him from getting control of that land. The line moved a few feet and Lively moved to lay down next to them, rolled over on his back and began to snore.

Lacey said "That is the most pitiful excuse for a dog I've ever seen."

"You should talk, with a powder puff for a pet."

Lacey sniffed disdainfully. "Where'd you get a bloodhound, anyway?"

Blackie lit his cigar. "He's a reject from the state prison at Huntsville."

"What?"

"He got fired," Blackie said with a nod. "The Texas Rangers were searchin' for some escaped prisoners and put Lively on the trail. They tell me he disappeared and when they finally tracked down their missin' convicts, Lively was curled up with them, sharing their food."

She couldn't control her scorn. "I reckon your dog is no judge of character."

He took a puff of his cigar and grinned. "He's not as judgmental as you are, sister."

She made a moue. "Let me guess. You were one of the prisoners."

"No, but my brother was one of the lawmen."

She blinked. "You've got a brother who's a lawman?"

"Is that so hard to believe?"

"You have to ask?"

Blackie knelt and patted the dog's long ears. "He was just too friendly to hunt people. Lively's like me; he believes in live and let live. The warden lost a hand of poker to me and he gave me the dog."

"Poker." Lacey sniffed. "I might have known."

It was late now, almost dusk. The pair and their sleepy dog were within a few feet of the front of the line. She could see several men and an army officer sitting at a makeshift desk made from an old door out in front of the shack. The pair moved closer and closer until they were at the front of the line.

One of the scribbling civilians glanced at the sun and then his pocket watch. "It's late. This Land Office is now officially closed." He stood up and yelled. "You folks will have to come back tomorrow."

"This is outrageous," Lacey shouted, "we've been standing here all afternoon."

"Can't help that," the man yawned. "We been sittin' here registering claims all afternoon. Time for a beer."

Lacey's indignation knew no bounds. "Beer? I might have known there were spirits involved somehow. Men always have to have their whiskey."

The men looked at each other, their eyes lighting up. "Whiskey sounds even better. We'll open up in the morning."

"But I can't stay here all night," she protested.

"You don't expect us to work without any light, do you?" growled one of the trio. "Anyway, lady, you ain't the only one. There's a long line behind you."

It was true. She was still protesting when the officials walked away. The rest of the people in line began to drift in all directions. "My word, now what do we do?"

Blackie grinned at her. "You still have that wagon-load of chickens?"

"Yes, I was going to deliver them when I got my claim filed."

"I don't reckon the army would miss one or two." Blackie started to walk away.

"You'd steal the army's chickens? That's outrageous."

"I'm a taxpayer, ain't I? I paid for some of those chickens. Come on, Lively. You comin', sister?"

"No," Lacey said and set her jaw stubbornly. "I'm going to camp right here and hold this place in line."

"For me, too?" He grinned at her.

"Of course not, you big lummox." Frankly, she wasn't sure how she would manage. Precious was squirming in her arms and meowing.

"Your cat's hungry and gettin' as grouchy as you are. Reckon I could go build a campfire and roast us some chickens on a stick while you hold the place in line."

"I said I wasn't going to hold your place in line."

He grinned at her. "You hold the place in line and I'll share my chickens. Is that fair?"

She felt she was losing this battle of wills. Precious meowed, squirmed and tried to get out of her arms. "I don't know. I don't like cooperating with you."

"Okay," he shrugged, "then go hungry. Come on, Lively."

The bloodhound got to its feet, shook the dust from its wrinkly brown hide, and ambled slowly after his master.

Lacey watched them go. Most of the people behind her in line had given up and gone off to get something to eat. They'd have to start all over in the morning, but darned if she would. She'd stay here until hell froze over to stake her claim. Lacey slumped down on a rock next to the Land Office shack and put the white Persian on the ground. The cat's pink ribbon was askew and for the first time Lacey could remember, Precious' snowy hair was dirty. Lacey was dirty, too, and she didn't like it. She was so tired, she might have wept, but that would have been a sign of weakness.

Around her, the night had grown dark but the spring air was warm. Ten thousand people moved about, building campfires, setting up tents. Here and there a horse whinnied or a baby cried. In the darkness she could see the glow of a hundred campfires as hardy pioneers began to cook. Across the whole land run territory, she realized suddenly, there were thousands more people than there was available land. Some of those would go home disappointed, their dreams of a free farm and a fresh start shattered. Well, she wasn't going to be one of them. She wished she had another drink of water and something to eat. She thought she smelled chicken frying and it made her mouth water.

After a while, Blackie and Lively came back, the dog carrying the biggest bone Lacey had ever seen. It would have been wonderful in a pot of stew, she thought with envy. Precious arched her back and spat at the dog, but the dog, having to decide between the cat and the bone, flopped down on the dirt and enjoyed his bone. Blackie himself had another cold drink in his hand and a gold toothpick in his mouth. The diamond ring on his right pinkie finger flashed in the light as he gestured. "My, that was mighty tasty."

"Stolen chicken probably does taste good to a thief." She kept her voice haughty.

"Yeah, it did." He was incorrigible; without shame. "I also took the wagon over to the army camp and let them unload it so we can return it tomorrow."

"*We?* I don't intend to give you a ride back."

"Well, I intend to give you one, so that makes me a nicer person than you, right?"

She must remember that arguing with a scoundrel was

a waste of time and reasoning. Her belly growled so loudly, that even the gambler must have heard it.

"Sister, I'll hold your place in line if you want to go get something to eat or I've got some leftovers. You want I should bring you some?"

"I don't need you to do me any favors. Besides, I don't trust you."

"Suit yourself," he shrugged. "I was tryin' to be a gentleman."

"Ha! You don't know what a gentleman is."

"I wouldn't talk about etiquette when the first time I saw you, your skirt was above your head and your underpants was showin'."

Some passing soldiers looked at her curiously and grinned before walking on. "Oh, you kid!" one of them yelled and another whistled.

"My word, can't you lower your voice?" Lacey buried her red face in her hands. Lively lay down next to her and his long tail thumped as he laid the bone across her foot.

"It seems Lively's willin' to share with you."

Without thinking, she reached out to pet the dog. "Nice dog," she whispered, "how could you take up with such a scoundrel?"

Her cat eyed the dog suspiciously and kept Lacey between them. Lacey's tummy rumbled again.

"Hey," Blackie squatted down, "can I give some of this chicken to your cat? She's hungry."

Lacey eyed the chicken he held out. "I—I reckon that's all right."

He laid it on a rock and Precious pounced on it. Lacey licked her lips and watched the cat eat.

"Well," Blackie said, "I'll go see if I can get some hay and water for the horse and find some amusement. Come on, Lively." He turned to walk away.

Lively didn't move. With a sigh, the dog curled up next to Lacey.

"You're stealing my dog," Blackie said.

"I didn't do anything. He just wants to stay with me."

"So let him." Blackie sauntered off.

"I won't hold your place in line!" She yelled.

He turned and winked at her. "Sure you will, sister." Then he strolled toward the busiest part of town.

Lacey glared after his broad back as he walked off down the street. The dog was asleep. She looked at the cat again. Could she? She who was so straitlaced and persnickety? "Precious, I hate to do this, but manners call for sharing."

Gingerly, she pulled a roasted chicken leg out of the pile in front of the cat and the cat turned annoyed yellow eyes her direction.

"Now, Precious, don't be selfish." Lacey took a deep breath and began to wolf down the chicken. She almost fought the cat for the last piece. She was already cramped and weary from sitting in the dirt, but she wasn't about to lose her place in line. From somewhere, she heard a tinny piano banging away and a woman's coarse laughter. No doubt, Blackie O'Neal had just said something amusing. No telling where he'd end up tonight, probably in some whore's bed. Maybe he'd be so drunk, he'd oversleep in the morning and she'd get her claim filed with no protest. She could only hope.

Unfortunately, as dawn broke and the settlement began stirring, Blackie returned. She awoke with a start to find him standing by her, blinking as if the bright light hurt his eyes. He carried his hat full of water. "Want a drink?"

"Out of your hat?" She shuddered.

"It's cold."

She knew it was a sign of weakness, but she was so thirsty. "Well, maybe just a sip." She put her face in it and gulped loudly.

"You sound just like the horse did when he drank."

She made a face and pulled back. "The horse drank out of this hat?"

"Well, he left you some."

"Eck." She made a face and wiped her mouth as he offered the remainder, first to his dog, then to the cat.

Now Blackie slumped down on a rock and groaned. "I shouldn't have played cards all night."

She had no sympathy for the wastrel. "My uncle always said 'If you can't run with the big dogs, you'd best stay on the porch.'"

"Your uncle was right."

Lacey scratched her neck. No doubt Lively had fleas. What had she come to? Stealing food from her cat, drinking after a horse, and getting fleas from a worthless dog? Her aunt Cimarron would never believe this because Lacey always liked everything so pristine and perfect. She was cross and sore as she stood up and tried to brush the dust off her skirt. She really needed to find the outhouse again, but the soldiers were opening the little land office and she wasn't about to leave. Instead, she stood on one foot and then the other.

"Careful, sister," Blackie warned, "you'll soak your drawers."

"Don't be crude. I'll not leave this line. You'd like that, wouldn't you?"

He grinned back at her. "Can't say I didn't try."

The line was forming again behind them as the officials set up the makeshift table.

"Next?" The official said.

Lacey rushed forward. "I wish to claim lot number three in the nameless township five miles south of here."

"Me, too," Blackie stepped up beside her.

"All right." The old man began writing. "And that's Mr. and Mrs.—?"

"We're not together," Lacey snapped.

The old man looked up and chewed on the tip of his pencil. "I see. That presents a problem."

"I drove in my stake first," Lacey said.

"No, she didn't," Blackie countered. "She arrived seconds after I did. Clearly, I was there first."

"Liar. You were not." Lacey said.

The two men at the table looked at each other. "One of you a sooner?"

"I beg your pardon?" Lacey said.

"I mean, did one of you break the rules and come in before the official time for the land run to begin?"

"Certainly not!" Lacey snapped, "I never break rules."

They turned their inquiring gazes toward the gambler. He grinned back at them. "Rules were made to be broken, gentlemen, but not this time. I'm not guilty. I rode a good, fast horse."

"In that case," the old man sighed, "this is another one of those contested cases. We've had a bunch. Government will have to decide who actually gets the lot. Takes about six months, maybe a year."

Lacey groaned aloud. "I was going to start building my newspaper office on that land this very day."

The official shook his head. "Can't do that, Miss, until the courts decide who owns it. Now if one of you would like to buy the other's claim out—"

"Not a chance," Lacey snapped, "but if the rascal here would like to sell—"

"Not a snowflake's chance in hell, sister," Blackie growled, "that's too good a spot for a saloon."

"A saloon?" Lacey sniffed. "There won't be any saloons once the Temperance Association dries up this Territory."

A groan went up from all the men behind her.

The men at the table looked at each other and sighed. "You two fill out these papers and you'll be notified when it finally comes up for review."

Lacey felt like weeping in frustration, but of course her emotions were always carefully controlled. "And what am I supposed to do in the meantime?"

"That ain't our problem, Ma'am. Next." He gestured to the man behind her.

There seemed to be nothing else to do but fill out the papers, turn them in, and walk away.

"You stubborn rascal," Lacey seethed, "I was clearly on that land first."

"You think just because you're a woman, I'm supposed to roll over and let you have it? You want it both ways, sister; equal rights when it's handy and special treatment for women when it serves your purpose."

"You're outrageous, you know that? Let me find a—a necessary, and then let's get out of here."

He lit a cigar. "So you're gonna share your wagon?"

"Do I have a choice?" She glared up at him. He had the broadest shoulders and a shadow of beard on his rugged face.

"Of course not. I was just bein' polite. I'll take the animals to the wagon and we'll wait for you there."

She paused, eyed him suspiciously. "Will you wait?"

He shrugged. "Might as well. Don't see no advantage in leavin' you behind now that the land is tied up by law."

She went to find an outhouse, then returned through the bustling crowds, half expecting to see the wagon gone, but he leaned against it, smoking a cigar. The cat and dog seemed to have settled their differences because both stared at her from the back of the wagon.

"Here," he said, "let me help you up."

"You touch me and I'll scream I'm being molested and the soldiers will come running."

"Fine, sister, then get yourself up here. I'll drive."

"Must I remind you that I am responsible for this wagon? I'll drive." She struggled to get up into the seat. It was difficult with her long skirts.

Blackie simply ignored her, climbed up on his side and took the reins. "No woman drives when I'm aboard."

"You are outrageous," Lacey seethed.

"I'm a Texan, what do you expect? Didn't your mama tell you 'You can always tell a Texan, but you can't tell 'em much?'"

"My parents are dead, I was raised by my aunt and uncle."

"Oh, sorry. My Ma died, too. Pa had it tough feedin' a passel of kids after he lost a leg in the war."

"The war?"

"Yep, one of Colonel Terry's Texas Rangers."

Horror swept over her. "A Rebel? Your family were sympathizers in the Rebellion?"

"No, sister, he was a Southern patriot in the War of Yankee Aggression." Shock gradually swept across his handsome features. "Don't tell me you're a damnyankee?"

She drew herself up proudly. "The Durangos were supporters of old Sam Houston when he tried to keep Texas in the Union."

He snorted. "I should have known." Blackie snapped the little whip at the horse as he turned the rig back south. "Get comfortable, Miss Durango, five miles is a long way." Under his breath, he muttered, "A damnyankee."

"I am not a damned Yankee, I am a true Texan whose family was smart enough to know that leaving the Union was poor judgment. I believe the South's defeat proved my point."

He heaved a sigh. "Do you always have to be right?"

"Only when I am."

They drove the next three miles in hostile silence.

Finally Blackie seemed unable to control his curiosity. "What's a woman doin' in a land rush alone anyway?"

"I'm not alone." She scooted as far to her side of the seat as she could. "My assistant, Isaac, is waiting for me back at the station. Hopefully, he's gotten our equipment unloaded so we can get out the first issue of the *Crusader.*"

"The *Crusader*? Sounds like every man's nightmare."

"For men like you, it probably is," she sniffed disdainfully. "With a crusading newspaper to lead them, the Ladies' Temperance Association will build a perfect town with no sin allowed."

"And no fun, either. I'm beginnin' to wish," he thought

aloud as he stared at the road ahead, "that you had fallen under that train."

"Aren't you sweet?" She smiled without mirth, "It's too bad that your horse didn't land on you when it stumbled."

"I think we understand each other, sister." He looked straight ahead as he drove.

"I think we do."

And so the battle was joined and each vowed silently not to give an inch. It was no trick too dirty as two Texans each schemed how to bring the other down.

Chapter Three

Meanwhile, back at the ranch . . .

Cimarron came outside to join her husband sitting on a bench watching the fountain in the courtyard. A brown Chihuahua was curled up in his lap. "Well, Trace, is there anything prettier than a spring sunrise in the Texas hill country?"

"You, darlin'." He put his arm around her. After twenty-four years, he was still madly in love with her.

"Oh, you charmer, you. You could sell whiskey to a church deacon." She smiled at him fondly.

"Which reminds me, you heard anything from Lacey?"

Cimarron shook her head. "Not yet, but you knows she's as independent as a cowboy who just got paid. I reckoned when she got back from that Grand Tour of Europe and went to work for that Dallas newspaper, she'd get over what happened."

"It's a little hard to forget. Half of Texas is still talkin' about it." He sighed and stared at the bubbling fountain.

"That's the reason she didn't feel she could settle around here," Cimarron's voice was sympathetic.

"Maybe if she'd get married . . . "

"After what happened?" Cimarron reminded him.

"You're right. Still, she ain't gonna like it up there in the Territory. You can take a gal out of Texas, but you can't take Texas out of the gal."

"Now, that's a fact." Cookie, their grizzled old cowboy limped around the oleander bushes at the corner of the adobe and joined them. As usual, his bushy gray whiskers needed trimming and he smelled faintly of vanilla.

"You through cooking breakfast for the cowhands?" Cimarron smiled at him and he grinned back. Everyone on the giant Triple D ranch knew how much he adored the missus.

"I did, but they must all be off their feed; none of them ate much."

Cimarron and her husband exchanged glances. Cookie had been crippled when a horse fell on him years ago and Trace Durango had made a place for him as the cook for their fifty cowboys. Unfortunately, Cookie couldn't fry an egg so a starving coyote would eat it.

Trace ran his hand through his black hair, now turning gray. "Reckon it's time you retired, Cookie?"

"And not earn my beans around here? I reckon not." The old cowboy was a proud one.

Trace smiled and returned to watching the fountain spray water in the air. He patted the small brown dog in his lap.

Cimarron decided to take the conversation in a new direction. "We were just discussing the fact we haven't heard from Lacey yet."

The old man spat tobacco juice to one side. "What got that fool girl thinking about takin' part in the land run?"

"Maybe still embarrassed about the weddin'." Trace said.

"Wal now," Cookie rushed to her defense, "that weren't all her fault. That dude she picked out—"

"My niece might be a mite impossible to live with," Cimarron admitted.

"A mite?" Trace threw back his head and laughed.

"Double damnation, Trace, it's just that she likes everything perfect, you know that."

"It was a perfect weddin'," Cookie nodded, "fanciest I ever seen. And it was perfect . . . wal, right up 'til the end."

Cimarron sighed. "No girl could have dealt with that embarrassment. And in front of all those people."

"Not to mention what happened later." Trace said. "It's her own fault she's now an old maid. I don't know why that gal keeps lookin' for perfection in everything; especially in a husband. She ain't gonna find a man who's perfect."

"You can take that to the bank," Cimarron muttered.

"What, darlin'?"

"Nothing." Cimarron smiled. "Maybe she'll be a success owning a paper."

"Ha." Cookie spat tobacco juice. "Who ever heard of a woman runnin' a paper?"

"It could happen." Cimarron said.

"Yes, and hell could cool off, too." Trace added.

"Well, double damnation, you must have thought she'd be a success or you wouldn't have loaned her the money to do it."

Trace petted the dog. "I just felt so sorry for her after the weddin' mess."

"Don't let her know that," Cimarron cautioned, "she's mighty proud."

"Of course she's proud, she's a Texan, ain't she?"

"But she was born in Boston, remember?" Cimarron said.

"Well, she and Lark were raised in Texas after her grandfather decided he couldn't deal with the twins, and that's what counts," Trace countered. "She's proud and stubborn. You know what they say, 'the meek may inherit the earth, but the proud will get Texas.' The meek don't feel at home here anyway."

"Don't let the padre hear you say that," Cimarron scolded. "He might think it was blasphemous."

"Naw." Trace shook his head, "he's a Texan, too."

"I am concerned about Lacey," Cimarron worried aloud. "A woman alone in an uncivilized land rush. If she gets in trouble, she's just like Lark, she won't let us know so we can help her."

Cookie sighed and surveyed the fountain. "Anybody heered from Lark?"

Cimarron shook her head. "Not in months. Of course, she was always a tomboy while Lacey was the perfect lady, so maybe Lark can take care of herself."

"Even Pinkertons haven't found Lark." Trace tossed away his smoke with a sigh. "I reckon she'll turn up when she wants to be found. She's a lot wilder than Lacey."

Cimarron nodded. "You're right; I'm more concerned about Lacey. Maybe we should go up to the Territory and see how she's doing."

"She wouldn't like that," Trace said.

The old codger scratched his gray beard. "You know, I always said, if I was a younger man, I'd have gotten in on that land rush myself."

"You, Cookie?" Both turned to look at him with surprise.

"Well, why not?" The old man said defensively, "Ain't I got a right to some dreams besides cookin' for a bunch of ungrateful cowhands?"

"I reckon I always thought you were happy as a dead hog in the sunshine on the Triple D." Trace stroked the pup.

"I am and I don't want you to think I ain't grateful, Boss, but I always had a hankerin' to open a cafe."

Both the others gulped.

"I heered that!" Cookie said.

"We didn't say anything," Cimarron said. "Did we, darlin'?"

"Nope." A muscle in Trace's jaw twitched.

"Wal, you was thinkin' it, Boss." Cookie said and stared off toward the north horizon. "You know, I'll bet that new town could use a good cafe. I could call it Cookie's Kitchen."

Trace hesitated as he lit a cigarillo. "It might be too much work for you, partner, and we'd miss you."

"Wal, I'd be back to visit and I could see about Lacey. I reckon somebody needs to."

Cimarron coughed, thinking of just what Lacey would say if the old cowboy showed up to check on her. Her niece was fiercely independent. "I don't know, Cookie, opening a cafe takes money—"

"Now what you think I been doin' with my wages all these years?" Cookie asked. "I been savin' them, that's what. I got enough to open a nice cafe."

Trace took a deep puff of his cigar. "Cookie, now you might want to rethink this—"

"I don't know why, unless you're needin' me to cook here at the big house again for you and the missus."

The others exchanged alarmed glances.

"Uh, Cookie," Cimarron said, "you wouldn't want to do Juanita out of her job, would you? She's got grand-children to support."

Cookie thought it over and nodded. "Reckon you're right. Wal, I might just mosey up to that Oklahoma Ter-ritory and look things over. If I see a good business opportunity, I might take it."

"Remember you're always welcome on the Triple D," Trace reminded him. "Long as we got a biscuit, you got half."

A Texan couldn't make a deeper gesture of commit-ment than that and Cookie was touched. "I know that, Boss, and I'm much obliged. The Durangos is the onli-est family I got, that's why I'm concerned about Miss Lacey. I could keep you informed about how she's doin' since she won't write."

"She won't like that," Cimarron said, wondering what she could do to dissuade the old man.

"Then let the young lady lump it." Cookie stood up. "I'll start makin' my plans right now. It may take me a week or two to get everything squared away, but the more I think about it, the better I like it. Cookie's Kitchen, best food in the southwest."

The pair watched him limp away and disappear around the corner of the adobe ranch house.

Trace swore in Spanish. "He'll poison the whole town."

"I heered that," yelled the old man.

"Now you've hurt his feelings, Trace," she scolded.

"If I could hurt his feeling, he would have left years ago." He pulled his wife to him and kissed her. "You got any tequila inside?"

"You know what your doctor said about tequila and cigars," she reminded him and kissed him back. The kiss lengthened.

"Well, I ain't too old for one thing," he murmured. "Why don't we move inside so half of Texas ain't watchin'?"

"I'm agreeable." She smiled at him.

They both got up, dumping the dozing Chihuahua on the patio. It promptly started for the house.

"You think I should let Lacey know Cookie's coming?" Cimarron asked as she linked arms with her husband and they strolled toward the front door.

"Uh, why don't we just pretend we don't know anything?" Trace answered. "Maybe Cookie will change his mind."

"Won't!" yelled the old man from around the corner, "I'm goin' to Oklahoma to rescue our Lacey."

Cimarron smiled as they went inside. Their cowboys would get a reprieve for awhile, but God help the settlers in the Territory who ate in Cookie's Kitchen. At least, the old cowboy would let them know how Lacey was doing.

Blackie smoked and watched dourly as the scene across the street unfolded. That annoying damnyankee gal and some short, ink-stained man were directing workmen unloading a printing press and many boxes at a site on Main Street. She looked fresh and determined this morning with her hair up in a bun, and wearing a no-nonsense plain dark skirt with a small bustle and a clean white shirtwaist with the new leg o' mutton sleeves. She wore horn-rimmed glasses and a determined expression.

Blackie was in a bad mood as he watched. Miss Iron

Corset, yes, that was a good name for that ornery gal.
She must have rented herself a lot on Main Street for her
damned reformer rag while she waited the outcome of
the contested land. If she thought she could be as stubborn as Blackie O'Neal, she had another think coming.
He decided at that moment that he would make her so
miserable, she would be happy to shout "calf rope," forget her prissy goals, and leave town.

That decided, Blackie looked about the bustling, busy
settlement this third day after the run and went to find
the owner of the lot directly across the street from Miss
Iron Corset's newspaper. His bartender, Moose, and Flo
and the girls would be arriving the day after tomorrow
to open and as yet, there was no saloon to put them in.
Maybe Blackie could rent that lot.

The whole settlement was a madhouse, most of the
businesses attempting to open along the dusty streets
were in tents, with a few already building more perma-
nent structures. Hammers echoed throughout the area
with horses and buggies moving up and down through
the higgledy-piggledy crooked lines of shacks and tents.

He scowled at the choice corner lot when he passed it:
a perfect place for the finest saloon in a wide-open, wild
settlement with a name like Whiskey Flats. Yes, he nodded
with a smile at the thought as he headed to the railroad
station, Whiskey Flats was a great name men would like.
It would signify the kind of town *real* men could gather in,
drawn like magnets to the liquor, gambling, and wild
women; the kind of women Miss Iron Corset would not
approve of.

At the railroad terminal, workmen were just unloading a freight car of fresh, pine-scented lumber. However,
when he tried to buy some, he was told Miss Durango
had come in only an hour earlier and bought most of
that load. The rest was headed to the new Peabody General Store that was already operating out of a big,
flapping tent at the end of Main Street.

He would not be outmaneuvered by that staid temperance leader. "I'll pay more." he offered.

The balding clerk hesitated. "I don't know," he said, "Miss Durango is planning on buildin' a newspaper office. Town needs a newspaper."

Blackie grinned and offered the man one of his own fine cigars. "You know what I'm plannin' to build? The finest saloon, gamblin' palace, and dance hall in the whole West."

"Dance hall?" The man took the cigar.

Blackie winked. "You know what I mean. Why, these gals that are comin' in on the train from Del Rio are the purtiest you ever saw."

"Texas gals? Texas gals are always the best."

"Ain't it the truth?" Blackie nodded and reached for his wallet. Given a choice between a town newspaper and a big saloon and bawdy house, of course there was no contest. Men would always be men.

Lacey was more than annoyed when she went to the train station to see about her shipment of lumber. The balding clerk mumbled an excuse and promised a later delivery. Despite her protests, she did not get her building supplies. Outrageous. She marched back along the dusty street to the big tent where Isaac was setting up the press. Her mood did not improve when she saw two wagon loads of fresh lumber being unloaded across the street under the watchful eye of that terrible Rebel who was contesting her for the choice lot. Worse yet, when he saw her, he grinned and tipped his hat. She, on the other hand, put her nose in the air and went into the tent. "That sleazy gambler has our lumber."

Isaac looked up from setting type. He was a small, stoop-shouldered Hungarian immigrant with ink always smeared across his homely features. "We get the paper out anyhow, yes?"

She paced up and down, ignoring Precious who attempted to rub against her legs. Every now and then, Lacey peeked out the tent entrance to watch the pile of lumber across the street grow and grow. Blackie O'Neal spotted her peeking and waved to her. Embarrassed to be caught watching him, she turned suddenly and fell across the cat, who fled with an indignant yowl.

"Miss Lacey, you hurt?" Isaac came around the press to stare down at her.

"Only my pride." She got up and dusted herself off. "That sidewinder Rebel, he's deliberately baiting me."

"He seems to be doing a pretty good job, yes?" Isaac observed.

"I will not let that tinhorn gambler get my goat," she declared, "that's exactly why he's doing it. I only wish I knew what he promised that railroad clerk to give him my lumber. I intend to help build a perfect town with no room for the likes of trashy saloons; I'll see to that."

She sat down at her desk, picked up a pen and pad and thought aloud. "Let's see, an editorial for our first issue: *"Welcome everyone to a new town, a new Territory and a new day. The old wild west is dead and good riddance. First, this settlement needs a name that will draw settlers, lawabiding citizens and families."* Absently, she lay down her pen and strolled to look out the back flap of the tent. While the front of the tent faced on the busy, dusty street and the hubbub of construction, the back view was serene with green rolling prairie. *"Yes, this settlement needs a name that will draw the kind of citizens we want, something like Pleasant View, Greenville, or Pretty Prairie."*

"Pretty Prairie, perfect." She returned to her very organized desk, picked up her pen and scribbled furiously.

Behind her, Isaac cleared his throat. "The people will get to vote on the name, yes?"

"The men will." She frowned in disgust. "But women's rights is something I will tackle later."

"If you don't mind me saying so," Isaac said, "the men won't vote for a name like Pretty Prairie. It's too— too—"

"Civilized?" Lacey chewed on the tip of her pen. "Not brutish enough? You're right about that, but there has to be a way to do this."

Isaac groaned aloud. "Miss Lacey, if you don't mind me saying so, let's not go tilting at windmills. Let's just get out the newspaper. First we need advertisers."

"On the contrary, the business of a newspaper is to tilt at windmills. The public has a right to know the facts."

"Opinion is not facts," Isaac reminded her gently. "Save your thoughts for the editorials, Miss Lacey."

"Of course. Now the first thing we need is a building instead of a drafty old tent." She heard a noise outside and went out to greet a driver who was delivering a small load of lumber. She looked at the huge stack across the street as she signed for the building supplies. "All right, you cheap tinhorn," she muttered, "two can play this game. You can't outsmart a Texas girl."

Maybe he hadn't yet hired workmen, and carpenters were surely in short supply with all the new construction.

"I'll be back in a few minutes," Lacey yelled to Isaac and started off down the street. Soon she had hired the last three available carpenters by offering what she considered outrageous wages and that afternoon, as she and Isaac set type for their first edition, the sound of hammers echoed around them outside the tent. She hated the noise and confusion but she would persevere. "This will work fine," she shouted at Isaac, "they'll build the building completely around our tent and then we'll take the tent down. I'll get more lumber somehow."

She made sure her top of her desk was neat as she sat down. Precious jumped into her lap to be stroked. She patted the cat, chewed her pen and smiled, imagining the look on that Blackie O'Neal's face when he found out he had lumber but no carpenters. The thought gave her grim satisfaction as she listened to the hammers ring. "About the town's name . . ."

. . . *bam, bam, bam.*

"Pretty Prairie would be a fitting name for this . . . "

. . . *bam, bam.*

" . . . settlement, and when we choose a city council . . . "

. . . *bam, bam, bam.*

" . . . this newspaper suggests to all law-abiding citizens that they should choose a name that shows a bright future."

. . . *bam, bam.*

She fiddled with her pen, and readjusted her horn-rimmed spectacles, deep in thought. She must really stop and take a pitcher of lemonade out to her carpenters after awhile.

Isaac cleared his throat. "What's that?"

"What's what?" She looked up from her writing.

"The noise has stopped."

Lacey paused and looked around. She could hear the sound of wagons passing in the street, a child laughing, a dog barking somewhere, but no hammers. "Maybe our carpenters have stopped for lunch."

Isaac pulled out his pocket watch. "At nine-thirty in the morning?"

The sound of hammers began again, but this time, they sounded farther away. "My word," Lacey said, "what do you suppose?" She got up, dumping the indignant white cat out of her lap as she went outside to investigate.

Across the street, that tinhorn nodded to her and toasted her with a tall glass, no doubt full of whiskey and ice. He was clean now, but he still looked like a gambler; bright silk vest, flat panama hat, a string tie, and a diamond ring on the little finger of his right hand. Didn't he know it was not proper for a man to wear diamonds?

"What am I thinking about? Blackie O'Neal and 'proper' in the same sentence?"

Abruptly what caught her attention were her three workmen now hammering away at the site across the street. She marched across, barely avoiding being hit by a beer wagon. "You!" She waved her finger at Blackie and her indignation knew no bounds. "You stole my carpenters!"

"Guilty as charged." Blackie grinned and sipped his drink. Miss damnyankee Iron Corset was almost pretty when she was angry, except her mouth was a thin, grim line. Not very kissable and that was always the first thing Blackie thought about when he looked at a woman's mouth. Oh, hell, it was what any man thought about. "You can have them back when they get my building finished."

Her nostrils flared like a fine racehorse's as she took a deep breath and glared at him over her spectacles. "My newspaper is certainly more important than a watering hole for whiskey-swilling toughs."

"Well, now, Miss Durango, that's a matter of opinion, now, ain't it?" He was loving this, after what the prim temperance crusader had put him through over the lot.

She took another breath and blinked rapidly. For a moment, he almost thought he saw tears there, but decided she wasn't feminine enough for that. She'd probably gotten dust in her eyes.

Now she whirled and her small bustle waggled invitingly as she marched over to yell up at the carpenters on the scaffold. "You there, whatever he's paying, I'll pay more."

The men hesitated, shamefaced, and looked toward Blackie, then went back to work. *Bam! Bam! Bam!*

"Didn't you hear me?" She called.

Bam! Bam! Bam! Apparently they didn't.

"It's no use, sister." Blackie grinned as he sauntered over and took in the scene with satisfaction. "They ain't gonna quit my job."

She whirled on him, arms akimbo. Yes, indeedy, Miss Iron Corset was almost pretty when she was furious. "What is it you offered them if not better wages?"

"Well, for starters, all the beer they could drink and a chance to meet my girls."

"Girls? What girls?" She looked around.

"They ain't here yet."

For a moment, she seemed speechless, which for the prim newspaper woman was probably a rarity, then a deep blush crept up the neck of her crisp white shirt-waist and spread across her face. "You mean—?"

He nodded. "You know what I mean. The kind of girls men like will be comin' in on the train from Del Rio."

"This is outrageous! You disgusting Rebel, I shall write an editorial!" She turned, nose in the air, and marched back across the street, narrowly missing tripping over Lively who was asleep in the middle of the road.

Blackie watched her go and smiled. She had challenged him and he was responding. If Miss damnyankee Iron Corset wanted to act like a man, Blackie was up to the challenge. He yelled at Lively to move out of the street and returned to supervising the construction. Later, he could sublet this building to someone else when he built an even bigger and better saloon on that choice corner lot. In the meantime, it had been a good morning because he had bested the annoying Miss Laccy Durango.

Chapter Four

Inside the tent, Lacey paced anew. "He's outrageous. The most stubborn man I ever met."

"Why don't you get us some advertisers and some local news and stop worrying with that gambler, yes?" Isaac suggested gently, "don't let him get your goat."

"You're right, of course." Lacey paused and peeked out the tent again. Again Blackie grinned and nodded to her. "That Texas loafer is not worth one moment of my attention. Maybe one of my stolen carpenters will drop a hammer on him. As hardheaded as he is, he probably wouldn't even feel it."

Isaac sighed. "Stop being obsessed with him."

"Obsessed? Obsessed?" Her voice rose. "He's trying to run me out of town, that's what. My idea for a perfect, law-abiding town is directly at odds with what he's got in mind."

"Miss Lacey," Isaac wiped a smudge of ink from his hand, "you can't dictate what kind of town this will be. Even rascals like that one have rights."

"I'll have to outwit and out-maneuver him," she said. "I'll send a wire to the Ladies' Temperance Association, get them to come. We'll convince the voters, all men, of course, that they really don't want all that drinking, gambling, and wild women."

The stooped, ink-stained man grinned. "Miss Lacey, you don't know much about men."

She snorted with derision. "Believe me, I do. I was

almost married once. What a rascal Homer was and he had me fooled into thinking he was perfect."

"The paper," Isaac said patiently, "remember the paper?"

"Oh, yes. I'll go down and meet the morning train, see if I can pick up some stories of new settlers. I reckon I'd also better wire Uncle Trace that I'm fine and the newspaper is about to put out its first edition."

She got her pad and pencil and a parasol to protect her complexion from the warm sun and began a brisk walk to the depot two blocks down the street.

She noticed Lively cross the street to join her, ambling along behind as she walked. "Honestly," she flung over her shoulder to the lazy dog, "I don't know why you choose to put up with that man. You're both dumb males, I reckon."

The dog wagged his tail and strolled with her to the depot. Inside, she sent her aunt and uncle a wire: *Dear Aunt Cimarron and Uncle Trace. Arrived safely. Stop. The newspaper is off to a great start. Stop.* She thought it over, decided not to mention the difficulties that rascal across the street was causing her. *Don't worry. Stop. I'll be fine. Stop. Love, Lacey.*

Then she fired off telegrams to other leaders of the Temperance Association: *I am fighting a tide of booze and rascals here. Stop. This is a call to arms for every right-thinking woman who'd like to live in a dry, civilized town. Stop. Please come help me hold the barricades against sin. Stop. Your President, Miss Lacey Van Schuyler Durango.*

When she went outside, waiting on the platform for the train to arrive was a tall Indian wrapped in a blanket and wearing war paint.

He looked at her and held up his hand. "How. Me Chief Thunder. You want buy brass buttons off General Custer's coat?"

"What?" Lacey blinked. "Now how would you have those?"

"My father cut them off after he scalped Yellow Hair."

She knew from reading newspaper accounts that George Custer had not been scalped. "What tribe are you?" Lacey asked with growing suspicion.

"Potawatomi."

"Well, Chief Thunder, I happen to know the Potawatomis are peaceful. The warriors at the Little Big Horn were Sioux and Cheyenne."

"Gimme a break, lady, I'm trying to make a living here." He had dropped the fake Indian accent and now his English was as good as hers.

She snorted. "Another rascal. So, who are you really and where are you getting the buttons?"

He grinned at her. "I'm Joe Toadfrog from eastern Indian Territory. Now if your name was Toadfrog, wouldn't you call yourself Chief Thunder? My dad was a half-breed trader who met a white girl and married her."

"Well, Joe, I suggest you get your story straight."

He shrugged. "I have the buttons shipped in from a New Jersey factory by the box and the stupid tourists don't know the difference. It's about time we Indians got even with the whites for stealing our land. Anyway, the extra change rounds out my income. Artists don't make much."

Her eyebrows rose. "You're an artist? Maybe you could do some art work for my newspaper."

"Oh, so you're Miss damnyankee Iron Corset."

"What?"

"Uh, I mean, the new lady newspaper person."

Miss damnyankee Iron Corset. There was only one person arrogant and fresh enough to call her that. "I see you've already met Blackie O'Neal."

He gulped in surprise. "How did you know?"

"Just guessed, I reckon." So that's how the Rebel was referring to her? She imagined reaching her hand down Blackie's throat and pulling his smart-alec tongue out so far it could be used for a red sidewalk. "You're a painter?"

He nodded. "Starving, mostly. I do signs, though, to make a living. Now and then I do a picture."

"Good." She heard a long, drawn-out train whistle and turned to watch the incoming train. "You can do a sign for the front of my building." She realized suddenly that Lively was asleep on the tracks. "Lively! Get up!"

About that time, the gambler himself came running up on the platform, whistling at his dog. The big bloodhound stood up slowly, stretched and ambled off the tracks as if he had all the time in the world to move. "Great God Almighty! That's a new low, sister, tryin' to get my dog killed."

"You think I'd stoop to that?"

"Hush it up, you two," Chief Thunder said, "here comes the train."

The train pulled into the station from the north, blowing steam and throwing soot and cinders as it ground to a halt with its whistle blowing. The conductor stepped down from the coach. "Here we are in the Unassigned Lands," he hollered at the passengers, "town of—?" He turned and looked at the people on the platform.

"Pretty Prairie," Lacey volunteered

"You must be joking," the gambler sneered. "Whiskey Flats, now that's more like it."

"What?" Lacey opened her mouth to protest, but people began getting off the train, a couple of cowboys, a nattily dressed traveling salesman with his sample kits, a family with squalling children.

Chief Thunder approached the salesman. "How. Me Chief Thunder. Have buttons from Custer's uniform to sell."

"Really?" The plump salesman paused and pushed back his derby. "Boy howdy, I'd like a souvenir like that. How'd you get 'em?"

The handsome Potawatomi looked somber and fierce. "My father cut them from General's uniform after him scalp him."

"Really? Hot diggety dog! How much?" The salesman was already reaching in his pocket.

Chief Thunder seemed to be sizing the man up. "One silver dollar for two."

The drummer hesitated.

"Throw in lock of his hair." He held up a blond wisp.

"Wow! Wait'll the boy's back in Cincinnati see this." The drummer could hardly get the money out of his pocket fast enough. The exchange was made.

When the drummer walked away with his treasures, Lacey raised one eyebrow at Chief Thunder.

He shrugged. "Hey, as Barnum used to say, there's a sucker born every minute."

She wondered where he'd gotten the light hair, but before she could ask, other people were departing from the train and the gambler and his dog, tail wagging, hurried to meet them. One of the biggest, baldest men she'd ever seen was shaking hands with O'Neal. "Hey, boss, glad to be here."

"Howdy, Moose, good to have you."

The Moose was bald as a marble and big as a mountain. He had a tattoo on his right forearm, a heart with "Ma" in the middle of it. Around him, young, flashily-dressed women were getting off the train, gathering their luggage. They were escorted by a matronly older woman with dyed red hair.

"Howdy, Blackie," the redhead hailed him and then came in for a hug. "Missed you."

"Good to see you, Flo. This is a great town."

"Better than the last one we got run out of?" She laughed with a husky voice.

The younger, highly-painted girls crowded around Blackie like bees around honey. "Ohh, Blackie, sweet, you got us a good place to work?"

Blackie grinned and wiped at the lip rouge on his face as he turned and glared at Lacey. "It'll do. I got a choice lot picked out, but someone is contestin' me for ownership."

"Now what range rat would do something mean like that?" Flo griped.

"Someone who landed on the lot first." Lacey snapped, surprising even herself.

Flo looked at her, surprise in her heavily painted old face. She might have been a beauty in her younger days. "Well, she's got gumption if she'll go up against Blackie; must be a Texan."

"Yes, I am." Lacey declared.

The younger women paid no attention to anyone but the smiling gambler as they gathered around him. "Ohh, Blackie, we're so glad to see you again."

They all tried to hug him and he was obliging. "Hey, Nell, hey, Sal. How are you doin', Dixie?"

Dixie was a young, painted blonde whose hair color looked suspiciously as if it had come out of a bottle. "I've missed you, Blackie." she drawled.

"And I've missed you all too, you little Southern belle, you. Atlanta doesn't know what they've lost."

"I got run out of Atlanta, remember?"

He shrugged. "Doesn't matter, Dixie, you'll love this new town, lots of men. Come on, I've got my new barouche. It came in on a freight car last night."

The Moose gathered up the luggage and the whole crowd trooped out to a big, fancy open carriage with bright red horsehair upholstery. Two fine black horses outfitted in shiny harness with lots of sparkling brass, pulled it.

Lacey took a deep, annoyed breath. Blackie had completely ignored her as if she didn't exist. His women had left a trail of heavy, cheap perfume on the air.

"Outrageous!" Lacy said to no one in particular as she watched the painted women giggle and take turns hugging Blackie, "he must have his own harem."

Chief Thunder coughed and shifted his feet. "Actually, Miss, they work for Flo, but they always share

Blackie's place because the girls bring in the galoots to gamble and drink plenty of booze."

"No doubt." Lacy snapped as she watched the crowd loading into the barouche with Lively barking and wagging his tail. "You seem to know a lot about them."

"Blackie and me go a long way back in some other towns. He's a charmer, ain't he?"

"Somehow, his appeal escapes me." She glared after the departing barouche. "When the decent citizens clean up this town, he and his girls will have to find some place to go."

Chief Thunder shrugged. "Wouldn't bother Blackie none. He's been run out of better towns than this one."

"I believe that."

"I reckon I've hit all the suckers I'll get this morning." Chief Thunder folded up his merchandize, left the platform and mounted his horse. As he rode away, she noticed the cream-colored horse he rode had a very short, ragged tail. Evidently the General's hair had been an excellent seller.

"My word." In all her astonishment at the arrival of Blackie's whores, she'd forgotten to interview anyone for the news article. Lacey took a deep breath, more annoyed with Blackie than ever and returned to her drafty, dusty tent to write an editorial about how this new town should be law-abiding with no saloons or other dens of sin.

The next morning, she had her first newspaper on the streets. Soon she would have small boys delivering, but for now, she set a stack of papers and an honesty box outside the tent so people could drop their nickles in and take a paper. Several men dropped in to congratulate "the little lady" on her enterprise and four upstanding matrons came by to tell her that they, too, were temperance believers and maybe they could get a chapter started in this new town. That encouraged Lacey tremendously.

"See," she said to Precious as she scratched the cat's

ears after she'd fed her, "we'll have a perfect town after all."

The cat bristled suddenly and Lacey turned to see Lively sticking his head through the tent opening. "Now, now, Precious, you mustn't hold it against the poor dog because his master is such an irresponsible rascal."

She gave Lively part of a leftover biscuit, patted him. "Must you drool all over everything?"

The dog's ribbon of tongue hung out and he wagged his tail. His chest hair was all wet. "You know, a baby bib would stop all that and be a lot neater. I'll have to get you one."

Lively only looked around for another biscuit and when none was offered, he lay down in the middle of the floor and dropped off to sleep. Isaac, hurrying through with an armful of papers, tripped over the dog and went down. The dog ran yelping out of the tent.

"Oh, Isaac, I'm so sorry. Are you hurt?"

"No, and I don't suppose the dog is, either." He stumbled to his feet, scrambling to gather the strewn papers.

At that moment, Blackie O'Neal pushed his way in, dark eyes blazing. "I thought you were ruthless, but I didn't think you'd kick my dog."

Lacey confronted him and glared back. "I didn't kick him. It was an accident. Anyway, if you'd keep him at home instead of letting him roam the town—"

"If you'd quit luring him over here, he'd stay on my side of the street."

"Oh, so now it's my fault?" She was as mad as he was. "It just seems you're too busy looking after whores to know what he's doing."

Blackie blinked. "Ladies don't usually use that word."

"Now how would you know anything about ladies?" The more she thought about that blonde called Dixie hugging him up against her big breasts, the more annoyed she became. "I intend to run your whiskey den out of this town."

"Go right ahead on," he challenged, "are you going to have temperance protesters marching out front, too?"

"Great idea!"

"Fine. It'll draw a crowd and I'll sell more booze."

"You're outrageous," Lacey said. "And by the way, I resent you calling me Miss damnyankee Iron Corset."

He paused. "Now who told you that?"

"Chief Thunder."

He didn't deny it. "Joe's got a big mouth. He should stick to selling Custer's buttons."

"You encourage him in that duplicity?"

"That's a mighty big word, Miss Durango, but considerin' you're a female who's too big for her britches—"

"It means to cheat people, to fool them."

"I'm not ignorant, sister, I know what it means."

"I reckon anyone who would steal chickens from the U.S. Army already knows about cheats—"

"As I recall, you and your cat ate some of that chicken."

Her face flamed. "I did not."

He smiled. "Oh no? You had chicken grease on your face. And don't call me a cheat, Miss Durango. I run an honest card game."

"This has nothing to do with the subject at hand," Lacey began, then stumbled to a halt and stared up at him blankly. He looked as blank as she did. They disliked each other so much, she realized that it didn't take much ammunition for them to begin firing at each other.

"Texans," Isaac sighed in the background.

Blackie took a deep breath. "You're mad because I got your lumber and stole your workmen."

She would not have admitted it under Apache torture.

Blackie turned to go. "Are you going to keep enticin' my dog away?"

"I beg your pardon. He showed up and I gave him a biscuit. You're probably so busy with your women, you forgot to feed him."

"I don't neglect my dog. I love dogs, you, you damn-yankee cat person." Blackie said and then he stalked out.

Isaac had been watching from the corner by the printer. "Why didn't you just tell him what really happened?"

"He probably wouldn't have believed me," she seethed. "Now let's try to ignore the tinhorn gambler and get on with getting out the next edition. Have you picked up any news?"

"Well," Isaac said, "someone dropped in to say Mrs. Anderson has new baby girl and the ladies sewing circle is planning its first meeting Wednesday, yes."

"Good." She grabbed her pen, "and I heard a committee is trying to raise enough funds for a school. That just shows Pretty Prairie is going to be a law-abiding, progressive town. Once a town gets a newspaper, a school, a church, and a public library, it's on its way."

In the background, drifting faintly on the warm air, she heard an off-key chorus of drunken men's voices, along with the hammering of the carpenters building the new saloon. "Oh, my darling, oh, my darling, oh, my darling Clementine . . ."

"Outrageous!" Lacey snapped, "you wouldn't think that saloon would be selling so many drinks this early in the day."

"Those pretty girls seem to be luring the customers in already."

Lacey looked at the little man with a stern eye. "Now how would you know that?"

He suddenly got very busy. "Well, that's what some folks say."

"Humph. Let's ignore the racket and do our work. Now, for our next editorial—"

" . . . you are lost and gone forever, dreadful sorry, Clementine . . . "

Lacey took a deep breath and picked up a pencil. "In

a civilized town," she read aloud as she wrote, "everyone works and is responsible."

"Oh, the Camptown ladies sing this song, doodah, doodah . . . "

"And the ideal town will have a mayor and a town council who are upstanding citizens . . . "

"Camptown racetrack, five miles long, oh, doodah day . . . "

She was determined to ignore the hammering and the drunken singing, even as women's voices joined it. "A referendum should be held immediately to choose a town name. Also, we'll need a safe and adequate water supply . . . "

" . . . Gwine to run all night, gwine to run all day . . . "

"My word, this has to stop." Lacey forgot about the town's water supply and stuck her head out the tent. There were wagons going up and down the street, a buggy or two, and several men on horseback. Across the street Lively lay on the wooden sidewalk as if dead, while from inside the saloon tent came the sound of singing and clinking glasses as the carpenters built a framework around them. They didn't look too sober, either.

"It sounds as if he's managed to get a piano," Isaac said behind her.

"With all the other racket, how can you tell?"

Precious evidently didn't like the noise. She flattened her ears back and meowed. Above all the sounds of gaiety, came the noise of her stolen carpenters creating the framework of the building around the saloon tent. "Outrageous!"

"I think so, too." A tall, handsome young man walked up outside, turned to follow her indignant gaze. "You're right, Miss. It's disgusting; yes, that's what it is."

She smiled at him. "I'm so glad you agree, Mister—?"

"Peabody." He doffed his derby hat and made a slight bow. "Eugene Reginald Peabody at your service, ma'am."

"Lacey Durango. Delighted to meet you, Mr. Peabody." She looked him over with growing approval. Mr. Peabody was perfect, just what a man ought to be. This ideal male had a slender build, brown hair, pale blue eyes and a wispy mustache. He wore a natty black suit, a derby hat and fine white gloves. The outfit was complete with spats, a boutonniere and a walking stick. Her heart fluttered. "You just arrived? You don't look like you're from around here."

"Hardly." He favored her with a superior gaze. "I'm a Harvard man, you know, and I'm going to hang out my "attorney" shingle later. First, I must help my uncle get his store up and running. He begged for my assistance."

"A lawyer?" She sighed with pleasure. "And so well dressed. We're used to men in muddy boots around here."

He snorted and twirled his cane. "So uncouth. Even the women are so—so provincial and poorly educated."

She wanted to make a good impression on this cosmopolitan gentleman. "I'm a graduate of Miss Priddy's Female Academy in Boston."

He looked down his thin nose and gave her an approving nod. "I've heard of it. Good school."

"Also I own the newspaper and I've traveled a great deal myself."

"Really?" His pale eyes lit up. "I knew you were sensitive and clever as well as beautiful the moment I saw you. By the way, I want you to know I heartily approve of your editorials. I stand foursquare in favor of temperance and women's suffrage."

Lacey gave him her warmest smile. This was the kind of ideal man she'd always dreamed of, one who certainly could quote poetry and was well-read. She thought about Blackie O'Neal with a frown. Probably that gambler didn't read anything but the *Police Gazette* with its racy drawings over at the barber shop. "Mr. Peabody, I'm so glad you've arrived and I hope I'll be seeing more of you."

In the background, the tinny piano accompanied raucous voices: "Buffalo gals won't you come out tonight, come out tonight, come out tonight . . . . "

The elegant Mr. Peabody frowned. "We honest citizens

will soon run crooks like that gambler out of town. I might thrash him myself with my cane, but I wouldn't want genteel ladies to witness such mayhem."

"You're sooo sensitive," Lacey gushed, "but I agree a fine gentleman shouldn't dirty his hands with the likes of Blackie O'Neal. Besides, he's a rough saloon brawler. The man who takes him on had better bring his lunch because it might take a while."

"Disgusting." The handsome dude's thin nose went even higher in the air. "Perhaps when I open my law office, I'll run for Congress. Maybe I can get a law passed for prohibition and against sin. Voters are always against sin."

"My very thought." She warmed to the newcomer even more. She'd love to see the Irish saloon brawler run out of town. Knowing the brash Blackie, he'd probably swagger along in front of the mob as if he were leading a parade.

"Oh, a kitty." The elegant Mr. Peabody attempted to pat Precious who promptly arched her back and spat at him. "Cats generally love me."

Lacey was embarrassed for her impolite animal. "I don't know what's bothering her today."

"Oh, well." The gentleman reached to turn his lapel so he could sniff his boutonniere, "I'm here to order a nice big ad in your paper for our Peabody General Store."

"Of course. Come in and we'll make some notes." She was gushing over the gentleman, but she could not stop herself. "May I get you some coffee?"

"Actually, in London, I got used to drinking tea, but of course I doubt you—"

"Oh, but I do." She led him into her office tent. "I've been in England, too, you know. What did you find the most interesting?"

"Ahh, everything." He waved one fine gloved hand in dismissal. "I wish I had more time to talk, Miss Durango, but my uncle has a very difficult time with the store unless I'm there to manage."

"Oh, I fully understand." She ran to heat a kettle of

water on her small kerosene stove. "We'll discuss our travels when you have more time. Now you write out your ad while I make you some tea."

Isaac frowned at her when she passed him. "Who's the fancy dude?"

"Shh! He'll hear you." She lowered her voice as she busied herself with the tea kettle. "He's the perfect catch. That is, if he isn't married."

"A dude, yes?" Isaac whispered with scorn and returned to setting up type for the paper.

Lacey brought young Mr. Peabody a cup of tea. He took off his gloves one finger at a time and put them in his pocket. She noticed that he held his little finger out as he sipped it. Such refined, sensitive hands. Blackie O'Neal had big strong hands that could easily turn into lethal fists.

"Miss Durango, I do hope there is some kind of social life for a single gentleman such as myself in this provincial little place."

She sighed and her heart beat faster. "Well, so far, I don't know, but we unmarried ladies hope to establish some croquet clubs or perhaps an occasional tea dance."

His pale eyes lit up and he smiled at her. "Croquet? I love it. I do hope sometime you'll be my partner."

"My word, that would be delightful. You know, Mr. Peabody, I've been thinking of organizing a box supper or some kind of community dance as fund raisers. This town is in dire need of a school and library."

"Very worthy." He nodded his approval. "I might help organize the businessmen to fund some of your endeavors."

Behind them, the singing from the saloon began again: " . . . Oh, it rained all night the day I left, the weather it was dry . . . "

Young Mr. Peabody frowned. "Well, *some* of the business people," he said, "I'm sure you'll agree there are *some* we'd just soon left town."

"I quite agree," Lacey said. "Mr. Peabody, I can see that we have a lot in common."

He smiled at her. "I hope you won't think it too forward if I hope that soon, you'll think of me as 'Eugene.'"

Be still my heart. She was so flustered, she dropped her pencil. "Not at all." She found herself giggling like an idiot school girl.

He stood up and twirled his cane. "As loath as I am to leave such pleasant company, I must be off. Uncle is just at a loss without me. Toodle-loo." He touched the brim of his derby and left, swinging his cane.

Lacey leaned back in her chair and sighed. "Dear me, I think I'm about to have an attack of the vapors. Such a perfect, perfect gentleman. Didn't you think so, Isaac?"

"Umm. A bit of a dandy, yes." He kept setting type.

"Oh, don't be so suspicious. Just imagine, well traveled and a Harvard man. The girl who lands him will get quite a catch."

Isaac only snorted and she stared at Eugene's tea cup. She imagined herself at a pristine dining table with a maid in uniform pouring tea from fine china in the perfect house while she sat across from her handsome, perfect husband, discussing current events and social functions. Outside, their beautiful, perfect children played on the landscaped lawn. Eugene would look across the breakfast table at her as he reached to kiss her hand and say—"

"You got that ad he gave you?"

"What?" She came back to reality.

"The ad," Isaac frowned.

"Yes, here." She handed it over and tried to return to work. It was difficult with memories of the fine gentleman mingling with the caterwauling from the saloon across the street. Her newspaper was off to a rousing start and now she'd be getting even more advertisers. Her life would finally be perfect. Or would be when she could build her new office on that corner lot and run that scummy gambler out of town. With Eugene as an inspiration, she sat down, dusted off her already perfect desk and wrote a scathing editorial about what a scandal and a detriment saloons were to a town.

Isaac read it and frowned. "This is pretty strong, Miss Lacey. Are you sure you aren't letting your personal dislike of the man cloud your judgement?"

"Of course not! There's nothing personal; I'm just thinking of this town's future." She was highly indignant that anyone might question her motives. "Print it!"

Isaac sighed. "All right, yes, it's your paper. But if it were mine, we wouldn't."

They printed up the edition and it went out the next day. When she looked out of her tent door that morning, she saw Blackie O'Neal standing on the street reading a copy. As they say in Texas, he looked mad as a rained-on rooster. When he spotted her watching him, he frowned and strode across the street toward her.

She took a deep breath. Uh-oh.

Chapter Five

Lacey took another deep breath and faced the gambler. "And how may I help you?" she asked a little too sweetly.

He seemed to take a deep breath, too, perhaps to control his temper. "I'll bet you think I'm upset over your editorial, Miss Durango."

"And you've come to give me a good tongue-lashing?"

"That's what you would expect, isn't it?" He grinned at her but it looked more like a grimace. "Actually, I've come to run an ad in your newspaper. Can we go inside?"

"What?" She'd been expecting anything but this. She felt stunned as he took her elbow and led her back inside her tent. Lively ambled behind Blackie, drooling as he lay down by her desk and promptly dropped off to sleep.

Blackie said "Now about the ad—"

"It does pay to advertise," she said, "but you see, I'm choosey about the ads the *Crusader* will accept."

He blinked. "Are you tellin' me you won't accept advertisin' for Blackie's Black Garter?"

"That's about the size of it."

"You might want to think that over, sister." He glared at her.

"I will not be intimidated, Mr. O'Neal."

Blackie stared down into her dark eyes. She was a little frightened, he could see, but she wasn't backing down. As much as he hated it, he felt a little admiration for the spunky girl. She had more guts than a slaughterhouse; much more than he had given her credit for, but after all, she was a

Texan. He had thought the constant and deliberate noise from his saloon would run her out of town, but it hadn't. He might have to change tactics with this prim spinster.

He gave her a charming smile, the kind that made most women's hearts beat faster, and had brought more than one into his bed. "Let's be reasonable, Miss Durango. You can use more income as you struggle to get this paper off the ground. And maybe advertisin' will help my business."

She must remember that he was as crafty as a coyote, even as she took a deep breath redolent of his shaving lotion scent. He was so very masculine, but of course, she preferred the sensitive type. "You are thinking I can be bought off for the price of an ad?"

"What?" He feigned surprise. "Why, ma'am, it never crossed my mind." She was smarter than most women. With those horn-rimmed spectacles sliding down her pert nose, she was almost as cute as a pup in a red wagon. "I just know a new paper needs all the advertisin' it can get."

"I'm getting plenty of business," she smiled back. "Mr. Peabody's nephew came by to put in a big ad for the general store."

"Oh, yes, the poor lame gent."

"He's not lame, he's a fine specimen of a man."

"Well, he was carryin' a cane. In Texas, that'd mean the poor hombre had a game leg."

What could she expect from a rough saloon brawler who wore a gaudy red silk vest and muddy cowboy boots? "Mr. Peabody will be a real asset to this community. He is very stylish."

Blackie smiled back. "I thought he looked like an undertaker."

He was baiting her and she knew it. "I don't suppose they see very many gentlemen in spats and derbies in the whiskey dives you frequent." She kept her voice icy. "I might even suggest he run for mayor as soon as we get this town named. I'm suggesting Pretty Prairie."

He threw back his head and laughed. "You're jokin', aren't you? The men are already thinkin' of namin' it Whiskey Flats."

She literally shuddered at the thought. "Outrageous. A name like Pretty Prairie will attract a better type of settler."

"It'll attract prim old maids, reformers, and nancy boys," Blackie retorted. "Anyway, no real man would vote for a sissy name like that and may I remind you that as of yet, thank God, ladies don't get to vote."

"I am well aware of that injustice, but that will eventually be remedied."

"Ha! You damnyankee temperance suffragette." He rolled his eyes.

"You uncultured brute, need I remind you the name of this paper is the *Crusader* and that's just what I intend to do. I will not accept your advertising and I will not stop attacking your vile business in my editorials. Now good day to you, you Rebel."

He seemed to be struggling to control his temper. "There are those who say your motives aren't so pure, sis. That you'd like to run me out of town so you can get the deed to that contested lot."

She felt the angry flush creep up her face. "I would not stoop to that. I have high principles."

"Sister, I think you're foolin' yourself. Come on, Lively." He turned to stride out, but his dog only raised its head and wagged its tail at Lacey. "Come on," O'Neal ordered.

"He won't leave until I give him a bite," Lacey explained and went around the corner to her makeshift kitchen and returned to give the big dog a biscuit. Precious, looking on from her place atop a file cabinet meowed and the dog wagged its tail at the cat.

"Lively," Blackie said sternly, "you must stop consortin' with the enemy." He glared at Lacey, "and you need to stop tryin' to alienate the affections of my dog." He paused in the doorway of the tent.

"Can I help it if he likes it over here?"

"Traitor dog. Come on, Lively." Blackie snapped his fingers at the hound and the pooch got up reluctantly. The two left.

"Well," Isaac came around from behind a printing press. "I don't know whether you should have turned down his advertising, we could use the money, yes?"

She drew herself up stiffly. "I have principles. Besides because of a past tragic experience, I cannot bring myself to push demon rum. She remembered with a frown. "The devil's brew causes a lady to do things that shame her."

Lacey paused, then realized Isaac was staring at her with curiosity. "Anyway, I wouldn't give that Irish scoundrel the satisfaction of seeing his name in my respectable paper. Blackie's Black Garter indeed."

"Have it your way." The printer shrugged and returned to his work.

Later that afternoon, Isaac came to her. "I heard some gossip at the barber shop, yes. There's a meeting tonight about the town name. Blackie O'Neal is organizing it."

"Aha! I reckon I galvanized that scoundrel into action. I'll be sure and be there."

"Ah, Miss Lacey, it's not a place for ladies. They are holding it in the Black Garter."

"Naturally," Lacey paced up and down, "he's trying to keep decent people from attending and voicing their opinions."

Isaac hesitated. "I hear he wants to advertise and the only way he can do it, since you turned him down, is to invite all the boys in and offer free beer. And of course, there's roulette, poker, and girls."

"That is aimed directly at me," she seethed. "He thinks he can influence all the men to vote for that outrageous name 'Whiskey Flats'. Surely the right-thinking men of this new settlement will not be swayed by such a cheap trick."

Isaac looked at her as if she'd lost her mind. "You must be joking, yes?"

"You're right; the brutes." She paused to think. "There has to be a way to sway the men in this town to the cause of Pretty Prairie."

Isaac shook his head. "Face it, Miss Lacey, this time, O'Neal's holding the winning cards."

"If he is," Lacey fumed, "it's because that tinhorn is stacking the deck. I might have a trick or two up my sleeve, too. I'm a Texan, remember?"

"And so is he," Isaac reminded her. "They say he's from the Big Thicket country; is that bad?"

Lacey paused. That was intimidating news. The Texas Big Thicket covered thousands of acres of swamps and impregnable brush in the eastern part of the Lone Star State near the Louisiana border. It was an ideal hideout for outlaws and moonshiners. Lawmen didn't like to venture into the Big Thicket, they often disappeared without a trace. Tough hombres came from the Big Thicket. Had she underestimated Blackie?

Lacey took a deep breath. "At any rate, I'll be at that meeting tonight both as a business owner and a newspaper reporter. In the meantime, if those carpenters are about finished with that house of sin, see if you can get them back on our building. Precious and I aren't too happy in this leaky old tent."

That evening, Lacey put on her most no-nonsense dark serge dress, a severe hat, took her pad and pencil and marched outside. She had to admit, the new two story building was an imposing structure. Dozens of horses were already tied to the hitching post out front. She paused, then took a deep breath for courage and strode across the dusty street, heading for the swinging doors.

Inside, Moose looked up from pouring drinks and yelled at the boss. "Uh-oh, here she comes."

Blackie went to the window and peered out. "Damn, I didn't think she'd have the nerve to come." He looked around at all the men sitting at the tables enjoying his free beer. "Gentlemen," he yelled, "watch your manners. A lady is about to join us. And Moose, stop servin' until she leaves."

The men set up a moan, but Blackie made a soothing gesture. "Don't worry, boys, she won't stay long."

Dutch, the little piano player, had stopped in mid-note and turned toward the door. The men paused in their card games and looked up. Blackie motioned to Flo and the girls who were scattered about the saloon, many sitting on the arms of men's chairs. "Go on upstairs, girls. We've got a meetin' about to start and there's a lady comin'."

"Well, now!" the pretty blonde Dixie drawled, swinging her hips as she paused. "What are we?"

"I mean a *real* lady," Blackie snapped, "and I don't want her mentionin' in her crusadin' paper how you gals was draped all over these businessmen, most of them married, who are here for this meetin'."

The men looked at each other in alarm.

"It's okay, boys." Blackie smiled reassuringly. "My girls don't tattle and they'll come back down after Miss Iron Corset leaves."

Blackie motioned and the girls headed up the stairs and the men quickly hid the cards. As Lacey Durango entered the swinging doors, Blackie was there to greet her, bowing low. "Why, Miss Durango, this is an unexpected honor."

"Unexpected? I reckon so since I had to find out about this meeting through the grapevine."

"Well," Blackie grinned, "we didn't send out engraved invitations. It ain't exactly a garden party."

The men all laughed but she didn't. They stirred uneasily and looked at each other.

Blackie said to her. "Perhaps you have been misled,

Miss Durango. This is a town hall meetin'. Please note the lack of any entertainment at all; strictly business."

"Uh-huh. I might believe you except I still smell cheap perfume on the air."

"It ain't cheap perfume!" Dixie's angry drawl echoed down the stairs. "I'll have you know a very fine gent gimme that in Atlanta."

"Dixie," Blackie frowned and yelled up the stairs. "Go to bed."

"By myself?"

The men all guffawed and Lacey felt the blood rush to her face. If this Rebel sidewinder thought he could embarrass her into fleeing like a scared jackrabbit, he was in for a surprise. She marched over, pulled out a chair at one of the poker tables, and sat down. Immediately the men at the table scattered like frightened quail, abandoning the whole table to her. She put on her spectacles and readied her pencil and pad, then peered over her glasses at the host.

Blackie smiled but it seemed forced. "Tell me, Miss Durango, are you here as a reporter or a business owner?"

"Both," she said. "May I have a glass of water?"

"Water?" Moose looked baffled. "Water," Blackie nodded. "Moose, I'm sure we must have some around here somewhere."

"I got iced tea," Moose said, "you know I always got a pitcher because—"

"Fine," Blackie interrupted, "get the lady some tea."

"No, thank you." Lacey said coolly. "I am not here to accept the hospitality of this very questionable establishment."

Dang her Yankee-lovin' hide, Blackie thought, there was no compromising this dame. She was an unbribable pillar of virtue without a breath of scandal to her name. He'd never met a woman like that in all his thirty years.

Lively raised his head from his corner as if suddenly recognizing her voice. The big dog got up and ambled across the floor, tail wagging, and put his head in her lap.

"Huh," one of the cowboys said, "look at the nancy dog."

For the first time, Blackie noticed the bloodhound was wearing a lacy pink baby's bib. It said *BABY* in pretty embroidery. "What the hell—?"

"Tsk. Tsk," she admonished him. "Did you know swearing indicates a lack of vocabulary?"

Blackie blinked, still staring at Lively. "What'd you do to my dog?"

She shrugged. "He was drooling all over the place and it was untidy. Mrs. Anderson had an extra baby bib."

The cowboys laughed. "Looks like the lady's got herself a dog. Right fetchin', that prissy pink bib."

"It is *my* dog," Blackie said, "the flea-bitten traitor. Now can we get down to business?"

About that time, the saloon doors swung open again and Eugene Reginal Peabody, in full glory and carrying his cane, paused in the doorway. He was perfect, Lacey thought with a sigh; a well-dressed, cosmopolitan gentleman who made all the other men in the room look like ragged barbarians.

"Is this where the town meeting is being held?" Eugene looked about uncertainly. My uncle asked me to attend."

"Who's the sissy dude?" One cowboy asked another.

"Dunno. Looks like an undertaker with that posy in his buttonhole, don't he?"

A ripple of laughter passed through the room.

"Stop that," the blacksmith muttered, "it ain't fair to make fun of a crippled hombre like that."

Blackie grinned. "Oh, fellas, I have it on good authority that the fanciest gents from back East carry stylish canes. Do come in, Mr. Peabody."

Lacey gestured to the uneasy gentleman. "Here, sit next to me, Eugene."

Blackie winked at her as Eugene walked hesitantly across the saloon with all the farmers and cowboys suppressing smiles. "Mr. Peabody, can I get you something to drink?"

"I'll have a glass of wine if it's a good year, or maybe some sherry."

"Sherry?" Moose paused in wiping the bar. "Boss, ain't that a lady's drink?"

"I'm sorry," Blackie was too solicitous. "You see, we've got a temperance leader present, so we can't serve alcohol. It would offend the lady. How about some iced tea?"

"Iced tea?" Eugene looked puzzled.

"It's not something they drink up north," Lacey explained while the men snickered.

"Mother's milk of the South," Blackie said.

"No, I— I think I'll just have water."

"Water?" Moose asked and blinked.

"You know, Moose," Blackie said, "that stuff we give to horses and wash with now and then."

Moose poured a beer mug full of water, brought it to the table, and slammed it down.

"May I have a napkin?" Eugene asked.

Now even Lacey winced, even though a perfect gentleman would expect a napkin. "Uh, Eugene, I'm not sure Mr. O'Neal even knows what that is. His clientele usually wipes their mouths on their shirt sleeves."

"How right you are," Blackie grinned. "Now if the gentleman is through askin' for stuff we don't have, maybe we can get started."

Lacey looked around at the gathered men. It occurred to her that some of them had had a good snoot full of alcohol long before she had arrived.

Blackie reached across the bar, picked up the bung starter used to open beer kegs, and rapped on the bar for order. He hadn't really expected the lady would have the nerve to invade this male bastion and now that she had, he wasn't quite certain how to handle it. He had tried to scare her out of town and it hadn't worked. Then he had tried bribery in attempting to buy an ad in her damned newspaper. That hadn't worked, either. She was not only stubborn as a jackass, she was smart. She might be almost as smart as he was. Naw; not possible. She was only a woman after all.

There was no compromising this woman. Miss Iron Corset was going to put a damper on what had started out to be a fun evening for all the men. The others knew it, too. They looked at each other and at the stiff, unbending lady with her notebook and pencil. Then they all sighed.

Young Mr. Peabody cleared his throat and stood up. "I have to say it is so good to have the press here to cover this historic event."

Lacey beamed at him. Such a perfect gentleman.

"Yeah, sure. We're all thrilled." Blackie glared at the young whippersnapper. The Yankee dude was probably about the same age as Miss Iron Corset, and as green as they came. Blackie looked around at the crowd. Cowboys, settlers, a soldier or two, a couple of railroad workers, and most of the businessmen in town. "Since I'm the host, I would like to suggest that we hold a referendum and name our new town Whiskey Flats."

One of the scruffy cowboys jumped to his feet, swaying a little. "Let's vote it in right now. Then can I have another beer?"

The prim newspaper woman paused in taking notes. "I'm sorry, but you're out of order, cowboy. When there's a motion on the floor, it has to be seconded and then discussed."

A low moan went through the crowded saloon. *Oh, hell,* Blackie thought in disgust. The men had hoped to have this business over with in about five minutes so they could get on with the more serious business of drinking, gambling, and ogling the girls who wouldn't come down until the prissy old maid left. He took a deep breath. He must not lose his temper with Miss Iron Corset even though he wanted to grab her, carry her out front, and toss her in the horse trough. "I'm sure Miss Durango knows more about proper procedure than we do. Very well, I made a motion, do I hear a second?"

The brawny blacksmith stood up. "I'll do that second thing. Now can we pee on the fire and call in the dogs? I've got five dollars in that poker pot."

The prissy gentleman turned to the lady and whispered loud enough for everyone to hear. "Disgusting. I don't even see a fire."

Amid roars of laughter, Lacey leaned over to him. "It's a Texas saying, Eugene. It means let's bring this matter to a close."

"That's right." Blackie turned and smiled triumphantly at Lacey. "Well, it appears this will get a unanimous vote anyway, so perhaps we could dispense—"

"No, wait." Miss Iron Corset peered at him over her horn-rimmed spectacles. "Now we have discussion— unless you'd like to withdraw your motion?"

"Withdraw?" Blackie said, "hell, no, anybody who knows Texans knows they don't ever withdraw. Why, at the Alamo—"

"Withdraw doesn't necessarily mean surrender," the lady pointed out.

"Sounds like it to me," Blackie retorted.

She sighed deeply. Dealing with this brute was like dealing with his hound dog. On second thought, Lively was probably more agreeable. "We now have a motion and a second," she said, "so now we have to have discussion."

A drunken cowboy near the back whined loudly. "And then can I have another beer?"

"Disgusting." Eugene said, but not very loud.

Perhaps it was her destiny to bring civilization and culture to this primitive settlement and these drunken brutes. She stood up. "As a citizen and business owner, I would like to discuss why Whiskey Flats is a bad name for this town."

"And then can I have another beer?" the cowboy yelled.

Blackie shot him a warning look. "We are gonna be

polite to the lady and hear her out, even though she can't vote so she's wastin' our time."

"Don't patronize me, you tinhorn," she shot back.

"Sister, don't try to impress me with your ten-dollar words." He grinned at her.

Eugene cleared his throat. "It means—"

"Never mind," Lacey said, "he's only trying to annoy me. Gentlemen, and I use the word very looucly, Whiskey Flats is a bad name for the town for the following reasons—"

"Great God Almighty. Is this gonna take a long time?" Blackie sighed.

"It will if you keep interrupting me," she snapped back. "Now, it's a bad name because it gives outsiders a poor image of what we're about. It conveys the image of a wild, whiskey-soaked, lawless town."

"Sounds good to me," one of the railroad workers grinned a little drunkenly and the crowd roared approval.

Young Peabody stood up. "You're disgusting. I'll thank you not to interrupt the lady. I for one, think she's right."

The brawny railroad worker half rose from his chair, his fists doubled. Blackie waved him back down and looked at Eugene. "Uh, Junior, unless you're pretty good with your fists, I'd be careful about your insults."

Lacey turned and beamed at Eugene. "You're so gallant, Eugene, such a perfect gentleman."

Blackie frowned. "Your perfect gentleman is liable to get hisself kilt if he ain't careful."

Lacey glared at Blackie. "You're out of order, sir. I have the floor. Businessmen, I urge you to think of the image of this town. Do you want a town that only draws cowboys and trail trash? If so, law-abiding citizens won't move here and the town won't grow. If the town doesn't grow, neither will your profits. I have a better name; Pretty Prairie. That name conveys a quiet, civilized settlement with orderly streets, white picket fences, and families moving in; in short, profits."

"Am I ever gonna get a beer?" whined the drunken cowboy plaintively.

Lacey decided to ignore him. "Not every male citizen is here tonight, so I don't see how you can hold a lawful referendum on the spot. Therefore, I am asking Mr. O'Neal to withdraw his motion."

"Now you know I ain't gonna do that," Blackie said.

"Fine, then I'll continue discussion."

A moan went up from the thirsty men. "Withdraw it, Blackie, anything to get her to shut up and sit down."

"All right, all right." He made a disgusted placating motion. "I withdraw my motion."

She beamed. "In that case, I would like to make one."

"You can't do that," Blackie snapped, "you're a woman and not even a voter."

"Someday women will be allowed to vote," Lacey smiled without mirth, "but in the meantime, I am a business owner, so I think I can make a motion that affects this town."

A cowboy nudged the judge who was dozing face down at a poker table. "Is that legal, Judge?"

Men began to roar in protest and Blackie grabbed the bung starter and rapped on the bar. "Order! Order!"

The grizzled judge woke up and stirred, lifted his face from the puddle of beer on the scarred table. "Order? I'll have another whiskey."

"Me too! Me too!" Came from a dozen parched throats.

Moose leaned his elbows on the bar and shook his head. "Boss says we can't open the bar until the meetin's over."

"Miss Durango," Blackie said, "can we get this over with? You're costin' me money here."

"All right, I move that the voters be given a choice between the two names, Whiskey Flats and Pretty Prairie, with the referendum to be held two weeks from today. Do I hear a second?"

Dead silence.

"Well," Blackie grinned at her. "I reckon even I know enough to know that it's dead if you don't get a second—"

"I second Miss Durango's motion." Young Peabody leaped to his feet.

A moan went up from the crowd. "Do that mean more talkin' and no drinkin'?"

"Not if you pass the motion to hold the referendum," Lacey shouted over the confusion.

A farmer stood up. "Let's do whatever it takes to sack this possum."

Eugene turned a curious gaze to Lacey.

She leaned over and whispered. "Same as, you know, on the fire and call in the dogs."

The farmer said "Everybody in favor?"

"Wait a minute," Blackie protested, "I think—"

"Aye!" The crowd shouted.

"Now can I have another drink?" The cowboy yelled.

Blackie sighed and nodded in defeat. "Moose, open 'er."

A cheer went up as the men rushed forward to the bar.

"Disgusting." Young Peabody wrinkled his nose.

Lacey gathered up her things and stood up. "Well, I reckon it now goes to the voters and may the best man win."

Blackie looked at her with almost a grudging admiration. The little Yankee-lover couldn't win this fight, she must know that, but she was game to try. No man was going to vote for a dudish name like Pretty Prairie and women couldn't vote. Miss Iron Corset smiled at him and he realized with a shock that she was quite pretty. She was just so opinionated and stubborn. Blackie wasn't used to that in a woman. "Well, sister, you won this battle, but you won't win the war."

"We'll see about that. Eugene, will you escort me home?" She stuck her pert nose in the air, took the dude's arm and they sailed out of the saloon, Lively following them.

"Damn it, Lively, come back, you're my dog, remember?"

The big hound turned and wagged his tail, drooling

down his pink baby bib. He ambled over and lay down in a corner.

A chorus of cheers as the men milled around and Flo and her girls came down the stairs. The piano began pounding out "Buffalo Gals" as the men bellied up to the bar and the roulette wheel began to whirl.

Blackie leaned against the bar and lit a fresh cigar. "Moose, you got to hand it to her, she was game to come in and face down all these drunks."

"Yeah, she was, Boss. The usual?"

Blackie nodded and accepted the drink, watching with satisfaction as the men drained their glasses and pounded on the bar for more. Miss damnyankee Iron Corset couldn't win this fight, but she was feisty as hell. Texans liked that in a woman. Was he getting loco? She was trying to put him out of business and Blackie wasn't used to losing; especially not to a petticoat. That she would lose the referendum was already a foregone conclusion, but he intended to make her a laughing stock. Maybe when he rubbed her nose in defeat, she'd be so humiliated, she'd take her damned reformer newspaper and leave town, relinquishing her claim. He'd build a saloon twice as big as this one on that choice corner lot.

Chapter Six

Lacey had finally gotten the carpenters to work on her building and though the constant hammering drove her to distraction, in about a week, she was finally in a real structure. What really annoyed her was that she could see the gaudy saloon from the newspaper's front window. She promptly installed curtains. However, nothing stopped the noise. Every time her door opened, a blare of off-key piano music, women laughing, and glasses clinking interrupted her solitude. Sometimes there was gunfire and fighting in the street. One night some cowboys rode their horses into the saloon. The sheriff seemed to ignore it.

As the days grew warmer, she was forced to leave the front door open in a vain attempt to catch a breeze blowing through. In her dreams now, she heard that off-key piano banging out every song Stephen Foster ever wrote. She devoutly wished she could bury Blackie O'Neal in the yard of "My Old Kentucky Home" or the "Camptown Races" so the horses could gallop across him.

The newspaper was selling briskly and that elevated her spirits. She would put a bundle of papers out by the door and an honesty box so people could buy a paper and drop their change in.

"Isaac," she said one night as she counted her money, "we're showing a profit, thanks in part to your expertise. You know, I've always wondered why you didn't open your own paper rather than work for me all these years?"

He hesitated. "I like working for you, Miss Lacey, and it's a good town."

"Hmm. Sometimes I wonder if the ruffians aren't going to prevail despite everything the good folk can do. I'm worried about the referendum."

He shrugged and wiped his thin face with an ink-stained hand. "I wish I knew how to help. You've got my vote, but I'm afraid most of the men will go along with Blackie on this one, yes."

Through the open door blared "Buffalo gals won't you come out tonight, come out tonight, come out tonight? Buffalo gals, won't you come out tonight and dance by the light of the moon?"

In disgust, Lacey went to the window and looked out into the darkness. A woman's laughter floated on the air and shadows danced across the upstairs windows of that den of sin. "I will best him yet," Lacey clenched her teeth. "We will clean this town up and make it a nice place for decent people."

"Miss Lacey, you can't legislate morality. This is a free country."

"Whiskey and wild women," she fumed, glaring at the shadows across the street. It looked like Blackie O'Neal dancing with one of his saloon girls. "Outrageous."

Lacey pictured how it would feel to be in his arms. She remembered the flash of his white teeth and the smell of tobacco and shaving lotion. Other women might be fooled by his charm, but not her. Blackie O'Neal was everything she despised in a man; a flawed, devil-may-care lady-killer with a drink always in his hand. She'd do whatever it took to force him to close up and get out of town. "I will write another editorial about the town name."

"Another one?" Isaac groaned.

And so she did; her strongest yet. Several straitlaced ladies came by to compliment her on her courage and wish aloud that they could all vote. In that case, Pretty Prairie would win in a walk. As it was, they were fighting an uphill battle reasoning with the men. Everyone knew men were weak creatures who thought with their . . . plumbing. Blackie was plying them all with whiskey, gambling, and pretty whores. The upright ladies of the settlement had no chance against odds like that.

They said so when the sewing circle came by her office one May afternoon.

"We just can't lose," Lacey told them, "this is too important."

Timid little Miss Wren, who was well-educated and of course still living with her parents, cleared her throat. "I don't know how we could persuade the men to vote our way."

"She's right about that." Mrs. Anderson transferred her baby to her ample hip.

The plump, near-sighted Ethel Wilson glared out the front window at the saloon across the street. "The business angle doesn't seem to matter. My husband, Julius, is the banker and he's set to vote for Whiskey Flats."

Miss Wren said shyly, "Maybe we could get all the ladies to stop doing their husbands' laundry unless the men promise to vote our way."

"My word, are you joking?" Lacey asked. "The average man wouldn't care if he wore the same dirty socks for a year. I doubt if they'd ever change their underwear if their wives didn't take it away from them and wash it."

"Isn't that the truth?" The barber's wife put in.

Ethel Wilson chewed her lip. "What if we quit cooking unless they promised—"

"You think a man will keep a promise?" Lacey remembered Homer and frowned. "Besides, men don't have any more taste than that hound dog of O'Neal's. If nobody cooked for them, they'd just open some cans or eat at our one cafe, that Chinese place over by the tracks."

"True," the ladies agreed.

Lacey chewed her lip, thinking. Across the street, a drunken cowboy staggered out, his arm around one of the saloon girls, that blonde one, Dixie. He paused on the sidewalk and began to kiss her, pawing at her bosom. After a moment, they went back inside.

Eugene Peabody arrived just then, paused in the doorway, staring back at the saloon. "Disgusting." He stuck his head in the door. "Ladies, I'm on my way to the post office. I just wanted to offer my support in any way I can. Toodle-loo." He tipped his hat and went on down the sidewalk.

"What a fine young man!" The ladies chorused. "Now there is a true gentleman."

Lacey felt a warm glow for Eugene. "Yes, he's perfect. Such a contrast to that outlandish rake across the street."

Little Miss Wren sighed. "But isn't he a dashing rake? Sort of makes my heart go pit-a-pat."

The circle of ladies stared at her with alarm.

Lacey said "Blackie O'Neal is a rascal, and no doubt, has talked many an innocent girl out of her drawers."

There was a moment of silence as the ladies seemed to picture that scene. Several sighed wistfully which annoyed Lacey even more.

"We are losing track of our mission." Lacey straightened her shoulders. "Think. Men don't care much about clean socks or even good cooking. What is the one thing the brutes can't do without?"

All eyes grew round.

"You can't mean—?" Mrs. Anderson began.

"Oh, my!" Little Miss Wren's face turned red as a settler's long-handled underwear.

The other ladies giggled nervously and avoided each other's gaze.

"Ladies," Lacey said sternly, "this is no time to let timidity and hesitancy rule. I suggest that the married ladies form a bedroom protest."

A gasp, followed by titters. "Oh, that's just too daring."

"Besides," Mrs. Anderson bounced her whimpering baby and thought aloud. "They'd just take their business over upstairs at the Black Garter."

A long sigh from the ladies and their faces turned sad with discouragement.

Lacey tapped her pencil and thought about it. Mrs. Anderson was right of course. She'd be damned if she did something to put even more money in Blackie O'Neal's pockets.

Through the door, the off-key piano banged out another chorus of "Buffalo Gals:" . . . "Buffalo gals won't you come out tonight, come out tonight, come out tonight . . ."

"You know," said one lady, "I'm beginning to loathe that song."

"And the saloon owner," Lacey declared.

"Now I didn't say that. He's a charmer. Why, he could talk a cow out of her calf."

"He's a rascal," Lacey reminded them.

Miss Wren sighed. "But such a tempting rascal."

Lacey was annoyed with the simpering lady. "Well, he doesn't tempt this Texan. What takes my eye is a polished, genteel gentleman."

"Well, he sure ain't that," declared Ethel Wilson. "He's a man; a *real* man."

"Amen," said a chorus of ladies and they all turned and looked toward the saloon with a sigh.

How could they be such fools? Lacey made a sound of annoyance. "May I remind you ladies that if we don't defeat that rogue and get him to leave town, that he's going to corrupt all your husbands?"

"Mine don't need much help," said the angular wife of the town blacksmith. "Neither do most of the rest."

As if on cue, a drunken railroad worker stumbled out of the Black Garter with lip rouge all over his face.

Lacey strode up and down, thinking. "If we instituted a total strike against the men; no cooking, no laundry, no cleaning and most of all, no bedroom privileges until they promise to vote our way, I think we could sway them."

"Easy for you to say," snorted Mrs. Anderson, "you

don't have a man to deal with. Besides, didn't we just agree they'd take their, ah, business to the Garter?"

Lacey stopped and a brilliant idea came to her. "Suppose we could get the girls who work at the Garter to join our Cause?"

A deep gasp. "Who would dare to approach those hussies and ask?" said the blacksmith's skinny wife.

"Besides," ventured Miss Wren, "it would be taking food right out of their mouths. Those girls get paid for doing . . . well, you know."

Nervous giggles and deeply flushed faces.

"We can't make the strike work if we don't get them to join us." Lacey conceded.

"Why would they care?" Ethel Wilson asked.

"Good question." Lacey paced some more. "Maybe I could convince the poor, downtrodden creatures that they are the victims of male brutes and that for the good of the future of all women, they need to join us in this protest."

Mrs. Anderson's baby began to whimper and she bounced it on her ample hip. "We all got groceries and maybe a little butter-and-egg money hidden away, but if the hussies don't earn money, they don't eat."

I'll have to think on this." Lacey stared out the window at the passing scene. A number of horses were tied in front of the saloon and a wagon and two buggies passed as she watched. Somewhere a child laughed and yelled, "Gotcha! You're it!"

As she watched, Blackie O'Neal came out of his saloon, looking dapper in a fine gray coat with a red silk cravat. It seemed to Lacey she could almost smell the scent of fine shaving lotion from here. Funny, he never smelled of whiskey although now, as usual, he had a tall drink in his hand and when he sipped, the diamond ring on his pinkie finger winked in the sunlight. When he spotted her watching him, he took off his hat, grinned, and bowed low. Then he turned and sauntered down the street.

Lacey whirled away from the window. How dare the Rebel rogue even acknowledge a respectable woman? She ground her teeth together and walked over to stroke Precious who lay sleeping on top of the printing press. "Yes, the key is getting the girls at the Carter to throw in with us."

"But wouldn't they rather have a wide-open town like Whiskey Flats?" argued Miss Wren.

Lacey asked, "What is it most women want more than anything?"

"A husband!" rang out a chorus of women.

"Right, except for yours truly," Lacey nodded. "Now if this were a respectable town, even the saloon girls would get marriage proposals. With no hussies, that rogue's business would suffer, maybe enough for him to close up his grog shop. You know, even Blackie's girls might have a shred of decency about them. Maybe they'd like to help win one for the ladies at least once."

"And then they won't have enough money to eat," said Ethel Wilson.

"But here is where we come in." Lacey insisted. "We will provide home-cooked meals for the girls."

"What?" The women looked aghast.

"We'll feed them so they can afford to deny all those men who want to buy their, ah, favors."

"It's unheard of," Mrs. Anderson said uncertainly. "I don't know what my husband would say."

"So don't tell him," Lacey said. "For once, we're going to outwit the men. It's worth it to best that scoundrel and to give this town a clean and wholesome name. Who is with me?"

"I am!" Miss Blanton, the milliner, stood up, fire in her pale eyes.

"Me, too," shouted Mrs. Wilson and Mrs. Anderson.

"Me! And me!" One by one, the ladies raised their hands. "Three cheers for Miss Lacey, our new leader!"

"Hip hip, hooray! Hip hip, Hooray! Hip hip, Hooray!"

They were all on their feet now, cheering and strengthened by their bold plan.

"I think," Lacey shouted, "we should march in front of the saloon to show the town loafers where we stand. When other women see us marching, they'll join our cause as will all the upright men of this settlement."

Another cheer rose as the ladies followed her out the open door of the newspaper and across the street, holding up the progress of a beer wagon and a mule caravan. Lively lay asleep on the wooden sidewalk in front of the Black Garter, but he got up, tail wagging, and joined them as they marched up and down. Men paused in doorways to watch and a passing rider seemed so astounded, he steered his horse into the back of the beer wagon with a crash. The horse reared and tossed him into a pile of manure.

"We need a song!" Lacey said, "how about the Battle Hymn of the Republic?"

"I think not. My Southern mama would roll over in her grave," Mrs. Anderson frowned.

"I know," Miss Wren said, "we can take 'Onward Christian Soldiers' and change it into: 'Onward temperance Ladies, marching as to war.'"

Mrs. Wilson paused uncertainly. "I don't know what Reverend Lovejoy would think of that."

"I know!" Lacey said, "we'll use one of the gambler's favorite tunes. Instead of 'Buffalo Gals', we'll sing 'temperance gals' and instead of 'dance,' we'll sing 'march'."

Everyone agreed and the ladies started marching in a circle, singing loudly, if not too well. People began peering out windows or coming out of businesses to stare. Passersby began to gather.

Blackie O'Neal had just come out of the corner barber shop and paused to lit a cigar. There seemed to be some sort of parade farther down the street and it sounded like someone was torturing some cats. He could see people gathering in front of his saloon. Puzzled, he began to stroll in that direction. His mild curiosity grew into annoyance as he realized that dozens of the town's most respectable matrons were marching up and down in front of the Black Garter. In fact, his own dog was walking with them, tail wagging Then he spotted Miss Iron Corset in the lead. *Oh damn.* This couldn't be good. Wherever she was there was always trouble.

He quickened his step, confronted her. "Great God Almighty! What's going on here?"

"A rally for righteousness." Lacey announced. My word, he was so tall and a little intimidating. She almost took a step backward, then remembered that she was the leader of these women and she must not waver. She began to sing again: "Temperance gals, won't you come out tonight, come out tonight—"

"I don't know what this is about, Miss Durango," he shouted over the off-key wailing, "but it won't get that lot for you."

"This is about something more important than land," Lacey yelled back, eyes blazing. "We have drawn the line in the sand and we give you men fair warning."

"Fine. But before you start shouting 'Remember the Alamo,'" Blackie said, "I wish you dear ladies would stop blockin' the sidewalk, you're interferin' with customers."

"We will not!" Lacey stood on her tiptoes and was still not tall enough to look straight into his dark eyes. "As other women rally to our cause, we will block this door forever if need be."

Blackie now seemed more amused than annoyed. He pulled out his gold pocket watch and checked the time. "Why don't you all just go home and cook supper for your husbands?"

"Aha! There will be no supper for men tonight," Lacey shouted. "Right, ladies?"

"Right!" They yelled in unison.

"Fine." Blackie said. "I'm sure the Chinese joint will be

pleased to hear that. Now let me through and you can march 'til the cows come home."

She didn't like it that he was suddenly being so tolerant. Blackie O'Neal obviously didn't see a small bunch of housewives as a big threat. "Aren't you going to try to have us arrested for trespassing?"

"I don't think so." He shook his head.

"Because if you were," Lacey said, "may I remind you this is a public sidewalk and there is no law against our marching and singing here?"

"Uh-huh. I see you've even enlisted my dog. I hadn't heard Lively was opposed to liquor."

At the sound of his name, the bloodhound drooled and wagged his tail.

Two cowboys rode up, started to dismount, then noticed the commotion. "Uh-oh," said one to the other, "I'd rather fight Injuns than walk through that bunch of old biddies."

"Me, too," said the other and they turned their horses and rode off down the street.

"Well now," Blackie said, looking annoyed, "this is gettin' serious. You've just cost me some customers."

"And we intend to cost you many more. Sing, ladies!"

He suddenly loomed larger then she remembered him, all wide-shouldered and smelling of tobacco and shaving lotion. His jaw was square and clenched, with just a trace of stubble. He was a man all right; all man. "All right, Miss Durango, you may march up and down out front with your silly ladies, but I think it's against the law to block the doors. Please move."

"I will not."

Silence fell over the little group and the gathering throng of onlookers as they watched the confrontation.

"Then I will move you."

"Don't you dare."

"Sister, never dare a Texan." Before Lacey realized what he was up to, he reached out and caught her by the waist, lifting her off the ground. He had big hands that almost spanned her waist and she had never felt so helpless as she did at that moment with her high-buttoned shoes dangling off the wooden sidewalk. He took one step and stood her in the gutter.

"Did you see that, ladies?" Lacey yelled. "This brute did me bodily harm."

Miss Wren sighed and edged closer. "Sir, if I block your way, could you do me bodily harm, too?"

"Vanetta!" Lacey scolded, "what are you thinking?"

"Women!" Blackie O'Neal snorted and strode inside the saloon, followed by his dog.

The curious crowd was still growing. "This is a protest!" Lacey shouted, "and it's going to grow. Ladies, are you with me?"

"Yes! Yes!"

"Good, then go home and stop cooking, cleaning, washing and most of all, you know what else."

The ladies blushed and giggled.

"By tomorrow, I want every woman in this township to be pledged to our cause." Lacey said. "Spread the word!"

A soldier wandered up. "Spread the word about what?"

Lacey smiled. "You're about to find out, soldier." The men had gotten bored watching the ladies' parade and had shrugged and wandered off.

Mrs. Anderson bounced her whimpering baby. "Are you going to do an editorial on this?"

Lacey shook her head. "We want the men to be slow to figure out what's going on. Each man will keep quiet, ashamed, and thinking he's the only one not getting any."

"Not getting any what?" Miss Wren asked innocently.

Lacey rolled her eyes at her. "Never mind, Vanetta. It isn't something you'd know anything about and I only know what I've heard my uncle's cowboys whispering about. Ladies, to arms and I will talk to the saloon girls myself."

"You gonna go in the Black Garter?" Ethel Wilson asked.

"Heavens no. I'd rather charge hell with a dipper of water than go in that den of sin and lust. I'll catch that madame, Flo, in a store, maybe. To arms, ladies! We owe it to our children and our descendents to put this town on the straight and narrow."

They all scattered and Lacey returned to her small room above the newspaper office. She could hardly sleep that night, she was so excited. Precious was curled up next to her, purring away. It was a hot night and her window was open. A chorus of drunken cowboys across the street sang: "Oh my darling, oh my darling, oh my darling Clementine . . . "

Outrageous. Well, Blackie O'Neal and all the rascals of this town were going to be in for a big surprise when the name Pretty Prairie won the referendum.

The next morning, Moose polished beer mugs while Blackie sat at a poker table nursing a cup of strong coffee and staring out across the street at the *Crusader* building. Lively was just coming out of there with a biscuit in his mouth. "Danged dog."

"Boss, I went out this morning to get supplies and something's afoot," Moose warned him.

Blackie shrugged. "I saw yesterday's silly little protest march."

"No, I think it might be bigger than that. All the men I've talked to think so, too, but nobody's quite sure what it's about. The ladies—"

"The ladies." Blackie snorted. "They're all scared to death that somewhere, somehow, some poor devil might be havin' a little fun. I am sick and tired of the ladies and especially Miss damnyankee Iron Corset who keeps stirring them up." He sipped his coffee.

"She does seem to have a mind of her own, stubborn Texas gal."

Blackie nodded. "She'd take on a rattlesnake and give it first bite. Then she'd write an editorial about it. You know she turned down my advertising? Sassy little thing."

Moose chuckled. "She's different, ain't she? Women usually can hardly wait to accommodate you and drop their drawers. The newspaper lady can't stand you."

"That works both ways." He pushed his cup away. "She's been the pebble in my boot ever since the first time I laid eyes on her."

"Spirited," Moose said, mopping the bar with a rag.

"Too damned spirited, and a Yankee sympathizer at that." Blackie complained and returned to staring out the window. Miss Iron Corset, in a crisp white blouse and plain long skirt was putting out newspapers in front of her office. As she moved about, the bustle on her backside waggled enticingly. He remembered how warm her body had been and how his two big hands had almost completely reached around her narrow waist as he'd moved her out of his path yesterday. She didn't weigh as much as a Colt pistol. There had been a sweet, clean scent about her, maybe her dark hair. When she had looked up at him, pouting in protest, he remembered that her mouth had been soft and full. "She's driving me loco."

"Who?" Dixie came down the stairs just then and sidled up to the bar. "Gimme some coffee, Moose," she drawled in her thick southern accent, "and hurry it up."

"I only got two hands, you tart." The light gleamed on his bald head as he busied himself with the cup.

Blackie looked Dixie over as if seeing her for the first time. Her bleached hair looked like an abandoned bird's nest and she wore a soiled flowered wrapper pulled around her. Last night's face paint smeared her cheap features. "Don't you ever wash your face?"

"What?"

"Never mind."

"Who's drivin' you loco?" She asked again and lit a cigarette.

"It ain't you." Moose scowled at her.

Blackie only half-listened to the exchange between the pair. They had never gotten along.

"Who're we talkin' about?" Dixie persisted.

"Miss Iron Corset." Blackie returned to watching the lady editor out the window. "She wants to name this town Pretty Prairie."

Dixie snorted in derision and blew smoke out her nostrils. Her voice was hard. "Ain't that sweet?"

"She's idealistic," Moose said.

"Aw, them reformers. She's probably a big hypocrite."

Blackie was abruptly annoyed with the whore. "Oh shut up, Dixie, I get tired of your yammerin'." He got up and strode to his office, slammed the door.

Dixie stared after him in surprise, smoke drifting from her nostrils. "What's eatin' him?"

Moose shrugged. "That newspaper woman. He ain't used to a woman he can't charm."

She laughed. "I'll bet that's the truth. Me, I'd do anything for him, but he don't seem to notice I'm alive."

Moose started to say something, decided against it. He had known Blackie since the boss was a hungry, runaway kid. Moose had bought him a meal and helped find him a job sweeping out a saloon. That was a long, long time ago and they had been friends ever since. Moose knew the boss wasn't nearly so tough as most people thought, but he didn't like people to know that. Blackie saw it as a weakness.

Dixie sighed wistfully and stared at the blank wall over the ornate bar. "You know, the last place had a fancy painting' hangin' up there."

Moose turned and looked. For once he agreed with the girl. "Uh-huh. You're right. I'll mention it to the boss."

"I might go back to his office and mention it myself."

Moose shook his head. "Leave him be. He ain't in a very good mood this mornin'."

"That ain't like Blackie."

"No, it ain't. It's become a battle of wills and since they're both Texans, it's a contest to see who'll cave in first."

"I'm sick of hearin' about her." Dixie snapped and tossed her cigarette in the spittoon. "Reckon I'll take my coffee and go upstairs. Nobody else is up yet."

Moose nodded, glad to be rid of her.

In a few minutes, Blackie returned, went to the window and stared out.

"You're wastin' your time," Moose said, "she's gone back inside."

Blackie felt embarrassed to be caught. "I was just wonderin' what the prim old maid would think up this mornin'. I've already got a plan for today that will annoy the hell out of her."

Moose sighed. "She's becomin' an obsession with you, boss."

"Well, Great God Almighty, I ain't ever had a woman buck me that way before. You know she had the nerve to turn down my advertisin'?"

"Yeah, you told me." Moose watched Blackie's expression. He had never seen him so down and distracted. Maybe he could get his mind off battling with that sassy wench. "Boss, I think there's something missing here."

"What?" He kept staring out the window, although there was nothing much to see.

"We got everything a great Western bar should have but one thing."

Blackie turned and looked around. "We got a piano, some poker tables, roulette wheel, a stage with red velvet curtains and plenty of booze, I—"

"Every Western bar has a nice nude hanging over the bar." Moose looked up.

Blackie turned and looked, too. "Hmm, I reckon you're right. The boys like something tasty to stare at while they drink; wishin' their old ladies looked like that. We'll have to get Joe to paint us a nekkid lady as soon as he gets the saloon sign finished. Where is he anyway?"

"Probably down at the depot," Moose said. "North train due in and it's usually full of Yankee city folk. He does pretty well selling them Custer buttons and hair."

"That old horse is gonna end up with no tail finally and then what will he do?"

"Get another horse?" Moose suggested.

Blackie didn't seem to be listening. "Them respectable women is up to something and that newspaperwoman has to be at the bottom of it."

"Aw," Moose wiped the bar, "you overestimate her."

Blackie shook his head. "That one is as wily as a coyote, which makes me nervous as a long-tailed cat in a room full of rocking chairs."

"If you say so."

"Did I tell you she wouldn't accept my advertisin'?"

"Uh, several times."

"The nerve of her. I'd like to put a burr under her saddle."

"Boss, forget it."

Blackie shook his head and suddenly his eyes lit up. "It's almost noon and it's Saturday. That means there'll be lots of people in town."

"So?"

"Wake the girls up and tell them to put on their fanciest duds. Then send word to the lively stable to get out that fancy barouche. We're all going for a carriage ride!"

Chapter Seven

"What?" Moose said. "There ain't no place much to go drivin'—"

"Sure there is," Blackie grinned. "up and down Main Street. Right past Miss damnyankee Iron Corset's newspaper, around the block and up and down again."

"What's the point, Boss?"

"Well, it pays to advertise and the *Crusader* won't accept my advertisin', so I'm forced to improvise."

Moose groaned aloud, looked as if he might argue, then shrugged and went to the foot of the stairs. "Hey, Flo, get the gals up. The boss is takin' you all for a drive."

"Why?" she yelled back.

"Because it's going to be a nice day and the boss thinks it would be good to get some fresh air."

"Fresh air?" Dixie's whining voice drifted down the stairs. "What the hell we supposed to do with fresh air?"

Blackie strode to the foot of the stairs. "Y'all get up. This is gonna be fun, whether you like it or not." He turned to Moose. "Send a boy for the barouche and make sure the harness is all shiny. Miss Iron Corset ain't the only one who can put on a show for the town." Then whistling, he went to his room in the back to shave.

It was a lovely warm May afternoon, Lacey thought as she walked toward the post office. The town was bustling with farmers and settlers in town for shopping and business. The northbound train should be pulling in soon and maybe there'd be some new settlers; wholesome people with families, the kind who would like living in a place called Pretty Prairie.

As she walked, Lacey heard laughter and singing and looked up. Coming around the corner was that elegant open barouche pulled by the two fine black horses. Sitting up on the driver's seat was that bald bartender of Blackie's. The red plush seats were overflowing with the girls from the Black Garter. They were dressed in their finest, a bit too flashy and showing way too much bosom, Lacey thought with indignation. It was a rolling display of brightly colored tarts, plenty of lace, a riot of scarlet, purple, and orange dresses. They also wore big hats with feathers and plumes and some sported fancy parasols.

Sitting amidst the highly-painted whores was Blackie O'Neal himself, grinning like a sultan in the midst of his harem. A circus wagon rolling down the street wouldn't have merited as much ruckus and attention as the loud and boisterous crowd from the Black Garter created.

"My word!" Lacey paused to stare as did all the other people on the bustling street. In fact, one cowboy was so entranced, he stepped into a mud hole along the wooden sidewalk and went down with a splash. The whole town seemed to come to a halt to gape at the fancy open carriage with its questionable cargo moving slowly down the street. The girls were singing and calling out to men they recognized.

"Hey, honey, ain't seen you this week."

"Hi, handsome, it's me, Dixie, I've missed you."

One man they yelled at was walking alongside one of Lacey's most ardent supporters. His face turned almost purple and his wife promptly began beating him about the head and shoulders with her parasol while berating him in a voice that could be heard all up and down Main Street. Blackie scolded his girls for that in a loud voice. When the barouche passed the astonished Lacey,

Blackie seemed to make a point of bowing his head and tipping his hat to her.

Outrageous. All she could do was blink and stare, totally speechless. Why, that no-account Rebel was flaunting his whores before the whole town. This must stop. Once the town had a respectable name and a town council, she'd see if her Ladies' Temperance Association could get that outhouse of sin closed and the town dried up so tight that there'd be no alcohol anywhere except in the local doctor's medicine bag. She realized that might result in a lot of abruptly sick men, but at least it would end disgraceful displays like this. Some of her temperance ladies were arriving on the afternoon train to aid the sewing circle and certainly seeing the tarts flaunting themselves up and down Main Street in a moving advertisement for sin would galvanize even the most hesitant to action. Abruptly Lacey saw the big banner down the side of the barouche that read: *Blackie's Black Garter Says Vote For Whiskey Flats.*

Dixie turned happily to Blackie as they passed. "Did you see that old maid newspaper woman's face? That look she gave you was colder than a mother-in-law's kiss."

"I didn't notice," Blackie said a little too quickly, staring straight ahead. "What Miss Iron Corset thinks don't make me no never mind. I just reckoned that if her paper wouldn't accept our advertisin', we'd advertise ourselves."

Dixie sighed and slumped back onto the red velvet seat. She'd been in love with Blackie for months, but he didn't seem to know she was alive. On the other hand, he seemed to care very much what the snooty newspaper lady thought. He cared too damned much. Now what could Dixie do to help get that frozen beauty to pack up and leave? Dixie decided she would do whatever it took to get Miss Iron Corset Durango to close her temperance paper and get out of town.

Lacey was still fuming as she walked on to the post office. Several of her ladies were there and joined her in her outrage at the carriage spectacle.

"Indecent!" whined Miss Blanton.

"Sinful!" piped in Ethel Wilson.

Eugene joined them. "Disgusting! Whatever you ladies decide to do, I fully support you." Then he tipped his hat and nodded to Lacey with a smile as he left the post office.

Be still my heart. The perfect pinnacle of virtue; one who could meet Lacey's standards. Might he possibly be an ideal husband?

She turned back to her posse of outraged ladies. "Yes, ladies, you have looked true sin in the face this very day."

Miss Wren sighed wistfully. "Sin does have the most charming smile."

Lacey frowned at her. "Now Vanetta, don't let him lure you into temptation with that wink."

"He was winking at you, Lacey," Vanetta Wren reminded her.

"Nevertheless, I consider myself a good judge of character and what this town needs besides a wholesome name is more men of spotless character such as Eugene Peabody. Just imagine what this whole town will be like with an image like Whiskey Flats. Why, we'd be overrun with rogues like Blackie O'Neal."

Miss Wren looked hopeful. "You think?"

"To arms!" Lacey said, deciding to ignore Vanetta. "It is your duty to go out and influence every woman in town to pressure her husband to vote our way."

"What about those women at the saloon?" Ethel Wilson asked.

Lacey took a deep breath for courage. "I will approach them myself."

"Do you dare?" asked Mrs. Anderson, bouncing her fretting baby on one hip.

"A true Texan would charge hell with a dipper of water," Lacey declared, "and I am a Texan. Remember the Alamo!"

Now the Alamo didn't have much to do with what the ladies were about, and some of them, non-Texans, weren't even sure what it was, but Lacey's enthusiastic war cry fired them up. The little group left the post office singing their battle song: "Temperance gals, won't you come out tonight, come out tonight . . . ?"

Yes, her ladies would win, Lacey thought. About that time, she heard the whistle of an incoming train and later that day, she remembered she needed to talk to Chief Thunder. She found him at the depot with his brass buttons set up on a display table and little tufts of yellow hair spread out before him. His poor horse didn't have enough tail left to switch flies, Lacey thought.

"Joe, could I get you to paint me a nice sign in front of the *Crusader* building?"

He nodded, intent on the incoming train. "Sure thing, Miss Lacey, but I got to paint Blackie's sign first."

She tried not to show her annoyance. "All right, just let me know when you can get to it."

"Sure." He said as the train pulled in from the south with a roar and a screech of brakes, cinders blowing from the black smoke stack. People began to get off the coaches: a young couple, a fat drummer, three soldiers, a family with young children. Chief Thunder approached the soldiers. "How. Me Chief Thunder. How would you like to be owner of rare brass button off Yellow Hair's coat?"

"Yellow Hair?" One of the soldiers paused, looked confused.

"General Custer, you dolt," Chief Thunder snapped as if he'd forgotten he was a Noble Redman. "Make you a deal you can't refuse."

With the three interested suckers, er, customers, gathered about fast-talking Indian, Lacey looked with curiosity at the others getting off the train. Maybe her ladies would be on it.

An old man hobbled off the coach: an old cowboy with gray whiskers and a limp. Lacey blinked in disbelief. "Cookie?"

He looked up from his worn carpetbag, seemed to recognize her and grinned mightily. "Miss Lacey? Is that you? Did the Durangos let you know I was comin'?"

She rushed to embrace him. "No, Cookie, this is a big surprise." As always, he smelled of vanilla, which she knew he preferred to plain whiskey, but in spite of his weakness, she was glad to see him. She hadn't realized how homesick she was for news of Texas. No ladies got off the train. Cookie picked up his carpet bag and they walked back toward town.

"Lordee," he looked around in wonder, "this is gonna be a big city, ain't it?"

"I hope so; a law-abiding place for families with neat houses and tree-lined brick streets. We've got homes and businesses going up." They paused at the corner and she frowned as she looked toward the contested, empty lot. Around them, hammers rang out and wagon loads of lumber rumbled past. "We've made a start, but we still need some work on our little church, a new school, and a library."

"They got a cafe?"

She shook her head as they resumed their walk. "Just a small Chinese place near the tracks."

Cookie frowned. "Them egg rolls and such ain't ever gonna catch on in America. What this place needs is a good cafe that serves homemade meals."

A horrible thought crossed her mind and she paused. Cookie's food was legendary at the Durango ranch. Uncle Trace said Cookie's cooking had poisoned half their cowboys. "Cookie, have you just come for a visit?"

"That, too," he nodded. "Your aunt and uncle just insisted I come check on you. Ace asked about you."

Lacey sighed as they walked down the street toward the newspaper office. "I'm sorry I missed Ace's wedding, I was in Europe on a Grand Tour, you know."

"I know. After what happened at your weddin', I can't blame you, young'un, for not showin' your face for awhile."

"Well, you didn't need to remind me." she said, her thoughts grim. "Besides, who would have thought Ace would get married so sudden like?"

"Reckon everyone was surprised at who he picked. Why, they got a baby now, Miss Lacey. You heard anything of your sister?"

Lacey shook her head. "You know Lark was as independent as a cowboy with fresh money in his pockets and quite the tomboy; no telling where she is."

"Wal, you two shore was different to be twins. Wherever your sis is, she'll take care of herself, she's a Texan and you know what the Good Book says about Texans? The meek might inherit the earth, but the proud will get Texas. The meek couldn't deal with it nohow."

"I'm not sure the Bible says that," Lacey laughed.

"Anyways, I come not only to visit but to open a cafe."

"You? A cafe?" Lacey blinked. Cookie might kill off half the men in the settlement before they could vote to name the town.

"Why not?" He took a chaw of tobacco. "I was bored to death at the ranch and I got enough money saved to open the place. You said yourself there was no good places to eat."

She coughed. "Running a restaurant is a mighty hard job."

"Wal, I may be old but I ain't dead; I can do it. And I'll run some ads in your paper."

If someone died from eating Cookie's cooking, could she be sued as an accessory after the crime? She had bigger problems than that right now. "Fine, Cookie. I'll take you over to the shack that passes for a hotel. We could use one of those, too. By the way, there's going to be a referendum in a couple of weeks to pick a name for the town."

The old cowboy spat tobacco juice and nailed a bug crawling along the wooden sidewalk. "Fine. What's the choices?"

"Well, some of the rowdier bunch want to call it Whiskey Flats, but the upright, respectable citizens prefer Pretty Prairie."

"Pretty Prairie?" His bushy eyebrows went up. "Sounds prissy."

"Now Cookie, it will give us a nicer image, bring in a better class of people."

He looked doubtful.

"A better class of people moving to town who'll need a good cafe," she said.

His grizzled old face lit up. "Miss Lacey, you might have a point there. Now get me to the hotel and I'll start inquiring about a building to lease."

"There's an empty one just finishing construction next to the Black Garter saloon."

His eyes lit up.

"The Garter is a terrible place," Lacey said, "run by the most outrageous man; Blackie O'Neal."

Cookie grinned. "Blackie? Wal, I'll be a son-of-a-gun."

"You know this rascal?" Lacey turned to stare at him.

"Knew his pa," the old man explained. "Moonshiner over in the Big Thicket. Lost most of a leg in the War, so he couldn't do much of anything except sire children. Think there was ten of 'em."

A moonshiner. Well, she wasn't at all surprised. "What happened to the mother?"

"Died, part Injun, she was. Kids sorts of raised theirselves. Reckon the old man's gone now, too."

"That Blackie is a perfect rascal," she complained.

"He's challenging me for ownership of the best lot in town."

Cookie grinned. "He was an engagin' little kid and proud as a pup with a new collar, even though he was dirt pore. Seems like he wanted schoolin' real bad. His Pa used to laugh about Blackie tryin' to learn to read by looking at the labels on snuff cans."

The image almost touched her heart and then she remembered who they were talking about. "He must not be much better than his pa, since he's peddling whiskey, too. Besides he's a libertine and a wastrel."

"Sounds like you two are at loggerheads."

"We are, and it's not just that claim squabble. He's trying to organize the men to name the town Whiskey Flats. Now, Cookie, you will vote with the ladies for Pretty Prairie?"

"For you, Miss Lacey, anything." He shrugged. "You got a sweetheart?"

She smiled modestly. "My word, Cookie, what a question. But now that you ask, there is a young man who's been to college; Harvard, no less, and he's a snappy dresser, carries a cane and everything."

The old man ran his hand through his graying beard. "Poor boy crippled, is he?"

"Why is it Texans think if a man carries a cane, he's crippled? Back east, it's stylish. He also wears spats and a derby. I think he's perfect."

Cookie glowered at her. "Sounds like a Eastern dude."

"Honestly, Cookie, you think anyone who doesn't wear cowboy boots is a dude."

"Remember you ain't got the best track record at pickin' men, Miss Lacey, and there ain't no such thing as a perfect man."

She felt her face burn at the memory. "Let's not talk about my wedding. It was humiliating enough. Because of Homer, I'm now crusading against strong drink."

"Now, a little medicinal spirits never hurt anyone none," the old man was defensive.

"Lips that touch liquor shall never touch mine."

Cookie grinned. "You'll miss a lot of fun that way."

"Cookie!"

"We'll visit later," he dismissed her by touching the brim of his hat with two fingers. "I got to get me a room and then I'll look around for a good cafe site." He limped away.

Lacey stared after him. "My word. A restaurant," she whispered under her breath, "He'll kill off so many men, there won't be any left to vote."

"I heered that!" He yelled back over his shoulder.

"I didn't say anything." She smiled and waved. Old Cookie was almost like the grandfather she'd never had. Well, she'd had one, but he hadn't wanted her or her twin sister, Lark. He'd kept the two older children when their parents were killed and sent the twins to her father's sister, Aunt Cimarron.

She turned and walked slowly back to her newspaper office. She didn't want to think about her cold and aloof grandfather, Silas Van Schuyler, or the humiliation of her wedding ceremony. Now that she thought of it, she hadn't really been in love with Homer, she'd been in love with love. Maybe Homer had rejected her just as her grandfather had because she wasn't perfect enough, although some of the blame fell on demon rum.

At that moment, she saw the older red-haired woman, the one she'd heard ran the upstairs, come out of the saloon and walk down the street toward the general store. Lacey took a deep breath for courage and started across the street. She didn't expect the saloon girls would throw in with the respectable ladies, but Lacey had to try. The alternative was living in a wild, wide-open place called Whiskey Flats. Lacey made a wry face and hurried toward the general store. Women should all stick together and she'd appeal to the madame in that vein.

Inside, she approached the woman. "Excuse me, I'm the owner of the local newspaper, Lacey Durango, and you are?"

The older woman turned from the counter and looked her up and down. She was a matronly woman except for too much face paint and her dyed red hair. Probably it was gray under that henna. "I know who you are. Blackie's been fit to be tied every time your name comes up. I'm Flo Clancy."

Lacey felt almost apologetic. "We're locked in a legal fight over a piece of land, I'm afraid."

Flo looked her over as if thinking. "Lot more to it than that, I reckon."

"What do you mean?"

"Could mean a lot of things. You're a Texan, ain't you?"

Lacey nodded. "I don't know what that's got to do—"

"Texans got a lot of pride; don't like to lose."

Lacey thought, *ain't that the truth?* But she said "Miss Flo, I need your help."

The woman looked her up and down. "Honey, with your looks and brains, you don't need anybody's help."

Lacey fidgeted. "You don't understand. Has Blackie mentioned the fuss over the town name?"

The other nodded. "Wouldn't tell him for nothin', but I thought Pretty Prairie was nice, made me think of the kind of town I grew up in back in Ohio; the nice kind I always hoped to live in."

Lacey looked into the worn face under all the paint. She wanted to ask how Flo came to this, but the other must have read her thoughts and waved her off. "Things happen, honey. Thought once I'd find a good man myself and settle down, but not many men want a gal who's been in my trade." She was suddenly tough and arrogant again.

"Miss Flo, the ladies of this town need your help. We're all women after all, and we should stick together."

"Respectable women ain't been too kind to me and my girls." She picked up a piece of lace off the counter and looked it over critically.

"It's this town name thing," Lacey explained. "If the women all stuck together, we could turn this raw frontier settlement into the kind of nice town you said you'd dreamed of long ago, white picket fences, houses with lace curtains at the windows, children playing tag in the yards. Pretty Prairie is a name that would draw families here."

The other sighed wistfully "Sounds good, but Blackie's dead set for Whiskey Flats."

"I know that and women can't vote. But if we stand together, women have power. We could make a difference."

"How?" Flo said and Lacey had a sudden feeling that Flo had never had much power over her own life and what she'd become.

"My group is going to form a bedroom boycott."

"What?" Flo's kohled eyes widened.

Lacey blushed even thinking about it. "What's the one thing men don't want to do without?"

"Whiskey." Flo said.

"No, more important than that."

"Cigars and food."

"No, the one thing men *really* want."

"You mean—?"

"Yes," Lacey laughed in triumph. "The ladies have agreed not to let the men have any unless they agree to vote for Pretty Prairie."

The other looked her up and down. "That's pretty daring." Her expression turned into one of admiration. "But my gals have a special problem; if they don't, ah, work, they don't eat."

"We've already thought of that," Lacey said conspiratorially and moved closer. "If your girls will join our strike, our ladies will bring in food so you won't go hungry."

"The respectable women of this town would do that?" She looked incredulous.

"It's for a good cause."

Flo considered. "Blackie will be madder than a stomped-on toad frog."

Lacey grinned at the thought. "Won't he, though?"

"You know," Flo said thoughtfully, looking Lacey over, "I wondered why you're such a thorn in his side and now I know. Blackie ain't used to being challenged or bested by a headstrong woman."

"It's time he got used to it." Lacey held out a dainty hand. "Shake?"

Flo grinned and clasped Lacey's hand with her own. "Honey, you got a deal. Let's win one for the women!"

They parted and Lacey was as pleased with herself as a kitten with a ball of yarn. Blackie O'Neal was going down in defeat yelling "calf rope," which was the equivalent of ultimate surrender in the Lone Star state. Highly enthused, she returned to her office and wrote an editorial about women taking control of their own lives.

She confided to Isaac about Flo's girls aiding the ladies in their crusade.

Isaac paused. "You know, Miss Lacey, I've stayed by you all these years trying to keep you out of trouble, but sometimes, I think it's hopeless."

"I always wondered why you stuck by me. I'm sorry I haven't been able to pay you better."

He shrugged. "I don't need much to live on; a little stew and coffee, yes?"

She looked down at her note pad. "That reminds me, I'm down for a peach pie and a pot roast."

"What?"

"Never mind. Just don't ask any questions." She got up and started for the back of their almost finished building. "Kitchen's not complete, but good enough. By the way, speaking of cooking, my family's old cowboy cook is in town. He's going to open a cafe." She shuddered at the thought.

"He a good cook?"

"Are you joking? He'd poison a hog, but nobody in the family ever told him so, they didn't want to hurt his feelings." Humming to herself, she began to mix her pie crust. It was a strange partnership, but she thought the girls at Blackie's and the more staid ladies of the town understood each other. It was a man's world, but women could win if they stuck together.

It was almost dark as she gathered up her pie and pot roast and sneaked down the alley to the back door of the Black Garter. As had been planned, she knocked once and then twice more.

Flo opened the door cautiously. "I'm sure havin' second thoughts about this, honey."

"How do you think I feel, slipping around like a bandit behind a notorious renegade's place?" Lacey asked.

About that time, other very respectable ladies came down the alley, each looking like a preacher caught with his hand in the collection plate. Each was carrying a basket of food.

"When is the upstairs boycott supposed to start?" Miss Wren asked, looking wide-eyed at Flo.

"This very evening," Lacey declared. "By the time of the referendum, the men'll be willing to promise anything."

Mrs. Anderson, for once, had left her baby at home. "Can we count on the girls at the Garter?"

Flo squared her shoulders. "You betcha. The men ain't gettin' none here. My gals and I stand foursquare behind your effort."

The ladies all shook hands solemnly as they had seen men do to close a business deal. Then they handed over their baskets and melted away into the evening darkness like rustlers.

Inside the Black Garter, the men were just beginning to drift in. Moose polished the mirror at the bar and looked toward Blackie who stood with one boot up on the brass rail. "There's something up, Blackie, I can sense it."

"Aw, Moose, you're lettin' that lady crusader put you on the run. That ain't like you. Once we best her reformers on the town name, she'd admit defeat and go back to coverin' ladies' book clubs and weddin' showers."

Moose scratched the tattoo on his forearm. "You underestimate her, Boss."

Blackie frowned. "Naw, I don't, just a prissy female. You know, Moose, I never did ask you why you've got 'Ma' on your arm. Most hombres would put 'Mother'."

Moose grinned, a little shame-faced. "The tattoo artist charged by the letter and I didn't have enough money at the time for that."

"Speaking of artists, is Joe workin' on the nude for over the bar?"

"Sure thing." Moose nodded. "He wants to know if the gal should look like Lillian Russell?"

"Naw, we might get sued. I got a better idea." Blackie paused and sniffed the air. "I swear I smell peach pie."

Moose set up bottles along the bar, getting ready for the evening rush. "You must be dreamin', Boss. You know Flo and none of the gals cook much unless I whip up something. They open a few cans or go to the Chinese place." He paused and sniffed the air. "Now you've got me thinkin' I smell pie, just like my Mama used to make. We always talked about openin' a tea room and a hotel together. I ain't never told her I work in a saloon."

"You got enough money put away for a hotel?"

"Sure, Boss," Moose grinned and nodded as he wiped glasses, "but if I left, I don't know who would look after you."

Blackie frowned. "I don't need no wet nurse, but I'd miss you."

It was dark outside now and men started drifting in. The little piano player came in, nodded to Blackie and Moose, took off his derby and sat down. "Anything special you want me to play, Blackie?"

Blackie got up from his table. "Anything, Dutch, just play it loud enough to annoy Miss Iron Corset across the street."

"That won't take much effort with the swinging doors open on such a warm night."

In minutes, the place was full of men leaning on the bar or at the poker tables. The piano banged away: "Oh, it rained all night, the day I left, the weather it was dry . . . "

One of the men said, "Where's the gals tonight, Blackie?"

Blackie shrugged, puzzled. "Beats me. Little slow gettin' downstairs tonight, I reckon."

A cowboy started up the stairs. "I know what I want!" he shouted.

Men below him guffawed and went back to their drinking and cards.

Blackie smiled with contentment. The Black Garter was doing a landslide business in spite of Lacey Durango's editorials. Her lady crusaders might as well unsaddle their horses and give up. Yes, the town of Whiskey Flats was going to be a wild and prosperous frontier town, as old-fashioned and uninhibited as Dodge City used to be. More men meant more saloon business. He'd heard someone had leased the half-finished building next door to the Black Garter and was going to put in a cafe.

The cowboy came back down the stairs. He paused half-way down and looked out over the crowd. He looked as confused as a steer in a stampede. "They said no," he shouted.

The piano stopped playing and as the words sunk in, men ceased their talk and turned and looked up at the baffled cowboy.

"Son," a railroad man yelled, "can you be more specific?"

"Reckon I can," the cowboy nodded, "they said, hell, no!"

"What?" Blackie threw his cigar into the nearest spittoon and started for the stairs with long strides. "Great God Almighty, what—?"

"They said unless this town gets named Pretty Prairie, the upstairs is closed for business."

Blackie began to curse under his breath. He didn't know how she'd done it, but Miss Iron Corset had gotten to Flo's whores. Damn that Lacey Durango anyway.

Chapter Eight

Blackie paused as he started for the stairs. "There must be some mistake." He grinned at the customers and signaled Dutch to resume playing. "Free drinks on the house!" he shouted and then he took the stairs two at a time. He burst into Flo's room. "What the hell's goin' on?"

"Ain't you gentleman enough to knock?" Flo was sitting at a small table with some of the girls and that wasn't egg rolls they were eating. In fact, it looked like the remnants of peach pie.

"That cowboy just said the girls turned him away," Blackie said. "Didn't he have any money?"

The girls looked at him in silence. There was a grim determination about them that unnerved Blackie and he had faced down tough gunfighters before without a bobble.

"He had money." Flo stood up, "but we ain't workin' tonight or maybe for any night for a long time to come."

"What?" Blackie was so astounded, he stood there, opening and closing his mouth like a fish gasping for air. "This ain't like you, Flo."

She grinned. "No, it ain't. Maybe we just decided we don't want to."

"I don't understand. Ain't you all well paid?"

They all nodded.

"Ain't this a nice place and workin' conditions good?"

They all nodded.

"Well, then what—?"

"We're on strike," Flo said.

"Strike? Don't be ridiculous," Blackie said. "Whores don't strike."

"Just watch us," Flo said. She looked around at the others. "Why don't we play some cards, girls, or maybe spend the evening washing out some stockings?"

"Great God Almighty! This is loco," Blackie said. "Men won't come into the Black Garter if there's no gals downstairs minglin' and if they ain't welcome upstairs."

"They'll appreciate us more when the strike's over." Flo began to file her nails.

"Which will be?"

Flo seemed to think on it. "Maybe in a week or two, or three. We'll let you know."

"Are you gals loco? Besides, you don't have enough money to go weeks without any business. You'll get hungry."

One of the girls let out a polite burp.

Flo smiled. "Maybe not."

He looked at the remnants of what appeared to be a wonderful, home-cooked meal. Something was amiss and there was only one person in town who was smart enough to create a ruckus like this. "That sassy piece from the *Crusader* is behind this, isn't she? Nobody else is clever enough to—"

"You sayin' I couldn't call a strike myself?"

"No, but you wouldn't, Flo, without her to put you up to it. Well, damn it to hell. We'll see about this!" Blackie turned and strode out of Flo's room. He slammed the door so hard, the whole building rattled.

Flo smiled and stared at the door. "He's madder than a wet cat and when he can't use his fists or that pistol he carries, he don't know what to do."

"Any more peach pie?" Dixie asked.

"No, but we got homemade jam and cookies from the banker's wife. Somebody make us some coffee and get out the cards. We got the evening all to ourselves," Flo said.

The girls all giggled conspiratorially as they gathered around the table to share the goodies.

Dixie watched and frowned. She hadn't said anything, and she'd be ostracized if she didn't go along with the strike, but she had a plan that didn't include the other whores. Dixie had been looking for a way to raise her chips with Blackie for a long time and maybe this was it. She'd have to wait for the right time.

Blackie was fit to be tied as he stomped downstairs. As word spread around the Black Garter that the girls weren't coming downstairs tonight and that men weren't welcome upstairs, it put a damper on things like a skunk at a garden party. The men drifted out early. Long before ten o'clock, Blackie, Dutch, and Moose sat in an empty saloon staring at each other.

"Well, Boss," Moose said, picking up empty beer mugs off the bar, "I told you something was up."

"Oh it ain't gonna last long," Blackie said with conviction. "They can't hold out on strike, they won't have any money for food."

"Can you toss them out in the street?" Dutch suggested. He was a little man in a bright pink shirt with lace sleeve garters.

Blackie shook his head. "No, I wouldn't do that to Flo and her girls and she knows it. I gotta think about this. I just know that uppity little damnyankee newspaper woman is mixed up in this somehow."

The next morning, Blackie was in a dour mood. As he sipped his coffee, he sat and glared out the front window at the newspaper office. Miss Durango opened her blinds and came out to put a stack of fresh newspapers outside and pick up the honesty box. She looked very perky in her white blouse and long skirt. Her dark hair was pulled back with a big blue bow. When she moved, the bustle on the back wiggled enticingly. Then she seemed to notice Blackie watching her through the window and she smiled and waved at him.

"Damn her hide." He stood up and moved to the bar, blowing smoke like an angry dragon. "Gimme my usual, Moose."

"Kinda early for anything but coffee." Moose set a tall dark drink full of ice on the bar. "Boss, you're lettin' her get your goat. You ain't proved she's behind this."

"She's the only woman smart enough to organize it. She's almost as smart as a man. Well, most men. I've got to do something to humiliate her so bad, she'll pack up and get out. This town ain't big enough for the both of us."

"That sounds like something Wyatt Earp or Doc Holiday would say."

"Does, doesn't it? I've known both of them. Don't think they'd let a mere gal buffalo them."

"Don't know about that, Boss. She ain't your average, run-of-the-mill petticoat."

"That's what's so annoyin' about Miss Iron Corset. I can't scare her, shoot her, beat her to a pulp, or have her ridden out of town on a rail. Townsfolks wouldn't put up with treatin' a real lady that way."

"Well, neither of us know much about real ladies. Except my mama." Moose sighed wistfully.

"I'm goin' uptown to the bank," Blackie muttered. "Maybe business will be better today."

He would have sworn he'd smelled homemade biscuits drifting from upstairs, decided he must be hungry. He'd see if that new cafe next door had opened up yet. Blackie put on his hat and went out the swinging doors.

There was construction going on next door, but the place wasn't open. An old cowboy with straggly whiskers limped up to him. "Howdy, stranger. Cookie's Kitchen ain't open for business, but I expect to be by tomorrow."

The old man smelled faintly of vanilla. They shook hands. "I'm Blackie O'Neal from next door."

The other nodded with a grin. "I should have known. Reckon you don't remember me, either, Blackie, but I knew your Pa. You was a young squirt last time I saw you."

Blackie frowned. Those memories of hardscrabble living were not pleasant. "I never go back to the Big Thicket and Pa's dead. I've made it on my own."

The old man nodded. "I know about you. Heard gossip already about the trouble between you and the lady what owns the newspaper."

Blackie shook his head. "She ain't gonna win this one. I intend to end up ownin' that lot. It's the best in town."

"Wal," Cookie leaned against the counter and watched the workmen hurrying about. "I got to tell you, Blackie, I knowed that young lady from a long way back. She's pretty stubborn herself, and you can't bluff her out of the pot."

"Damned female." Blackie muttered. "Well, I'm headed up to the bank. You need a sign painted, Chief Thunder is the local artist and painter."

"Much obliged. I'm hopin' to be open by tomorrow. Good, home-cooked food. Do the cookin' myself. Used to be the ranch cook for the Triple D outfit."

"Then you really know a lot about Miss Lacey Durango?" He didn't mean to ask, but he couldn't stop himself.

"Sure do. Sassy little gal."

"Too sassy," Blackie growled, "no wonder she ain't married."

"Wal, that's a tragedy we don't talk about in the family," the old man said.

"She's absolutely loco on the subject of whiskey."

The old man nodded. "If you knew about her past . . . " Cookie suddenly seemed to remember that that wasn't something he was supposed to discuss with strangers and his voice trailed off. "Anyway, knowing her like I do, I reckon you'll yell 'calf rope' before she does."

"Not a snowflake's chance in hell." Blackie promised and turned and went out the door.

At the bank, men were standing about, muttering and complaining.

" . . . and when I asked why supper wasn't on the table, Fern said, 'fix it yourself, you male pig . . .'"

"Sounds like my Lydia, she didn't clean up the house or make the bed yesterday and she said she's on strike . . . "

"Worse yet," whispered the banker, "my Ethel wouldn't even let me in bed last night. I slept on the couch."

The others looked at each other as if each had a shameful secret he didn't want to discuss.

A cowboy said, "you know, the girls at the Black Garter wouldn't come down and serve drinks last night."

At the mention of the saloon, they all turned and looked at Blackie.

He tried to grin and make light of it. "I'm not sure what's afoot, fellas, but it's just some silly female notion. Things'll be all back to normal by tomorrow, or Saturday at the latest."

"They better be," said a cowboy. "If the girls ain't bein' friendly, I must as well stay at the bunkhouse and drink my beer."

There was a murmur of agreement among the men.

This meant real trouble, Blackie thought as he finished his business and left the bank. Women withholding housekeeping chores, cooking, and more importantly, sexual favors was more than unthinkable, it was shocking. Come to think of it, he hadn't had any favors from anyone in a while. It wasn't that girls like Dixie hadn't offered, it was just that he'd had his mind on another girl, the annoying, stubborn one. She had to be behind this unheard-of strike. No other woman would have even thought about such a thing. Worse yet, if women got used to the idea that they should have some say in things, men would lose all their privileges. He sure hadn't made much headway trying to run Miss Iron Corset out of town. Maybe he ought to change tactics and try charming her out of her drawers instead.

He paused in the warm spring sunshine to consider that possibility. Was he going loco? Besides the fact that she couldn't stand the sight of him, if he did manage to get her clothes off, she'd probably stop in the middle to give him a lecture. Not that she'd know anything about bedding a man. Miss Durango was evidently as chaste and pure as a stone statue. He dismissed the idea and returned to his saloon. Out front, Joe was finishing up the new sign and hanging it. "What do you think, Blackie?"

"Good," Blackie nodded, cheered by the inviting naughtiness of the sign. "Ought to bring in a lot of trade."

That was if the girls upstairs got over their mad. He noticed a number of the most respectable women in town going toward the *Crusader's* office. Each stopped and gaped open-mouthed at his new sign, then pursed grim lips, shook her head and went into the newspaper building. One of them must have said something to Lacey Durango because she came outside, took a horrified look, her mouth dropping open.

Good, she was shocked and infuriated. That meant it was a very good sign. She shook her finger at him as if he were a misbehaving school boy, then went inside.

What a maddening woman. He wanted to grab her up and spank her until the dust flew from her bloomers. "Joe," he said, brightening with a sudden idea, "How you doin' with the nude painting to hang over my bar?"

"Working on it. Very voluptuous. Lillian Russell got nothin' on this babe."

"Good. Come in. I want to talk about an idea I've got." His idea for revenge made him smile to himself as he and Joe went inside to talk.

Lacey could hardly believe her eyes as she stared at the new sign going up over the entry of the saloon across the street. When the ladies had come in and told her, she'd been sure they were exaggerating, but it was now evident they were not. *Blackie's Black Garter,* read the lettering, but on the sign was a very shapely lady's, er, limb, the foot wearing a high-heeled shoe. A black lace garter was around the thigh.

For a moment, she was so shocked, she was speechless. She knew Blackie O'Neal was watching her reaction so she shook her finger at him and flounced back inside. When she peered out the window, she saw him pat Chief Thunder on the shoulder and then they both went inside the saloon. Sopping up whiskey, the both of them, no doubt.

"Miss Durango," said the banker's wife, "can we begin?"

"What?" Lacey jumped and realized she'd been standing too long staring after the maddening brute while the ladies waited patiently. "Yes," she turned around, now very efficient. "All right, how did last night go?"

The ladies tittered and some faces turned red.

Ethel Wilson cleared her throat. "I didn't know we had so much power over men. Julius was just begging, but I made him sleep on the couch."

Mrs. Anderson tended to her baby. "It won't hurt my old coot to do without some. We already got six kids."

Each lady related a story of no cooking, no cleaning or laundry, and, especially, no bedroom favors. The lack of bedroom favors was the only thing the men seemed to notice.

Lacey nodded in triumph. "With Flo and her girls aiding us, we'll soon bring the men to their knees. Sometimes I think men don't think about anything besides, you know."

"No, I don't know." Miss Wren sighed wistfully, "but I'd like to find out."

"Vanetta!" Lacey scolded. "Now ladies, remember, we must keep this boycott going and to do so, we have to keep the girls at the Garter in groceries. They're dependent on us or they can't continue in this strike."

"I'm making a big pot of stew," Mrs. Wilson said. "Julius thinks it's for him, but it'll be long gone out of the house by the time he closes the bank."

"I've got a big salad," said another.

"I've got homemade rolls and butter from my own cow," said a third.

"I've got some fresh cold milk and a chocolate cake," another said.

"My word," Lacey exclaimed, "we're putting together a real feast. I'll cook some potatoes and fresh vegetables."

The ladies laughed conspiratorially. "We're going to have some hungry men again tonight, and none of them can cook enough to boil an egg."

"That's because they've always taken you for granted," Lacey reminded them. "By the time the vote comes up next week, they'd vote to call the town anything we wanted if you'd just go back to cooking, cleaning, and well, you know." In spite of herself, she felt her face flush.

"That new cafe is opening next door to the Black Garter," one said, "they'll all go eat there."

Lacey started to say something, thought better of it. She wasn't about to cost her old friend, Cookie, any money. "Let's just say, ladies, that after they have a few meals in Cookie's Kitchen, they'll really appreciate you. Now, let's all get to work. Meet me in the alley at dusk and I'll carry the food inside for Flo's girls."

They all shook hands awkwardly as they had seen men do, then they departed in twos and threes.

Blackie sipped his tall, cool drink and watched through his front window as the women came out of the newspaper office across the street. "I wish I knew what in tarnation those women are up to."

Behind him, Joe laughed. "Worries you that newspaper woman is so stubborn, doesn't it?"

He swore under his breath. "That is the dad-blamedist female I ever met. You're clear now about the paintin'?"

The handsome Indian paused as he finished his beer. "I don't know, Blackie, it don't seem quite right—"

"You're havin' a twinge of conscience after spendin' years sellin' Custer's hair and buttons to gullible whites?"

Joe shrugged. "They stole most of our land. I reckon they'll steal the rest in a few years and give it to white folks. Anyway I like Miss Durango. Besides, I got to face her tomorrow when I paint her sign."

"Miss Iron Corset ain't gonna know about this, she'll just know she's being snickered at. After all, respectable old maids like her don't come into saloons except that one time. She'll be so humiliated when she finally hears, she'll pack up, clear out, and good riddance."

"You got a point there," Joe set his beer mug down. "Well, I got to go. It's almost time for the train and I got to cut some more of General Custer's hair."

Moose came in from the back room just then. "You better get you another horse, Joe, that one ain't got enough left of his tail to switch a horsefly."

"I'm lettin' General Custer's tail grow out," the Indian said, "I'm using his mane now." He went to the swinging doors. "I'll have your nude for you in a couple of days, Blackie. Anybody tried the new cafe next door?"

"I had lunch there while ago," Moose said, shifting the toothpick to the other side of his mouth.

"What'd you think?" Blackie asked.

Moose hesitated. "It was different."

"That bad, hey?" Joe went out the swinging doors.

"I'll be in my office." Blackie started toward the back of the saloon.

Moose said "It's shaping up to be a slow day. None of the boys seem to be comin' in."

"With Flo's gals on strike, we ain't gonna sell enough drinks to make a dime. I'd just soon not be disturbed." Blackie went into his office and sat down at his cluttered desk. He felt at home in these quarters with a bedroom off the office. There was a big walnut desk with claw feet, shelves of books, and a small watercolor on the wall. The watercolor was restful. He leaned back in his chair and looked at it with a wistful smile. Someday, he was going to get out of the saloon business. He had his own private dream, but it wasn't a hotel and tea room like Moose's.

With a sigh, he got out his ledgers, cleared a spot amidst the clutter of his desk top and studied the numbers. After about an hour, there was a soft knock at the door. *Now what?* "Come in, Moose, I told you I didn't want to be—"

He paused in surprise as Dixie tiptoed into his office and closed the door. "Can I come in, Handsome?"

"Looks like you're already in." He said, a bit short.

"We never get to talk much." She came around the desk, shoved some of the clutter aside and sat down on the edge of the desk so that her skirt hiked up, showing her ankles. She wore a tight orange bodice that didn't look good with her bleached hair and when she leaned forward, he could see the vast expanse of her ample bosom. Yet he could see dirt on her neck and she reeked of strong perfume and smoke. Such a contrast to the clean, prim brunette across the street.

"Dixie, what do you need? I'm really busy right now." Once he had been tempted by the young blonde, but for some reason, not any more.

"It's not what *I* need, Blackie, honey," she drawled in her southern accent, "it's what *you* need. I could make you very happy." She ran her tongue across her lips very slowly and suggestively.

"Look, Dixie," he stood up, "I'm already happy. Now, if you'll excuse me—"

Before he realized her intent, she stood up, put her arms around him, and kissed him very slowly, lingeringly. At one time he might have taken her right there on the top of his big desk, but now her hot kiss didn't cause his body to react, which surprised even him. He stepped back, reached for a handkerchief, and wiped the greasy rouge off his mouth. "Save it for the customers, Dixie, I've got work to do."

"What's wrong with you? I'm offerin', don't you see?"

"Yeah, I know. Now get out of here, I'm busy."

"It's one of the other girls, right? Maybe that redhead, Flossie, has been in your bed—"

"Look Dixie, I don't mix business with pleasure. If you don't know that, ask Flo. Store owner who samples the merchandise cuts into the profits."

She was fuming and he knew it. "I ain't never had a man turn me down before. You need me, Blackie, you need me to let you know what's goin' on around here."

"Oh?" He sat down and leaned back in his chair, grinned up at her. "Is there something goin' on?"

Now that she had his attention, she seemed to forget her pique and smiled archly at him. "You know there is. It's that prissy newspaper editor."

Miss Iron Corset. Of course. "I'd like to wring her neck. Every time I turn around, she's like sand in my scrambled eggs."

"That high-class old maid has gotten all the women in town involved in namin' this town Pretty Prairie."

"Women can't vote; we all know that." Blackie reached for a cigar and lit it, shaking the match out.

"Yeah, but if the men don't get no food, no cleanin', no roll in the hay, they'll vote any way the women want."

"That's the meanest thing I ever heard of, but it's pretty damned clever." He smoked and considered. "And even Flo and you girls are in on it?"

Dixie nodded. "I had to go along so I wouldn't be the only one objectin'. Everyone's sworn to secrecy."

"That's fine for a bunch of housewives, but you girls won't have any income—"

"Miss Newspaper Lady has gotten the respectable

women of this town to slip us homemade meals so we can last."

"Peach pie and homemade biscuits," Blackie muttered, remembering the delicious smells wafting through the saloon.

"What?"

"Never mind. How's the food gettin' in?"

"That newspaper dame brings it around to the back door and the girls slip it up the backstairs without you, Moose, or Dutch knowing about it."

"Damn her hide."

Dixie grinned. "You hate her, don'cha? Men don't like stubborn, smart women, do they?"

"I'll fix her wagon," Blackie vowed. "Thanks for lettin' me in on the secret, Dixie."

"Whatcha gonna do, Blackie?"

"I'll have to think about it. Go on upstairs."

"Okay, Handsome," she purred. "Just remember I'd do anything for you. Any time you want me—"

"Sure, sure." He dismissed her with a nod. "Go on."

She walked out of his office, swinging her hips and looking back over her shoulder with kohled eyes heavy with desire and invitation.

Blackie hardly saw her; his mind was intent on another woman, a tall girl with black hair. Damn that infernal temperance crusader. While he was furious at her sneaky plans to defeat him, he couldn't help but admire her cleverness. A woman like that would give a man tall, strong sons who were as smart as they were resourceful. Sons? Was he losing his mind? No man would ever get Miss Iron Corset to shut up long enough to make love to her. He shuddered at the thought. She'd want to give the man instructions on how to do it even though she had no experience. Blackie looked around at the shelves of books and sighed. There'd been no peace in his life ever since Lacey Durango had jumped off that train and challenged him. Maybe it was time he got out of the saloon business and lived his dream.

"Blackie, are you loco?" He asked himself aloud. "You gonna let that petticoat defeat you and run you out of town?"

He sat in his office until almost dusk, then he got up and went to the door and looked into the saloon. It was almost empty and probably would remain so as long as Flo and the girls were on strike. Yep, that newspaper woman deserved what she was about to get. Blackie grinned, thinking of the painting that would liven up the place and be a wonderful revenge. Then he tiptoed to the back door and waited.

After a few minutes, there was a soft knock at the door. Dixie had been right. Another knock.

"Flo?" called a soft voice.

Blackie opened the door abruptly. "Gotcha!"

Miss Iron Corset dropped the bundle she carried and shrieked as Blackie reached out and grabbed her.

Chapter Nine

Blackie acted on impulse. He grabbed her wrist, yanked her up against him and put his hand over her mouth. "Shut up, woman, you'll have someone callin' the sheriff."

In answer, she sank her little teeth into his hand.

"Oww. Great God Almighty! You bite like a coyote!" He turned loose and shook the injured hand.

She straightened her mussed dress. "That's what you get for pawing me, you villain."

"I wasn't pawin' you."

"My word, you lie, too." Her dark eyes blazed in self-righteous anger. "You are an outrageous, lowdown cur, sir."

He sighed loudly, acutely aware that this confrontation was going on in a public alley. Right now, there was only a tough-looking yellow tomcat watching, but who knew if her shriek might draw a curious crowd? "Come inside, Miss Durango and we'll talk."

"Oh, come into my parlor, said the spider to the fly. I will not." She had stooped and was picking up the packages she had dropped.

He felt foolish and bent over to help pick up the items. Warm scents of goodies wafted to his nose. His mouth watered. "Come in and talk. Maybe I owe you an apology."

"Maybe?" She paused and glared at him. "I am on a mission of mercy and will not be deterred."

"Must you always talk like a dictionary? Here, I'll carry your packages inside."

She hesitated as if uncertain.

He took her arm and they were standing close enough that he could smell the clean scent of her dark hair. Her warm skin smelled like violets. It was such an innocent scent. Blackie hadn't known many innocent women. He suddenly had the most insane urge to kiss those full, soft lips.

Blackie, are you loco? he asked himself. But of course the urge was only because the ripe and voluptuous Dixie had rubbed herself all over him and he was only human after all. "Look," he said, "if we keep standing here, someone besides that tomcat's gonna see us and then your reputation will be ruined, Miss Durango."

"Yes, I agreed heartily, Mr. O'Neal. Being seen talking to a blackguard like you is enough to ruin any woman's reputation. All right, you may help me carry the packages."

He grinned. "May I ask what's in them?"

"No, you may not."

"It is my saloon you're carryin' things into."

"Oh, shut up, that's not relevant."

"You're talkin' like a dictionary again."

"What do you expect from an educated, liberated woman?" She stared past him through the open door into his office. "My word, all those books. I must say I'm surprised."

She would ruin his reputation as a tough, ignorant gambler. "Books?" he shrugged. "Don't know what's in them. Bought 'em by the boxload and had them shipped in from Kansas City just for looks and to impress people."

She frowned. "I might have known." She took her packages. "Please, you blackguard, unhand me."

He realized he was still holding onto her arm. "Excuse

me, Miss Durango." He stepped back. "Do be on your way."

He watched her walk off down the alley, her bustle swishing enticingly. She still carried her packages. Lacey certainly had the nicest shape he'd seen in a long time. It was a shame for the Good Lord to waste looks like that on a prim, uptight old maid. Well, after the election, maybe she'd throw in the towel and leave town. Certainly no woman wanted to be laughed at and humiliated. He turned and went back inside.

Watching from the upstairs window, Dixie sighed. Even from here and in the almost darkness, she had seen the play of electricity between the two. She was so jealous, it made her grind her teeth with rage. She began to think how she could get rid of Lacey Durango before the attraction got any stronger. No, maybe Miss Iron Corset was just a challenge, that was all. Blackie was used to women willing to do anything to get into his bed. He couldn't expect that from the newspaper woman . . . or could he? Dixie sighed again.

Behind her, Lil said, "What's the matter?"

"Dinner's gonna be a little late," Dixie muttered and decided to play down the scene she had witnessed. "That newspaper woman came to the back door and Blackie must have heard the noise, went to the door and she slipped into the shadows. She'll have to wait 'til he settles down again to get that food up the stairs."

"We can wait," Flo said. "I must admit it's excitin' to defy the men this way. This feelin' of power is good."

"Yeah, don't it, though?" Dixie yawned. What had felt good was brushing up against Blackie, imagining what it would be like to go into his embrace, have him caress and kiss her. Then later . . . Dixie took a deep breath at the thought. She was going to end up in Blackie's bed, no matter what happened. Once he'd tried Dixie's experienced charms, he wouldn't have eyes for anyone else. She'd see to that. In the meantime, she needed to do something about that prim old maid.

Lacey waited until dark before she tried again with the food. This time, it was Flo who answered her furtive knock at the back door. "Had some trouble the first time; somehow, Blackie seemed to know I was coming."

Flo took the basket and breathed in the scent deeply. "Umm. Must have been gambler's luck, I reckon. You know all my girls are standin' behind you on this."

There didn't seem to be much noise from the saloon. Lacey asked, "How's business?"

"Terrible," Flo admitted. "The few customers that do come in are as sad as orphaned pups. They all figure that if the gals ain't available, even as waitresses, they might as well drink at home or back at the bunkhouse. Worse than that, I hear none of the wives is cookin' anything and you know most men can't boil a pot of water. That new cafe is doin' a landslide business."

"Cookie," Lacey snorted, "the traitor."

"You know him? I went in for lunch once and thought he was kinda cute."

"Cookie? He's so old, he's almost white-headed."

Flo grinned. "Honey, just because there's snow on the rooftop don't mean there's no fire in the furnace."

Lacey raised her eyebrows in surprise. She realized again that Flo was no spring chicken herself. "He's been the cowboys' cook for years on my uncle's ranch. Cookie is really a pretty nice guy."

Flo sighed and turned away from the door. "It's lonely, runnin' a place like this. I always wanted to marry some nice fella and settle down, but I had younger brothers and sisters to support and I did what I had to do. Women like me don't get much chance at nice guys."

Lacey's heart went out to the madam. "You've still got

a chance at happiness, Flo. Here, I brought you and the girls some food." she handed over her bundles. "Isn't it fun, though, to upset the men's plans this way?"

Flo nodded. "Blackie ain't used to not gettin' his way. If he ever figures out that you're behind this . . . " She made a knife gesture across her throat.

Lacey decided not to give her the details of Blackie surprising her at the door. "I think he suspects something's up. Anyway, I'm not afraid of that bully. Even if he is a Rebel rascal, he wouldn't harm a lady."

"No, he wouldn't, but he could sure figure out a way to make you miserable."

"He's been the fly in my buttermilk ever since I contested him over that lot, but if he thinks I'm going to yell 'calf rope' and give up, he'd believe pigs can fly."

Flo looked up and down the alley. "You'd better go, hon, before someone sees you."

"Blackie in his office?"

"Naw, I think he's next door at the cafe eatin'."

"I must talk to Cookie. How dare he feed the enemy?"

"Men always sticks together, you know that. Thanks again for the vittles."

"You're welcome." In the darkness, Lacey sneaked back around to the street and peered toward the cafe. It was busy, all right. Many of the men were inside including Blackie, Eugene Peabody, and even Isaac. She decided to scout deep into enemy territory by going inside. Immediately, the men stopped talking and stared at her. Cookie himself was busier than a one-armed cowboy trying to saddle a horse.

"Hey, young'un," he yelled, "come on in and eat."

Before she could answer, a dozen men scrambled to their feet. "Here, Miss Durango, take my chair."

"Here, Miss Durango, I'd be much obliged if you'd sit at my table."

"Why, Miss Durango, sit right down here."

Blackie O'Neal didn't get up or even look up. He went ahead with his eating and ignored her.

"No thanks, fellas, I just dropped by to visit Cookie."

"Can I see you in the kitchen, Miss Lacey?" Cookie pulled her to the back. "Young'un, what you women got goin' on? All the men are gripin' about how none of them are getting any cleaning, cooking or . . . " His whiskered face turned scarlet as he paused. "Or nothing else," he mumbled.

"My word, Cookie," she smiled innocently as she watched Blackie eat. She'd seen hogs with better manners. The gambler glared at her and slowly and deliberately stuffed a big bite in his mouth and wiped his face on his sleeve. Blackie grimaced but swallowed it anyway. Lacey shuddered at the thought of steak grease on that expensive, perfect coat and turned her back to him. "Cookie, are you accusing the ladies of striking?"

"Is that what you call it?" Cookie said. "Wal, it's sure good for my business."

"You old traitor," she lowered her voice, "you're working against me."

"Aha," Blackie said behind her, and she jumped. She hadn't heard him get up from his chair and stride up behind her. "You admit you're at the bottom of this."

"That's an outrageous accusation," Lacey protested. "I said no such thing."

"You're the only cussed female in this settlement who's smart enough or ornery enough to organize this."

She smiled, delighted to be the burr under his saddle. "Are you saying a woman might be the equal of a man?"

"You're puttin' words in my mouth, Miss Durango. What I'm sayin' is you have been the pebble in my boot since that first day when we collided on that claim."

"You should have been a gentleman and let me have that lot," she reminded him.

"Not if hell froze over," he vowed. "And to think I was

havin' second thoughts about the painting . . " He stopped in mid-sentence as if he'd said too much.

"What painting?"

He swore under his breath, turned and returned to his table, began to cut up his burned steak as if he were imagining sticking that fork in her.

In the kitchen, she noticed the back door was propped slightly ajar. That ragged yellow tomcat came inside and began eating a saucer of leftovers. She was scandalized. "Cookie, you let a cat in your kitchen?"

Cookie paused. "He's a stray that was livin' out of the garbage can. I kinda took him to raise."

At that instant, perhaps on hearing Lacey's voice, a white cat stuck its head around the door.

"Precious?" She hurried to scoop her cat up in her arms. "Why, you're all dirty!"

Cookie admitted "She's been sneaking over here, Miss Lacey. I think she finds tom charmin'."

"That awful alley cat?" Lacey was horrified as she looked down at the big yellow tom. His ears were torn but he walked across the floor in a swaggering motion. "I feed Precious the best fish and roast beef, so she can't be hungry."

"Wal, you know, Miss Lacey, ladies do love a rascal."

"Not *all* ladies." Lacey said firmly, looking into the dining room where Blackie ate with his fingers. He was as bad as the yellow tom, no manners at all in that ruffian. "I'll try to keep her up from now on. The very idea, Precious, hanging out in garbage cans with a tramp like that."

"Meow," whined Precious and tried to get away.

"Meow." The yellow tom seemed to grin up at her pedigreed darling.

"Oh, no you don't." Lacey scolded, "Precious' future is Sir Fluffy Boots in Kansas City." She headed back through the cafe toward the street. As she passed Blackie, she muttered, "Cookie's a terrible cook, I hope he poisons you."

"I heered that!" Cookie yelled from the kitchen.

Blackie glared up at her. "I don't seem to have much choice except when Moose decides to stir up something, 'cause Flo don't cook no more. I'm sure I have you to thank for that, sister."

"You're welcome." She took her cat and threaded her way through the crowded cafe toward the street. She had to step over Lively lying asleep by the front door. Precious meowed in protest as Lacey headed toward the *Crusader's* office. "Now Precious, I have a wonderful, pedigreed, blue-blooded Persian in mind for you. I absolutely forbid you to see that rascal alley cat again. Garbage cans—the very idea!"

Precious squalled and tried to get out of her arms. Evidently, like most ladies, the wild male was just too fascinating to resist. Lacey determined she simply would not allow her lovely pet to be compromised by that alley cat.

The next day, Lacey put out an issue of the paper with an editorial encouraging "ladies to stick together through trying times." She saw men gathering around to get copies of the paper, as if it might hold the clue as to why the ladies were all on strike. Lacey stood at the window and watched the men dropping their money in the honesty box. "My word, Isaac, looks like this edition will be a sellout again."

Isaac came to the window and joined her. "The men in this town are fit to be tied and they've been trying to get the secret out of me, but I'm loyal to you, Miss Lacey. That gambler has told them you're at the bottom of this, but I'm not sure they believe him. You seem so sweet and innocent, yes." He smiled at her.

"Isaac, you're one of the few men entrusted with this secret. The ladies won't drop their bombshell until the day before the referendum."

Isaac pushed up his wire-rimmed spectacles and left a smudge of ink on his thin face. "Who else did you tell?"

"Well, the preacher knows about it, but he swore he wouldn't tell and I told Eugene Peabody. He seemed so aligned with our cause."

I don't know about him," Isaac complained. "I think he's a self-serving toady."

"Now how can you say such an outrageous thing? Eugene is a perfect gentleman compared to that rogue across the street. Why, he's told me many times how he supports the liberation of ladies and after all, he's a Harvard man. A girl could do much worse."

Isaac appeared about to argue the point, then shrugged and returned to work on the printing press.

Lacey sighed and thought of Eugene as she went to the front window and stared out. Eugene was nice, solid and respectable. Oh, so respectable. To the point of dullness.

Lacey, how can you even think such a thing? Why, if you were looking for a husband, Eugene would be a good choice. As soon as he gets his uncle's business on solid ground, he'll open his law office. A marriage to that well-educated, well-traveled gentleman would be perfect: a position of respect in the community. There'd be no surprises or excitement living with him like there would with that gambling rascal.

Speaking of the rascal, Blackie came out of the saloon, as usual, carrying a tall, iced glass in his diamond-studded hand. His drooling dog accompanied him.

The drunkard. Already in his cups and it wasn't even noon yet. However, he never appeared drunk or smelled of liquor. He must gargle that expensive shaving lotion. Lips that touched liquor would never touch hers, she vowed again, remembering the humiliation of the wedding and the party afterward.

The gambler walked across the street toward her office. Well, "walk" was not the correct description, she decided with a frown, "strutted" was more like it. He was a Texan, all right—God's gift to the world and its women. He came up to the box of newspapers, saw her standing behind the window and took off his hat, made a low bow. Then he put his hat back on, put his nickel in the box and took a paper. He nodded to her again with a mocking grin before turning back toward the saloon. Lively ambled along behind his master as they threaded their way between buggies and beer wagons. She wished one of those beer teams would run Blackie down and squash him flat. It would be ironic justice.

She turned away, annoyed with herself that she was remembering the touch of his big hands when he'd grabbed her in the alley. She had almost had a feeling at that moment that he was going to kiss her, but he hadn't. Good thing, she told herself or she would have called the sheriff and had him arrested as a masher.

The plan was going according to schedule as the days passed. The ladies and the saloon girls were still on strike. The ladies, joined by the lately arrived temperance members, met at the newspaper to confer.

"My house is so dirty, I can hardly stand it," wailed Mrs Anderson, holding her baby.

"I'll bet it's not bothering the men in your family one iota," Lacey said.

"Nor mine." The other ladies nodded.

"You know," Ethel Wilson offered, "I think men could live in a pig pen as long as somebody cooked for them and, well, you know." Her face turned red and the other ladies laughed in mutual embarrassment.

"Ladies," Lacey encouraged them, "our time is almost here. The referendum is day after tomorrow. Now is the time to let the men know what they have to do to get their maids and cooks back in the kitchen and the bedroom. I'll do an editorial in the morning paper."

"Oh, this is so exciting," said little Vanetta Wren. "I've never been so naughty before."

"Women would all be better off," Lacey said, "if they'd

raise less kids and more hell. Our next goal will be to turn Pretty Prairie into a dry town, run the saloons out permanently."

They all looked at her in awe. "What an ambitious plan. Our husbands and Blackie O'Neal will be furious."

"I'm not afraid of that rascal," Lacey countered. That wasn't exactly true, she thought, remembering that one time he had suggested that what she needed was a good spanking. He was the only man she'd ever met who might be man enough to do it. "All right, ladies, to the battle lines. It is time to let the men of your family know that if they don't vote for the name Pretty Prairie, they may never get another home-cooked meal—or anything else."

The ladies scattered. As she watched them go, she saw Blackie O'Neal standing at his saloon window watching the ladies leave. Again he raised his glass to her in a salute.

"My word, does that man ever get through even an hour without a drink?" She muttered.

About that time, some workmen came out the door and began to hang a banner across the front of the Black Garter. *Big Rally Tonight,* the banner read, *Vote for Whiskey Flats, a man's kind of town.*

Outrageous. "We'll see how long men can hold out. They won't vote with Blackie if it's going to cost them cooking, cleaning and bedroom privileges."

About that time, a wagon drove up out front of the saloon with Chief Thunder driving. He nodded to the workmen and they came over and helped him unload a big, canvas wrapped object. Lacey watched with curiosity. Something new for the saloon, no doubt. Well, that was nothing to her. She had correspondence to get out. She sat down at her neat desk and rearranged the pencils in perfect order. Precious usually lay on top of her desk, but she wasn't there. "Isaac, have you seen the cat?"

"Saw her slipping out the back door while ago."

"That stupid cat, she's not used to crossing busy streets, she'll get run over."

"Thought I saw her headed toward the cafe."

That terrible yellow alley cat. Why couldn't Precious learn that rascals might be enticing but were dangerous to nice girl cats? Lacey marched across the street and around the block. Sure enough, there was her beautiful, well-fed white Persian digging in a garbage can along with the ragged tom cat. "Shoo! Shoo!" She made a chasing motion to the big yellow tom as she gathered up her white pet that now reeked faintly of garbage. "You terrible rascal," she scolded, "don't you know the lady's too good for you?"

"Is she?" that familiar, deep masculine voice asked.

Still holding the cat, Lacey whirled around. Blackie O'Neal leaned against the door jamb of his open back door.

Lacey drew herself up proudly. "She certainly is. That tom has a lot of nerve tempting my blue-blooded Precious."

"Sometimes high-class ladies are just too temptin' for a rascal to resist," Blackie grinned.

She had forgotten how white his teeth were and how dark his eyes. They had a little glint in them. Her heart seemed to skip a beat and she stepped backward. "That doesn't mean the lady has to be tempted. When Precious comes to her senses, she'll realize Sir Fluffy Boots is a more sensible choice."

He grinned even more. "Sensible, maybe, but not near as much fun."

She felt the flush burn her cheeks. "My word, what do you know about cats?"

"Not much, I just know about rascals."

"You can say that again!" Still carrying her protesting cat, Lacey turned and flounced out of the alley.

Behind her, Blackie watched her go. That was the damnedest female it had ever been his misfortune to meet up with. She was a Texan, all right, everything about her was defiant and proud and stubborn. She was not going to let him win and he wasn't used to losing. That thought annoyed him so much, he brushed aside any reservations he might have had about sullying a lady's honor. At this very moment, Moose and Joe were hanging the painting on the wall behind the ornate bar. By tomorrow, Miss Iron Corset would be the laughing-stock of this town and maybe, just maybe, she'd be so humiliated when she found out, she'd pack up and get out of town. Whiskey Flats could return to being the wild, untamed, men's stomping grounds it should have been in the first place. "It's a dirty trick, sister, but you deserve it. I can hardly wait to see what happens when you hear about that paintin'." He was mighty pleased with himself as he shut the door and went into the saloon to admire the nude.

Chapter Ten

The next day as Lacey walked to the post office in the bright May weather, she nodded to people she passed on the wooden sidewalk. The ladies nodded back, but a number of men hesitated, gaped, looked embarrassed, and fled without speaking. After she passed, she had a distinct feeling that the men were gathering in little groups and talking. In the post office, two men smirked at her and one old rascal said, "Oh, you kid!" under his breath as he took his stamps and walked out. *Now just what was going on?*

Eugene Peabody entered the post office, stared at her in apparent shock and finally said "Disgusting! I never would have dreamed you would do such a thing."

"Do what, Eugene?"

"You know very well. Everyone is talking about it." With that, Eugene gathered up his mail and left.

Lacey watched him go, more puzzled than ever. Blackie O'Neal might be right, she thought grudgingly. Eugene was more prissy than perfect. She had no idea what was happening, but if it was bad, she knew Blackie O'Neal had to be at the bottom of it.

Some of the men outside the barber shop actually leered at her and laughed as she passed them. Lacey was more and more uneasy. What had happened? All that afternoon, when she looked out her big front window, she would catch men staring back at her curiously. One old lecher even winked at her. *Outrageous*. Perhaps Blackie had been spreading rumors about her.

Late in the afternoon, Joe Toadfrog came by and talked with her about painting the sign for the *Crusader*.

"Now," she said, "I don't want anything too shocking like that sign you did for that dreadful rum shop." She nodded toward the lady's leg, er, limb, with its stocking and black garter that hung over the vile establishment across the street.

"No, Miss Durango, you just tell me what you had in mind." He seemed to be avoiding looking her in the eye. Strange, since Joe had always seemed so friendly and open before.

"What about a stalwart lady carrying a banner and the banner reads: *The Crusader, A Newspaper for a Progressive Town?*"

"Yes, Ma'am, I'll get right on it."

"Joe," she hesitated. "Have you noticed anything strange going on?"

"I don't know what you mean, Ma'am."

"Men keep staring at me, leering or laughing. It's almost as if my petticoat were showing, but I've checked and it isn't."

The Indian coughed and looked away. "Men don't need much excuse to laugh, Miss Durango."

"Hmm. You're right, I reckon. Well, get on with the sign. I've got a paper to publish." She went back inside, sat down at her organized desk and mulled over how to effectively place her ladies to picket that sinful establishment across the street again. The sooner she ran that wicked saloon out of business, the better the town would be. She smiled as she pictured a bone-dry town that would welcome wholesome, respectable people like Eugene Peabody. Drunken cowpokes and gamblers would move on to other wild, reckless frontier towns.

Eugene Peabody. She stopped and chewed her pen, wondering what had upset him so and sent him prissing out of the post office? *Had Blackie started some wild rumor that Eugene had heard?*

As evening came on, more and more men stopped by her big front window to stare in at her. "My word," she muttered and frowned, "haven't those galoots ever seen a lady at a desk before?"

She still hadn't finished her editorial when Isaac came from the back, wiping his ink-smeared fingers on a rag. "I'm tired out, Miss Lacey, you ready to quit for the night?"

She shook her head. "You go on. I've got a lot of work to do before I close down." She glanced out the window at the growing darkness. Blackie's house of sin seemed to be doing an extra-bustling business tonight. There were many horses tied up at the hitching post out front. Men came out of the saloon, laughing and slapping their thighs. Some of them pointed toward her office and roared with drunken laughter. "Outrageous. Didn't their mothers ever teach them it was rude to point?"

"Probably not," Isaac said. "Well, I'm going over to Cookie's Kitchen for a bite to eat."

"Watch out, the old codger has poisoned half the cowboys on the Triple D spread."

"It isn't so bad when you get used to it. Besides, except for the Chinese joint, there's no place else to eat."

"You need a wife," she said absently.

"I'm happy working for you, Miss Lacey."

"Uh-huh." She returned to her work. "Leave the front door open, it's hot in here."

After Isaac was gone, the laughter and noise from the saloon drifted through the open door. The music interfered with her concentration. "Oh, it rained all night the day I left, the weather it was dry; the sun so hot, I froze to death, Susanna, don't you cry . . . "

Lacey ground her teeth together at the distraction. She wished Blackie O'Neal would freeze to death, him and his demon rum and his gamblers. Yes, she would organize her

Ladies Temperance Association to picket his den of sin again. As word spread across the Territory, more upright, righteous ladies would come and help with the crusade. They would make it hotter than a west Texas summer for all the saloon keepers, but especially the scoundrel across the street. If the ladies could run Blackie out of town, the other saloons would soon follow.

More laughter. She looked up, annoyed. Three cowboys were standing outside her office window, leaning on each other and laughing as they looked in. She got up and went to the open door. "Gentlemen—and that salutation is quite liberal, I assure you—please move on. You're distracting me from my work."

"Hey, baby, I'd like some of them grapes." One hiccoughed and staggered. They all howled with laughter like drunken coyotes.

"Grapes? This is not a grocery store." Lacey drew herself up with dignity. "Now please take your rum-soaked carcasses back to that vile whiskey shop across the street or go home and sleep it off."

The cowboys tottered off down the street, still laughing and singing. Lacey shook her head and closed the door. Outrageous behavior. A civilized settlement like Pretty Prairie would never put up with that. She returned to her desk. Precious hopped into her lap and she stroked the cat absently. Lacey sniffed and sniffed again. Her darling white kitty smelled faintly of garbage. "Precious, have you been slumming again?"

The cat actually seemed to smile and purred at her.

A few minutes later, Isaac burst through the front door, "Oh, Miss Lacey."

She looked up, alarmed. "My word, what's wrong? Are you sick? I warned you about eating at Cookie's place—"

"No, I just came from the Black Garter, and—"

"What were you doing in that dump, you traitor?" She leveled a steely gaze at him.

"All right," he scuffed one shoe on the wooden floor, "I never told you, but I like a beer now and then, and—"

"Oh, Isaac, I'm so disappointed in you."

"Miss Lacey," he burst out, "would you please hush and let me tell you something, yes?"

"All right, what is it?"

"That O'Neal fella has really done something terrible."

"That's news? Blackie O'Neal has certainly been one step ahead of the law all his life. Why, I suspect he's been run out of half the towns in Texas. He as much admitted it to me."

"He's hung a painting over the bar; a painting of a nekkid lady."

Lacey snorted. "Isaac, you're starting to talk like a Texan. Anyway, I hear that's the usual subject in saloons. I reckon Chief Thunder painted it for him. Drunkards like to stare at nudity while they drink, I reckon."

"The nekkid lady is surrounded and covered with fruit."

"Fruit? Like . . . like grapes?" She had a sudden, horrible premonition.

"Yes, Miss Lacey." he hesitated and took a deep breath. "Worst of all, the lady, well, it's you."

"What?" She stood up so suddenly Precious went to the floor and let out an indignant yowl. "What?"

"I tell you, Ma'am, there's a nekkid painting of you hanging over Blackie's bar and all the fellas is laughing and asking him how he got you to pose for it."

"My word." For a moment, she was too stunned to say anything. She remembered how men had treated her all day, snickering and pointing. Blackie O'Neal was attempting to use ridicule to run her out of town. *Outrageous.* "I am going over there," she announced and headed toward the door.

Behind her, Isaac pleaded, "I'm not sure I'd do that, Miss Lacey. Maybe you should get the sheriff—"

"The sheriff is probably in there having a beer, too,"

she complained, "male varmints all stick together." She marched out the door like a soldier going into combat.

Lacey strode across the street, avoiding little piles of horse manure as she walked between the horses tied at the hitching rail. Three men coming out of the saloon paused, took one look at her face and fled, obviously certain that something terrible was about to happen and they didn't want to be there for it. Other men standing outside talking, paused and looked at her curiously as she stomped across the wooden sidewalk and through the swinging doors.

Inside, it was hot and noisy, saloon girls dancing on the small stage while a little man banged out a melody on the piano: "Oh, dem golden slippers, oh, dem golden slippers . . ."

The place smelled of cigar smoke, stale beer and cheap perfume. "Make way!" Lacey shouted, "let me through, please!"

Men fell silent and moved back, as if suddenly invaded by Belle Starr. Some of them were evidently horrified to see a real lady in a modest white shirtwaist and plain black skirt moving through the gaudily dressed saloon girls. Lacey paid little heed to any of them as the men fell away. She kept her gaze on the giant painting hanging over the bar as she moved closer. In the background, the girls stopped singing about Golden Slippers and the piano trailed off.

Lacey reached the bar and gasped. From an art standpoint, the painting might be quite good, except as Isaac had pointed out, the lady was nekkid as the day she was born. The woman reclined on red velvet eating a piece of fruit, but her rotund form was quite bare except for a bunch of purple grapes at the most important part of her anatomy. The smiling face looking back at her was her own. She felt herself blanch and for a moment, she was speechless. "Oh, my word."

About that time, Blackie came out of his back office.

"What's going on out here? Dutch, why'd the music stop? Moose, what—?" He seemed to see Lacey for the first time. For a split-second, he almost looked ashamed and embarrassed, then recovered and sauntered toward her, his cigar at a jaunty angle. "Well, Miss Durango, what brings you to my establishment? Would you like a drink?"

"You have one on me!" Lacey snapped and grabbed one off the bar. Before the gambler could react, Lacey threw the drink in his face and stalked out. It seemed a long way to the door in the silence, but she kept her head high and walked with dignity although tears were blinding her. Behind her, the silence was deafening. She made it outside, almost tripping over the sleeping Lively, then with her eyes brimming with tears, she stumbled across the street. She went inside, locked the door and drew the shades.

"Miss Lacey," Isaac said, "I'm so sorry, I didn't know what to do."

"You—you can go, Isaac." She kept her voice cool and in control. "It was of little consequence, although it is amazing to what lengths that rascal will go to try to humiliate me."

"If you want my opinion," the little man said, "this has gone beyond a fight over a lot or even a crusade against liquor. This has become a personal thing between you two."

"I didn't ask for your opinion, but you're right. Sparks just fly when we cross each other's paths. I have never felt such emotion before. I'd like to tie the rascal to a red ant bed, in Comanche-style torture."

"I reckon he must feel the same way. He's sure going to a lot of trouble to annoy you."

"Go on, Isaac." She wanted to be alone. "I'll deal with this."

"How? Writing another editorial?"

"I'll figure something. After all, I am a Texan." She collapsed in her chair and Precious jumped into her lap. Once she heard the back door close behind the departing Isaac, Lacey buried her face in the cat's soft fur and gritted her teeth. She would not cry. She would be tough like a man. After all, this wasn't the first time a man had humiliated her. There'd been that awful scene at her wedding and then the one at the fountain later that evening. If she'd survived that, she could survive anything. She took a deep breath and began to plot her revenge. She imagined burying Blackie O'Neal on that disputed lot and building the foundations of her new newspaper building right on top his worthless carcass so she could tread up and down his arrogant body every day.

Across the street, Blackie wiped the liquor from his face with a fine linen handkerchief as the girl sailed out of the bar, head held high. No one said anything in the awkward silence. He was suddenly very much ashamed of the trick he'd pulled and it didn't seem as hilarious as it had when he'd first hung that painting. Lacey Durango might be the most annoying female he'd ever had the misfortune to cross paths with, but she was a lady after all. Still, no Texan knew the meaning of the word "retreat." "Moose, drinks on the house!" he shouted, "and Dutch, play something. I'm in my office."

As he turned and elbowed his way through the crowd, the noise level began to rise again as the piano started up.

Dixie pushed through the raucous crowd and grabbed his arm. "I saw what she done, Blackie, she had no right to—"

He shook Dixie's hand off, weary of the cheap, coarse girl. "Maybe she did, Dixie, maybe I went too far."

She blinked in surprise. "I ain't never heard you sound like that, Blackie, you sounded like you're apologizin'—"

"Who, me?" He threw back his head and laughed. "You're right, Dixie, she had it comin'. Now give me a kiss."

"Now you're talkin,' Handsome." She put her arms around his neck and kissed him with her painted lips, rubbing her big breasts against him. In his mind, he saw pale pink, soft lips and a brave, indignant figure of a woman marching out of his saloon, the blue bow on her dark hair slightly askew.

He shook Dixie off. "That's enough, honey, save it for the payin' customers."

"But, Blackie—"

"You heard me." He went into his office and shut the door. Great God Almighty. Damn that newspaper woman, didn't she deserve to be laughed at? He'd always done whatever it took to win and that choice lot was a valuable piece of property. The fight had escalated to more than that, it had become a test of wills and he didn't intend to lose to a girl. Yeah, he smiled, the temperance leader deserved to be made the butt of tough men's jokes. Yet he was still bothered by that nagging voice inside as he lit a cigar.

The next morning, early, Lacey hunted down Joe at the depot. "I saw the painting."

The handsome Indian gulped and looked embarrassed, avoiding her direct gaze. "I'm real sorry about that, Miss Durango. I told Blackie I thought it was a bad idea and he wavered some, but I think that Dixie gal urged him on."

"Hmm. I thought she was on the side of the ladies, but I reckon she's just out for herself. Well, never mind." Lacey thought about it a moment. Could it be that the saloon girl was in love with Blackie? Naw, that Irish rascal was about as appealing as a polecat. "Joe, I want you to do a painting for me."

She explained what she wanted.

"You gonna hang it in your office?"

Lacey shook her head. "No, I'm going to see if I can catch Blackie gone and then I'll make him wish he'd yelled 'calf rope' and left town."

"I don't know what you're up to, Miss, but I don't—"

"You'll be better off if you don't know, Joe. I reckon Blackie will be madder than a rained-on rooster."

"You can take that to the bank. He may come down on both of us like Sitting Bull on Custer."

"Enrage Blackie, you think?" The thought cheered her. "Paint it anyway. I owe the rascal one."

He sighed in defeat. "All right, as soon as I meet this next train and sell some buttons, I'll get right on it. You're sure more than a match for him. He ain't used to women who stand up to him."

"I'm a Texas girl, so he should have expected it," she called back as she turned and strode off the platform.

Now she went to the general store. Eugene rushed to meet her. "Oh, Miss Durango, I'm so sorry about what happened yesterday. I should have known you would have never posed for a painting like that."

"Seems you jumped to conclusions and judged me before you had all the facts, Eugene." She was cool to him.

Old Mr. Peabody came in from the storeroom. "Well, young lady, isn't that what your paper has been doing?"

Lacey felt an uneasy twinge. Had she been too judgmental? Of course not. "Mr. Peabody, this town would be a lot better off without the likes of Blackie O'Neal."

"I reckon he's got a right to live, too, Ma'am," the old man said. "You crusadin' females might cut him some slack."

"Now, Uncle," Eugene said, "I for one think she's right."

"Oh, hush, Eugene. If you weren't my nephew . . . "

"Mr. Peabody," she said, "Pretty Prairie is going to be a civilized, quiet town and we can't have that with people like Blackie O'Neal in residence."

"That's right, Uncle." Eugene said with a self-righteous nod, "with the likes of him tempting the weak with his demon rum and sinful women—"

"I don't need no sermons, especially from you, Eugene," the old man said.

"Well, that was rude," Lacey burst out, "especially since Eugene has done you the favor—"

"Miss Lacey," Eugene interrupted, "I think you'd better run along now. We've got work to do."

"Humph!" Old Mr. Peabody said. "It's about time you thought of that, Eugene."

It seemed to her the old man was being terribly ungrateful after his nephew had foregone opening his law firm to help out with his uncle's store, but she decided old Mr. Peabody was just out of sorts. She turned to leave.

The older man sighed. "What is it going to take to get a little cooking and cleaning done, even for a widower?"

"Vote for the ladies' choice in naming this town," Lacey said, "in the meantime, you can eat at Cookie's Kitchen."

The older man shuddered. "My hired girl, Mildred, can't cook very well, but Cookie's food makes hers seem tasty."

"I don't know," Eugene said, "Cookie's food is beginning to taste pretty good to me. Of course, if I had a wife . . . " His voice trailed off and he smiled at Lacey.

Mrs. Eugene Reginald Peabody. The embroidered initials on her linens and silver would be E.R.P. Somehow, that wasn't too appealing, but he was such an elegant gentleman, that made up for it. She remembered Blackie wiping his face on his sleeve. So much for linens. As for silver, all Blackie knew about that were the dollars thrown into a poker pot. "You're so gallant, Eugene; a perfect gentleman."

He smiled and bowed. "Thank you, Miss Lacey. I'm so sorry I misjudged you. Why, if I didn't have a bad back, I'd go down to that disgusting saloon and whip that rascal, make him take that painting down and burn it."

Oh dear. Blackie O'Neal would wipe up the floor with Eugene and she'd be responsible. "Thank you, Eugene, but I wouldn't want you to dirty your hands. I've already got a plan to deal with that scoundrel. Good-bye now."

It wasn't until she had taken her leave and was returning to her office, that she wondered how Eugene had known about the painting in the first place? Well, he might have heard gossip from men who did frequent the Garter.

She brushed that thought aside and went to the saloon. She entered hesitantly, but it was morning and there was no one in the front except Moose who was sweeping up. She noted the notorious painting had been taken down, and she was too proud to ask what had happened to it.

Moose blushed scarlet when he saw her. "I'm real sorry about the painting, Miss Lacey, I told Blackie it wasn't a good idea. My Mama would be real upset with me over this."

"Never mind, Moose, it's not your fault." she assured him. "Where is the scoundrel anyway?"

"In his office catching up book work. We're going to Purcell this weekend to get fresh supplies. Flo and Dutch will be holding the fort for a day or two."

"Oh, you're going, too?"

He nodded. "Blackie's thinkin' about adding some fancy wines and cheeses. I know about such things because I took a correspondence course. I always hoped to open a fancy hotel and tea room."

She didn't answer, her mind busy. So the scoundrel and his second-in-command were going to be gone. Maybe that would be time enough for her to take her revenge if she could enlist Flo's help.

"Miss Durango," Moose said, "I hope you and Blackie get this thing settled. It's keepin' the whole town stirred up."

"It'll be settled when this town is a quiet, law-abiding place with no saloons." Lacey wheeled and left. She intended to make Mr. Blackie O'Neal both an ass and the laughingstock of this township. She was humming to herself with pleasure as she imagined the look on his face when he walked into the saloon after his trip and saw a new painting over the bar. It would be a picture of him, that Texas rascal, and it wouldn't be flattering.

Chapter Eleven

It was evening as Blackie and Moose got off the train from Purcell and walked down the street toward the saloon.

Yes, the town was really growing, he noted with satisfaction. The Black Garter was turning a nice profit despite Miss Iron Corset's crusade. Now if he could only build a bigger saloon on that choice lot, she would make even more money so eventually he could retire and do what he really loved out in the Texas panhandle. Oh, well, that was some years into the future, maybe. He noted the number of horses tied up out front of the Garter and smiled. Usually Monday night was slow. There had to be some reason for the big crowd tonight. Maybe some of the men had come to see the notorious painting, but having humiliated her, Blackie had taken it down. At least, that's what he had told himself. Somehow, he had decided he didn't like other men leering at it. The painting was now safely locked in his office where only he would see it.

He started toward the swinging doors and his dog got up, tail wagging. "Hey, boy, you know how sissy you look wearin' a baby bib?"

Evidently, Lively didn't care. He licked Blackie's hand and Blackie paused and looked across the street. Was she watching him behind those curtains? What did he care? More laughter from inside. Yes, indeed, the boys were certainly in a good mood tonight. He thought about the

nude painting with a smile and tried to picture Lacey
Durango without any clothes on. Certainly she would be
much more slender than the Rubenesque nude in the
portrait. His imagination lingered over the image of
Lacey naked and it made him take a deep breath.
Grapes . . . he smiled at the thought. Of course the
chances that any man had ever or would ever see the
newspaper owner naked were as slim as a royal flush
twice in a row.

Blackie paused and looked across the street. He
could see the slight glow of a lamp downstairs where
her desk was. The prim old maid must be working late.
Indeed she was the hardest working girl he'd ever met.
Also the most stubborn. Pretty Prairie indeed. He almost felt sorry for her because of course she was going
to lose the referendum. About that time, she came to
the window and looked out. She appeared tired but
she was pretty, even though she had a big smudge of
ink on her face. Blackie hesitated, unsure what to do
now that she had seen him. She might come out and
give him a piece of her mind.

Instead, she smiled and waved at him. Blackie was
taken aback. Surely she hadn't forgotten about the nude
painting. Yet here she was smiling and nodding to him.
Hell, who could understand women? Blackie nodded,
tossed away his cigar, and tipped his hat to her. Three
cowboys came out through the swinging doors of the
Black Garter, spotted him and one pointed. The other
two held their sides and laughed until they seemed ready
to fall down. Too *drunk*, Blackie thought in disgust. He
must speak to Flo and Dutch about that. Blackie had
rules about letting customers drink too much. The three
cowboys stopped two other men entering the bar and
said something to them. All five laughed as they walked
away.

From across the street, Miss Iron Corset smiled and
waved again. Blackie began to get an uneasy feeling. She

was grinning like she'd just been dealt an ace-high straight. Now what was that little rascal up to? Whatever it was boded ill for him and his customers, he was sure of it.

With Moose right behind him, he started through the swinging doors. Even from here he could hear the peals of laughter from inside. Boy, the crowd was in a good mood tonight. That was great for profits. The saloon was so crowded, he had to elbow his way through the jovial mob. Dixie was singing loudly but not too well, and the place was alive with people and hazy with blue smoke. As Blackie passed, men fell silent and edged away. Blackie elbowed his way through the crowd to the bar. "Hey, Flo, I'm back. Gimme the usual."

She paused, blinking in surprise. "Uh, coming right up, Blackie. You and Moose have a good trip?" She sounded nervous as she slid the tall cold glass down the bar. Around him, conversation gradually died as men edged away from him. Blackie didn't even look up. He wasn't much in the mood for conversation tonight. The girl across the street had ruined his mood with her suspicious cheerfulness. In the background, the piano gradually stopped playing and the noise faded away.

Beside him, Moose let out a long breath. "Oh, my God."

"What?" Blackie didn't look up.

Dixie pushed her way through the crowd to him. "Blackie, it ain't my fault. I didn't know nothin' about it."

"About what?" He wished she'd go away. He didn't want to deal with the slut tonight; she grated on his nerves.

"About that. You ain't noticed it?" Blackie looked up from his drink and followed the motion of Dixie's hand. She was pointing up over the bar. For a long moment, he was not sure what he was looking at in the blue haze of smoke. Certainly the painting was not the nude . . . oh, Great God Almighty.

He could only blink in disbelief as he stared. Around

him, men edged away as if afraid of what was about to come. Hanging in place of the female nude was a painting of the biggest, fattest hog Blackie had ever seen. It lay in a mud puddle and it wore a Panama hat cocked over one eye, a cigar sticking out of its snout, and a diamond ring on its dirty hoof. But its face . . . its face was Blackie's own, grinning back at him.

The silence was deafening. *Touché.* He didn't know how or where, but that little rascal across the street had to have had a hand in this. He was so angry, his hand was shaking as he picked up his drink. "Moose," he thundered, "take that damned thing down! Flo, I'd like to see you in private!"

Men made way for him as Blackie strode back to his office, trailed by the henna-haired madam. Behind him, he heard the buzz as men discussed the event. Half of him wanted to congratulate the sassy girl on her coup, the other half wanted to wring her dainty neck. He went into his office and sat down behind his cluttered desk. "Close the door," he ordered.

From out front, the merriment was building again. He gritted his teeth, imagining the men pointing and laughing. Flo balanced first on one foot, then the other. "I don't suppose you'd believe me if I told you it just appeared on the wall right before the evening crowd came in?"

"Sure, Santa Claus brought it. Do I need guess who was behind this?"

"Maybe it was Chief Thunder's idea." She toyed with her cameo brooch, not looking at him.

"I think not, although I'm sure he painted it. Flo?"

She put her hands on her ample hips, still apprehensive but angry now. "Well, you big lug, you started it. That paintin' you hung was hittin' below the belt, Blackie."

"Do I need to remind you, you work for me?"

"I'm a woman first, Blackie. I figured you had it comin' after you put up that paintin' with her head on it. You can fire me if you want."

"And let her think she got to me?" He grinned weakly, "Flo, we been friends too long to fire you. Maybe I did have it comin', but who'd have thought she'd pull a stunt like this?"

"Blackie, she ain't your average girl."

"Ain't that the truth?"

More laughter from the saloon. He shook his head and sipped his drink. "Go on back out front, Flo, and tell everybody I thought it was a funny joke."

"You don't look like you thought it was funny," Flo said.

"You know what would be funny?" Blackie snapped, "takin' that little rascal across my knee and wailing the daylights out of her like the guy did in *The Taming of the Shrew*."

"What?" Flo paused in the doorway.

"It's Shakespeare."

"Reckon I don't know him."

More laughter from the front. No wonder that prim old maid had smiled and waved to him. He'd been outsmarted and outfoxed by a woman, aided by his own employees. "Never mind, Flo, just get out of here and don't let that gal pull you in on any more of her schemes."

"She don't need much help, Blackie. She's a smart little lady." She grinned and left.

He had to agree on that. Great God almighty, was there no end to the daring of that prim old maid? Blackie sighed and reached for one of the well-worn books in his bookcase. He wanted to read that scene again where the guy got fed up and spanked the fiery Kate. "Everyone would laugh if they knew I read Shakespeare," he muttered. "Bet there's nobody in town who knows the Bard."

Well, there was one person. He'd wager Lacey Durango knew the classics, but he'd die before he'd let her find out how well he'd educated himself. "It must have taken a heap of plannin' to pull this off. If the joke weren't on me, I'd laugh about how clever it was."

But it was on him and it was all her fault. He slammed

the book down and got up. Out front, the singing and
the noise grew louder. It grated on his nerves more than
ever. He longed for peace and solitude, a good horse
under him and a starry sky above. He uncovered the
nude painting in the corner behind his messy desk. The
naked Lacey seemed to grin in triumph at him and her
grapes looked inviting, although he had never really
liked grapes.

Was he loco? He ought to stride across the street and
confront the feisty newspaper editor, but he wasn't quite
sure what to say. "Congratulations on besting me," would
be in order, but he wasn't ready to yell "calf rope" to a
mere girl.

About that time, he heard someone coming; he
quickly covered the portrait and sat down at his desk.

Dixie entered his office without knocking, her bright
scarlet skirts swishing as she swung her hips. "I didn't
have no part in that, Blackie, it was that newspaper
woman behind it all."

He scowled at the tart. "Yeah, I know. Flo and me had
a talk. No gal but Lacey Durango would be smart
enough to outwit me. 'Course she's a Texan."

"You ain't mad?" Her painted face was incredulous.

"Hell, yes, I'm mad. Now go earn your pay. I'm not
feeling like much talk tonight." He stood up, made a gesture of dismissal.

"Whatcha reading?" She didn't move, but looked at
the book with wide eyes.

"*The Taming of the Shrew,* nothin' you'd ever read."

She laughed. "I don't even know what a 'shrew' is,
Blackie. I got an idea of something more fun than
readin' some stupid book." She sidled up to him and put
her hand on his chest.

"Get out, Dixie," he said. "I'm busy."

"You don't never have time for me," she complained.
"You ain't had time ever. You used to act like you might
be interested before we got to this town."

He tried to brush her off. "I've been busy gettin' the saloon up and runnin'.'"

"You used to always find time for gals, no matter how busy you was. You know what the girls are sayin'?"

He didn't much give a damn what the whores were saying and said as much.

"Yeah?" Dixie looked up at him, standing so close, her big breasts brushed against his chest. "They say you got the hots for what you don't have and can't get, that uppity high-class newspaper woman. I'll bet I could get your mind off her." Before he could react, she slipped her arms around his neck and kissed him, pressing her eager body against his.

For just a moment, his body reacted instinctively and he pulled her hard against him, kissed her almost brutally. Yet something was missing. Gradually, he pulled away from her and sighed. "Go on back to work, Dixie. You got customers to entertain."

Dixie looked livid. "You ain't gonna get in Miss Iron Corset's drawers, if that's what you're wantin'."

Her words infuriated him. "Are you loco, you crazy slut?"

Dixie stepped back as if he'd slapped her. Now she smiled and drawled, "No, but I reckon you are. All right, Blackie, but all of the girls is willin' and able when you finally come to your senses. That Durango woman ever finds a husband, it'll have to be some respectable rancher or business owner. She wouldn't stoop to being hitched to a bum who runs a saloon."

"Get out of here, Dixie!" He shouted at her and Dixie turned and fled. Blackie strode over and slammed his door. He looked around his office, feeling suddenly very tired and lonely. He wanted to talk to someone who read books and knew who Shakespeare was and wouldn't laugh at his hobby. "I'm too tired to play poker tonight," he muttered, "I think I'll go to bed."

* * *

He had to put a pillow over his head to be able to sleep. His mind was torn between wanting to spank Lacey Durango and congratulate her for outsmarting him. Well, if she thought this would win the referendum for her, she had another think coming. Damn her, anyway.

Tomorrow was the referendum and all the men knew what was at stake. He ought to be out in the saloon campaigning, but he didn't feel like it. Anyway, it didn't matter. No man worth his salt was going to vote for a prissy name like Pretty Prairie.

Lacey was up early, smiling to herself as she imagined the look on Blackie O'Neal's face last night when he saw the painting of the pig. For a moment, she almost pitied him with all the men laughing and pointing. Then she recalled the ridicule he'd put her through over the nude and shook her misgivings away. Today was the day of the big vote and the ladies had worked hard to swing the men to their way of thinking. Today was one last push for the undecideds. "Isaac, you got the signs ready?"

The stooped little man nodded. "Sure thing, Miss Lacey. Eugene Peabody said he'd come by and get some."

"Thanks, Isaac, and don't forget to vote."

"I won't." He was out the door with an armful of signs that read: *End the Ladies' Strike. Vote for Progress. Vote for Pretty Prairie.*

"Someday, women will get the vote," she muttered, "and we won't have to resort to all this blackmail."

There was something going on out in the street. Lacey went to the window and looked out. Blackie's big, fancy barouche had pulled up to the saloon and Moose, Blackie, and some of the men were hanging signs all over it. *Vote Today!* the signs read, *Whiskey Flats is Our Kind of Town. Don't Let Women's Apron Strings Choke You.*

Outrageous. Well, at least he wouldn't be able to get Flo

and her girls to ride in his buggy. No, she was wrong. That blonde, Dixie, came out of the Black Garter, all dressed in bright scarlet silk. She looked toward the newspaper office almost as if she wanted to make sure Lacey was watching. Then she kissed Blackie's cheek, leaving a smear of lip paint. He laughed and helped her into the carriage.

"My word. How can he make such a spectacle of himself?" she fumed.

Now coming down the street were the good ladies of the town, most carrying the signs Isaac had distributed. Out in front marched Eugene Peabody, beating a big drum. She should have known she could count on Eugene, bless his heart. Lacey hurried out to meet her righteous parade. "Good day, ladies, and thank you, Eugene, for helping us. Besides you, the preacher, and Isaac, no man has come forward for our cause."

Eugene beamed at her and then frowned as he looked across the street toward the Black Garter. "Disgusting. That saloon crowd has no shame. Never you mind, Miss Lacey, after tonight, they'll all fold up and leave town."

"Let's hope so, although I doubt that Blackie O'Neal is one to run from a fight."

"I ought to whip that rascal for you," Eugene said.

"Uh, I don't think that would be a good idea," Lacey hastened to say, glaring across the street at Blackie. He looked every inch the rogue as he sat his carriage with the whore. He tipped his hat to Lacey and the big diamond on his hand flashed. Someone should tell him men didn't wear diamonds except maybe as a stickpin in a tie.

Eugene said "You think I can't whip him? I'll have you know I've had lessons in the manly art of self-defense." He put up his fists is an exaggerated manner.

Eugene looked positively ridiculous posing that way, but she didn't say so. She was also certain that Blackie had come up through the School of Hard Knocks and would wipe Eugene's face in horse manure right here in the middle of the street if it came to a fight. "Oh, no, Eugene, it's just that I can't stand the sight of blood."

"Oh, of course. You're such a delicate lady. Are you going to march at the front of our demonstration?"

"Certainly. Ladies, get in some kind of order and we'll parade around the block and up Main Street."

"I'm really enjoying this," said Miss Wren with excitement, "It surely beats cleaning house."

"Good." Lacey smiled. "If we could get ladies across the nation organized like this, we could get the vote."

Eugene paled. "That might be going too far, Miss Lacey."

She had a sudden feeling that Eugene wasn't as progressive as she had thought, but that wasn't today's problem. "All right, ladies, wave your signs. Eugene, are you ready with the drum?"

He nodded. "Let's go, Miss Lacey."

Blackie O'Neal's fancy open barouche with its banners pulled out just ahead of them so that Lacey and her parade were marching through fresh horse manure. My word, how ornery could the man get? Well, there wasn't anything she could do about that now. Her ladies began to sing in protest as they marched down Main Street. "Temperance gals, won't you come out tonight, come out tonight, come out tonight? Temperance gals, won't you come out tonight and march by the light of the moon . . . ?"

Boom, boom, went the big drum as they passed shops, the post office, and the bank. *Boom, boom.* Eugene beat the drum as they marched and sang.

Lacey smiled and waved to men on the street. "End the ladies' strike!" she shouted, "vote for a wholesome town! Vote for Pretty Prairie!"

Ahead of them, she could see Blackie's barouche with that whore throwing kisses to the men. She looked back at Lacey, smiled archly and scooted even closer to Blackie on the scarlet plush seat.

Outrageous, Lacey thought. *Boom, boom, boom* went the big drum as the parade marched up and down the street and around the block. People on the sidewalk stopped to stare at the procession. Whether it was because of the banners or the fact that most of Blackie's saloon girls were now marching side by side with the most respected matrons of the town was hard to say. Lacey smiled and waved. "Get out and vote!" she called to men she passed. "End the strike by supporting a wholesome, law-abiding town like Pretty Prairie."

Blackie glanced back over his shoulder. There she was in the lead with that prissy store clerk banging on a big drum and all the self-righteous ladies of the town marching with her. *Ladies?* Why, Flo and most of his own whores were walking in her parade. Talk about traitors. Well, he could rely on one gal anyway. He turned and grinned at Dixie as they drove down the street and she cuddled up even closer.

"It's you and me, Blackie, we think alike."

"We sure do, Dixie." He looked back over his shoulder again at the defiant Lacey and put his arm around Dixie's bare shoulders. As they passed, men stopped and gaped. "Get out and vote today for Whiskey Flats!" he yelled. "Keep this a wide-open town like men want. Don't turn it into a sissy's retreat."

He couldn't compete with Lacey's strike, of course, but he could remind men what they were fighting for. After all, men were basically uncivilized animals. They wanted to be able to scratch when it itched, walk across clean floors with muddy boots, burp when they felt like it, chase women, drink and play cards. Civilized women like Lacey wanted them to wash, behave like gentlemen, and be responsible and respectable. When men got civilized, the wild frontier days would end. It was a scary thought.

"Vote for Whiskey Flats," Dixie cooed to the men they passed, and winked and blew kisses.

Blackie grinned. Let Miss Iron Corset compete with that. The referendum was a shoo-in. Why had he been worried? The whole unlikely parade toured the town's main streets twice before they ended the march. Blackie pulled up in front of his saloon, climbed down, and handed the reins to Moose. He looked to see Lacey ending her parade in front of the newspaper office. She looked his way. "Come on, Dixie, honey," he said loudly and reached to help the blonde from the seat. He hugged her to him and she kissed him impulsively.

When he glanced toward Lacey again, she was kissing Eugene Peabody's cheek. "Thank you, Eugene, for helping us."

The prissy back-East dude seemed so pleased, he looked like he might faint amid the mud and horse manure.

Blackie snorted. "Go on inside, Dixie, I've got to go vote." He made a big show of walking toward the post office. Inside, there was already a line. Good, there was going to be a big turnout. The ladies didn't stand a chance. He could almost pity Lacey Durango for her game try. "Boys," he shouted, "free drinks tonight at the Black Garter when the polls close!"

A cheer from the men. Yes, this election was a shoo-in. If there wasn't so much at stake, he could almost feel sorry for Miss damnyankee Iron Corset.

He marked his ballot, dropped it in the box and went outside. It was going to be a clear, hot day. But a victorious one. Blackie grinned and sauntered down the street toward the saloon. All he had to do now was wait for the results tonight. Tomorrow, the town would have an official name: Whiskey Flats. *Too bad, Miss Durango, but you never had a snowball's chance in hell of winning. That will teach you to go up against the master, Blackie O'Neal.*

Chapter Twelve

It was the grimmest news white males had heard since George Armstrong Custer had gone down to defeat at the Little Big Horn. That night, after the ballots were counted, the men gathered in little groups along Main Street to discuss what went wrong.

Blackie was fuming. "God Almighty! I can't believe only a handful of us men had the balls to vote for Whiskey Flats!"

Julius Wilson, the banker, cleared his throat. "Well, now, Blackie, I was under pressure at home—"

"Me, too," piped up the barber. "I wasn't gettin' no cleaning, cooking, or—or anything else."

It was the "anything else" that had sunk the victory, Blackie knew, even though most of the men were not going to admit they caved in and voted for the women's choice. "That newspaper woman, that reformer, did this. I reckon the next thing on her agenda is to dry up this town."

The faces of the men around him paled visibly. "You mean—you mean no more, er, ah—medicinal alcohol?"

"That's exactly what I mean," Blackie snapped. "She's out to clean up this burg and make it a wholesome, law-abidin' place."

"That's not a bad thing," fat Mr. Anderson ventured. All the men turned to glare at him and he retreated. "I mean, from a chamber-of-commerce point of view, it'll cause the town to grow."

Blackie snorted. "It'll grow all right; all civilized and quiet. No more shootin' up the town or cowboys ridin' horses into saloons on Saturday nights. Instead, they'll roll up the sidewalks by dark. Why, all the men will be expected to be home with the missus every night and wash every Saturday whether they need it or not."

More than one man paled at the thought, although Blackie wasn't sure which was worse—spending more time with the little wife at home or the thought of washing.

"Wal now," said Cookie, leaning against the red-and-white barber pole, "Maybe we drink too much anyways."

"Why should that worry that old codger?" old Mr. Peabody said under his breath to no one in particular, "he drinks vanilla anyhow."

"I heered that!" yelled the old man.

The barber brightened. "I reckon now we can go home and tell the ladies they've won and we all might get a little—well, you know."

All the men straightened up and smiled.

"Don't bother rushin' home," Blackie grumbled. "The ladies ain't there." He jerked his head down the street toward the little park. "They've got a victory march startin'."

And sure enough, the ladies, their little parade lit by the torches they carried, were marching down Main Street, singing their temperance battle cry, led by Eugene with his drum and by the Reverend Lovejoy. The only other two males in the victory march were Isaac and Lively.

Yes, even his own dog was strolling alongside Lacey, wagging his tail and wearing that damned pink *BABY* bib.

"Blackie, ain't that your dog?" the blacksmith asked.

"Well, he used to be before she bribed him with biscuits," Blackie said in disgust.

"I'd like to throw horse apples at them women," muttered a cowboy.

"That ain't the way to treat ladies," Cookie said.

Blackie sighed. The idea of pelting Lacey Durango with horse manure was mighty appealing right now. "You

can bet this win will be in her newspaper and even more
of them temperance females will arrive by train from all
over the country. We got too many now."

The ladies marched past, their torches lighting up the
night. Some pushed baby buggies. Even the gals from the
Black Garter had gotten out the fancy open barouche and
were in the procession.

"Blackie," said Julius Wilson, "ain't that your carriage
and your whores?"

"Yep." Blackie struck a match on his boot and lit a
cigar. "I just can't control Flo and the girls any more
than my dog."

"Temperance gals, won't you come out tonight," sang
the ladies as they marched past, "come out tonight . . . "

Boom, boom, boom. Eugene marched right next to the
triumphant Lacey.

"The dude," Blackie growled. "I can see why Reverend
Lovejoy and Isaac feel obligated to march with the ladies
against demon rum, but Eugene is a big hypocrite."

"He's more than that," griped old Mr. Peabody, then
seemed to reconsider and didn't say anything else.

Blackie watched the ladies dourly. "Next thing you
know, they'll be organizin' to get the vote. Worse yet,
Miss Iron Corset has the bit in her teeth with this victory
and she'll be workin' toward dryin' up the territory;
maybe the whole country."

"You mean . . . ?" The men shuddered.

"I mean prohibition," Blackie said the dreaded word.

There was a horrified intake of breath from the as-
sembled males.

"In that case," hiccoughed one of the cowboys, who
was so drunk he couldn't have hit the ground with his
hat in three tries, "we'd better fill up now."

"Best idea of the night," the barber nodded, and the
men started toward the saloon.

The ladies walked the block again, singing and waving
their banners. Blackie had to admit that Lacey Durango

looked fetching with her red, white, and blue dress, her small bustle waggling and her eyes alit with the fire of victory.

"Ethel," yelled the banker, "you get out of that gol-darned parade and go home and cook me some supper!"

"Ain't a-gonna! Cook your own danged supper!" Ethel, also a Texan, yelled defiantly and waved her banner.

"And so it starts," Blackie sighed. "You see what we're facin', gentlemen? A rebellion on the homefront and all because of that newspaper woman. Great God Almighty, I can't believe I've lived long enough to end up in a town with a name like Pretty Prairie."

"Look on the bright side," the barber grinned, "to-morrow, my old lady starts cooking again."

"And I'll get my socks washed," said the horseshoer.

A cowboy smiled dreamily. "And the girls at the Black Garter will be inviting the boys back upstairs." He paused hopefully. "Won't they, Blackie?"

"How the hell should I know?" He gave a disgusted snort, "ask Miss Iron Corset."

Shy Miss Wren passed by in the parade, carrying a torch.

"Vanetta!" yelled her father, "you get out of that con-founded parade and go home, you hear me?"

"I'm not going to, Daddy," Vanetta shouted back with spirit, "I'm having too much fun. I may even get a job."

"A job?" Mr. Wren clutched his chest as if having a heart attack. "Women ain't supposed to go to work and have their own money."

"Fun!" A cowboy said, "Respectable ladies ain't sup-posed to have fun, they're supposed to do for men; cookin' and washin'. I don't like this idea of them takin' over."

"Get used to it," Blackie said. "If we can't find a way to stop Miss Iron Corset, you're gonna see this town be-come so respectable, that average men can't stand to live here. Come on, boys, the drinks are on the house."

Even that didn't raise their spirits as the dejected, defeated men shuffled toward the saloon. Blackie knew most of them had voted the way the ladies had told them to, but each had thought the others would vote for Whiskey Flats. They were astounded at their own gutlessness and the ladies' victory.

Blackie shook his head as the men entered the saloon. Lacey Durango was stubborn; the most stubborn female he'd ever had the misfortune to run across; almost as stubborn as he was himself. Now he began to have serious doubts that he might not outlast the Iron Corset to gain ownership of the contested prized land. The women were taking over this town and he didn't like it.

Lacey and Isaac stayed up most of the night getting the special edition out. People were lined up on the streets at dawn to read the news. The banner across the top of the paper now read: *The Pretty Prairie Crusader.* The big headline crowed:

Progressive town looks forward to becoming a modern metropolis. Landslide victory for the more respectable town name proves citizens want a civilized, more refined town.

Blackie scowled as he read the news aloud. "It only proves men are helpless to withstand the pressure when nobody cooks or washes their socks."

Cookie limped up to stand at his elbow. "It's the 'other' that really got them."

"Women!" Blackie snorted. He looked up in time to see Miss Iron Corset looking back at him through the newspaper office window. She smiled and waved gaily to him.

He decided to pretend he had not seen her. Around him, men were plunking their money in the honesty box and grabbing papers to read the details. "She keeps selling

Take A Trip Into A Timeless World of Passion and Adventure with Kensington Choice Historical Romances!
—Absolutely FREE!

Enjoy the passion and adventure of another time with Kensington Choice Historical Romances. They are the finest novels of their kind, written by today's best-selling romance authors. Each Kensington Choice Historical Romance transports you to distant lands in a bygone age. Experience the adventure and share the delight as proud men and spirited women discover the wonder and passion of true love.

4 BOOKS WORTH UP TO $24.96— Absolutely FREE!

Get 4 FREE Books!

We created our convenient Home Subscription Service so you'll be sure to have the hottest new romances delivered each month right to your doorstep—usually before they are available in book stores. Just to show you how convenient the Zebra Home Subscription Service is, we would like to send you 4 FREE Kensington Choice Historical Romances. The books are worth up to $24.96, but you only pay $1.99 for shipping and handling. There's no obligation to buy additional books—ever!

Save Up To 30% With Home Delivery!

Accept your FREE books and each month we'll deliver 4 brand new titles as soon as they are published. They'll be yours to examine FREE for 10 days. Then if you decide to keep the books, you'll pay the preferred subscriber's price (up to 30% off the cover price!), plus shipping and handling. Remember, you are under no obligation to buy any of these books at any time! If you are not delighted with them, simply return them and owe nothing. But if you enjoy Kensington Choice Historical Romances as much as we think you will, pay the special preferred subscriber rate and save over $8.00 off the cover price!

We have **4 FREE BOOKS** for you as your introduction to
KENSINGTON CHOICE!
To get your FREE BOOKS, worth up to $24.96, mail the card below or call TOLL-FREE 1-800-770-1963.
Visit our website at www.kensingtonbooks.com.

Get 4 FREE Kensington Choice Historical Romances!

♡ **YES!** Please send me my 4 FREE KENSINGTON CHOICE HISTORICAL ROMANCES (without obligation to purchase other books). I only pay $1.99 for shipping and handling. Unless you hear from me after I receive my 4 FREE BOOKS, you may send me 4 new novels—as soon as they are published—to preview each month FREE for 10 days. If I am not satisfied, I may return them and owe nothing. Otherwise, I will pay the money-saving preferred subscriber's price (over $8.00 off the cover price), plus shipping and handling. I may return any shipment within 10 days and owe nothing, and I may cancel any time I wish. In any case the 4 FREE books will be mine to keep.

Name_____

Address_____ Apt._____

City_____ State_____ Zip_____

Telephone (____)_____

Signature_____

(If under 18, parent or guardian must sign)

Offer limited to one per household and not to current subscribers. Terms, offer and prices subject to change. Orders subject to acceptance by Kensington Choice Book Club.
Offer Valid in the U.S. only.

KN025A

papers like this, she'll be the richest person in town. Damn her stubborn hide, anyhow." He turned and walked away. Look at the bright side, Blackie, he told himself, at least the girls upstairs would go back to work and the saloon would fill up again. All that would put money in his pockets, but somehow, that didn't cheer him. He had never been bested by a woman before and he wasn't quite sure how to handle it. "Miss Iron Corset is almost as smart and stubborn as a man," he muttered as he walked, "and maybe as good at business, too."

Lively walked along behind him, panting. It was now June and it was as hot as hell with the lid off, Blackie thought. Being a Texan, he felt right at home with that kind of weather. What was it that damnyankee general had said? "If I owned both hell and Texas, I'd rent out Texas and live in hell." Well, what else could you expect from a damnyankee from one of those cold, northern states?

Inside, Lacey wiped her hands on her printer's apron and smiled in satisfaction as she watched Blackie O'Neal reading her paper. "Isaac," she turned to speak to her assistant, "we keep selling like this, we're going to be able to build the finest building in town on that corner lot."

"If you get it, that is," Isaac said.

"I'm going to outlast him," she declared as she watched Blackie reading the paper outside the window. "He's seen now that I'm as tough as he is."

"You're a matched pair, all right," Isaac agreed, "like two locomotives on the same track headed for a collision; that can't be good."

"Actually, I'm enjoying myself hugely."

She saw Blackie look up from the paper. She smiled prettily and waved. He frowned and turned away. "You know, he's a typical Texan—stubborn, proud."

"And he's all man," Isaac reminded her, "he doesn't like being bested by a woman."

"Then he'd better get used to it," she said. "Pretty Prairie is going to be a rallying place for all the lady crusaders in the Territory. Maybe in the whole country. Should my next crusade be for prohibition or women's rights?"

Isaac groaned aloud. "Can't you just run the paper?"

"While the ladies have all this power?" Lacey snapped, "now that we've got a respectable name for this town, we need a school before autumn and a public library. Reverend Lovejoy has a modest church building, but it could use a stained glass window."

She went over to her perfectly organized desk and reached for a pen. Precious lay curled up on her desk. "I swear, Precious, have you been eating out of the garbage with that old yellow tom again? You're getting awfully heavy . . ." A thought crossed her mind and Lacey shook it off. No, her darling, blue-blooded Persian would never surrender to the charms of that feline rascal . . . would she? Of course not.

Lacey sat down at her desk and began writing:

What the progressive town of Pretty Prairie needs next is fewer saloons and more families taking up residence. What will bring in more families, you ask? A good school for all the little children. We must find a way to raise enough money to build a school before autumn comes.

How could the respectable ladies raise money? Very few women had money of their own, the husbands controlled it all. *Outrageous,* she thought. When she called her next ladies' meeting, she would suggest the women feed their men more potatoes and less meat. A thrifty housewife could save a few pennies that way to contribute toward the school. Still that wouldn't be nearly enough. "I will ask the businessmen of this town to contribute," she thought aloud. "Eugene will come through for me and maybe he can convince the others."

Isaac frowned. "You watch that Eugene, he's a slick one, yes?"

"My word, you must have been mixing with that scurrilous saloon bum," Lacey snapped. "Eugene Peabody is a wholesome, wonderful man."

"You gonna marry him?"

"What an outrageous question," Lacey sputtered, "but some girl would be lucky to get him; he's perfect."

"No man's perfect," Isaac said matter-of-factly, "but if you love them, you overlook the shortcomings."

"Well, I'm looking for the perfect man and maybe Eugene is the one." Lacey felt her face burn as she imagined getting into bed with Eugene. Somehow, this pristine husband material didn't set her pulse racing like the flawed saloon owner did. The thought shocked her. Why, she wasn't much better than her stupid cat. "Anyway, I'm not planning on marrying anyone for a long time."

"If you're waiting for the perfect man, you may wait forever," Isaac warned.

She was not perfect herself, she knew. That had to be the reason her grandfather had rejected her and sent her and her twin sister to live with their aunt and uncle in Texas while he kept the older two children. She must strive to do better. Eventually, her grandfather would realize that she was worthy, too; especially if she came to visit bringing along a superior husband.

"You know, Isaac, I've never understood why you don't get married."

"Now, how could I, when you need me so bad to help with the paper, yes?" He wiped his inky fingers on his apron.

"Reckon so. You got any ideas on how to raise money for the school house?"

He shook his head.

She shifted her thoughts to that problem. "I know," she stood up suddenly, excited at a new idea, "we'll put on a street dance! All the young ladies will take part because it will give them a chance to meet all the men in a respectable way. The men will all come because they'll buy tickets and get to dance with the ladies. Even Reverend Lovejoy will approve because it's for a good cause."

"I don't know. That daughter of his—"

"Now Mable is only sixteen and innocent as the driven snow."

"Everyone says she's sixteen going on thirty-five and the snow may have drifted a bit," Isaac said.

"Oh, I'm sure she'll behave herself." Lacey assured him. Mable Lovejoy was ripe for her age and had a way of looking at men that made Lacey uneasy. She wondered if Reverend Lovejoy was as aware as Lacey was that Mable had been known to wink at cowboys?

"You gonna dance with the cowboys?" Isaac asked.

"I reckon I can, although I'm sure most of the cowboys will want to dance with the younger girls. Certainly I can count on Eugene to buy tickets to dance with me."

"I'll buy some tickets to dance with you, Miss Lacey." He blushed and smiled.

"Isaac, you're a jewel. You've been so loyal and such a good employee all these years when you could have left and started your own newspaper."

Suddenly, he got very busy. "Aw, I wouldn't want to work without you, Miss Lacey."

She was now thinking about details of the dance. "For refreshments, we'll serve cookies and lemonade."

"Lemonade?"

"Stop making such a disagreeable face, Isaac. Respectable young ladies won't want to dance with men who reek of beer and whiskey. You know what they say and it's certainly true: 'Lips that touch liquor will never touch mine'."

"In that case, most women would never marry."

"Don't be such a pessimist. There have to be a few fine men like Eugene out there who have never let a drop of spirits touch their mouths."

"Not in this town," Isaac said wryly and returned to setting type.

"That's because of that rum shop across the street and its flawed owner." She scowled as she thought of the charming rascal and the ever-present drink in his hand. "This afternoon, I'll call a meeting of the ladies to plan the street dance. You know, now that we have a little park with a bandstand behind the barber shop on the corner, we can set up the Odd Fellows' little band there."

"The barbershop quartet will want to take part, too."

"I reckon we'll have to let them, although they aren't all that good—except for Eugene, of course. He has a beautiful high tenor voice. We'll give the dance a lot of newspaper publicity." She had a sudden thought. "We might even let the most daring of our volunteers sell kisses."

Isaac paused. "Don't know what Reverend Lovejoy will think of that."

"My word, Isaac, I mean innocent little pecks on the cheek. After all, it's for a good cause."

"You better watch young Mable then, she'll have some of those cowboys down on the grass behind the bandstand."

"Isaac!" She was scandalized. "I said little pecks on the cheek and I meant it. After all, we're not going in competition with the girls at the Black Garter."

Within days, excitement had spread through the town over the big street dance on Main Street next Saturday night. All the young girls were tittering with excitement at the daring idea of dancing with all the men and actually selling kisses at a booth. The men in town thought it was a great idea too . . . until each found out his own young daughter, sister, or niece was planning to work in the kissing booth. However, each man began saving his silver for the event. It wasn't often a man could dance with and kiss all the nubile young females in town without his wife busting his head in. However this was for such a good cause, even the most watchful wife couldn't complain.

Blackie paused to glower at the poster Flo was nailing up on the wall outside the saloon. "God Almighty, Flo, don't tell me you and the girls are gonna take part in Miss Iron Corset's dance?"

"We certainly are, although some of the more respectable members of the community might raise their eyebrows. Lacey Durango invited us personally."

He turned on the sidewalk to glare across the street at the newspaper office. "Is there nothing in town that infernal woman is not involved in? Next thing you know, the ladies will be electin' her mayor."

Flo smiled and winked. "She'd make a good one. Admit it, Blackie, you're just sore because she bested you in the referendum."

"She didn't play fair."

"Ha! She fought with what ammunition she had available, which was considerable. You comin' to the dance?"

"Reckon not!"

"Wal, I am." Old Cookie came out of his cafe, limped over to grin at Flo. "Hope to git a chance to dance with you, Miss Flo."

She actually blushed and tittered like a young girl. "Now, Cookie, you don't have to say that to be nice."

He ran his hand through his tangled beard and reddened. "I mean it, Miss Flo, you're a fine figure of a woman. Can't imagine why some man hasn't married you."

"I'm a mite old," Flo said, "and I been in a questionable line of work—"

"You're just in your prime," Cookie said, "and sometimes bad luck gets the best of anybody."

She brushed her hennaed hair back, as shy and flustered

as a young girl. "Cookie, you're a real gent. I'd be right pleased to dance with you at the school charity."

He grinned, proud as a pup with a new collar. "And I'll be right pleased for the honor. You can hang one of them posters inside my cafe."

Blackie snorted. "Well, don't hang one in my saloon."

The old man looked at him in surprised disapproval. "You ain't in favor of schoolin'?"

"I ain't in favor of Miss Iron Corset." Blackie said.

Flo laughed. "Blackie's still sore as a stepped-on rattlesnake about the referendum. He ain't used to losin' to women."

"Who is?" Cookie grinned, "but I knowed Miss Lacey from a long ways back, so I knowed she was mule-headed enough to win."

"What that woman needs to occupy her time is a husband and some kids." Blackie said. "She's purty enough, how come she ain't hitched?"

"She almost was," Cookie said, "but at the wedding—" He seemed to think it over, didn't finish.

"Yes?" Blackie was intrigued. Lacey Durango was pretty, so it was odd that she wasn't married.

"Never mind." Cookie said and turned to limp back inside his cafe, "I reckon it ain't nobody's business 'less Miss Lacey herself wants to tell it."

Blackie stared after him, annoyed with himself because he was curious. "That old codger probably doesn't know anything."

"I heered that!" Cookie yelled from inside the cafe.

The days until the street dance passed quickly. Indeed, Blackie thought dourly, the cowboys who came in for a drink talked of little else. There were posters up all over town and in every single business except his. He seemed to be the only person taking no interest in the event.

Flo acted like a young school girl when she came into

his office, face all alight. "All the girls is big on the dance, they're hopin' to snare husbands."

He reached down to pat Lively who was asleep next to his chair. "We're already losin' too many girls to all these cowboys lookin' for wives," he griped. "We lose many more, you'll have to close the upstairs."

"Well," she sighed and brushed back a wisp of dyed red hair, "I been wanting out of this business a long time, Blackie. I never gave serious thought to any man wantin' to marry me until that fine fella next door began makin' eyes at me."

He'd never thought about Flo leaving. "You mean, marry that old codger, Cookie?"

"He's a fine figure of a man," she said hotly, "and he's got a good business 'cause the cowboys got used to eatin' his grub. I used to be a pretty fair cook myself; I could help him make it even bigger."

Blackie groaned aloud. "I don't know what's got into everybody. You and the girls talkin' about gettin' respectable, Moose talking about wantin' to open a hotel. I like things just the way they've always been."

She leaned against the doorjamb and looked at him almost sympathetically. "Things change, and people, too, Blackie. Like it or not, civilization is comin' to this wild, untamed land."

"Well, I ain't gonna change. Runnin' a bigger and fancier saloon, that's what I want."

She shook her head. "When you're a lonely old man, that gonna give you satisfaction? What about sons and grandkids?"

He snorted and reached for a cigar. "That's for old geezers, not a gambler; I'm still in my prime."

"But you won't always be, Blackie. Don't you want a woman to love you?"

Blackie lit his cigar and laughed. "What you talkin' about, Flo? You know any woman I wink at will give me all the lovin' I need."

"I didn't mean saloon girls who'll bed you for the night. I meant someone who'd *really* love you."

"Now you're talkin' like one of them silly romantic novels women read."

"Uh-huh." She turned to go. "Seriously, Blackie, ain't there something in your heart of hearts that's more important to you than runnin' a saloon?"

He took a deep puff of his cigar and grinned at her. "You cut into my heart, Flo, you'd find a handful of poker chips and a deck of cards."

"You're impossible, you charming rascal. Remember, if you care to attend, the dance starts at dark."

"If all the gals go, who's gonna entertain all the cowboys at my place tonight?"

She paused in the doorway. "I got news for you, Blackie, you ain't gonna have enough business tonight to bother openin' the doors. All the men will be at the dance."

"That damned newspaper woman, she's determined to cost me business, run me out of town."

"Blackie, it ain't always about you. I reckon she's really thinkin' of the good of the town."

"Ah, I don't believe anybody can be that good and unselfish. Everybody looks out for hisself. I know I always had to." He growled and leaned back in his chair.

Moose came in just then, handed him a tall, cool drink. "We thinkin' about closin' this evening, Boss?"

"You, too?" Blackie took the drink.

"Well, I was hopin' to join Flo and the girls at the dance; it'll be fun. Besides it's good public relations for us to close down tonight and support the fund raisin' for the school."

"Is nobody on my side any more?" Blackie scowled as he tossed his cigar in the spittoon. "What do I care about a school?"

Moose scratched his tattoo. "Uh, boss, it ain't my business, but if Lacey Durango weren't behind this dance, would you feel that way?"

"And can't I get through a single hour without someone mentionin' that dad-blamed woman's name? Get out of here, both of you. I got ledgers to work on."

They both left and Blackie sighed and reached to scratch the head of his sleeping dog. He suddenly felt old and abandoned. *In your heart of hearts, Flo had said.* Yes, he had a secret dream that he never shared with anyone. He turned in his chair to stare at the watercolor on the wall behind him and smiled. Yes, there was a dream. The money he made operating a saloon was just a means to an end. He almost had enough now to realize that dream. Maybe in a couple of years . . . No, he shook his head.

Blackie studied the big diamond on his hand. It was almost the first thing he'd bought when he got a little money and he never planned to take it off. It was his security. As long as he had that fancy stone, even if his luck turned bad, he'd never be broke and hungry again.

He walked over, uncovered the nude painting and stared at it. "I ain't gonna lose this fight with you, Miss Iron Corset," he vowed to the painting, "and you can quit tryin' to tempt this Texan with them grapes. I don't like grapes."

Am I loco, talking to myself? He covered up the painting and went back to his messy desk. "You know, Lively, I'm sick of the saloon business, but I ain't gonna let that dame best me." The dog raised its head and thumped its tail. "I reckon maybe I need a couple more years of big profits before I can quit."

That new location on that prize lot would bring in big profits. Somewhere down the road, that dream waited. Of course, there'd need to be a special woman and kids to go with it. So far, there'd never been a woman he wanted to share that dream with and so, it waited. And waited. And waited. Now that damned newspaper woman stood in the way of the bigger profits.

"That sister ain't gonna make me yell 'calf rope,'" he

vowed. "She may have won the first round with her prissy town name, but there's more battles to follow and she ain't gonna win."

He got up and went up front in the growing dusk. The saloon was empty. Moose wiped beer mugs behind the bar. "I told you, Boss, we got no business."

"You'd think fellas would come in for a drink before that damned dance," Blackie went to the front window and looked out.

"Real ladies won't dance with men who have liquor on their breath," Moose said.

"Well, I reckon we know who's behind that, now don't we?" Blackie asked sarcastically. "She gonna be at the dance tonight?"

"Reckon she will, all the men are wantin' to dance with her. I hear Eugene Peabody bought ten dollars worth of tickets. Everybody's talkin' about that."

Blackie snorted. "She must really be strong for her cause if she'd dance with that damnyankee dude."

"You've heard the gossip; folks say she's sweet on him."

"She's smarter than that," Blackie said and looked out the front window at the gathering crowd. Paper lanterns had been strung up and down the street which had been blocked off from traffic. Even the horse manure had been swept up. People clustered around a stand where ladies sold lemonade and cookies. Another gaily decorated booth advertised *Kisses, 10¢.* "I reckon Miss Iron Corset don't know Eugene comes in here for drinks and even goes upstairs?"

Moose hesitated. "We don't usually tell stuff on our customers, Boss, you know that."

"'Course I know it," Blackie snapped. "Otherwise, most men would be afraid to come in here when their wives and sweethearts think they're at the Odd Fellows meetin' or a city council supper. I just reckon if Lacey knew what a big hypocrite that prissy store clerk was, she wouldn't give him the time of day."

Moose shrugged his big shoulders. "Why should you care? Wouldn't you like to see her made a fool of after all the trouble she's caused you?"

"Sure I would." Blackie said and paced up and down. "Maybe she gets humiliated enough, she'll pack up and leave town."

"She didn't when you hung that painting." Moose shook his head. "She's pretty stubborn."

"But she's proud; Texas proud." Blackie almost smiled as he remembered the way she walked with her head high, leading the victory parade. He realized suddenly that Moose was staring at him, head cocked. "What?"

"Nothing, Boss. Can I close now? I told you we ain't gonna have any customers tonight."

"Damn cowboys would rather have lemonade and ladyfingers than good whiskey."

Moose snorted. "You're one to talk. Besides, Blackie, it ain't the refreshments, it's the lure of respectable women, the kind a man would like to take home to Mama. All a cowboy's got to do tonight is plunk down a dime and he can hold one in his arms for a few minutes and pretend she belongs to him."

"Well, he won't get nothin' but that," Blackie grumbled, "When our gals would give him more than a smile and a hug."

"Our gals is at the dance, too," Moose reminded him.

"Aw, go on and close up," Blackie griped, "we don't want the other men of this burg to think we don't support buildin' a school."

"Thanks, Boss." Moose began to take off his apron. "First a school, then a public library. Miss Durango says—"

"Miss Durango! Miss Durango!" Blackie was beginning to lose his temper. "I am God Almighty sick of that woman and her high-and-mighty opinions about everything. Who does she think she is, a man?"

Moose grinned. "She don't look like one, does she? Never saw a filly get to you this way before, Boss."

"Never had one that wanted to go toe to toe with men before, offer opinions, and expect men to listen. Too damned headstrong for a gal. Go on, Moose, I'll lock up."

Moose grinned, nodded and strode up to his room to get cleaned up. Blackie sighed and began to turn down the gas lights. From outside on the warm night air drifted the music of a small band playing loudly but not too well: " . . . oh, Genevieve, sweet Genevieve, the days may come, the days may go, but still the hands of memory weave the blissful dreams of long ago . . . "

He had dreams but no blissful memories. And not likely to, spending his life in a saloon.

Well, hell, there was no point in sitting in here in the dark all by himself. Lively looked up at him and thumped his tail. "What're you lookin' at, stupid dog? I reckon I might as well go to the dance so the other business owners will know I support a school."

Schools. Schools meant women and children and civilization taming the wild whiskey towns and the rugged men. He looked into the future and saw all the rough frontier towns becoming Pretty Prairies because of stalwart, brave, determined pioneer women like Laccy Durango. Well, this was one wild hombre who wouldn't be changed. "There's a few of us real men left who might be tempted by a pretty piece of calico but we won't be tamed." He opened the front door.

Outside, the music quickened and people began to clap as a square dance formed.

"Come on, Lively, let's go." He and the dog went outside. Coming out of the newspaper office across the street was the Iron Corset. Blackie almost didn't recognize her. Gone was the no-nonsense white, starched shirtwaist and the hair pulled severely back on her neck. Tonight she wore a soft, shimmering blue dress that left her shoulders bare and had a neckline that dipped to show the rise of her bosom. Her hair hung in ringlets with a bunch of blue flowers tucked along the curls.

"Damn, tonight, she looks . . . she looks like a real woman; all soft and fluffy."

He must remember that under that softness was a Texas tornado who was as tough and stubborn as he was himself. Blackie took a deep breath and walked out to the dance.

Chapter Thirteen

Blackie gave this whole problem some serious consideration as he entered the crowded street. He wasn't winning a single battle going toe to toe with Miss Iron Corset, so he needed to change his strategy.

To himself, he muttered, "Now Blackie, what's your best asset? Don't all the gals tell you you're so charmin' you could talk a dog off a meat wagon or do a cow out of her calf? Then Mister, it's time to turn some of that charm on Miss Lacey Durango. You ain't winnin' the old way, so you might try charmin' her out of that choice lot."

The paper lanterns threw shadows across the dancers out in the middle of the street. The warm June breeze carried the scent of wildflowers from the prairie surrounding the town. The little band played loudly, if not too well. Older people clustered along the sidewalks, talking among themselves and watching the dancers. The streets were awhirl with girls in bright dresses and young cowboys wearing their Sunday best. Blackie scanned the crowd. Lacey Durango was greeted by Eugene and now danced by in his arms. Somehow that annoyed Blackie but he wasn't sure why. Eugene was whispering in Lacey's ear and she threw back her head and laughed. It sounded soft and musical like wind chimes.

Blackie strode over to the ticket booth where several ladies were sorting tickets. "How much to dance with Miss Durango?"

Mrs. Anderson was behind the counter, bouncing her baby on her ample hip. "You? Now there's a switch."

Blackie felt himself flush under her withering gaze. "It's for a good cause," he mumbled.

"She's mighty popular, you'll have to wait your turn." said young Miss Lovejoy and she looked him over with such a bold gaze that Blackie ran his finger around his collar. She licked her full lips. "I might be available, though."

Across the street, Blackie saw Reverend Lovejoy look up and frown at him. "I'm sorry, Mable, I don't think your daddy would like that."

"But I would." She winked at him.

He was horrified, but nobody saw what the bold young woman had done except himself.

Ethel Wilson informed him, "I think young Mr. Peabody has bought up *all* Lacey's dances."

That Yankee dude. "I'll deal with him." Blackie scowled.

"That's be ten cents for each dance," Mrs. Anderson calculated. "But we've got a lot of other young ladies who—"

"I just want to dance with Miss Durango," Blackie snapped. God Almighty, he didn't want to dance with decent respectable young ladies. He wasn't even sure what he was doing here. He felt as popular as a wolf in a chicken pen. He bought his tickets and went to stand on the sidelines to wait. When Miss Iron Corset saw him watching her, she reached and patted Eugene on the arm in a gesture of familiarity. The elegant young man threw back his head and howled with laughter and then she laughed, too.

"Howled like a coyote," Blackie grumbled to himself, "they can't be havin' that good a time."

Old Cookie danced by with Flo in his arms. He didn't dance very well with that bad leg, but Flo didn't seem to mind. She was looking into his eyes like he was Casanova. Isaac stood by the lemonade stand watching the couples dance, but Blackie noticed his sad gaze never left Lacey Durango. Miss Wren stood on the sidelines looking forlorn, but nobody asked her to dance. Blackie considered it, then decided her pa might not appreciate a known blackguard such as himself dancing with his daughter. Besides, if he encouraged the plain spinster, he'd be stuck with her all evening.

Lacey danced by in her light, airy blue dress, leaving the scent of violets lingering on the warm air. Blackie took a deep breath and sighed at the scent. He was used to the strong perfumes Flo and the girls at the Garter favored. This gentle scent was so much more inviting.

The music stopped and the couples retreated to the sidelines.

He heard Eugene say, "I'll go get some lemonade, Miss Lacey."

She was fanning herself with a lace hankie. "Oh, Eugene, I'd love some."

Blackie waited until Eugene had faded into the crowd before striding over to face her. "I believe this next dance belongs to me, Miss Durango."

Her smile faded. She couldn't have looked more alarmed if he'd been Jesse James about to rob the town's bank. "I—I believe the next dance belongs to Mr. Peabody."

"Well, he ain't here, is he?" The music started again and even as she was protesting, Blackie swept her into his arms and danced away. He was a good dancer, and he knew it. Somehow, she just fitted into his arms. "My, Miss Durango, you are ravishin' tonight."

Lacey looked up at him, speechless for once. He was an excellent dancer and her small hand just fitted into his big one. Although she was tall, he stood more than a head taller so that her face brushed against his wide shoulder as they danced. His body was strong and muscular and he pulled her closer so that she felt the warmth of him all the way down her length. He was totally in command of the situation, which unnerved her. On the

sidelines as they danced, she saw Eugene standing with
two cups of lemonade. He looked as forlorn and sad as
Blackie's bloodhound. Of course Eugene might be perfect, but he wasn't brave enough to cut in on the scrappy
gambler who had stolen his partner.

She looked up at the big Irishman. "Mr. O'Neal, you
surprise me. I wasn't expecting you to forgive and forget
about the referendum."

"Why?" he grinned down at her and she wondered if
she hadn't noticed what fine white teeth he had and the
way he smiled with full, sensual lips. "You bested me,
Miss Durango, and I take my hat off to you for it. I'm not
a sore loser."

She warmed to him although a small warning bell
began to ring in her head like the one on the volunteer
fire department's red engine. She knew very well that he
was a rascal who couldn't be trusted. Yet he smelled of
some wonderful cologne and she let him pull her closer;
too close for it to be respectable. Over on the sidelines, Eugene was frantically trying to get her attention, which was
difficult, considering he was splashing lemonade as he gestured. She decided to ignore Eugene.

However, she noted young Mable Lovejoy seemed to
think Eugene was signaling her and crossed to stand
next to him. Glumly, he offered that young lady his extra
lemonade. She took it with a smile and linked her arm
through his.

"I think Mr. Peabody is upset with your stealing his
dances," Lacey murmured.

"Oh?" Blackie grinned down at her. "Are you?"

"Uh, I'm not quite sure. Dancing with you could ruin
my reputation."

"Have you thought how much fun that could be?" He
whispered, his face against her hair. It sent a delicious
thrill running up and down her back that was quite unexpected. "Besides, if the dude isn't willin' to fight for
his lady, he don't deserve her."

"That—that sounds so primitive, like you were going to carry me off to your cave."

His breath was warm on her ear as he murmured, "That might be arranged."

She tried to put a little distance between their bodies, but he was so strong and he didn't allow it. "People will talk," she protested. She could feel the heat of his strong hand on the small of her back. She felt engulfed and overwhelmed by this big man as they danced. Warning bells now rang loudly in her brain like both volunteer fire wagons were dashing madly down the street, pulled by lathered horses. This rascal was known to be a devil with the ladies and she should be sensible enough to slap his face and walk away indignantly. However, then poor Eugene might be called upon to protect her honor and Blackie O'Neal would wipe up the street with the stylish dude.

The dance ended and she tried to pull away, but the gambler did not release her hand. "Miss Durango, you dance better than the gals at the Garter."

"I don't reckon you dance with respectable girls much."

"No ma'am. Never known many." His voice was soft.

She hesitated. Eugene was looking at her like a dejected hound dog while Miss Lovejoy chattered on and on to him. The real hound dog, Lively, was wandering through the scene, begging cookies from the crowd. "I—I really should dance with some of the other men."

"Oh, but I have a half-dozen tickets yet to use," Blackie protested.

"There are lots of other young ladies who would be thrilled to dance with you." She tried to disengage her hand again, but he did not release it.

"I only want to dance with you," he whispered and took her in his arms again as the music started.

She knew she should insist that he free her to mingle with the other gentlemen, but somehow, she couldn't bring herself to do that. Blackie had his face against her hair. "You smell wonderful," he sighed, "I don't know why some man hasn't married you and carried you off."

That broke the spell because she suddenly remembered Homer. She stopped dancing.

"What is it? Did I say something wrong?"

"Nothing. I— I— well, I was almost married once. The wedding was the most humiliating event of my life and afterwards—never mind." She broke away from him and returned to the sidelines.

Blackie had never felt so inept and stupid. Here he was, the most charming man in Texas, and he'd just caused a lady to flee the dance floor. Worse yet, she had now taken Eugene's hand and he looked like a grateful pup. They were out on the paving together now, engaged in almost frantic conversation and laughter.

Blackie was in a dark mood. He'd set out to charm a headstrong girl out of her claim to that lot, and maybe even her drawers, and she'd left him standing on the dance area alone. Now the prissiest, greenest dude was waltzing her around the street. A hatred began to build in Blackie's heart for the young man for holding Lacey in his arms. How dare that fancy, eastern dude dance with her? She had been so soft and had smelled so good. Blackie wanted her back in his arms.

"Hey, Handsome," Dixie drawled at his elbow, "Dance with me."

"Sure, Dixie, sure." He let her pull him out into the middle of the street. She danced close, too close. He could feel the blonde's big breasts against his chest. Her scarlet dress was too tight and cut too low. She reeked of some cheap, strong perfume and, even in the lamplight, he could see her neck was dirty.

Dixie chattered away, but Blackie hardly listened. He was watching Lacey Durango dance with young Eugene Peabody.

"Ain't you listenin' at all?"

"What?" He jerked to attention, looked down into Dixie's painted face.

"You've tripped over my feet twice already," she griped. "You was always a good dancer, Blackie, so you ain't payin' attention. I don't think you've heard a word I said."

"Sure I have, Dixie," he lied.

The music ended and a square dance caller stood up near the band. "Now everybody form two circles," he yelled, "Gents on the inside, ladies on the outside. The band will play and when it stops, you dance with the one in front of you. That gives everybody a chance at different partners."

"I don't want no partner but you," Dixie frowned.

Blackie smiled in relief. "Now, Dixie, we got to follow the rules." He shook her hand off and got in the circle. Out of the corner of his eye, he watched Lacey Durango. When the music stopped suddenly, he was two ladies down from her, but he pushed through and took Lacey in his arms. "So we meet again."

She looked annoyed. "I think you broke the rules. You were actually standing in front of Miss Wren."

"Was I?" He raised his eyebrows innocently and smiled. Before she could protest more, he swept her into his arms and danced away.

Lacey sighed and surrendered to his embrace. He really was a difficult man to argue with, as pigheaded as any man she'd ever known. They whirled past Eugene who was now dancing with Miss Wren. Eugene looked as sad as a dead hog.

"Blackie," Lacey said before she thought, "you're simply outrageous."

He liked the way she said his name. He didn't think she'd ever called him Blackie before. "Ain't I though, sister?"

"Your grammar leaves something to be desired," she corrected.

Miss Iron Corset would never change, he thought, but she could be charmed, just like any woman. "I thought I told you, Miss Durango, I came up through the School of Hard Knocks. My mama died at an early age and I was kinda on my own."

"Oh, I'm sorry. I had forgotten that."

In spite of her feistiness, she was kindhearted, Blackie thought happily and held her even closer. Yes, he couldn't win against Miss Iron Corset by going toe to toe with her; she was as stubborn as he was, but he might charm her out of that land. He sniffed the clean scent of her hair again as they danced. While he was at it, he might even charm her out of her drawers.

After another dance, Lacey pulled away, protesting. "I've got to go take charge of the kissing booth now."

"A kissing booth?"

"Yes," she nodded, "some of our young ladies have been daring enough to offer up kisses for money, you know, for the school."

He took a deep breath at the thought. "Of course, for the good of the school." He followed her over to a small booth where giggling young ladies stood taking money. Shy, awkward men were lined up. They lay down their dimes and each nodded to the blushing girl of his choice. The chosen one giggled and extended her cheek. The young man kissed her cheek and stumbled away, quite overcome with his own daring while the girl blushed and giggled some more.

Lacey Durango said, "Miss Lovejoy, I'll take over selling the tickets now."

Mable's pale eyes lit up. "And I'll sell kisses. Line up, boys."

Lacey hesitated. She wasn't sure if Reverend Lovejoy knew that Mable was working this booth and might not approve. After all, the buxom girl didn't have a mother to guide her. "All right, gentlemen," Lacey said, "who's next? Pick a girl of your choice. Only one dime to kiss a pretty girl."

Eugene came through the crowd. "Miss Durango, here's my dime. May I have a kiss from you?"

"Of course, Mr. Peabody." She took his dime, put it in the little box and extended her cheek.

Eugene Peabody seemed as nervous as a long-tailed cat in a roomful of rocking chairs. He hesitated, licked his lips, then kissed Miss Durango's cheek and stumbled backward with a delighted sigh.

Somehow that annoyed Blackie. He didn't like the idea that that greenhorn had even touched her cheek. "You call that a kiss?" he snorted. "I'll give a twenty-dollar gold piece for a kiss."

Everyone around the booth drew a surprised breath

"Mr. O'Neal," Lacey said as if talking to a small, stupid child. "The charge is only one dime."

"But it's for a good cause," Blackie reminded her and laid out his money in a grand gesture.

"All right. Now which young lady do you choose?"

The half dozen young ladies giggled and blushed.

"You, Miss Durango."

"Very well then." She put the money in the box and leaned toward him, offering her cheek.

"For twenty dollars, I ought to get more than that," Blackie said.

Before she was quite aware of his intentions, Blackie swept her into his embrace and kissed her full on the mouth. She was so surprised, her lips opened and he kissed her thoroughly, overwhelming her with the heat and the sensation. Around her, she was only dimly aware of the gasp of surprise from the crowd. For a long moment, she was overwhelmed by the warmth of his mouth, the scent of his shaving lotion, the strength of the man. Finally, she managed to pull away, gasping. "That—that was outrageous!"

Blackie grinned at her. "I thought it was pretty damned good myself."

She reacted instinctively by slapping him hard. He

looked surprised as his head snapped and he rubbed his cheek.

"Sir," Eugene Peabody stepped up, "I must protest—"

"Oh shut up," Blackie said, "before I wipe up the street with you, you Yankee dude."

"You disgusting brute!" Eugene said, "I may have to call the sheriff."

"You just do that, Junior, since you're not man enough to fight me yourself."

Lacey's eyes turned dark with anger. "You brute, if you don't leave, I shall call for the sheriff myself."

"No need," Blackie said, "I was leaving anyway." He turned and strode away, back toward his saloon. He'd really made a mess of things. He'd meant to be merely charming enough to sway her opinion of him just enough to get that land. Instead, when he'd had the chance to kiss her, he'd gotten carried away. It had been a long time since he'd kissed a woman like that or had even wanted to. Miss Iron Corset had surprised him with the need she built in him. Damn her anyhow.

"Wait up, Blackie!" Dixie called behind him.

Instead, he kept walking, Lively running ahead.

She caught up with him and grabbed his arm as they approached the darkened saloon. "I saw that. It ain't like you to let a woman humiliate you like that in front of a crowd."

"No, it ain't, is it?" He looked back. In the dim light of the lanterns, it appears half the town was watching him. "Come here, Dixie." He grabbed her and kissed her, laughing easily as if the incident on the street had meant nothing to him. "Come on, in, Baby, we'll have our own party."

"You bet!"

They went inside and closed the door. Immediately, Dixie came into his arms, kissing him, her mouth forcing his lips open, hers open, hot and wet, and greedy with need.

"Find the light," he said.

"To hell with the light," she whispered against his mouth, "let's go up to my room."

His body reacted to her ripe, full one and he let her kiss him again with her scarlet-painted mouth. But even as he kissed her, it wasn't the same as that moment when he'd held Lacey, soft and giving and innocent in his arms. He pulled away, took out his handkerchief and wiped his mouth. "Go on upstairs, Dixie."

"Okay, you comin'?"

Was he? His body yearned for the heat and the release Dixie would provide. Outside, the music drifted softly through the darkness to the inside of the closed saloon.

" . . . oh, Genevieve, sweet Genevieve, the days may come, the days may go, but still the hands of memory weave the blissful dreams of long ago . . . "

Blissful dreams. He remembered again the soft, sweet taste of Lacey Durango's mouth. Great God Almighty, he'd started out to charm Miss Iron Corset and ended up making a fool of himself. "You go on, Dixie. Maybe I'll be up later."

"*Maybe?* I'm gonna bring out the stallion in you, honey." She smiled up at him and started up the stairs.

"Umm, sure." He gave her a dismissing nod, eager to be rid of her, then stood in the darkness, listening to her going up the stairs. Funny, once he would have taken those steps two at a time. Now, his mind was on another woman, one who would never invite a man into her bed without a wedding ring. Miss Iron Corset, indeed.

"Well, Lively, you as tired as I am?" The dog's tail thumped. Blackie felt his way through the darkened saloon to his office and sat down at his desk with a sigh. "Okay, you were going to charm her and she ended up slappin' your face. That ain't like you, Bucko. You ain't had your face slapped since you were a half-grown boy. Women could hardly wait for you to kiss them." But not Lacey Durango. She was different. But whether through sheer stubbornness or charm, he intended to outmaneuver that woman and end up with that land. It was going to be harder than he had thought to tempt her.

"You're a damn fool, Blackie," he reminded himself, "there's a hot, eager girl who knows how to please a man waitin' upstairs and here you sit in your office listenin' to the music from outside."

The dog yawned at him and he reached to scratch Lively's long ears. Then he leaned back in his chair, closed his eyes and listened to the faint music carried on the warm summer air. In his mind, he held her again, her with her softness and fragrance and the soft blue dress she wore. He ran his tongue over his lips and recalled the kiss. He'd give a hundred dollars to kiss her again like he had kissed her tonight. He'd give five hundred to have her kiss him back. Damn her anyhow.

Lacey had stood watching with mixed emotions as the gambler strode away. He had both humiliated and overwhelmed her with his possessive embrace and heated kiss. No man had ever kissed her like that and she never dreamed she could respond that way. She had liked it; had yearned to return that kiss, deeply, passionately. The thought had shocked her so much that she had acted instinctively, slapping him hard when she pulled out of his arms.

Still standing next to her, Eugene said, "Miss Lacey, are you all right? I should have whipped that gambler within an inch of his life. I've had lessons in the manly art of self-defense, you know."

She had watched Blackie walk away, the saloon girl catching up with him and linking her arm through Blackie's in a too familiar gesture. "Eugene, he would've beaten you until you didn't know 'come here' from 'sic 'em'."

"What?"

"Uh, nothing. It's something Texans say; that's all."
She brushed back her hair, suddenly very conscious of
the stares around her. "Forget it. It's over. Let's get back
to making money for the new school. Here, Miss Wren,
you take over the ticket booth."

"I'll walk you home," Eugene said anxiously.

"No, no, I'm fine. I can get Isaac to walk me home.
You stay here and help Miss Wren. I'm sure Vanetta
would love to sell you some kisses."

Vanetta giggled and blushed. "How about a dollar's
worth?"

Eugene paled visibly. "Uh, it wouldn't be fair for me to
take up all your time, Miss Wren, not with these other
fellas waiting."

Lacey frowned at him. "Don't be shy, Eugene, give
Miss Wren the dollar."

"All right, Miss Lacey, if you say so." He handed over
the money reluctantly and accepted the favors with the
expression of a man who'd rather be licked in the face
by Lively the hound.

Lacey slipped away and mingled with the crowd. She
looked back toward the darkened saloon. There was just
enough light inside so that she could see the silhouette
of two people in an embrace. It could only be the pair
that had just left here, Lacey thought, recalling the familiar way the tart had taken Blackie's arm. Well, Dixie,
would satisfy all the passion Lacey had tasted in Blackie
O'Neal's kiss. Somehow, the thought angered her. "How
dare he grab me like that! He's outrageous."

The couple in silhouette disappeared. They've gone upstairs, Lacey thought, upstairs to the bedrooms. Somehow,
the thought upset her. She was suddenly very tired and a
little sad. He was a no-account, sorry gambler who ran a
rum shop and wanted to build a bigger one on her corner
lot. Well, she'd fix him. He might think she was going to
let him have that land, but he had another think coming.

It would be over Lacey's very dead body and she wasn't ready to die yet.

Isaac hurried up. "You need me, Miss Lacey, yes?"

"No," she waved him away. "Stay and enjoy yourself, Isaac. I don't really need anyone to walk with me."

"But I'd like to—"

"No," she wanted to be alone. "Stay here and find someone to dance with."

"I don't care about that, Miss Lacey, I only came because you were coming, yes?"

"That's sweet of you, but I've been too much of a burden to you. Stay and have fun."

He sighed. "If you say so."

"You're a good employee, Isaac." She patted his arm absently and walked away. Lacey went into the newspaper office and closed the door, torn by her emotions and uncertain what she was feeling. A new crusade, yes, she needed to throw herself into a new crusade. She and her Ladies' Temperance Association ladies needed to start a push to run demon rum out of this lovely town of Pretty Prairie. And leading the parade, hopefully wearing tar and feathers, she intended to have Mr. Blackie O'Neal.

Chapter Fourteen

The Fourth of July dawned warm and bright. Lacey was full of good humor as she put on a red, white, and blue figured dress, then went downstairs to pack a picnic. "Isaac, you coming?"

The little man shook his head. "Eugene would resent me coming along. Anyway, the noise of the fireworks gives me a headache. If you don't mind, Miss Lacey, I'll stay here with Precious."

"If you'd mingle more, you might get a sweetheart," she scolded. "I worry about you being alone."

"No more alone than you, yes, Miss Lacey?"

She frowned. "I choose to be alone; that is, until I find the perfect husband."

The stooped little man grinned at her. "Maybe I'm waiting for the perfect woman. In the meantime, I'll work for you, Miss Lacey, yes?"

"Suit yourself," Lacey said, "but with your talent, you ought to start your own newspaper."

He shrugged. "I am pleased to work with you." Isaac returned to setting type. "Now get along to your picnic. I see that silly Mr. Peabody driving up in a buggy."

"You don't like him, do you?" Lacey went to the window. Sure enough, Eugene was just arriving.

"Not much; but that doesn't matter if you like him."

Lacey stared out the window. Past Eugene and his little buggy, she could see Blackie O'Neal loading his fancy open barouche with the girls from his saloon.

That outrageous Irish stallion. "I reckon when the entire town was invited out to the Double Bar ranch for the holiday, it meant even that rascal could attend."

She hadn't forgotten how, a few days before, Blackie had grabbed her and kissed her at the street dance. She was annoyed with herself that she hadn't forgotten it. She had dreams about it at night and woke up wet with perspiration and gasping for air.

Eugene came to the door and stuck his head in. As usual, the handsome dude was dressed in the height of fashion: a plaid suit, new spats, a fine derby, boutonniere, and carrying a walking stick. "Happy holiday, Miss Lacey, you look very festive in red, white, and blue. Are you ready for some fun and excitement?"

Excitement. Somehow, she couldn't put that emotion with Eugene Reginal Peabody—he was dependable and steady as a peddler's horse. "Thank you, Eugene. I'm ready to go. You can carry the basket. I'll get my parasol."

They went out to the buggy and Eugene helped her up, his hands lingering a moment too long on her waist. His hands were small, quite soft and very sweaty. She thought of Blackie O'Neal's big, strong hands with a sigh.

"Look at that spectacle," Eugene said with a disapproving clicking of his tongue as he stared across the street. He got in the buggy, picked up the reins. "Disgusting. They ought to be run out of town."

"Be a little kinder, Eugene. After all, the girls did help swing the vote for 'Pretty Prairie.' I don't know any of them but Flo very well, but I think most of them are just unfortunate victims of circumstance."

"You're way too sweet and generous, Miss Lacey," Eugene sniffed. "I can't believe your friend, Cookie, is actually calling on the madame." He adjusted his derby and glared at the barouche again.

"Flo's really a nice person. I understand Cookie was picking her up in his new surrey this morning. They were going out early to help Chief Thunder with the food."

Blackie's fancy barouche, overflowing with whores and the drooling hound dog, had already started down the road toward the ranch with Moose driving and Blackie in the back surrounded by his adoring whores.

"Now we'll have to eat their dust all the way," Eugene grumbled.

"We'll simply ignore them," Lacey said loftily and twirled her parasol.

"Right."

The little buggy with its ugly bay horse pulled away and kept a steady clip behind the fancy barouche for a mile. Lively seemed to recognize Lacey and barked, his tail wagging as he hung over the back of the open carriage. Blackie turned to look her way, grinned, took off his hat and nodded to her. Around him, the girls squealed and laughed, more than one reaching over to give him a big kiss.

"Disgraceful!" Eugene said with a snort.

"Outrageous!" Lacey opined as Eugene snapped the little whip.

The girls in Blackie's fancy carriage were laughing and singing. Blackie threw back his head and laughed with them. Somehow that annoyed Lacey no end. "You're right, Eugene, we'll have to eat their dust all the way to the ranch, can't you pass them?"

"I'll try." Eugene snapped his little whip and the bay horse broke into a trot as he swung out to pass the barouche. Immediately, the open carriage also picked up speed, and both vehicles were abreast of each other, trotting along.

"Yoo-hoo!" yelled the girls, giggling and waving. "Yoo-hoo!"

Lacey nodded to them, puzzled since she didn't know the ones who were waving. "Honestly, I wonder why they're being so friendly?"

Eugene ran his finger around his stiff collar, his face turning scarlet as he stared straight ahead. "I wouldn't have the faintest idea."

Blackie craned his neck and positively leered at her, then he traded places with Moose and took over the driving himself. Lacey stared straight ahead and gave no indication that she saw him. He was a renegade and a rascal, she thought, with all the girls' lip paint smeared on his handsome face.

The two vehicles were still side by side on the narrow road. Now coming from the other direction was a big wagonload of hay.

"Eugene," Lacey warned, "you'll have to drop back and give that farmer room."

"I will not!" Eugene tried to hurry his horse, glancing over at the fast-moving barouche. "I intend to pass that gambler and make him eat our dust."

"Eugene, you'd better drop back," she warned, realizing that Blackie was a better driver, had better horses, and wasn't about to let the shopkeeper pass him.

Eugene stared straight ahead, his mouth a grim line as he cracked his whip. Both buggies were side by side, moving at a swift pace. Moving steadily toward them was the big hay wagon.

"Eugene, you're going to cause a wreck!"

"I'm not going to let him win!" Eugene cracked his whip again.

Lacey gritted her teeth and got a grip on the seat. "Eugene, you're a damned fool!"

Now it was too late to pull back in line, the hay wagon abruptly loomed big and solid in their path. Lacey closed her eyes as their bay horse shied and went off in the ditch, the buggy turning over and spilling its contents.

When she opened her eyes, she was flying through the air with the saloon girls shrieking in the background. Then she hit the ground and tumbled over and over. She came to a halt, in an undignified tumble of petticoats and red, white, and blue skirts. Eugene lay nearby, and when he sat up, he had been lying on his fine new derby. It was as flat as a tortilla.

Both the farmer and Blackie reined in and came to help. Blackie bowed before her. "Miss Durango, are you hurt?"

"No. No thanks to you and your racing."

"I beg your pardon," he held out his hand to her, "I was on the right side of the road, it was *your* escort who was racing me." There was nothing to do but let him pull her to her feet. "Are you hurt?"

"Nothing but my dignity." She began to brush the dirt from her skirt.

"Here, let me help you." He leaned over and picked up her parasol. It was badly squashed, but still Blackie made a grand gesture as he handed it to her. "The farmer seems to have righted your buggy, and the horse seems to be unhurt. Allow me to escort you back."

She hesitated. All the whores in the big barouche were grinning at her, all but the blonde one called Dixie. Eugene was engrossed in explaining to the farmer why he hadn't pulled back to avoid a collision.

"This is not a very good start to the holiday," Lacey complained.

Blackie put his big hand over the one she laid on his arm. "On the contrary, I think it's a great start to the day. By the way, sister, your bonnet is askew."

She reached up to straighten it. Eugene saw her, smiled and came forward to assist her up into the righted buggy, but Blackie very deliberately elbowed him aside and lifted her lightly to her seat. "Peabody, you should drive more carefully, especially when you have a lady passenger."

"I don't know what you'd know of ladies," Eugene sniffed.

Blackie grinned even wider, that infectious, charming smile of a man sure of himself and his effect on women. "I know one when I see one. Good day, Miss Durango, I trust we'll meet again at the barbecue."

As Eugene and Lacey watched, he swaggered back to his fancy carriage and was helped aboard by the giggling whores. Then they drove away.

"I hate that man," Eugene grumbled, "so damned sure of himself. Oh, excuse me, Miss Lacey, I didn't mean to curse in front of you."

"That's quite all right, Eugene," she nodded as they pulled back out on the road. The horse seemed uninjured. "That Blackie O'Neal could make a saint curse. He is the most maddening, most arrogant, most—"

"A typical Texan," Eugene said with great self-righteousness. He had evidently forgotten she was a Texan.

She was annoyed with Eugene. "You know what Texans say, 'And on the seventh day, God saved the best for last and created Texas.'"

"Why, Miss Lacey, that's blasphemous." He looked shocked and surprised.

"Oh, shut up, you— you Eastern dude, you," she muttered under her breath.

"Did you say something?"

She managed to regain control of her temper and gave him her most bewitching smile. "I was just talking to myself about what a lovely day it's going to be."

"Won't it though?" He smiled at her. "You know, there will be contests and races with some prizes. I intend to win them for you."

"Thank you, Eugene, I'm honored."

Ahead of them, dust rose from the road from the big barouche and coated the pair in the buggy. The whores were singing and laughing. Blackie glanced back at her, then joined in the singing. He laughed like a crazed hyena, Lacey thought in disgust.

Within the hour, they reached the Double Bar ranch where other buggies were drawn up in the shade of trees. Children ran up and down, chasing each other and laughing while their harried mothers tried to spread picnic lunches. Men played horseshoes or stood in groups talking. Lacey noted with disgust that many a man's eyes lit up and they grinned like possums when they saw Blackie and his girls arriving. Even Cookie didn't seem to notice Lacey had arrived. The old cook and his lady were busy helping Chief Thunder with the meat.

Eugene reined in, stepped down, and tied their horse to a tree. Then he came around to help her out. "Looks like a capital day for the celebration, Miss Lacey. Where shall we spread our blanket?"

"As far away from Mr O'Neal as possible," she declared, trying not to watch the charming scoundrel. His girls were spreading a picnic and he was sitting on the blanket among them. "Like a foreign potentate," she muttered, "with women fawning over him and rushing to please him."

Eugene drew himself up self-righteously. "Disgusting! He ought to be run out of town."

There wasn't a man with balls enough to do that, Lacey thought, especially the prissy Eugene, but she didn't say so. "Never mind, Eugene, we'll just ignore them and maybe they'll go home early."

That didn't seem likely. Blackie appeared to be having a grand time, and the girls were scattering to flirt with some of the cowboys. Even Cookie was now strolling with Flo, grinning like a cowboy who just won a big poker game. Over at the barbecue spit, Chief Thunder was turning a whole side of beef over a slow fire.

There was a lovely creek nearby and on its bank, Lacey began laying out their picnic. "I've got fried chicken, Eugene. Eugene?"

She looked up. Her escort was staring at Blackie's girls like a hungry hound looking at a ham bone. Speaking of the hound, Lively, in his baby bib, was wandering from picnic to picnic, tail wagging, begging food from every family.

"That dog," Eugene said, "has no more manners than its owner. I hate dogs, blamed messy nuisances. I'm a cat person, just like you, Miss Lacey."

"Of course." She'd always thought Lively rather adorable, but she didn't say so. They settled down to eat. Besides crisp fried chicken and baked beans, she'd packed

homemade pickles, homemade bread, chocolate cake
thick with rich icing, and some icy cold tea full of lemon
slices.

"Delicious," Eugene grinned. "Miss Lacey, you really
belong in some man's kitchen. I could just see you in
mine, cooking all day for me."

Somehow, that didn't seem like much fun, especially
for a liberated woman, but she didn't say so. She ate
while sneaking glances at Blackie O'Neal who was wolf-
ing down barbecue, dainty cookies, and tiny cucumber
sandwiches. Now who among those girls would make
tiny cucumber sandwiches? When he caught her looking
at him, he grinned and winked.

She felt her face go scarlet and glanced away. That
maddening man. He made her feel so uneasy and unsure of herself. That wasn't normal for a Texan.

The afternoon was pleasantly warm as Lacey packed
up the remnants of their lunch. The grizzled foreman of
the Double Bar strode out into the middle of the clearing. "Line up, folks, we'll have some games, and then
later a trail ride, and tonight, some fireworks and more
barbecue."

The children squealed with delight and clapped their
hands.

The foreman held up his hands for silence. "First off
is the three-legged race. Let's make this excitin'. You
gents tie up with your sweethearts and we'll see how fast
each pair can run."

The women giggled with embarrassment and the men
looked at each other and winked. Blackie and Dixie were
pushing forward, laughing. Someone stepped forward
with a rope and Dixie giggled and took it, hiked her skirt
coquettishly and tied her ankle to Blackie's. He laughed
and put his arm around her.

"Come on folks," urged the foreman, "don't be shy,
fellas, this is your chance to get close to your sweetheart
without her mama objecting."

More laughter. Two more couples came forward. Blackie glanced back at her and Lacey could see the challenge in his merry eyes.

"Come on, Eugene, let's enter this race." She grabbed him by the hand and pulled him to his feet.

"Oh, I don't know, Miss Lacey, it seems so undignified for a lady—"

"You going to let that scoundrel win this without a fight? Come on, Eugene."

He was still protesting as she pulled him to the starting line and reached for a rope. She tied their ankles together and looked over at Blackie. He was watching her. She pretended not to see him. "All right, Eugene, now put your arm around my waist. We'll have to be really coordinated to win this."

Very gingerly, Eugene put his arm around her. His arm felt thin and flabby and his palm was sweaty.

The foreman lined everyone up. "That oak tree down there is the finish line. There's a silver cup for the winners. Everyone ready? Ready, set, go!"

She was not going to let Blackie O'Neal win this. Lacey put her arm around Eugene's thin frame and they began to jump. Unfortunately, Eugene was not well coordinated. He stumbled and went down, taking her with him in a flurry of white petticoats. "Come on, Eugene, get up!" She had him on his feet again and they were jumping, but awkwardly. All the other couples were ahead of them. Blackie and Dixie were in the lead, their arms so entwined, they looked like they'd grown together, Lacey thought with a frown. When Dixie stumbled, Blackie through sheer strength, caught her, lifted her and kept hobbling forward. They won by twenty yards. When Lacey looked toward the finish line, Blackie and Dixie had just crossed it and she was showering him with kisses. "My hero!" she shrieked. "My big he-man hero!"

"Disgusting!" Eugene panted next to her.

"Agreed," Lacey frowned, "she's licking his face like a hungry bear cub eating a honey comb."

The race was over. Lacey untied the rope. "Let's sit back down, Eugene, you look like you might faint."

"It's hot out here," Eugene griped, "I'm used to working inside."

Perfection was becoming a prissy dude, Lacey thought as they returned to their blanket under the tree. But of course, maybe she was expecting too much brute strength from an educated gentleman. Speaking of brutes, Blackie was glowing with pride as he wiped his sweating face and accepted his prize, kisses and a trophy from the rich rancher's daughter. Somehow, Lacey found that annoying. It wasn't as if he didn't get enough kisses from the whores who worked for him, she thought, remembering that silhouette in the darkened saloon window.

There were a few more games, then the foreman stepped up again. "We've got some bronc ridin' coming up. Now you gents who think you know something about ridin' the wild ones, come on up here and saddle up."

"Hey, Blackie," yelled one of the cowboys, "you're used to riding the wild ones, you gonna enter?"

"The foreman meant horses!" Another man yelled and all the men chuckled while the ladies frowned and fanned themselves.

Eugene sniffed. "Of course he won't enter. That gambler is only at home riding a chair at a poker table."

"I don't know about that," Lacey said before she thought. "He's a Texan and most Texans can handle a horse."

Blackie got to his feet, swaggered out to the center.

Eugene snorted. "He's such a show-off. If I didn't have a bad back, I'd ride that bronc myself."

"Sure you would," Lacey said. She wasn't a terrific rider like her sister Lark, but she knew a bad bronc when she saw one. This big buckskin had his ears laid back and his back humped. The man that climbed up in that saddle might get thrown clear to Dallas.

The first cowboy couldn't even get into the saddle before the buckskin tossed him into the dirt and tried to stomp him.

"Look out!" Blackie yelled.

The cowboy rolled to avoid the flashing hooves.

"Well, now," drawled the ranch foreman, "you've seen what a sweet disposition this pony has, ought to be on a merry-go-round."

The crowd laughed.

Another cowboy tried, but just barely got into the saddle before the bronc tossed him into the middle of the creek. He floundered around in the deep part before emerging dripping wet.

"Who's next to ride?" The foreman challenged.

"Oh, Blackie," squealed the saloon girls with him, "Oh, Blackie, you gonna try?"

"Oh my word, of course he won't," Lacey said in disgust. "He'd have to be loco to try that crazy bronc and besides, I don't reckon a gambler is that good a rider, even if he is a Texan."

Blackie must have heard her because he turned and grinned at her. "I'll see if I can top him out for you."

The crowd gasped and then cheered.

"Well," Eugene said, "I guess that damn fool is going to get killed."

Somehow, Eugene's words annoyed her. "I didn't see you offering to ride it."

"I'm not a damned fool," Eugene said. "And I've got a bad back. Surely you don't admire that rascal for risking his neck?"

"Of course not." Lacey said but she took a deep breath. Blackie had peeled off his jacket and taken off his tie. He stood there now in tight pants and a Western shirt open at the neck. There was dark hair on his chest and his face was tanned from the sun. She noted half the women in the crowd were looking at the swaggering Texan and sighing wistfully.

Blackie looked the horse over for a long moment. "Hey, boy," he said gently and offered his hand to the buckskin bronc. It promptly tried to bite his fingers. Blackie jerked back and then reached to rub the horse between the eyes. "You've had a bad time of it, haven't you, boy?"

The horse seemed to quiet a moment, and in that moment Blackie swung into the saddle. The foreman turned the bridle loose and the big buckskin exploded across the grass, bucking and spinning, each jump higher than the last. Each time he came down, a sound like the thunder of buffalo hitting the dirt rang out, and then the buckskin threw back his head and bucked some more. Blackie hung on, arrogant and sure of himself. The crowd cheered as the horse bucked and Blackie stayed with it. Lacey hadn't seen such good riding since her days at her uncle's ranch. She forgot that she was angry with Blackie O'Neal; she forgot he was an unmitigated rascal; she was on her feet, cheering him on like the rest of the crowd.

The horse bucked and reared and bucked some more but Blackie hung on until the horse surrendered and stopped bucking, trotting in a circle while the crowd had a moment of awed silence, than began to cheer. Blackie rode the buckskin into the middle of the circle, reined in, and dismounted. Then he handed the reins to the foreman. "He's almost lady-broke now. Why, I'll wager even Mr. Peabody could ride him."

"Not likely!" someone yelled.

Eugene flushed and Lacey felt both humiliated for him and angry with Blackie.

The Irishman swaggered back to his saloon girls. They gathered around him oohing and aahing in adoration while the men cheered some more. Sweat made his shirt cling to his powerful chest. He looked at Lacey and smiled, his white teeth flashing in his dark face. Something inside her made her catch her breath. Now people were coming over to congratulate him, the men shaking his hand, the ladies sighing and fluttering their eyelashes at him.

"Disgusting." Eugene said, "you'd think nobody had ever seen a man ride a bronc before."

"Well, not like that," Lacey admitted.

It was getting late in the afternoon. The foreman announced that there were horses available for those who wanted to take a trail ride across the large ranch.

The cowboys began leading out horses for the crowd. Blackie said "I'll take that buckskin I just rode."

Eugene winced. "Let's not do that, Miss Lacey. Why don't we go back to town?"

"But I'd love to go riding," Lacey protested.

"I heard that." Blackie strode up, grinning. "I'd be delighted to escort you on the ride, Miss Durango."

Eugene puffed up like a stomped-on toad. "Miss Durango is with me and we were just about to select horses."

"Of course we were." She gave Blackie a look as cold as a Texas norther. "I know a little about horses, having been raised on a ranch."

She walked over to the horses. In truth, Lacey was only a so-so rider; not nearly as good as her tomboy twin sister, Lark. A nervous black mare laid her ears back at Lacey.

Behind her, Blackie said, "Watch out for that one, sister, she looks like she's got the disposition of an angry old maid."

"In that case, she's perfect for me, isn't she?" She glared at Blackie. "Wrangler, put a sidesaddle on that one."

The young cowboy looked doubtful, but began to saddle the edgy mare.

"Okay, sister," Blackie shrugged. "If she throws you on your fanny, don't say you weren't warned."

"How dare you use a word like that to this young lady?" Eugene said, "I demand you apologize."

My word, Eugene must have a death wish today, Lacey

thought. *Blackie might spread him all over the pasture.* "Uh, Eugene, it's all right," she said.

The gambler made a sweeping bow. "I do apologize if I offended the lady. Back in Texas, we'd of said something stronger than 'fanny'."

Wasn't that the truth?

Eugene was looking over the horses as if they were all bloodthirsty monsters. "Oh, Miss Lacey, maybe you should chose a gentler horse. That mare looks too much for a lady."

With both men cautioning her, she was determined to ride this mare if it harelipped half of Texas. "I'm much obliged for all the male advice, but I can handle her. All I need is a hand up now."

Both men rushed forward, but Blackie elbowed Eugene out of the way. She didn't think Eugene had the strength to boost her anyway, but she wasn't about to let Blackie put those warm, strong hands on her waist. He did anyway, and for a split-second, he stared down into her eyes and she had the strangest feeling that he was thinking about kissing her. "Uh, Mr. O'Neal, the gentleman usually cups his hands for the lady's boot, remember?"

"Oh, of course." He bent and put his hands together for her small foot, then lifted her up to the saddle.

She stared down at him, uneasy at the electricity that was passing between them. She had the strangest feeling that he was about to pull her from her horse and kiss her breathless. She pictured that in her mind and drew a sharp breath. She had to break the spell, so she looked over to her unhappy escort. "Eugene, pick yourself a horse."

Blackie grinned. "Cowboy, we're dealin' with a dude here. Ain't you got a lady-broke horse you use for kids?"

"Yep."

With Eugene glowering, the cowboy led out an old bay nag that seemed to doze off to sleep as Eugene struggled to climb aboard.

The other riders were already strung out along the

trail as the three started off, Lively walking along with them and barking.

Eugene said, "That mutt will probably spook the horses."

"Not your horse," Blackie said, "I don't think blastin' powder thrown under her would make her to break into a trot."

"Do you mind?" Lacey frowned at him. "Mr. Peabody and I prefer to ride together."

"I can take a hint." Blackie rode on ahead.

"Blackie, what about me?" Dixie called.

Immediately, a dozen cowboys rushed to the blonde's side.

"Here, Miss Dixie, lemme hold your horse for you."

Here, Miss Dixie, I'd be powerful pleased if I could escort you on the trail ride."

The girl looked disgusted, but she let one of the cowboys help her up on a horse.

The nubile Mable Lovejoy had gotten on a horse and now rode up to join Lacey and Eugene.

The shopkeeper looked as nervous as a whore in church on Sunday. He sawed on the reins as they started away, evidently uneasy at riding a horse, even an old, sleepy one.

Ahead of her, she saw Blackie, riding as if he'd been born on a horse. Dixie rode up to join him, but she evidently rode no better than Eugene. Somehow, Lacey was annoyed at the easy, familiar way Dixie talked to Blackie.

Next to her, Eugene sweated and sawed on the reins. "You're riding too slow, Eugene, I think I'll ride on ahead. You and Miss Lovejoy can ride together."

"Be careful!" Eugene warned.

"Eugene, I've been riding since before I could walk." She urged the nervous mare forward and very deliberately edged Dixie out of her path on the narrow trail. Pouting, Dixie dropped back to join the stragglers, such as Eugene and Miss Mable Lovejoy, whose horses were barely walking.

"Well," Blackie grinned at her. "Finally someone who can sit a horse."

She felt she had to challenge him. "Why don't we pick up the pace a little?"

He shrugged. "It don't make me no never mind, sister."

She nudged her black mare and broke into a canter. Immediately, Blackie quickened his pace, too.

Behind her, Eugene wailed, "Miss Lacey, you be careful now."

"Oh, shut up, Eugene." she yelled back.

"Tsk, tsk, sister," Blackie winked at her. "That ain't too ladylike."

"Sometimes I get tired of being a lady," she snapped.

"Let's take off on that trail to the right." Blackie said. "They tell me there's a beautiful view of the sunset from the crest of that far hill where the creek bends, make a pretty paintin'."

"I didn't know you were the type who'd appreciate a beautiful painting, Mr. O'Neal."

He laughed. "I'm just goin' by what Chief Thunder tells me. I only appreciate saloon art like any ruffian."

"That does not surprise me." Why had she been so impulsive about riding with this rascal? In the first place, she was only a fair rider, not an expert like Lark. And in the second place, she should be staying with her escort and as far as possible away from this charming rogue after the way he'd kissed her at the street dance and the way he might have been about to kiss her as he helped her on her horse. People were liable to talk.

Well, she could handle Mr. Blackie O'Neal. She'd show him she was independent and immune to his charms. Something about the way he turned his head and grinned at her made her want to show him just how feisty she was. She urged the peppery mare from a canter into a lope.

In the distant growing dusk of evening, she heard Eugene's frantic wail. "Miss Lacey, you be careful there!"

Careful? She was always careful and cautious. Tonight she wanted to do something daring, throw caution to the wind. She loped on ahead along the trail with Blackie riding next to her. She was enjoying herself as the horses loped, the wind blowing through her dark hair that had loosened from its proper bun.

Blackie yelled at her. "You're riding a mite fast for a lady with a sidesaddle. I have to hand it to you, you look good on a horse."

She smiled at him in challenge, then reined her horse to a walk. "Compliments will not get you that lot, Mr. O'Neal."

"What lot?" He grinned at her in that most appealing, annoying way.

"You know very well what lot."

"Did it ever occur to you that I just like your company?"

"Since when?"

"Maybe since I've gotten to know you better, I find you more interestin' and at least, more challengin'. I like a proud, independent woman."

She found herself warming to him, despite the fact that she knew his reputation with women. "It's a nice evening," she said as they rode along the trail in the twilight. They had left Eugene, Mable Lovejoy, and Dixie somewhere on the trail behind them. Even slow-moving Lively had been left behind. "It's a nice evening."

"It's a very nice evening," he agreed.

Behind her, somewhere in the distance, she could hear Eugene calling, "Miss Lacey? Are you all right? Come back here!"

She didn't bother to answer as she and Blackie rode along.

About that time, Lively topped the hill and ran toward them, barking frantically. Her mare neighed and reared at the unexpected noise.

"Watch out!" Blackie shouted as the dog ran closer, barking and barking.

Before Lacey could react, the panicked mare reared, whinnied in panic, and took off at a mad gallop. Lacey hung on for dear life as the mare galloped across the prairie. She'd said she was a top rider and now she was going to get thrown and killed for her deception. She bit her lip, closed her eyes, and hung on as the horse galloped madly across the rough, uneven ground. Up ahead, she could see a gully and she wasn't sure the maddened mare would be able to jump it.

Behind her, Blackie yelled, "Hang on, I'm coming!"

He wasn't going to be in time, Lacey thought and her hands were wet with sweat as she clung to the saddle. She was going to get herself killed. What an undignified mess she'd be, lying dead on the ground in a tangle of petticoats with her face smudged and bloody. Worse yet, Eugene would lean over her coffin and say primly, "I told you so!"

She'd lost her reins and now the black mare galloped completely out of control. Lacey glanced back, gave Blackie an imploring look. If anyone could save her, it would be that expert horseman, but would he? After all, if she got killed, he'd get that prize lot.

Chapter Fifteen

Even though it was undignified, Lacey screamed as the horse galloped. The gully ahead loomed wide and rocky in the growing darkness and she wasn't going to be able to stop the panicked mare.

Blackie had watched for a split-second, then realized the girl was not joking. He was galvanized into action, spurring the buckskin to give chase. He had to stop Lacey's horse before she reached the gully. Her dark curls blew back as she tried frantically to stop her runaway horse.

Blackie was galloping abreast of her now. Her beautiful face had gone white as she hung on for dear life. "Lacey!" he shouted. "Turn that horse!"

She shouted something, but her words were lost on the breeze. The gully loomed closer. Then he realized she had lost her reins. There was only one more thing he could do. "Come to me!" He held out his arm but the girl looked from him to the ground flying beneath her feet and hesitated. Both of them realized trying to jump to Blackie's horse was incredibly dangerous. "Lacey, come to me!" Blackie demanded and held out his arm again.

She hesitated, looking at him, almost too terrified to make a decision. Up ahead, she could see the gully looming deep and wide. Her frightened horse would never make that jump successfully with her on its back.

"Lacey, come to me!" His face was pale with apprehension but he looked strong and capable. Dare she take the chance? How much did she trust his ability?

"Here I come!" She loosed her foot from the stirrup and leaned toward him as he reached for her. For a split second, her heart almost stopped in terror as she turned loose of her horse and jumped toward him. For a heart-stopping split-second, she seemed suspended in midair, then his strong arm grabbed her. He was as capable as she had thought he would be. His powerful arm held her, lifting her up to the front of his saddle as he reined in. Ahead of them, the black horse saw the gully, hesitated, then stumbled, fell, clambered to its feet and stood lathered and blowing a long moment before turning back toward the barn and trotting away.

"I thought I was a goner!" Lacey leaned against Balckie's wide chest as he reined in his snorting, lathered horse.

"Are you all right?" He stared down anxiously into her face.

"I—I think so." She looked up at him, the evening shadows on his handsome features didn't hide his concern.

She had an almost overpowering urge to kiss her rescuer, but resisted. It was only gratitude after all. "I—I was doing just fine, thank you. I was about to bring my horse under control. It wouldn't have happened in the first place if your stupid dog, Lively—"

"Yeah, sure, sister. I saw how you were controllin' that mare." He wheeled his horse and started back toward the trail at a slow walk, Lively was now barking and running in circles around the buckskin. "Great God Almighty, why the hell didn't you tell me you weren't an expert rider?"

"Ha! A Texan admit that? My uncle was so embarrassed for me, he could hardly stand it."

"You little fool," he muttered. "You almost got us both killed. Reckon your horse is back at the barn by now."

It was very comfortable and warm against his chest. She snuggled deeper and closed her eyes. He smelled of sunlight, tobacco, and shaving lotion. She had never felt so protected and safe. She suddenly thought of something and sat bolt upright as they rode. "My word, I must look a mess."

He grinned down at her. "You do, but who cares?"

She tried to brush back wisps of hair with her hands. "I like everything to be perfect."

"Life isn't perfect and people aren't, either. That's a silly thing to worry about, considerin' you were almost killed."

He made sense, of course, but still she was very conscious of her tangled hair and smudged clothes. Certainly, her stern grandfather would not have approved.

They rejoined the waiting group.

Eugene looked angry. "Miss Lacey, are you all right? Your horse just ran past us."

"Fine, no thanks to you," she snapped. "I notice you didn't come to my rescue."

"How could I when you had gotten so far ahead of us?" He paused and frowned. "Besides, I have a bad back."

Lacey realized suddenly how undignified and unladylike she must look cuddled up against the gambler's chest. One of the cowboys had caught her winded horse and brought it to her now. "I'll ride back on my own, thank you."

She pulled away from the shelter of Blackie's arms and slid down the side of his buckskin horse. While the cowboy held her black horse for her, she mounted up and fell in next to Eugene and Mable. "It's not what it looked like, Eugene. The rascal simply came to my rescue."

"Disgusting scoundrel!" Eugene said.

Behind them, she heard Blackie snort.

"Everybody," the wrangler said, "I think we've had enough excitement for the day. Maybe we'd better head back."

It was dark as the riders returned to the big campfire. Eugene helped Lacey from her horse. "We had a little excitement," he announced, "Miss Durango's horse ran away. I was about to rescue her, but someone got there first."

She hadn't thought Eugene was about to rescue her at all. If it hadn't been for Blackie O'Neal . . . she turned and smiled at the gambler and across the fire, he winked at her in such an intimate way that it made her blush to the roots of her hair. She noticed Dixie's scowl and realized the saloon girl had seen it, too.

Now the ranch served barbecue around the fire, hot and juicy with big hunks of homemade bread and spicy beans cooked over the campfire. Then the fireworks were set off to the "ohs" and "ahs" of the crowd. Finally the people dispersed slowly, heading back to their homes and the town.

Eugene helped her up to the seat of their buggy. "It's been a long day," he said.

She started to answer, but was drowned out by the laughter and singing of Blackie's girls in the big open barouche as it passed them, returning to town.

"Disgusting!" Eugene said.

"Maybe we've misjudged him," Lacey said dreamily, remembering how it felt to be in the circle of his embrace.

"I hope you're not being naive enough to fall for that knight-in-shining-armor routine," Eugene said and cracked his little whip. "He'll try to have his way with any woman he meets, but he's after that valuable lot, you know." The buggy jolted as they pulled out on the road.

Lacey blinked. "Uh, of course." She stared straight ahead as they drove. She had almost forgotten she and Blackie were adversaries. "But he probably did save my life back there on the trail."

Eugene snorted. "Texas men always think they got to act like big heroes," he said, "I was coming after you myself, but he got in my way."

She didn't say anything. He was right about some things at least. Blackie might have been playing to the crowd so they'd all think better of him. Still if she had been killed, Blackie would have gotten that choice lot without her there to contest it.

The next day, Lacey did write up the Fourth of July festivities, but played down her adventure:

This editor's horse ran away with her at the trail ride. Mr. Eugene Peabody attempted to rescue her, but she was eventually rescued by another citizen.

Isaac scowled at her as they put the papers out for the boxes. "You could have at least mentioned your rescuer's name."

She felt guilty. "My word, what would people think? Me being rescued by the proprietor of that saloon and bawdy house?"

"It's not as if nobody in town hadn't already heard about it, yes?"

"I'm sure Mr. O'Neal doesn't give a fig about whether he appears in the pages of my paper. He probably doesn't even read it."

The next Sunday, Eugene picked her up as usual in his buggy to drive her to church. She wore a fluffy pink dress and a big hat with roses on it. Blackie O'Neal never came, of course, but he did have the decency to close down on Sunday. As they sat in the pew, Lacey noted the voluptuous daughter of the minister sitting as part of the choir. Mable Lovejoy seemed to be staring out at someone in the congregation. Finally, she gave a bold wink. Lacey glanced around, wondering which young man was the object of the buxom girl's attention? She had seemed to be looking toward Lacey and Eugene, but when Lacey craned her neck, she realized there was a handsome young farm boy sitting directly behind her.

After the sermon, silver-haired Reverend Lovejoy raised his hand for silence. "You all know we've been attempting to raise enough money for a large stained glass window in the west wall behind the pulpit." His very pink face smiled. "Well, I'm pleased to announce an anonymous donor has come forward and pledged a thousand dollars. Looks like we'll get that window after all."

The crowd gasped, then began to applaud. A shout went up, "Tell us who he is, Reverend, so we can thank him proper-like."

The minister shook his head. "I promised to protect his identity. He is a modest person, wanting no personal glory from his generosity. Now let's sing one verse of: "Praise God From Whom All Blessings Flow" and end the service."

As they filed out of the small frame building, Lacey turned to Eugene. "Who do you suppose donated the window?"

Eugene shook his head. "Remember Reverend Lovejoy said he wanted no publicity, but it has to be a successful businessman who would donate that much."

A successful businessman. Of course that might be a description of the man escorting her. She looked at him. "Eugene, do you know more than you're telling me?"

He hadn't the foggiest idea what she was talking about, but he didn't let on. "What?" he said cagily and grinned.

"Eugene, is it you?"

"Me?" For a moment, he blinked at her, but she was smiling and clinging to his arm all dewy-eyed. Of course it wasn't him. If he had an extra thousand dollars, which he didn't, he certainly wouldn't waste it on a hunk of glass for a stupid window. "I'm not saying it is, I'm not saying it isn't."

"Oh, Eugene, how wonderfully generous of you." She almost squealed with joy, holding his hand very tight. She was beautiful when she was excited like that. Beautiful enough to seduce if he got the chance.

"Shh!" He looked around furtively and put his finger to his lips. "This must remain a secret. I don't want any publicity about this, which means you can't print a thing in your paper."

"But people will want to know who made this gift," she protested.

"I did it because I love the Lord and the people of

Pretty Prairie," Eugene said sanctimoniously. "You must not breathe a word."

"You're wonderful!" Impulsively, she reached up and kissed him.

Blackie had just come out of his saloon and was standing on the sidewalk watching the crowds coming out of church down the street. He smiled when he saw Miss Durango. She looked fetching in a pale pink dress and a hat with big flowers on it. So feminine, which hid the steel of her disposition under that curvaceous body. Then he frowned as he saw how she clung to Eugene Peabody's arm. He could only guess what they were discussing, but Eugene looked mighty pleased with himself. Abruptly, Lacey reached up and kissed him. God Almighty, what had he said to get that kind of reward?

Blackie remembered the kiss at the fund-raiser and sighed. It had been unforgettable, worth the slap that came afterward. Now he remembered how she'd felt in his arms when he'd rescued her from the runaway horse. His feelings were slightly ruffled about her deliberate slight of him in the news story while mentioning Eugene who had hung back like a lily-livered coward. She was not very grateful and she should have been. Still, Blackie never liked publicity when he did a good deed. He was afraid he would look soft or that people would misinterpret his motives.

With Lacey kissing the dude like that, Eugene must have done something really great. If things kept on, she'd probably marry the prig and raise perfect, priggish children. That thought did not improve Blackie's mood. Of course, he assured himself, it was only because if she married Eugene Peabody, Blackie would never get that prize lot. Eugene would not allow it.

The next day, Lacey was floating on cloud nine as she set type to inform the town about the coming stained glass window. Eugene was so kind and generous. She had certainly underestimated him. She laid out the type for the headline:

CHURCH TO GET WINDOW. Generous anonymous donor steps forward, leaving town to wonder which businessman has made the gift? This reporter thinks she knows who the donor is, but the person she interviewed refused to admit his good deed, saying only that he loved the Lord and the people of this town. Window is to be delivered in a couple of weeks.

"Done." She sighed and pulled off her apron. "Isaac, you can finish setting the type for the other stories so we can get the paper out on the streets. By the way, have you seen Precious?"

"No," Isaac came around a stack of newsprint. "Haven't seen her since yesterday."

"That worries me," Lacey frowned, "I thought she was asleep up on a pile of books somewhere, but she hasn't shown up for breakfast. Ever since she took up with that trampy tom, he's been teaching her bad things like digging in garbage cans. Precious? Here, kitty, kitty. Here kitty."

"Meow." From some distance, she heard a faint answer.

"Precious? Where are you, Precious?"

"Meow."

Why didn't the Persian come? Lacey walked toward the faint sound. She hoped she wasn't sick. It wasn't like the plump cat to miss a meal. "Precious?"

"Meow."

Mystified, Lacey followed the sound. It led her to the bottom drawer of a big filing cabinet in the back of the shop. The drawer was half open. "Kitty, kitty?"

"Meow," came from the drawer.

Relieved, Lacey slid the drawer open. For a moment in the dim light, she only saw her white cat curled up in the drawer. "Why, you rascal, where have you—? Oh my word!"

Isaac yelled from the front. "What is it, Miss Lacey?"

"Outrageous!" Lacey gulped as she knelt down and peered into the drawer. "You—you feline harlot, you."

Three squirming little yellow kittens nursed at Precious' side. The cat didn't look ashamed at all. In fact, she looked right proud of herself.

Isaac came up behind her and let out his breath. "Well, looks like the tom taught her something else besides digging in the garbage. Guess you can forget about Sir Fluffy Boots, yes?"

"But I had such big plans for her. Precious, shame on you!"

Precious didn't look embarrassed for her lapse from grace. She almost seemed to purr as she began to lick the kittens.

Isaac laughed. "That old yellow tom must have been so charming, she forgot all about a fancy dude like Sir Fluffy Boots."

"I ought to kill that tom cat," she muttered.

"I think Cookie would object to that," Isaac grinned, "he sets a heap of store on that yellow cat."

"Then I ought to take these bastard kittens over and dump them on his doorstep." One of the yellow kittens raised its head and mewed plaintively. "Well, they are cute," she admitted and picked that one up. She stroked its tiny head a long moment before putting it back with its mother. "Precious, you shouldn't have let that charming rascal turn your head. Now look at what's happened."

Precious didn't seem at all concerned. She licked her kittens and then Lacey's hand.

"Well, come on and let me feed you," Lacey sighed. "I reckon there's no accounting for taste."

Isaac shrugged. "She's not doing any worse than most

females would have done. They'll pass up the respectable male for the charming rascal every time."

"Ha!" Lacey said, "Some of us are smarter than that."

"Maybe." Isaac countered and returned to his type
setting.

In the mail several days later, she got a note from
Blackie congratulating her on her new family. Damn his
hide anyway. She was embarrassed enough about
Precious' transgression without him rubbing salt in the
wound. She ought to leave some kittens on his doorstep.
Oh course, they were so adorable, she soon decided she
couldn't part with even one.

The hot days of July continued. Eugene continued to
call on her. She could almost set a clock by his punctuality.
He was precise, dependable, and so dull. She made it a
point to avoid bumping into Blackie O'Neal. She didn't
like feeling obligated to him for rescuing her from the runaway horse. Besides, there were other feelings that made
her uneasy whenever he crossed her mind. Things had settled down to everyday life in a small, quiet town. Except on
Saturday nights when there seemed to be a lot of noise,
music and fighting across the street at the Black Garter.

One Monday morning, she complained to the sheriff
about how particularly loud it had been last Saturday
night. "This is outrageous. I think you ought to close that
place about eight o'clock."

"Even on Saturday, Miss Durango?" The wiry old fellow took off his western hat and scratched his gray head.
"Seems to me the cowboys ought to be allowed to let off
a little steam—"

"The ones gathering at the Black Garter are rascals," she
protested, "and that Blackie O'Neal is the worst of all."

"Well, Miss, I reckon everyone knows about the trouble between you and Blackie over that lot—"

"You don't think I would take this personally?" Her face flamed. "I'm complaining as a concerned citizen."

"Uh-huh. Wal, now, you come down to my office and swear out a complaint and in the meantime, I'll talk to Blackie and see if he and the boys can tone it down a little."

"Demon rum; that's what it is," she declared with a self-righteous sniff, "my L.T.A. ladies may picket the place again. Maybe that'll run him out of town."

The sheriff grinned. "Hardly think a few ladies trottin' up and down and singing hymns are gonna stop the cowboys from celebratin' on Saturday night."

"We'll see." She marched inside and wrote an editorial about how a civilized town should rid itself of gamblers, saloons, and alcohol.

The next Saturday, she had her Ladies' Temperance Association organized to picket on the wooden sidewalk in front of the Black Garter. As they marched with their signs, singing hymns loudly if not too much in tune, a group of cowboys rode up, hesitated, and rode on.

"See?" Lacey shouted, "already tonight we've saved those poor cowboys from squandering their hard earned dollars in this vile den of sin."

The banker was passing by. He stopped, stared and shouted "Ethel? Is that you, Ethel? Why ain't you home cookin' and cleanin'?"

"I'm saving this town from demon rum!" the stout housewife shouted back, "Julius, you can scrub your own bathtub."

"I swear," said the barber, who had come out to stand on the sidewalk, "I don't know what the world's comin' to when ladies start protesting. Next thing you know, they'll dry up the whole country."

"God forbid," said two cowboys who were standing watching the spectacle.

"We're gonna do more than that, we're gonna get women the vote!"

"Hallelujah, amen!" shouted the ladies.

"Ethel!" shouted the banker. "Oh, Ethel, what will everyone think?"

Eugene Peabody was just closing the store and strolled down to join the ladies. To Lacey, he said, "I think it's wonderful these ladies are willing to stand up and be counted."

"Good," said Lacey and handed him a picket sign. "You can join us, Eugene."

He was clearly not happy. "But, er, it's an all-ladies' march."

"Not any more," Lacey said, "not with you in it."

Eugene gulped. "It might cost me business. You know men are very touchy about their drinks."

"Eugene, you're either with us or against us. Now will you help us?"

Eugene fell into line and joined the march up and down before the saloon, but he was clearly uneasy about it.

Abruptly, Blackie O'Neal came through the swinging doors and his face looked like a thunderstorm. "What's goin' on out here?"

The ladies hesitated and Eugene shrank back behind Lacey. The saloon owner was a formidable opponent, but Lacey squared her shoulders bravely and stepped forward. "We are protesting your selling demon rum. If you are thinking of calling the sheriff, I remind you the sidewalk is public property and we have a right to march up and down here."

"That's right," the ladies echoed. Eugene didn't say anything.

Coward, Lacey thought.

Blackie took a deep breath. "Oh, is that it?"

Moose appeared in the doorway behind him, looking over the crowd.

"Yes," Lacey said, "and don't think you're going to scare us with that big bartender of yours."

"Why, ladies," and Blackie gave them his most dazzling grin, "I wouldn't dream of it, would I, Moose?"

"That's right, Boss." The big man smiled. "Shall I bring out some refreshments now?"

"Do," Blackie gestured, "I'm sure the ladies must be thirsty in all this heat."

Lacey glared at them both. "Our lips do not touch the devil's brew." Behind her, the ladies murmured agreement.

"I wouldn't dream of offerin' ladies liquor," Blackie grinned again. "How about some iced tea or lemonade?"

"What?" Lacey blinked.

"Iced tea," Blackie smiled at all the ladies. "The mother's milk of the South, and Moose has made dainty sugar cookies and little cucumber sandwiches. Start servin', Moose."

With a wide, snaggle-toothed grin, Moose came out carrying a big tray of cups, followed by Dutch, the piano player, carrying another tray of cookies and sandwiches. "Hope you like 'em, ladies, my mama's own recipe."

"How sweet," cooed Miss Wren.

"How thoughtful," said Ethel Wilson, the banker's wife.

"Don't trust them, ladies," Lacey warned, "they're just trying to make us forget what we're here for."

"Delicious," said Mable Lovejoy, "why, Mister O'Neal, you're so much nicer than Miss Durango said."

"I'm sorry to hear she doesn't like me," Blackie replied with a sigh, his face sad. "But then, you realize that if she runs me out of town, she gets that contested land?"

"I resent you're suggesting there's anything personal in this." Lacey shouted.

"Isn't there?" He gave her that dazzling grin.

She was beaten and she knew it. Protest forgotten, the ladies were sipping iced tea, munching cucumber sandwiches cut in fancy shapes, trading recipes with Moose and looking at her suspiciously. "Ladies, remember we are here to protest demon rum. Remember, Mr. O'Neal excels at being charming." She certainly knew that for a fact.

"Mmm," said Ethel Wilson, "Mr. Moose, you must give me the recipe for these delicious sand tarts."

"I'd love to, ma'am." Moose smiled and offered her another from the platter, "and I'd like the recipe for those blackberry tarts you brought to the Fourth of July picnic."

"Speaking of tarts," Lacey said, and glared at Dixie who stood in the doorway.

"Iced tea, Miss Durango?" Blackie smiled again, and around her she heard all the ladies sigh.

"Isn't he handsome?" whispered one.

"Isn't he charming?" sighed another.

"Ladies," Lacey said, "what about our protest?"

Mrs. Anderson handed a cookie to her baby in its buggy. "It doesn't seem very polite to accept this charming man's refreshments and then picket his establishment."

"Hear! Hear!" murmured the ladies between bites of Moose's food.

Yes, it was a lost cause. How cheaply the ladies had been bought off. Now that all the cookies and sandwiches were gone, the ladies began drifting away, murmuring their thanks and fluttering their lace handkerchiefs at Blackie. "You know, you don't seem like a bad sort," said Miss Wren with a sigh.

Blackie made a sweeping bow. "Ladies, do come again. Moose is workin' on a new recipe for angel food cake."

Moose nodded. "With lemon zest icing."

"Devil's food would be more appropriate," Lacey said.

"Don't you know it!" Blackie grinned at her.

The ladies were still oohing and aahing over the refreshments as they drifted away.

Lacey stood there glaring at Blackie as Moose gathered up the empty cups and went inside.

Eugene said "I— I've got to get home. My uncle is expecting me." He fled the scene like he'd gotten a scorpion down his neck and into his pants.

"You rascal!" Lacey leaned her picket sign against the hitching post and faced Blackie. "You're charming these unsuspecting ladies into liking you."

He gave her that devilish grin. "Why, Miss Lacey, I merely thought the ladies would be in need of refreshments after all that marching and singing."

"I am going to write another editorial about you." Lacey threatened.

He winked at her. "You just do that. And Miss Lacey, next time you bring the ladies out to picket, give me some advance warning. Moose has a new recipe for these tiny little chicken salad sandwiches with watercress and the best jelly roll—"

"I hope you choke on that jelly roll." Lacey turned and marched away, seething. The ownership of the choice lot was no longer important to her, nor were her temperance convictions. It weighed heavily on her that she was now obligated to Blackie for saving her life in the runaway and the fact that she could not stop having wild and confusing dreams about the man. This had become more than a clash of wills between her and Blackie O'Neal and she figured she was as stubborn as he was. He might charm those other women into simpering idiots, but she wasn't about to be taken in by this ladies' man.

Chapter Sixteen

The hot days of mid-July were upon the little settlement of Pretty Prairie. Lacey's subscription list continued to grow as did the three yellow kittens. Eugene Peabody occasionally took her for a buggy ride and to church. The town was prospering, more people arriving every day. Chief Thunder was doing a landslide business in selling fake buttons from the late hero's coat. General Custer's horse's tail had gotten so short, wisps of mane were now being sold. The Black Garter continued to operate across the street, much to Lacey's annoyance and she went out of her way to avoid its owner.

One Saturday, she was in the bank when she ran into that whiskey-selling rascal. He was standing admiring the mural Chief Thunder was painting in the lobby. As usual, he had a tall, cold drink in his hand. "Hello, sister, and how are you today?"

"Fine." She answered coldly, then turned her back on him and surveyed the mural which depicted the historic land run across one long wall. "My, Joe, I had no idea you were so good."

"I paint signs to eat, but I'm an artist at heart," the Potawatomi said proudly and stepped back, paint brush in hand, to survey his work. "What do you think, Blackie?"

Lacey almost snorted. "Now why would you expect the proprietor of a saloon to know anything about art?"

"Miss Lacey," Joe said, "Blackie is a fellow—"

"Never mind," Blackie interrupted him with a shake

of his head. "I think," Blackie mused, "the sky could use a few more clouds and this front horse doesn't look realistic enough. Bay would look better against that background than a black one."

To her surprise, Joe nodded somberly. "You're probably right. I'll be back in a minute, I've got to get a different brush." He turned and left.

Lacey sniffed. "So now you're an art critic?"

"Well," he grinned, "I just know what I like."

"Joe Toadfrog is extremely talented," she reminded him, "and I think you're arrogant to be offering him advice."

Blackie grinned again, that maddening charming grin. "May I remind you that he asked for my opinion, Miss Durango? By the way, your charming ladies have not been out to picket me again. Weather too hot for them?"

She took a deep breath and drew herself up proudly. "You know very well why. If I bring them, you'll have Moose out there giving them iced tea and cookies. Next thing I know, they're trading recipes with him and I look like a damned fool."

"I didn't say that. You did." He sipped his drink.

"And you, gulping whiskey and it's not even noon yet. You're as worthless as your dog."

"Lively's not worthless."

At the sound of his name, the hound raised his head from where he lay sprawled on the bank floor and wagged his tail lazily.

"By the way," Blackie grinned, "how are your kittens?"

"That is a sore point with me and you know it."

"No such thing, I was simply inquirin'—"

"Poor Precious was taken advantage of by a charming rascal of a trampy yellow tom cat."

"She may have enjoyed it." Blackie was positively leering at her.

Lacey felt the blood rush to her face. "That's an outrageous comment to a lady."

"I don't see why . . . unless another lady is worried about bein' taken advantage of by a charmin' rascal."

"Ha! In your dreams."

"I beg your pardon?"

"Do not try to charm me, Mr. O'Neal. I would rather not be seen speaking to you in public."

About that time, Eugene entered the bank. "Ah, Miss Lacey." He took off his derby. "Am I in time to offer you a glass of iced tea or lemonade down at the cafe?"

She turned and glared at Blackie. "You certainly may. It's so refreshing to know a *real* gentleman."

Blackie smiled. "I never claimed to be a gentleman, Miss Durango."

Eugene looked very uncomfortable. "Is—is this masher annoying you, Miss Lacey?"

"That's all right, Eugene," she said quickly. "I would not want you to get blood all over the bank floor engaging in fisticuffs with saloon trash."

"I'd wipe up the floor with him and you know it," Blackie said while still smiling sweetly.

Eugene backed away quickly and in doing so, stumbled over Lively who rose up with a growl and grabbed Eugene by the pants leg.

"Mad dog!" Eugene cried, struggling to retrieve his pants from the hound's mouth. "That beast should be destroyed."

"Eugene," Blackie said and this time he wasn't grinning, "you make any move to hurt my dog and you'll look like a stampede ran over you."

Eugene's pale face turned positively white. "Did you hear that threat?" He gasped to Lacey, "why, I ought to call the sheriff—"

"Lively," Blackie said, "let go of the big, brave man."

The dog let go, yawned and lay back down on the floor. In seconds, he was fast asleep again.

"Eugene," Lacey said, taking his arm, "let's get out of

here. Don't lower yourself to trading insults and threats with a common saloon gambler."

Eugene's thin face was drenched with sweat and she had a feeling it wasn't the heat. He pulled out a handkerchief with a trembling hand and wiped his face. "If you insist, Miss Lacey." As they left, he called back over his shoulder, "good thing there was a lady present. I didn't want to do anything violent in front of her."

"We could meet in the alley later." Blackie offered.

"I—I'm going to be busy later," Eugene gulped and hurried out of the bank with Lacey. Other bank customers turned and looked at them curiously. Lacey had never felt so conspicuous in her whole life.

"Never mind, Eugene, he's an uncivilized brute." She looked back over her shoulder and Blackie winked broadly at her. "My word, he's outrageous."

"Disgusting!" Eugene said.

"Never mind." She had no doubt Blackie, that rough and tumble saloon gambler, could and would wipe up the floor with Eugene Peabody.

They had a glass of iced tea at the cafe and then Eugene said, "if you'll excuse me now, my dear, I must get back to work. Things have been so busy at the store lately."

She smiled and watched him leave. Cookie came over to wipe off the table. "Can I get you some more tea, Miss Lacey? Lunch crowd's startin' to come in and we're about to get busy."

She shook her head with a smile. "I've got to hand it to you, Cookie, I never thought you could make a go of a restaurant."

The old man gave her a snaggle-toothed grin before he left her table. "It's Miss Flo, she's got a talent for cookin' and she comes over to help sometimes."

"You've been seeing a lot of her lately, haven't you?"

Cookie blushed. "She's a right nice woman and just bad circumstances got her where she is. I been thinkin' about askin' her to marry me."

"You? Get married?"

"Wal, don't look so shocked." The old man drew himself up proudly. "I ain't too old and the cafe is doin' well."

"I just wondered if Blackie could run the Garter without her?"

He nodded. "She's havin' a hard time keepin' girls anyhow. Cowboys keep marryin' them and takin' them out of the Garter. I hired one or two myself to work as waitresses."

Lacey smiled. "If that continues, Blackie won't be able to keep that part of the Garter open."

"The saloon business ain't where his real interest lies anyhow, or so Flo says."

"Oh?" She couldn't imagine that Blackie O'Neal had any interests besides drinking, gambling, running a saloon and making her life miserable.

"Here comes the lunch crowd," Cookie said. "By the way, you want to give away old tom's kittens, I'll take one."

She shook her head. "I've fallen in love with them. They're so cute, despite their dubious heritage."

He grinned. "Fancy ladies never could resist a rascal." Then he hobbled away.

Lacey looked out the big window. Half a dozen cowboys had tied up at the hitching post and were coming inside. Within minutes, the place was busy with cowboys shoving up to the counter for sandwiches and stew.

Nubile young Mable Lovejoy came in just then, saw Lacey at her back table, and came over. "Hello, Miss Lacey, may I join you?"

"Please do." Lacey indicated a chair. "How have you been?" She had genuine concern for the girl whose father didn't seem aware of how boy-crazy Mable was. "Are you coming to the box supper next Saturday night?"

"I think Daddy will let me since it's for a good cause." The girl took a chair, leaned on the red-and-white checked oilcloth. "I'm trying to decide whether to pack fried chicken or roast beef sandwiches."

"You have a sweetheart who'll be bidding for your box?"

"Oh, Miss Lacey," the girl lowered her voice and looked around as if afraid of being overheard, "I do have someone in mind, he's positively charming, but I'm not sure what Daddy would say."

"Oh, the Reverend might be a little overly protective, but I'm sure you're worried for nothing."

"But my beau's older than I am, you see, and I'm not sure Daddy would approve of him."

Lacey wrinkled her brow, trying to remember the age of the farm boy at church she had thought Mable was winking at. He hadn't seemed that much older. "Well, all you can do is try. I'm sure if he's a good choice, it'll be all right."

"Miss Lacey, I don't think Daddy would ever think he was a good choice. Daddy is very strict since Mama ran off with that ribbon salesman five years ago."

Who on earth could Mable's beau be? The voluptuous girl was looking at Lacey as if expecting advice and Lacey wasn't sure what to say. "Is he ready to commit to you?"

"I don't know. He's hinted he might soon, but you see, there's another girl and he hates to hurt her. I do, too."

Lacey shrugged. "Everyone has to follow her heart. You might be doing the other girl a favor."

The pretty Mable looked relieved. "You know I'd really like to travel to exotic places instead of just handle the collection plate and keep books for the church. I don't want to end up an old maid like—"

Her voice trailed off and she colored.

"Mable," Lacey said and she tried to keep the annoyance out of her voice. "I am not an old maid, I am a career woman."

"Excuse me, Miss Lacey," the girl turned red with awkward confusion, "but all the men say you're getting a little long in the tooth and you ain't spoke for yet."

Lacey felt a flush creep up her neck. "I could have plenty of men; I just haven't found one who meets my standards."

"Daddy says the Angel Gabriel couldn't match up to

what you expect from men, 'cause there ain't none of them perfect. Excuse me for repeating that."

Lacey was a bit miffed. "Perfect? I'd settle for one who wasn't just a stupid brute. In general, men are loathsome creatures who track dirt into the parlor, burp, and scratch all the time, like a dog with fleas. Why, even old Cookie, who is a long-time friend, would be a disaster as a husband—"

"I heered that!" Cookie sang out from the kitchen.

The girl leaned closer. "Miss Lacey, even though he's older, do you think it's okay if he courts me secretly for a while? We ain't doing nothing except go for an occasional buggy ride and meetin' secretly behind the church sometimes."

"I reckon that's pretty innocent," Lacey said absently, still wondering who the mysterious older beau could be.

"Good." Mable stood up. "I'll tell him that when I see him later. I'm hoping he'll buy my box at the social next Saturday." She turned to leave. "Oh, Daddy says the big stained glass window is due next week. I've got the money ready to pay for it."

"That's good. I'll mention it in the paper." Lacey said and Mable smiled and went out the door. The lunch crowd was filling every table. Next to her, Cookie slapped down a plate of soggy biscuits and burned stew before a cowboy. The cowboy took a deep sniff and sighed. "Just like Mama used to make. I gotta hand it to you, Cookie, your grub makes me homesick."

Cookie grinned. "Just keep coming in, Hank, I'll keep fillin' you up."

Well, there was no accounting for tastes, Lacey thought. Certainly the cooking would get better if Flo stepped in to help. She nodded to Cookie and pushed her way through the crowd and went outside, crossed the street to her office. Inside, she said to Isaac, "I'm concerned about that little Mable Lovejoy, she's got some mysterious suitor."

Isaac laughed gently. "You ought to be relieved that she might get married. She looks a little wild to me, sidling up to all the men. Now that Vanetta Wren is the one who needs help finding a man. That's the homeliest face I've seen that wasn't wearing a bridle."

"Well, beauty is only skin deep," Lacey reminded him.

"Yes, but as they say in Texas, ugly goes all the way to the bone, yes?"

"Isaac, you're terrible. I've been trying to help Vanetta find a job. You know, she would make a great librarian if the town ever builds a library."

He nodded. "So far, there's no money to build it and no good land to put it on, but maybe someday."

"One thing at a time," Lacey said, "Pretty Prairie can only grow so fast." Precious climbed up in her lap as she sat down at her orderly desk and one of the yellow kittens mewed until Lacey reached down and picked him up, looked him over critically. He was an ornery-looking tom kitten, a dead ringer for the alley cat across the street. "Oh, Precious," she sighed, "how could you?"

Precious seemed to grin at her and began licking the feisty kitten. Lacey chased them both off her lap and turned her chair to stare out the window. Blackie O'Neal came out of his saloon. As usual, he held a tall, cool drink. The diamond ring on his hand winked in the hot sunlight. Around the corner came Moose on the seat of a small buggy. He got down and handed the reins to Blackie. Blackie climbed up in the buggy, snapped the reins and started down the street. When he saw Lacey watching him, he took off his hat and bowed in her direction. Embarrassed at being caught staring, Lacey turned her chair around. "Now why would he be going out with a buggy instead of riding a horse? That doesn't make any sense."

"Maybe he's taking someone for a drive," Isaac suggested. "Anyway, what do you care?"

"I don't," Lacey said, reaching for a pen. "It's just unusual, that's all." She began to write a headline: CHURCH PASTOR REPORTS STAINED GLASS WINDOW TO BE DELIVERED SOON. She must interview Reverend Lovejoy and see if she could get some details. No one yet knew officially who the mysterious donor was, but when she had congratulated Eugene on his generosity, he hadn't denied it. Now there was a fine man, a paragon of virtue. How dare the preacher say that Lacey was looking for the perfect man as if it were a crime?

That made her think of Mable. How dare that girl think of Lacey as a long-in-the-tooth old maid? Did the whole town think of her that way instead of as a career woman? Mable. Now, who could she be secretly seeing?

They only went for buggy rides or met secretly behind the church sometimes, Mable had said. An older man she was not sure her father would approve of. In her mind, Lacey saw Blackie O'Neal driving away alone in a buggy. *Where was he going? Was he meeting someone?* The pencil fell from Lacey's nerveless fingers. "My word, surely Mable didn't mean she was seeing Blackie O'Neal?"

Was he even now taking young Mable out in the country for a drive, and who knew what else? What should she do? Should she tell Reverend Lovejoy? She thought about it, shook her head. Mable had talked to her in confidence, and she didn't really want to get the girl in trouble at home. Yes, that would be just like that handsome, dashing rascal to take advantage of a young, naive girl like Mable. When Lacey got a chance, she would give that gambler a piece of her mind.

She kept an eye on the saloon as she worked, waiting to see when Blackie returned. Across the street, it was late afternoon and traffic at the Black Garter was picking up. Because of the heat, she had the front door propped open. Every time the swinging doors opened for some cowboy, the tinkle of glasses, the laughter of women and a smattering of song drifted on the hot air.

Lacey noted it was almost dark when Blackie returned with his buggy. He looked very satisfied with himself. *What had that scoundrel been up to?* She felt responsible for Mable. First chance she got, she must give her some advice about dealing with rascals. Certainly Lacey had had dealings with one. She thought about Homer and frowned. Well, maybe he hadn't exactly been a rascal, just weak and unable to deal with a strong woman.

Isaac called from the back. "You almost got that article about the library benefit written so I can set it in type?"

"Uh, yes, in a minute." She began to scribble furiously, ashamed that she had been sitting here staring out the window, watching for Blackie O'Neal's return. It was only because she was concerned for Mable, she told herself. BOX SUPPER TO BENEFIT PUBLIC LIBRARY, she wrote.

Even though the town council still does not have the land to build a library, they are going ahead with their fund-raising efforts. So ladies, start cooking and tell your man to get ready to bid your box up since it's for a good cause.

She paused and chewed the tip of her pen, smiling. She'd fix something really good, decorate the box and of course, she could expect Eugene Peabody to bid it high. Mrs. Eugene Reginal Peabody. E.R.P. He was a sober, industrious chap with a good business. And a Harvard man. Then she thought about crawling into bed with him and shuddered in spite of herself. Somehow, she couldn't get excited about sleeping with him. She imagined their dull, perfect children with Eugene's brown curly hair and thin features and somehow, it wasn't appealing. Now if that baby boy had the black hair and big grin of a rakish devil like . . . was she out of her mind? Outrageous thought.

"I've got the article ready," she called to Isaac, and then she got up and slammed the front door to keep out the merriment that was drifting on the hot air across the street from Blackie's Black Garter.

It was a warm Saturday afternoon toward the end of July. Lacey tried to be excited about tonight's box supper, but somehow, eating with Eugene seemed about as exciting as watching tumbleweeds blow.

Isaac came to the front window and looked out. "Looks like there'll be a big crowd, from the number of wagons and buggies in town. The mayor and the councilmen are already blocking off Main Street for the event."

"There'll be a band, too, and of course the barber shop quartet," Lacey came to the window. "This is going to be a really big event."

"Yes, now if they only had a lot to build the library on," Isaac said.

"They'll find one," Lacey said, "maybe one of those sites over on Maple Street."

"Too far from the center of town, yes?" Isaac asked.

"You're right; it needs to be downtown. You coming to the social?" Lacey asked.

He hesitated, then shook his head. "No, I'll find something to do; maybe go over my finances."

Lacey bit her lip. "I'm sorry I haven't been able to pay you a little more—"

"That's fine, Miss Lacey, I'm happy working for you."

"But I know you turned down a good offer last year with that Kansas City paper and you keep talking about owning your own paper."

The little man shrugged. "You need me right now, Miss Lacey, and I like this town, yes?"

"It is a good town." She sighed wistfully. "I miss Texas, though. You can take a girl out of Texas, but you can't take Texas out of the girl."

Isaac went to the front window and looked out. "You figure all the girls at the Garter will bring box suppers?"

"Probably, even if they have to buy them at Cookie's Kitchen."

"I hear Blackie is closing the saloon for the event—generous of him."

"I doubt that," Lacey snorted. "He probably figures he won't be doing much business anyway, so he might as well close for the evening."

Isaac looked at her. "Maybe you're too quick to judge the man."

"Ha! What's to judge? He's a whiskey-swilling, card-playing rascal."

"He might have some good points you don't know about."

"I doubt that. What this town needs is for him to pack up and move on. The town will be better off without people like him."

Outside, local men were stringing up paper lanterns lit by small candles and setting up tables.

Isaac said, "I think they could use some help. I'll go see what I can do. You got your box ready, Miss Lacey?"

She shook her head. "I've got the box all decorated up so maybe some of the men will bid high. All I've got to do now is fry the chicken. I've got half a chocolate cake with a creamy pecan filling and some homemade potato salad."

Isaac laughed. "Sounds good. I'll spread the word so you'll get some high bids."

She shook her head. "It's supposed to be a big secret, you know. The fun is that the boxes won't have names on them, but I've alerted Eugene that mine is pink."

Isaac said "I imagine most of the ladies will be telling their men which box is theirs so the men won't be bidding blind."

"Of course." She watched Isaac go out the door, then went to inspect her box and smiled with satisfaction. She had wrapped the lid in pink tissue paper and festooned it with pink ribbon and wild flowers. "It'll be just fine. Now I'll get my chicken fried up."

It was dusk dark on that warm night as she surveyed the contents of her box one last time. Besides the fried chicken, the potato salad and chocolate cake, she had added bread and crisp dill pickles. She smiled with satisfaction and put the lid on, finished wrapping it up in a pretty pink package. "Now all I've got to do is get dressed." She knew Eugene would bid on her box. She wasn't all that thrilled to be sharing a box with him, but after all, he was a respectable man and a pillar of the community. *Not like some people.* She frowned as she thought of that scoundrel across the street. Maybe he wouldn't come to the box supper. "My word, Lacey, of course he will," she muttered to herself. "After all, he came to the street dance, didn't he?"

For just a moment, she remembered the heat and passion of his kiss and the way she had felt in his embrace when he rescued her from the runaway horse. She took a deep, wistful breath, then was annoyed with herself. She put on a pale green dress with matching hair ribbon, then picked up her box and went out into the evening. Traffic up and down the street had been blocked off and paper lanterns festooned the night. Tables laden with lemonade, iced tea, and homemade candy were by the big table where the ladies were setting their boxes. Already eager cowboys were standing around, waiting impatiently as the crowd gathered. As Lacey set her box on the table, she noticed there were several other boxes decorated in pink. She hadn't been so original after all. To Mrs. Wilson, she said, "Need any help, Ethel?"

"Oh, no, thanks. Miss Wren, Mable Lovejoy, and the committee have plenty of help right now." Mable walked up just then and Mrs. Wilson handed her Lacey's box. "Here's Miss Durango's box supper."

"Very pretty," Mable smiled. "Mine is pink, too."

"There are several pink ones; confusing to the men, but fun." Lacey smiled at the girl then surveyed the crowd, already planning her article for the next edition of the *Pretty Prairie Crusader*. ENTHUSIASTIC CROWD RAISES LARGE SUM FOR FUTURE LIBRARY.

She heard laughter and turned to see Blackie O'Neal and some of his saloon girls crossing the street, laden with lunch boxes. For once, the windows of the saloon were dark. Well, that was a relief, she thought, the event wouldn't have to compete with the saloon for the men's attention tonight. Dixie put a pink box on the table. It had a rose on the top.

"I didn't know you could cook," Lacey blurted.

The blonde looked at her coldly. "I can't. Moose fixed me some tiny watercress sandwiches and some petty fors, whatever the hell those are."

Lacey heard her name called and turned to see Eugene coming toward her, all smiles. As usual, he was dressed in a good suit with a boutonniere, his derby hat, and was twirling his cane. "Ah, Miss Lacey, I'm really looking forward to sharing your box supper tonight."

"Uh-huh," she nodded without much enthusiasm. "Remember it's pink with wildflowers. I really fixed something good."

He smiled again. "I won't be bidding on it for the food," he smiled. "It's your company I'm aiming for."

"Oh Eugene, you're so gallant."

Eugene looked past her shoulder and frowned. "Well, I see the saloon crowd is here. They've got their nerve, mingling with decent folk. Disgusting."

"Now Eugene, the girls really helped us with getting the town named and, after all, most of them are just victims of circumstance."

"Huh!" Eugene sniffed. "That Black Garter is like a magnet to trail trash. Look over there now."

There was some kind of commotion going on in front of the saloon. A big bruiser wearing dusty Western clothes and accompanied by two other riders was banging on the door of the saloon. "What the hell's going on here?" he bellowed. "Had to leave my horse around the corner and now I can't even get a drink!" He rattled the door handle again.

Even as she watched, Blackie hurried over to the big man, stood talking to him a minute. After a few words, the three tough-looking cowboys strode back around the corner and disappeared.

"Wonder what that was about?" Eugene said. "I guess that O'Neal promised them all the liquor they could drink later."

"You're probably right, Eugene. Why, if we could get that saloon closed, Pretty Prairie wouldn't attract that kind of people."

"Disgusting," Eugene agreed and turned away to speak to the owner of the barber shop. Lacey looked across the crowd at Blackie. As usual, he had a tall, cold drink in his hand. He held it up as if toasting her and gave her a broad wink.

Outrageous. She turned away, making it clear she was snubbing him.

The crowd had grown to several hundred people, all milling about and talking. Children ran through the crowd and somewhere, a baby cried.

The banker went up to the big table laden with boxes and took off his shoe, banged on the table for silence. "All right, men, we've got all these beautiful boxes to bid on, and you know it's for a good cause. Besides, if you're the lucky bidder, you get to enjoy the company of the lady who packed that box."

Girls in the audience tittered and some of the cowboys guffawed and shuffled their feet in embarrassment.

Across the crowd, Eugene looked toward Lacey and mouthed the words "pink with wildflowers?" She nodded back.

Blackie stood on the sidelines watching the bidding. He wasn't too thrilled about being here, but he'd promised Dixie he'd come bid on her box and he knew Moose had packed something really good. There was a great talent going to waste—Moose really should be running a fine hotel. When he reached his own financial goal, he would offer to stake Moose to a start.

The boxes were going down before the auctioneer's hammer pretty fast now. The crowd let out a gasp as a cowboy paid two silver dollars for a lacy blue box and the pretty new school marm came up to stand beside him, blushing.

It was easy to see that some men's wives had given them orders about which box to bid on. The banker himself bid on Ethel's box, but he didn't look too happy about it.

Speaking of happy, that lady newspaper woman didn't look particularly happy. Maybe she was afraid nobody would bid on her box. After all, she'd probably give the unlucky hombre strict guidelines on how to eat it. That twerp, Eugene Peabody would buy it.

Blackie was glad he didn't have to eat supper with Miss Iron Corset. Now which box belonged to Dixie? She'd said something about pink and flowers. He should have listened more closely. He tried to look across the crowd to catch Dixie's eye, but she was talking to Flo and not looking his way. The banker was holding up a box.

"Umm, this smells good, fellows, what am I bid?" The men began to bid. Blackie lit a cigar and stooped to scratch Lively's ears. He'd run that trail bum, Snake Hudson, off without much trouble, telling him he'd give him and his buddies free drinks if he'd come back tomorrow night.

"Sold!" The banker shouted, bringing his gavel down with a bang. "Reverend Lovejoy, come up and claim your dinner and will the young lady who packed it come up please?"

A titter began in the audience and Blackie looked up to see what was going on. Homely Miss Vanetta Wren pushed her way through the crowd toward the front. Poor Reverend Lovejoy looked very uncomfortable as he went up to pay for the box. Blackie had a sudden desire to fade into the crowd and skip the rest of this tiresome event, but because of public relations with the town fathers, he could hardly do that. Besides, he'd promised Dixie he'd buy her box.

What color had she told him her box would be? Pink, oh, yes, Blackie thought in a panic, it was pink, and maybe it had flowers on it, but what kind? How many boxes like that could there be?

The banker was holding up a pink box decorated with wildflowers. "Pretty as the lady who packed it, I reckon. Mmm, boys, smells like fried chicken to me. What am I bid?"

Across the crowd, Blackie saw Eugene raise his hand. "Fifty cents!" Eugene shouted.

"Wow, we've got a big spender," the banker laughed, "Remember, boys, this is for a good cause. I need a higher bid than that."

Now why would prissy Eugene be bidding on Dixie's box? The dude must know whose it was. Blackie was annoyed. He wanted to best Eugene and make him look like a fool. "A silver dollar!" Blackie shouted.

"Two silver dollars!" Eugene shouted confidently.

Then a cowboy offered two fifty and Eugene upped it to three dollars.

"Five dollars," Blackie shouted, determined that Eugene would not win this one.

The crowd took a collective breath. No one had bid so much tonight for any box.

"Well," said the banker, "seems like a lot of men want to eat supper with this young lady. Do I hear another bid?"

Blackie glanced over at Miss Iron Corset. She looked positively livid. "Six dollars!" she shouted.

"Miss Durango," said the banker, "Women's liberation has not progressed to the point that ladies are allowed to bid."

Now why would Miss Iron Corset be bidding on Dixie's box? *Just to run the cost up to raise money for the library.*

"Six dollars then," Eugene shouted.

Blackie glowered at him. That prissy shopkeeper would not outbid him for that box, and Blackie didn't much care who it belonged to. "A twenty dollar gold piece!" He shouted and the crowd murmured so loudly, the banker had to rap for silence. "Now that's what I call a bid. Going once, going twice. Sold to Mr. O'Neal. Come up and claim your supper, sir, and the young lady who packed this box."

What had he done? Twenty dollars to eat with Dixie when he didn't even like the tart. Well, at least he had bested that prissy Eugene Peabody and that was all that mattered. Blackie began to push his way through the crowd to claim the pink box. When he reached the front, he realized suddenly that Lacey Durango stood there beside it, glowering at him like she'd like to lift his scalp. "Don't tell me this is your food?" he gasped.

She looked mad enough to take on a rattler and give it first bite. "It certainly is, and I hope you choke on it!"

Chapter Seventeen

An excited buzz ran through the crowd as the word traveled faster than gossip at a sewing circle.

Lacey took a deep breath and glared up at Blackie. In the meantime, Eugene appeared, pale and helpless, shrugging his shoulders at her as if uncertain what to do to rescue her. Lacey looked plaintively toward Banker Wilson. "No chance there's a mistake?"

Banker Wilson shook his balding head. "No, ma'am, and Mr. O'Neal has paid a fortune for the privilege of eating with you."

With the crowd watching, there was nothing to do but hand her box to the scoundrel. Blackie took it, looking like he'd been slugged with a Colt pistol. Obviously he wasn't too excited about the turn of events either. In the background, Dixie's pretty face looked furious.

Blackie O'Neal paid his money and accepted the dainty pink box as if it were about to explode in his hands. In the background, the auctioneer started again. "All right, gents, here's another pretty box, what am I bid for it?"

Lacey didn't hear anything else as she stood awkwardly before the gambler. "This is outrageous," she seethed. "How in the hell did you get my box?"

"A lady cursing? Tsk. Tsk. Let me make one thing clear, sister, there was some mistake. I thought I was bidding on another young lady's supper."

"Oh." That thought hadn't occurred to her. It was a

bit insulting. "All right, I can be a good sport about this," Lacey said. "After all, it's a for a good cause."

"I can be a good sport, too," he grinned and winked. "I just hope the food's worth twenty dollars."

"Was what was in that other box worth what you were bidding?"

"I have no idea," he said honestly, "and I couldn't figure out why prissy Eugene was bidding on that same box. Come on, let's get this over with." He took her arm and led her away from the crowd.

"My word, if I'd known you were going to end up with my supper, I'd have packed rat poison."

"And, sister, if I'd known I was gonna have to eat with you, I'd gladly eat it."

"That's not a gentlemanly thing to say."

"I thought we had already established I'm no gent."

They went over to a grassy place and spread a blanket. Behind them, she heard Eugene call out the winning bid and go up to accept a box that looked somewhat like Lacey's. Mable stood there grinning like a possum. Eugene looked toward Lacey, evidently baffled and uncomfortable as he went forward.

"I think there's mischief afoot," Lacey grumbled, "maybe someone's been mixing up the boxes."

"Well, no kidding." Blackie said.

Mable, she thought, remembering what the girl had told her. *An older man her father wouldn't approve of.* "You ought to be ashamed of yourself."

"I'm seldom ashamed of anything, sister, you know that."

Dixie's pink box had just been bid on by a rather embarrassed but pleased-looking cowboy. In the meantime, Eugene looked confused as he accepted the third pink box while Mable took his arm and they went off and sat down at a picnic table. Cookie got into a spirited bidding duel with the gunsmith but came out victorious with Flo's box. He actually swaggered as he went forward to claim his prize. Even in the dim light, Lacey could see the older woman was positively blushing.

"Great God Almighty," Blackie grinned, "looks like love has come to the most unlikely pair. Next thing I know, Flo's gonna leave and marry that old codger."

"She could do worse," Lacey sniffed and flounced down on the blanket.

Blackie opened the box. "You got anything in here worth eatin'?"

She was immediately defensive. "I'll have you know, Mister, that I'm a pretty good cook. There's fried chicken and some really good cake."

"You want some?" He was gobbling greedily.

"Is there going to be any left when you get through?" She kept her voice cold.

"May I remind you that I paid a small fortune for this box? Some good food is the least I can expect." He looked surprised as he ate. "You're right, you're a fair cook; maybe almost as good as Moose."

"I'm the best cook you'll ever know."

He dug into the potato salad. "I hate to admit it, Miss Durango, but you may be right. What other hidden talents do you have?" He was positively leering at her.

"Nothing you're going to find out about." She reached over, grabbed a piece of fried chicken, and began to eat. "Who was that big drunken cowboy who was beating on the door of your saloon awhile ago?"

Blackie shrugged and wiped his mouth. "Some tough who's just passing through, I reckon, name of Snake Hudson. Seems to be a pretty bad hombre."

"Saloons attract that type," she sniffed.

"So do towns with prosperous banks," he reminded her. "Are you gonna get the ladies to picket the bank next?"

"Oh, shut up and eat. Let's get this over with."

"Tsk, tsk. I didn't think ladies ever told anyone to shut up."

"That's when they're dealing with gentlemen." In the dim light of the paper lanterns, she could see Blackie's profile. He really was a handsome devil, and when he smiled at her, his teeth seemed so white, framed by that full, sensual mouth. He reached for some homemade bread and their hands touched. His hand was strong and warm. She jerked hers back as if she'd touched a red-hot poker. He grinned at her as if he realized how upsetting his touch was. That rascal.

Across the crowd, Eugene looked at her, apparently upset and helpless as he ate with young Mable Lovejoy. Well, at least by making this sacrifice, maybe Lacey was protecting young Mable from this lecherous older gambler.

The banker stepped back up on the podium. "All right, folks, now that you've almost finished eatin', the band is gonna play a few numbers. You gentlemen who bought your lady's box now get a chance to cuddle her up out here as you dance with her."

Blackie wiped his mouth and smiled at Lacey. "Shall we?"

"You must be joking."

"I paid a twenty-dollar gold piece for supper and a dance," he reminded her as he reached over and caught her hand, pulling her to her feet.

"One dance is all you're going to get." Her tone was so icy, it should have frozen him, but he ignored it and pulled her out onto the new brick street.

"Now, sister, did I say I expected anything more? Besides, I might not want it even if it was offered."

She was livid, but she managed to control her temper. "I'm sure I couldn't compete with one of your whores."

"Does that mean you'd like to try?" He pulled her close against him and began to dance. It was a slow waltz.

"Outrageous." She tried to jerk away to put a little distance between them, but he was strong. He had her pulled tightly against him so that she could feel his lithe, muscular body all the way down hers. His big hand completely encompassed her small one. Lacey toyed with the idea of kicking him in the shins, decided she couldn't get enough distance between them to put any power behind the kick.

"Why don't you relax, sister?" he whispered against her ear. "Dancin' with you is like dancin' with a coiled steel spring."

He was too strong for her. There was nothing she could do now but relax against him, letting him mold her against his big frame, his mouth close to her ear as he hummed the soft tune the band played. He smelled like woodsy shaving lotion, tobacco, sunshine. She smiled in spite of herself and closed her eyes.

"Miss Lacey," Eugene hissed as he danced by, "everyone is looking."

She jerked up straight and glanced around. Nobody seemed to be looking but Eugene, who was steering the nubile Mable around the dance area like he was pushing a wagon. The Harvard man didn't dance any better than he rode a horse.

"Don't pay any attention to young Peabody," Blackie whispered. "He's just mad because you ain't dancin' with him."

"He's right." She was once more uptight and rigid, putting distance between herself and the gambler. "This is totally—"

"Outrageous," Blackie finished with a grin. "But Miss Durango, it's for a good cause."

The music stopped and she looked up at him. His mouth was full and sensual. She felt suddenly very feminine and helpless. She had a sudden feeling that he was going to kiss her, and of course, she must not allow that. It scared her to feel so vulnerable. Almost with regret, she pulled out of his arms. "All right, you've had your dance and your supper. I hope it gives you indigestion."

He let go of her with a smile. "I never thought I would say this, Miss Durango, but I'd say this evening was well worth what I paid."

"I hope you enjoyed it, because that's all you're geting." She flounced away with as much dignity as she could muster.

Blackie watched her go. Funny, he hadn't wanted to let her leave his arms. Somehow, under that Iron Corset image, there was a very soft and vulnerable woman. While he had danced with her, he'd had an almost uncontrollable urge to kiss that sweet, full mouth. He remembered with pleasure the other time he had kissed her. He was also certain that, again, she would have slapped him into next week.

Now Miss Iron Corset was talking to Eugene Peabody, who was looking daggers at Blackie. The shopkeeper took Lacey's arm and they walked away into the darkness.

Blackie sighed, annoyed with the Yankee upstart. Blackie had intended to walk her home. Maybe, just maybe, at her door, she might have let him kiss her.

Was he goin' loco? She'd have let out a squawk like an indignant hen with a coyote chasing it. Great God Almighty, he must be getting soft in the head. If he wanted kisses and more, Dixie and any of the other gals would be eager to offer. Somehow, that didn't appeal to him. He started walking back across the street to the saloon.

Flo caught up with him. "Wait up, Blackie, I got news."

"Oh?" he paused.

"Cookie asked me to marry him this fall."

Somehow, he'd known that was coming. "You gonna?"

She nodded. "He's a nice guy and I ain't gettin' any younger. I want you should give me away."

"I reckon I'm supposed to wish you well, Flo, and I do, but I hate to lose you."

"I'm lonely, Blackie, and tired of the way I live. You ought to be, too."

He patted her shoulder. "I am," he agreed. "But I ain't found nobody to share my dream, so I keep puttin' it off."

She gave him a warm smile. "Dreams are fragile, Blackie. Sometimes if you delay too long, you lose them."

He sighed and looked off toward the horizon. "Maybe you're right. I'm beginnin' to look at my own future, and I don't like what I see. So what if I build a bigger and better saloon? I'm downright tired of spendin' my evenings at a card table."

She reached up and kissed his cheek. "I always knew you was soft inside, Blackie."

"No, I ain't."

"I know better. Will you give away the bride, come maybe September or October?"

"Sure. And I'll dance at your weddin'."

Dixie joined them. "What's this about a wedding?"

"I'm getting married," Flo told her.

"To that old geezer?"

Flo scowled at her. "You should be lucky enough to find a real man who cares about you, you slut."

Dixie smiled at Blackie and winked. "How about it, Blackie? We could make that a double wedding."

Blackie coughed and shrugged. "Stop making jokes, Dixie. I'm just gonna give away the bride. You know no bit of calico will ever put a halter on me."

"I seen the way you was dancing with that lady newspaper woman," Dixie frowned. "You looked like she could put hobbles on you and make you like it."

Blackie laughed again. "I ain't lady-broke, this old stallion, Dixie, and you know it. I was just sweet-talkin' her, that's all, so I might get that corner lot we've been fussin' over."

"Ohh," Dixie nodded and linked her arm through Blackie's. "I might have knowed."

The three of them trooped off to the saloon.

Behind them, Lacey looked back over her shoulder as Eugene walked her home. The gambler, Flo, and that blonde tart were standing and talking in the street. There was laughter, and Dixie linked her arm familiarly through Blackie's. No doubt she was going to give him a little more dessert when they got upstairs at the Black Garter.

She was so busy looking behind her, she stubbed her toe and stumbled. Eugene caught her arm.

"Miss Lacey, look where you're walking," Eugene scolded, "you don't seem to be paying much attention."

"Uh, I was disconcerted from having to share a supper with that Blackie O'Neal tonight." She hoped Eugene couldn't see the blush going up her face.

"That was very sporting of you," Eugene said. "It must have been very distasteful and disgusting."

"Uh, yes, of course." In her mind, she was once again in Blackie's arms with his mouth close to her ear. Her mind stayed with that dance as Eugene talked on and on about the hardware business. They came to her door.

"Perhaps we might go for a stroll Monday night after supper," Eugene took both her hands in his.

"Mmmm." Lacey said, thinking about how damp and soft Eugene's hands were compared to Blackie's. Once again in her mind, she was in the gambler's embrace.

" . . . so if it's all right," Eugene said.

"What?" She jerked back to attention.

"Miss Lacey," he frowned, "I don't know where your mind is tonight. I just asked if I could kiss you!"

"My word, I—I don't think we know each other that well, Eugene," she gulped and hurried inside the newspaper office, closing the door in his face.

Eugene stared after her with a sigh. He was no fool. It was plain that she was fascinated and tempted by that rascal of a gambler, and that there was no way Eugene was going to end up with the beauty in his bed or as her husband, part owner of her profitable newspaper. A shame, too, since he understood she was related to the prosperous ranching Durango family which meant she probably was in for a nice inheritance. Eugene wasn't ready to give up yet. He had one more idea to sway the luscious Lacey back to viewing him with favor. She'd promised to stroll with him Monday night and he'd put his plan into action. If that didn't work, he already had another woman and another plan in mind. Whistling with satisfaction at his own cleverness, Eugene strolled away.

On Monday morning, Lacey didn't seem to be able to keep her mind on her work.

"Miss Lacey, what's wrong with you today?" Isaac asked.

"What?" She jerked to attention, realized she had been sitting in her office chair for an hour doing nothing but stroking Precious and staring out the window toward the saloon across the street while the kittens gamboled around her feet. "Oh, I—I was thinking about an editorial."

"Uh-huh. You've got a silly look on your face, sort of like a moon-sick calf."

"My word, Isaac, I'm just trying to collect my thoughts."

Eugene stuck his head in the front door, smiled. "I'll be by about eight."

"What?" Lacey blinked. She hadn't the slightest idea what he was talking about.

He frowned. "Remember? You promised to go for a walk tonight."

"Oh, certainly. I—I'll be ready." She managed a weak smile. Going for a moonlit walk with Eugene didn't seem

very exciting. He had almost kissed her last Saturday
night and she'd avoided it. It would certainly come up
again. She didn't know why she was hesitating; after all,
he was perfect husband material. "Run along now, I've
got to write an article about how much money the box
supper raised for our future library."

Eugene frowned. "That was something, you ending up
with the gambler. That must have been someone's idea
of a joke."

"Some joke. If he thinks he'll get on my good side by
paying so much for my box, that scoundrel is sadly mis-
taken."

"He's trying to charm you so you'll give up your claim
to that lot," Eugene reminded her. "And you being an innocent woman—"

"Eugene," she said, his male arrogance annoying her,
"I did not come in on a pumpkin wagon. I'm really quite
astute at business."

"Of course," he didn't sound as if he believed it. "Just
remember that lot is worth a lot of money."

"Yes, I realize that better than you. Now I've got work
to do, Eugene. I'll see you tonight." She dismissed him
and Eugene walked away down the street. Lacey sat
down and picked up her pen. LIBRARY FUND RAISER DRAWS
BIG CROWD, she wrote.

> The social and box supper was enjoyed by all and
> raised a large sum—uncounted as of yet. Miss
> Mable Lovejoy, who took charge of the money, will
> add up the sums.

She leaned back in her chair and sighed as she remembered. Of course Eugene was right. Blackie O'Neal
would do anything to charm her into giving up her
claim to that choice lot. Why, he might even attempt to
seduce her. She drew in a sharp breath at that daring
idea. Last Saturday night her defenses had been down,

and he could have easily waltzed her off into the darkness to the grassy shadows on the other side of the band stand in the park and kissed her. They might have sat down to talk on that grass and he might have kissed her again. She could imagine that big hand of his toying with the lace at the top of her bodice as he kissed her until she was breathless and trembling and ready to surrender. And maybe he would have put his lips close to hers and whispered . . .

"Did you get that order for ink refilled?" Isaac asked.

"What?" She blinked, pen halfway to her lips.

"I said, did you remember to order more ink for the press?" Isaac stood there, wiping his hands on his apron.

"Oh, no. You'd better take care of it."

"I don't know what's wrong with you lately," Isaac complained, "your mind seems to be a million miles away."

"I'm just so busy, that's all."

Isaac shrugged and returned to the back to set type.

"Meow?" Precious jumped up into her lap and she stroked the cat absently. "I can see how any female could be so tempted by a handsome rascal, she would give in," Lacey muttered, "but I don't want a bunch of kittens of my own."

"What?" Isaac called.

"My word, I was just talking to the cat," Lacey said, embarrassed.

Suppertime came and went. It was Monday evening and things were always slow across the street at the Black Garter on Monday. As Lacey waited for Eugene to arrive, she watched out the front window. There were only a few horses tied in front of the saloon, but music and laughter drifted across the street from the place. No doubt Blackie O'Neal was inside playing cards with his usual big tumbler of demon rum before him and a slut like Dixie sitting on the arm of his chair, running her hand familiarly across his shoulders. The thought set Lacey's teeth on edge.

Eugene arrived. He had brought her a small sack of cheap hard candy from the general store.

"Thank you, Eugene. You know, I'm really not in the mood to go for a walk."

"Don't be silly," he countered, taking a cinnamon ball and crunching it between his teeth. "A walk will do you good and it's a nice evening. There's hardly anyone out tonight."

"All right," she sighed. She took Eugene's arm, and he put the sack of candy in his other hand along with his cane. They went out the front of the newspaper office and strolled along the boardwalk down the block. All the businesses were closed except the saloon and there was almost no one on the street. They strolled along, looking in shop windows and talking. In the background faint music drifted from the saloon.

"Disgusting," Eugene declared, helping himself to another cinnamon ball. "Sooner or later, I'll have to give that gambler a good thrashing. Why, it was shocking how close he was holding you at the library social."

"Uh, Eugene, I don't think I'd try to take on Blackie O'Neal if I were you." She had a mental picture of the virile Texan wiping up the street with Eugene and tossing him into a horse trough, cinnamon balls and all.

"I know a lady such as yourself must find bloody fisticuffs upsetting," Eugene said as they walked, "but if he does anything like that again, be warned that I may just have to challenge him."

She had a vision of her perfect husband material floundering about in the horse trough. "Oh, please don't, Eugene." They strolled farther up the street and turned in front of the post office, headed back down the other side.

"When we get close to that terrible den of evil, Miss Lacey, we'd better cross the street," Eugene warned.

"Of course." At least in another block, she'd be back at the newspaper office and could plead a headache and go in, she thought.

It was a hot, moonless night and there was no one on the street at all now. Eugene crunched another cinnamon ball between his teeth. Lacey winced, it sounded like a squirrel cracking nuts. If he tried to kiss her, she would get that taste of cinnamon, and she wrinkled her face at the thought. Eugene was talking and talking and talking. Maybe she could walk a little faster and get this evening over with.

"Why are you hurrying so?" Eugene scolded. "I thought we might go to the little park behind the barber shop and talk awhile."

There he would definitely try to kiss her, cinnamon breath and all. The thought paralyzed her. "Uh, Eugene, I think I'm beginning to get a headache. Why don't we call it an evening?"

"Already?" He paused, put his cane over his arm and pulled out his pocket watch, peered at it in the darkness. "No, we can't go in yet."

"Why not? It's not as if we were waiting for anyone."

"Uh, well, I don't know, I just thought we were enjoying each other's company."

Lacey sighed. He glanced at his watch again.

"Eugene, is there somewhere you have to be?" She tried not to sound too hopeful.

"What makes you ask that?" He put the rest of the cinnamon balls in his pocket.

"Well, you just keep looking at your watch as if you were expecting someone."

Was that a look of guilt or just anxiety on his thin face? Down in front of the saloon, a big cowboy had just staggered out onto the wooden sidewalk. He turned and looked toward them.

Lacey felt a stab of apprehension as she recognized the big bully from Saturday night who had tried to kick in the saloon doors to get a drink. What had Blackie called him? Snake something. "Uh, Eugene, I think we'd better cross the street and avoid that brute's notice. He looks like he's drunk."

"You may be right, Miss Lacey, but never fear, I can protect you." He squared his thin shoulders and took her arm. They crossed the street and started back up the block. However, instead of mounting his horse and riding out of town, the big cowboy seemed to be staring at them.

"My word," Lacey muttered, "I think he's looking at us."

"Ignore him," Eugene said. "If we don't show any fear, he'll go on."

Instead, Snake swaggered across the street, walking toward them. "Hey, pretty lady."

"Uh-oh," Lacey stopped. "We're in for some trouble."

Eugene drew himself up proudly. "Never you fear, Miss Lacey. I won't let that brute bother you."

"Maybe we'd better start yelling for help," Lacey suggested. "The sheriff's office is around the corner and—"

"You yell for help and this big bruiser's friends may come out of that saloon to join him. I can whip one, but I'm not sure I could take on a bunch of drunken cowboys."

She glanced sideways at him. "Eugene, you're going to get yourself smashed flatter than a cow pie." She was very nervous now, watching the big cowboy stumbling toward them.

"Disgusting comparison," Eugene said, then to the approaching drunk. "See here, you brute, get out of the lady's way."

Snake stopped, swaying on his feet. He was ugly, with a bad scar that slashed across his dirty forehead. Even from where she was, she could smell the liquor on him. "Hey, pretty lady, you wanta go for a little ride with me?

I gotta horse." He gestured back toward the hitching rail.

"Outrageous!" Lacey snapped, "Get out of town before I yell for the sheriff."

Eugene stepped forward. "You drunken brute, you." He went into a fighter's stance. Somehow with Eugene, it looked ridiculous. "Step out of the lady's way now or I'll have to pummel you, and you'll regret it."

Lacey was certain Eugene would be the one to regret it. Maybe the saddle tramp was so drunk, he wouldn't want to take on her escort. "You heard Mr. Peabody, he'll wipe up the street with you."

Snake threw back his head and guffawed. "Hey, baby, come here and give me a little kiss." He grabbed her arm.

"See here, " Eugene stepped bravely forward, looking a bit like a ridiculous John L. Sullivan as he pranced around, his fists doubled up.

"I've changed my mind, dude," Snake grumbled and he pulled Lacey to him. "How about a kiss, baby?"

Eugene grabbed the cowboy, tried to spin him around. "All right, you asked for it." He threw a weak punch.

The cowboy laughed, doubled up his fist and hit Eugene in the nose, then he grabbed the struggling Lacey.

Eugene stumbled backwards, put his hand to his nose. "Blood. Blood! I've been hurt. Blood!" He was wailing as he turned and ran, stumbling in his haste.

"Eugene!" Lacey shrieked as she struggled. "Come back here! Don't leave me! Come back here!"

The big cowboy put his hand over her mouth and cut off her shriek. He grinned down at her as she struggled. "Honey, you're purtier than I remember. Let's you and me go off and have a little fun."

Her heart hammered in sheer terror as she struggled, but he picked her up like a doll, and began staggering toward the dark shadows of the little park behind the barber shop. There wasn't a soul on the street, and the only sound was Snake's labored breathing. He reeked of liquor, and the hand over her mouth tasted of sweaty dirt. She was really terrified now, knowing what awaited her when the drunken cowboy got her into the deserted shadows away from the street.

Chapter Eighteen

"Great God Almighty! What's that racket?" Inside his saloon, Blackie threw down his hand of cards, got up so fast he turned his chair over, and ran out the door. For a moment in the darkness, he saw nothing. Then, as his sharp eyes grew accustomed to the darkness, he saw just the barest hint of movement disappearing around the corner.

He didn't think, he acted. Someone was in serious trouble. He took off at a run, rounded the corner to see that big saddle tramp, Snake Hudson, fighting with some woman. He saw only the barest silhouette of her. As she half-turned, struggling in the moonlight, he recognized her. Lacey Durango.

"Snake, what the hell's going on out here?"

Lacey looked toward him, white-faced and scared in the moonlight, her blue dress torn. "Help! Please . . . !"

At that instant, Blackie gave no thought to danger, or the fact that the drunken cowboy was much taller and heavier than he was.

Lacey glanced up as she struggled, saw Blackie O'Neal silhouetted against the moonlight, and felt a great surge of relief. She screamed out for him, and he ran toward her, pulling her away so that she stumbled and fell in a heap. He grabbed Snake by the arm and spun him away. "You dirty bastard, that's no way to treat a lady!"

"She's mine!" Snake growled, as he charged Blackie. They went down in a tangle, rolling over and over around the park benches and against the band stand.

Blackie was on his feet now, his face dark with fury. Snake staggered to his feet. Blackie hit the big drunk hard, knocking him backward into a park bench that splintered and collapsed under him—but Snake came roaring back like an enraged bull.

What could she do to help? Lacey looked about for a tree limb or anything she might use for a weapon, but found nothing. She ran from the park back to the street. Then she spotted Eugene's cane lying abandoned, grabbed it up, and went charging into the fray.

Snake slapped her away. "Stay out of this, bitch!"

She went down, half stunned.

Blackie snarled as he hit the other man, knocking him end over end. "That's no way to behave with a lady, you trail trash!"

Blackie was outmatched, Lacey thought. She had to help him. She stumbled to her feet, grabbed the cane again, and began beating the cowboy about the shoulders even as Blackie landed a solid blow. The big drunk went down like a felled bull. Blackie stood over him, breathing heavily and wiping blood from his mouth. "Get out of town, you drunken bastard, before I beat you to death!"

With a gasping sob, Snake stumbled to his feet and ran for his horse. Blackie watched him go, breathing hard.

"Oh, Blackie, are you all right?" She ran to him, trying to hold back her tears.

He took her in his arms, holding her tightly against his big chest. "What the hell are you doing out at night alone?"

"I—I wasn't alone," she sobbed, "Eugene went for help."

"Then you might as well have been alone," he said softly and tilted her face up to his with one big hand. "Don't cry, sis, you're all right now."

It seemed so natural to close her eyes and tilt her face

up to his. His big hand cupped her chin as he kissed her gently. His mouth was warm and soft on hers. Without thinking, she opened her lips to his kiss as he pulled her tighter still, kissing her thoroughly. For a long moment, they clung together as she returned his kiss breathlessly. "Well, I'll be damned," he said. When she opened her eyes, he was looking down at her as if he'd never seen her before.

She blinked, amazed and speechless at the electricity that had just passed between them. She didn't want to leave his protective embrace. Lacey took a deep breath and very slowly pulled out of his arms.

"Sister, are you all right?"

She nodded, too emotional to speak. After a moment, she managed to say, "Thank you. There's no telling what would have happened if you hadn't come—"

"I know what would have happened." His voice was as grim as his face.

They heard the sounds of a running horse as Snake galloped out of town. Curious townspeople, attracted by the fight, were coming out of buildings to stand and gape. About that time, Eugene came around the corner, accompanied by the sheriff. "I'm here, Miss Lacey, I brought help."

Blackie snorted. "You're a little late, Peabody. Only a gutless wonder would run away and leave a lady to deal with that big drunk."

"I didn't run away," Eugene defended himself. "I went for help."

"Uh-huh." Blackie said.

"Who was that?" the sheriff asked.

Eugene spoke first, "That disgusting drifter, Snake Hudson."

Lacey looked at him, a question in her mind. "How'd you know who it was?"

"Well," Eugene hesitated, "I remember seeing him at the box supper. Are you all right, Miss Lacey?"

"Of course she's all right," Blackie snapped. "No thanks to you."

"Eugene was going for help," she defended her escort because she was embarrassed for him. She abruptly realized she was now beholden to the charming gambler for saving her twice, and that didn't sit too well. "Never mind, Eugene, I know you were doing your best."

"Ha! He ran off like a coyote with its tail on fire." Blackie snorted. "Leavin' the lady to fend for herself."

There was a growing crowd gathering and they laughed.

She felt embarrassed for Eugene. She took his arm. "I'm sorry, but I broke your walking stick."

He picked it up, crestfallen. "That was a fine, imported cane."

Blackie wiped blood from his lip. "I'd like to take that cane, Eugene, and stick it up your—"

"My word," Lacey snapped, "can't you ever act like a gentleman? I was dealing with the situation and didn't ask you to interfere."

Blackie raised one cynical eyebrow as he lit a cigar. In the light, she could see how bruised and bloody his rugged face was. "Listen, sis, after Eugene here abandoned you, if I hadn't interfered, that big drunk was just about to rip all your clothes off and—"

"And if he hadn't been drunk on liquor from your saloon, this whole thing might not have happened."

"Sister, with you, I can't win, can I?"

Eugene examined his shattered cane, evidently distressed at the damage. "I would have arrived in time to save her."

"Don't know about that, Mr. Peabody," the old sheriff sighed. "That Snake Hudson is a bad hombre. He killed a couple of men, I hear."

Blackie nodded. "He's hightailed it out of town. With girls in every saloon, don't know why he got it in his head to go after Miss Durango."

The sheriff took off his Stetson and scratched his head. "Don't seem too smart, does it?"

Lacey looked at Blackie, annoyed. "Do you find it so impossible to believe he was attracted to me?"

Blackie looked up her up and down slowly in a way that sent shivers up her back. "Not at all, sister."

Eugene drew himself up. "Sheriff, have you any more questions for the young lady? If not, I'll walk her home."

The sheriff shook his head. "I'll just be on the lookout for Snake, but knowing Blackie, I reckon he gave him such a beatin', he won't be coming back to this town any time soon. Now, you folks break it up. Show's over." He gestured for the crowd to disperse.

"Come, Miss Lacey." Eugene offered her his arm and she took it. Turning to go, she hesitated, and turned back to Blackie. "I'm much obliged," she said, thanking him in the Texas manner.

He smiled at her in a way that pulled at her heart and made her feel slightly giddy. "You're welcome, Miss Durango."

She and Eugene walked away.

Eugene said, "Are you all right? I really was coming back, I just realized he was so big, I couldn't—"

"That's all right, Eugene," she assured him, "I knew you had gone for help." *Had he, or was he running to save his own hide? One thing was certain, if Blackie O'Neal hadn't showed up, something terrible would have happened.* She shuddered, imagining that big brute tearing her clothes off and throwing her down on the grass of the small park.

"It just seems very strange," Eugene muttered.

"What?"

"That big brute came out of the Black Garter and attacked you when there were willing girls at the saloon."

"That's what Blackie said."

"Aha!" Eugene paused and looked at her. "Has it occurred to you that that sleazy saloon gambler might have set this whole thing up?"

"What?" she blinked. "Why would he——?"

"If he supposedly came to your rescue, you'd feel kindly toward him."

"I reckon I do," she said.

"And if you felt kindly toward him as the big hero, you might give in and let him have that choice lot."

"What?" She paused and let his words sink in as she looked up into Eugene's triumphant face. "It never occurred to me——"

"Of course not. Being a helpless female, you'd feel like a knight in shining armor had come to your rescue and you'd give him anything he wanted."

Anything he wanted. For just a moment, she remembered Blackie's lips on hers and the emotions that had overpowered her. "Surely he wouldn't stoop to that."

"Oh, you think not? He pretends to fight the big oaf so he'll look like your rescuer. He's pretty clever."

The logic of it overpowered her as reality crashed down. "I reckon you might be right, Eugene."

"*Might* be?" He snorted. "What a charade that slick rascal put on. Disgusting."

She suddenly wanted to cry. "I—I'm ready to go home, Eugene, it's been a terrifying night for me."

"Certainly, my dear." He patted her hand. "Remember, I did bring the sheriff. I was going to rescue you myself."

She didn't say anything else as Eugene walked her home. Yes, it did make sense that Blackie would do that, do anything to soften her since he wasn't making any headway on getting that land. On the other hand, the blows and the blood had seemed very real. She went inside, closed the door, and locked it. She sat down at the desk, tears starting to her eyes.

"Meow?" Precious jumped into her lap and in the darkness, she felt the kittens gamboling around her feet.

Lacey hugged the cat to her. "I almost fell for a charming rascal just like you did," she sobbed against the cat's

fur. "I reckon Eugene is right—that gambler's just trying
to fool me into signing over that lot."

Her heart didn't want to believe it. She went to bed
but couldn't sleep. Over and over in her mind, she re-
lived the terror of the drunken brute grabbing her and
tearing at her clothes, then watching Blackie fight him.
She took a deep shaky breath, remembering the feeling
of that protective embrace. What a villain, to scare her
and take advantage of her that way. She couldn't sleep.
She got up, lit the lamp, got a robe and went downstairs
to sit at her desk. Pretty Prairie Needs More Street
Lights to Combat Crime, she wrote.

> This editor was recently manhandled by a rough
> drunk coming out of the Black Garter. The town
> needs more street lights, more law enforcement,
> and fewer saloons where drunks get full of cheap
> red-eye and then go out and attack innocent citi-
> zens.

The next day Eugene hurried through the door of the
newspaper. "I left Uncle in charge so I could come by. I
wanted to see if you were all right."

Somehow, she didn't want to talk to Eugene this
morning. "I'm fine, a little sore, and the dress will need
repairs, but I'm all right. I'm very busy working on the
paper, Eugene." Somehow, she didn't want to give a lot
of thought as to whether he'd actually been going for
help or had fled like a cowardly cur.

"All right, then, do you want to do anything tonight?
We could play checkers."

Playing checkers with Eugene sounded like as much
fun as getting her teeth pulled. "I don't think so, I've got
a lot to do. Why don't you just pick me up for church
Sunday morning?"

"Fine. But I can't bear to go almost a week without
seeing you."

"Well, I'm very busy this week." Her perfect man was becoming annoying.

As Eugene was about to leave, the Reverend Lovejoy and his daughter stopped by the newspaper office. "Young lady, I heard you had a bad scare last night. Heard that O'Neal fellow was quite a hero."

Eugene snorted. "Some of us have our doubts about that. Myself, I was going for the sheriff and supposedly, that saloon owner came running. Mighty convenient, if you ask me."

The reverend looked puzzled, but Mable sighed and smiled at Eugene. "I just knew what everyone says wasn't true."

"Uh, Mable," her father cautioned.

"What are they saying?" Eugene demanded.

Lacey stepped into the awkward situation. "Yes, Mister Peabody did what any sensible man would have done, he went for help. I'm writing it up now for the next edition."

"Oh, by the way," the preacher said, pushing his gold-rimmed glasses back up his thin nose, "here's another story for you: the stained glass window is due to be delivered tomorrow. We'll have a special ceremony at the service on Sunday."

Lacey smiled. "That's wonderful. Have we got enough to pay for it?"

He nodded. "Thanks to our kind benefactor."

Eugene winked at her. Eugene, the kind benefactor, Lacey thought with a smile, how generous he was.

"In fact," said the minister, "I've been a little nervous about us holding all that money along with the box supper money. I reckon I should put it in the bank."

"Is that a good idea?" Lacey asked, "I mean, keeping that much money in your house?"

"I've got a small safe at the house," the minister said, "and no one but me and little Mable here know the combination, so it'll be safe enough."

Eugene cleared his throat. "Are you sure, Reverend?

If there's any doubt, I've got a gun, I could come stand guard all night—"

"I don't think it will be necessary," Reverend Lovejoy assured him.

Lacey had a feeling Eugene with a gun would be more danger to himself than to a robber, but she kept quiet.

"Never can tell what kind of villains are lurking about," Eugene said sternly. "If you change your mind, just let me know. I'm a fair shot."

Lacey suspected he couldn't hit the side of the barn with a scattergun, but she didn't say so.

Mable looked up at Eugene and smiled. "You're so brave; just like Sir Lancelot."

The Reverend cleared his throat. "Come along, Mable. I've got to write a special sermon. The window is magnificent, and being shipped all the way from Kansas City on the train."

"I can hardly wait to see it," Lacey said. "All that's lacking now to be a real town is a public library, but that will come."

"Well, we'd better go," the older man said. "Come along, Mable."

"I've got to go, too," Eugene said, "Store's real busy. Toodle-loo." He turned and strolled down the street.

Lacey watched the three of them walk away. *Toodle-loo.* There was something silly about a man saying that. In Texas, real men didn't speak much, they went into action. That made her think of a certain charming gambler and the way he'd handled himself in that fight last night. All for her benefit. What an actor. What a rotten rascal.

Across the street, traffic was already picking up at the Black Garter. A half dozen horses were tied up at the hitching rail and music blared through the swinging doors. A typical night at the saloon. Blackie ought to be very happy. Why, he had almost had her fooled into thinking he really was a heroic guy instead of a schemer who would do anything to get what he wanted. Life with him would be one hectic adventure after another while life with Eugene would be a perfect picture of domestic tranquility; very safe and predictable. And very dull, she thought with despair. What was wrong with her? Was she no smarter than her cat?

The rest of the week, she busied herself with her work and ladies' meetings. When Eugene wanted to call on her, she had begged off, telling him how busy and tired she was. He told her she should get fresh air and eat more bran. She sighed at the thought. Blackie O'Neal probably ate plenty of rare steak and didn't know what bran was.

Again it was Saturday night and the racket from the saloon across the street was appalling. She washed her hair, got a good book and went to bed. Alone. Of course alone, she scolded herself, she was a perfectly respectable girl. Her grandfather would be proud of her, maybe. In the meantime, the music and singing from the Black Garter grew increasingly louder. Women laughed and sang. In her mind, she again saw that blonde, Dixie, lounging on the arm of Blackie's chair while he played poker. The girl ran her hand familiarly across the broad shoulders and massaged his neck. Somehow, the image annoyed Lacey. The music grew louder as the night wore on. Lacey finally had to put a pillow over her head to drown out the piano playing "Camptown Races." She'd grown to hate Stephen Foster in the last few weeks. *Doodah. Doodah. Damn it.*

It was a indeed a busy Saturday night in the Black Garter: cowboys laughing and slapping pretty girls on their backsides, the piano playing loudly if not too well, Moose at the bar serving thirsty customers. Blackie sat at a poker table, shuffling a deck. A movement near the back door caught his eye. "Boys, play this hand without me."

He tossed in his hand and stood up, pushed his way through the crowds to the shadows near the back door. He reached out and grabbed Eugene Peabody by the arm as the man started up the back stairs.

"I thought I told you to stay out of my place since I caught you cheatin' at cards?"

Eugene grinned nervously, trying to pull away. "Take it easy, O'Neal, I was just headed upstairs to have a little fun with Dixie—"

"Does Miss Durango know you come in here?" Blackie scowled at him.

"Of course not," Eugene straightened his plaid jacket, grinned. "That's something you don't tell a lady."

"I might tell her, you low-life skunk."

"She'd never believe you," Eugene said. "She thinks you're a rascal, and I'm an upstanding citizen."

"You're probably right," Blackie admitted, "she always thinks the worst about me. By the way, I've had time to think about Snake Hudson—"

"What about him?" Eugene avoided his glare. "I was bringing help—"

"That's not what I mean," Blackie said. "I saw you talkin' to Snake the other night when you were both in here, and I've been puttin' two and two together."

"You can't prove anything." Eugene backed away.

"Maybe not, but it got me to thinkin' that there was no better way to impress a lady than savin' her from a villain. Only it didn't go accordin' to plan, did it?"

"He hit me!" Eugene said. "Made my nose bleed. Snake got drunk and changed the plan."

Blackie reached out and caught him by the lapel. "That girl almost got hurt because of your connivin' to look like a hero. If I hadn't heard the noise and come outside—"

"She'll never believe you if you tell her," Eugene pulled out of his grasp and backed away.

"I reckon not," Blackie growled. "But sooner or later, she'll find out what a rat you are. Why, you'd steal the butter off a sick beggar's biscuit or the milk out of a baby calf's bucket. Now get the hell out and don't you ever come back or I'll beat you like cornbread batter."

"I'll tell the sheriff on you!" Eugene backed away.

"You do that, but by that time, you'll be picking up those pretty teeth off the floor and I mean it, Peabody. Also I want you to stay away from Lacey Durango, you're not near good enough for her."

"And I suppose you are?"

"Me?" Blackie touched his silk vest, "Why, she wouldn't spit on me to put me out if I was on fire. She's lookin' for a perfect gentleman."

"That newspaper business must be worth some money," Eugene said, "and her family owns a big ranch. Suppose I'm not willing to walk away from a chance like that?"

Blackie gave him a look that would freeze a rattler in its tracks. "Then I'll tear you apart so that God can't find enough pieces to put you back together again."

"All right, all right, I'm going," Eugene backed away, turned and fled out the back door.

Blackie stood glaring after him. "Damned hypocrite, and her too naive and innocent to see him for what he is."

"Well, Blackie," Dixie said behind him, "it ain't like you to run off a payin' customer."

Blackie shrugged. "He's a jackass."

She shook her head. "That ain't it and you know it."

He turned to go back to the poker table. "Don't think so much, Dixie."

She caught his arm. "It's that damned newspaper woman; you got a thing for her."

He tried to brush her off. "Are you loco, Dixie? That bossy damnyankee gal's been nothin' but a fly in my buttermilk since the first time I saw her."

"Then come on upstairs with me," she smiled up at him, "I could make you real happy."

"Forget it, Dixie, I ain't in the mood."

She pouted. "You ain't never been in the mood since the day you met her. What's she got that I ain't?"

"Hell, I don't know. She's just Texas stubborn and independent like me, I reckon. I'd like to turn her across my knee and whip her little butt, but she'd probably bite me on the leg while I was doin' it."

"You ain't never gonna bed her, Blackie, because you run a saloon and she hates liquor."

"I won't always run a bar," Blackie said, "I got plans."

"I do too, Blackie," she said softly and her blue eyes got dewy and moist as she slipped her arms around his neck. "You and me, we could go places together. I'm smart and ambitious. We could go to Kansas City or maybe San Francisco and open a big gambling palace."

He shook his head and reached to disengage her arms. "What dreams I got don't include you or a big city, Dixie. The dreams I got include Texas."

"You Texans," she sneered, "you think heaven's in the Lone Star state. Okay, we could try San Antone or Dallas—"

"No," he shook his head. "No city, no gamblin' halls."

"And no Dixie," she said in a whisper.

He looked at her a long moment, reached to wipe a tear from her smudged, kohled eyes. "And no Dixie," he agreed, then turned and walked back to the poker table.

Dixie watched him go. Yes, he was stuck on that damned newspaper woman. The only way Dixie might ever have a chance with him was to get rid of that uppity girl. Then Dixie might have a chance with Blackie. No matter what he said, she could imagine the good life in a big city with fine clothes and plenty of jewelry, a fancy gambling palace. Yes, she'd bring him around to her way of thinking as soon as she figured out a way to run Miss High-and-Mighty Durango out of town.

The gunsmith staggered toward her, more than a little drunk. "How about it, Ma'am, go upstairs?"

She could use the money, and maybe she could steal his wallet without Blackie finding out about it. She looked longingly toward the gambler, but he was already back at the poker table, shuffling cards. She forced herself to smile as she took the gunsmith's arm. "Sure, handsome, why not?" She didn't look back as they stumbled up the stairs.

The next morning, Lacey got up and reluctantly dressed for church. It would be nice to see the beautiful new stained glass window, but somehow, she wasn't looking forward to attending with Eugene. Of course that rascal across the street never went to church, although she had to concede that he did close his saloon on Sundays.

She fed Precious and the yellow kittens, then went to the door and looked out. Eugene was late. Well, maybe he'd had trouble getting the horse harnessed. Eugene wasn't too good with horses. She saw Reverend Lovejoy pass by, almost running the opposite direction from the church. In minutes, the sheriff was walking back with him.

What on earth was happening? Along the street, people were stopping to gather in small groups, talking. Then old Mr. Peabody walked up and joined the reverend and the sheriff in animated conversation. Eugene had still not shown up.

Finally her curiosity could take no more. Lacey went out to join the excited little knot of people standing on the street around the reverend. There was an excited buzz of conversation. Lacey said, "What has happened?"

Reverend Lovejoy looked both distraught and embarrassed. "It—it's Mable, Miss Durango, she left a note. She's run off and taken the money."

"What?" Lacey said. "My word, what on earth—?"

"Worse than that," the sheriff announced, "she's run off with a man!"

She had a sudden memory of Blackie O'Neal and his mysterious trips out in the country with that buggy. Surely he wasn't enough of a villain to run away with the church's funds and a young girl. *Or was he?*

Chapter Nineteen

Blackie, a tall, cool drink in his hand and followed by his dog, strolled up to join the crowd. Lacey let out a breath of relief and felt sudden guilt. So he wasn't the one who had run off with Mable.

Mr. Peabody hurried to join them. The sheriff took off his hat and scratched his head. "John, I'm sorry to tell you that your nephew seems to have run off with Mable Lovejoy."

"Eugene?" Lacey gasped.

Old Mr. Peabody nodded. "And that ain't all, sheriff. The young rascal cleaned out my cash register late last night, too. I reckon that's what I get for trying to help my brother out when Eugene got in trouble back home."

Lacey blinked. "Trouble? My word, I wouldn't think a Harvard graduate—"

"Harvard graduate? He tell you that?" Mr. Peabody shook his head. "He ain't ever been out of Iowa until he come here. I think he's been embezzlin' money from the store from the start."

She thought of Eugene's fine clothes and his righteous indignation. "I—I can't believe it. He was such a perfect gentleman."

Blackie grinned. "And you bein' such a good judge of character, too. Why, weren't you thinkin' of marryin' young Peabody?"

All the men looked at her. She wanted to kick Blackie in the shins for bringing up her relationship with

Eugene. "He called on me a few times, that's about it."
She looked at Reverend Lovejoy. "How will we pay for
the stained glass window now? We only paid a deposit
and the company said we could pay the rest when it was
delivered."

The preacher pushed his gold-rimmed spectacles up
his thin nose. "Maybe they'll get caught before they
spend the money. My poor Mable is so innocent, so easily led astray. Her mother was wild, though. I reckon
Mable's headed for a strict girls' school when we catch
her."

The sheriff took off his Stetson and scratched his
head. "With the money gone, I reckon we'll have to return that fancy window."

Blackie sipped his drink. "If everyone put in a little, we
might be able to do it."

Lacey curled her lip in disgust. "Don't tell me a saloon
owner would donate to buy stained glass for a church?"

Blackie only smiled at her. "You're very judgmental,
Miss Durango, or has someone already told you that?"

"I'll donate a hundred dollars," Lacey said, "To get the
ball rolling."

"Hold up. Maybe nobody will have to donate nothin',
if we catch them." said the sheriff. "I've already wired the
law along the Kansas and Texas borders to be on the
lookout for the pair. We can't do much more than that."

The preacher nodded. "I just can't understand how a
sweet, innocent girl like my Mable could be duped."

Blackie looked at Lacey and winked. "I imagine
Eugene can be pretty charmin'. Certainly, he fooled a lot
of women who should have known better."

She had a terrible urge to yank one of the bricks out
of the new street and hit him with it, but decided the
sheriff would arrest her. "Reverend Lovejoy, who's going
to preach this morning?"

He shook his head. "I—I'm not really up to it. Maybe

the assistant pastor can take over for today. Mr. O'Neal, can we talk?"

The two men turned and walked away, talking earnestly. "My word," Lacey said to the sheriff and Mr. Peabody, "I can't imagine what that pair would have to talk about."

"Don't know," said Mr. Peabody, shaking his head. "I reckon I'd better get back to the store and begin checking my books for even more loss. Eugene was in the same trouble back in Iowa. This time, he'll most likely go to jail."

Everyone turned and left the street.

Lacey was almost kicking herself. How could she have been so wrong about Eugene? And if she had been, could she have been wrong about other people? She turned and watched Blackie and his dog walking along with the preacher. Naw, not a chance. Once a rascal, always a rascal.

The next day, word came over the telegraph that Eugene and Mable had been apprehended at the Kansas line and most of the money had been recovered. Eugene would be heading to prison, and young Mable was to be sent to a strict girls' school.

The stained glass window was paid for and installed behind the pulpit that very week. The next Sunday, Lacey sat with the congrgation and admired it. Everyone in the church commented about its beauty.

After the service, Lacey said to Reverend Lovejoy, "The scene is so beautiful, and not at all like most church windows. Why, that brown and green prairie stretching as if for eternity and the sun setting all red and gold behind those hills is breathtaking. It gives you a feeling of serenity and peace. It's perfect for Pretty Prairie. Only a truly sensitive artist could have captured that emotion."

Reverend Lovejoy hesitated as if about to say something. Finally he said, "It is beautiful, isn't it? God moves in mysterious ways his wonders to perform."

"I'll write a nice article in my paper about it," Lacey said. "Everyone in town is wondering who the anonymous donor was. Are you sure you don't want to reveal that so I can give him some publicity?"

The man shook his head. "Sorry. He doesn't want any. That must always be a secret between me, him, and the Lord."

"Once I had thought it was Eugene Peabody. I had no idea he was such a scoundrel."

The preacher took out a hankie, took off his eyeglasses and wiped them. "It's difficult knowing what's in a man's heart. Maybe we all judge without knowing enough."

"Anyway, it's beautiful," Lacey said. "Everyone is coming from miles around to take a look."

"Let's just hope they come inside the church for the services," Reverend Lovejoy said. "That will make it worthwhile."

Lacey put out her paper later that week and as usual, she and Isaac went about town at night putting the papers in front of stores, then emptying the honesty boxes.

The next morning, people came into the office. "Miss Durango, the paper must have sold out. I didn't get one."

"That's unusual," she smiled, "but good news for me. Maybe there's some down in front of the barber shop."

About that time, the barber came in. "You got extra papers, Miss Lacey? There don't seem to be any in front of my place."

Lacey was puzzled. "My word, we must have really had a run on them. Isaac, go empty the honesty boxes and redistribute some of the papers from other locations. They can't have all sold out."

In a few minutes, Isaac was back. "Miss Lacey, there

doesn't seem to be a paper anywhere and no money either."

"What?" Was someone who disliked her playing a prank? "We'll reprint, Isaac, and put them out again. It's probably just children larking around."

However, the next batch of papers disappeared, too, and again, there was no money in the boxes.

"Miss Lacey," Isaac shook his head as he delivered the news, "this can't keep up or you'll be broke and unable to buy more supplies. You'd have to pack up and leave town."

She sighed. "Start another issue, Isaac, and let me give this some thought." She went to the front window and stared out. Blackie came out of his saloon, followed by Lively. As usual, the man had a tall drink in his hand. "That drunk," she muttered, "is a disgrace to the town. Now who would like to bankrupt me and run me out?"

Of course. It was as plain as long ears on a mule. The only person who had been at odds with her all these weeks was that scandalous saloon owner. "Blackie O'Neal," she muttered, "I can't accuse you yet, but when I get some evidence, I'm going to file charges. We'll see who runs who out of this town."

Thursday night, she tried to stay awake and watch some of the boxes of papers from her front window, but she dozed off and again in the morning, they were gone. "Isaac, I'm going to do a little detective work."

"Why don't you just file a complaint with the sheriff and let him investigate, yes?" Isaac suggested.

"I told him about it and he said he'd get around to it sometime. With a Westerner, that means between next week and never. By then, I'll be broke. I've got to handle this myself. I'm certain Blackie O'Neal is behind this."

"He might be a rascal," Isaac agreed, "but he's fair, yes? I don't think he'd stoop to something like this."

"Ha! I think he'd stoop to anything to get that lot, and what better way than to bankrupt me?"

She waited until almost dark and then went snooping along the alley behind the saloon. If Blackie was taking hundreds of papers, what could he be doing with them? They'd be a big thing to hide.

Cookie's Kitchen seemed to be doing a landslide Friday night business, judging from the noise inside. The big yellow tom sat atop a garbage can licking his fur. "You rascal, you've seduced my fancy darling."

The cat almost seemed to grin at her. He had the same expression she'd seen on Blackie O'Neal's face. Well, Lacey wasn't as easy to persuade as Precious.

There was a big trash bin behind the saloon. She managed to lift the lid and peer inside. "Outrageous!"

Just as she'd suspected, the bin was full of copies of *The Pretty Prairie Crusader*. Her indignation knew no bounds. Grabbing up an armful of them, she marched through the backdoor of the saloon and into Blackie's office, threw them down on his desk before him.

He looked up, as startled as his dog. "What the hell—?"

She was seething as she stood arms akimbo, glaring at him. "This is a new low, even for you."

The dog raised its head, then crept under the desk.

Blackie leaned back in his chair and smiled. "Please Miss Durango, do tell me what you're so outraged about and why did you bring me all those papers? I can only read one at a time."

"You rascal! You thief! How could you have been stealing all my papers?"

"What? Great God Almighty, sister, surely you don't think—?"

"Aha! Don't play innocent with me. Someone has been stealing all my newspapers and emptying the honesty boxes. You were the only person I could think of who would be dishonest enough to steal from an honesty box."

He stood up. "Sister, I don't know what this is all

about, but you must have a pretty low opinion of me to think I'd stoop to that."

"Low? Why a snake couldn't crawl under you. If you didn't do it, why are there hundreds of my papers in your trash?"

He looked both baffled and annoyed at her onslaught. "I'm sure I wouldn't know, Miss Durango, but maybe I could help you get to the bottom of this—"

"Outrageous! That'd be like letting the fox help investigate who was stealing chickens out of the hen coop. I'm going to prefer charges, Mr. O'Neal and you're not going to be able to talk your way out of it. I'm on to you, sir, and . . . " She paused, staring at the painting hanging on the wall behind him. It was a beautiful serene painting of a prairie with all its brown and greens and a breathtaking red and gold sunset behind it. "Oh my Lord, this is blasphemous. You've had Chief Thunder copy the stained glass window from the church."

"But I—"

"Copying the church's window to hang in a saloon! That is the most terrible thing I ever heard of, even worse than trying to run me out of business by stealing the papers."

He took a deep breath and looked weary. "You think I'd stoop to either?"

"Of course I do. Do you have nothing to say in your own defense?"

He hesitated. "If I told you, would you believe me?"

"Of course not."

"Then I'll just keep quiet, Miss Durango, and you can think what you will."

"The whole town will hear of this," she threatened.

"Miss Durango," and now his voice thundered, "If you slander me, I might sue you. As for the painting . . . "

"Well?"

"Never mind. Think what you will."

"Outrageous!" She stormed out of his office, out the back door and down the alley. She returned to her place and paced up and down. Tomorrow, she would report everything she knew to the sheriff. *We'll see who runs who out of town,* she promised herself. She was seething with righteous indignation, yet inside was a deep sadness. She had thought Eugene was perfect and he had turned out to be a crook. She had known Blackie O'Neal was a rascal, but she hadn't thought anyone could sink this low.

Blackie stood staring after the girl as she left. Then with a deep sigh, he flopped down in his chair and stared at the untidy pile of newspapers on his desk. "Lively, she hates me—really hates me."

The dog thumped its tail and looked up at its master.

Dixie sauntered into his office. "Well, what was that all about?" she drawled. "I thought I heard Miss High-and-Mighty in here raisin' a little hell."

"More than a little," Blackie conceded and then slowly lit a cigar. "She's found some of her missin' papers in the trash behind my saloon and jumped to the conclusion that I've been stealin' them."

Dixie laughed and sat down on the edge of his desk. "So, did ya?"

He shook his head. "I'd like to run her out of town, all right, but I figure I've got to play fair."

"Play fair? Naw! That ain't the way to win, Blackie. You must be gettin' soft."

"Maybe I am," he said after a long moment. "She's been nothin' but trouble since the first time I laid eyes on her. But on the other hand, I have to admire her for tryin' to make it in a man's world."

Dixie laughed uneasily. "Watch it, Blackie, she's beginnin' to melt you."

Blackie stared at her a long moment, thinking as he

smoked his cigar. "Now even if I did steal the papers, which I didn't, I wouldn't be stupid enough to leave a bunch of them in the trash behind my place where she might find them. I'm thinking someone wanted her to find them so she'd hate me more than ever."

Dixie got up off the desk, avoiding his gaze. "You think too much, Blackie. You know she blames you for that attack by Snake Hudson, too. Eugene said so."

He looked at her. "What do you know about Snake?"

"Only that he bragged to me that Eugene Peabody put him up to that so Eugene could look like a hero. Only Snake got the hots for the girl, and being drunk, he forgot his original deal and went after her for real."

"I suspected as much, but couldn't prove it. That rotten—!" Blackie cursed.

"Honey, we ought to clear out of this one-horse town, go on to some bigger place. You know I got a yen for you."

He didn't answer for a long moment. "Now who would have reason to make her hate me?"

"Lots of people, I reckon," Dixie didn't look at him. "Well, I got to go. It's time for me to sing—"

Blackie tossed his cigar into the spittoon and stood up, grabbed her arm as she started to leave. "Dixie?"

"It wasn't me," she stammered, "it wasn't!" She began to cry. Her heavily painted eyes left dark, crooked smears as the tears ran down her pretty face.

"Dixie?"

"All right." She threw her arms around his neck, still sobbing. "I seen how you're lookin' at her, seen how she's beginnin' to look at you. I love you, Blackie, and we're two of a kind. You don't need no fancy, high-toned, educated girl who wouldn't spit on you to put out the flames if you was on fire. We belong together."

Before he could react, she pulled his face down to her tear-stained one and kissed him passionately.

He pulled away from her, reached up and unclasped

her hands, scowling. "Dixie, this is just too much. I'm gonna have to fire you."

"What? It won't do any good!" she snarled. "She ain't gonna believe you didn't do it. You ain't ever gonna get to be respectable in Miss Iron Corset's eyes."

"Don't call her that." Blackie snapped.

Her eyes widened in disbelief. "You've changed, Blackie. You're the one who started that nickname. It's funny, you know that? You ain't guilty of nothin', but she'll never believe it."

He was struggling to control his temper although he knew Dixie was right. Lacey Durango would never trust him, no matter how much he denied and protested. He had always won every battle he had gotten into . . . until he had gotten into a contest of wills with Lacey Durango. He stared at the cheap, defiant tart before him. He was sick of her, sick of this whole scene. "Dixie, you're fired. Have Moose pay you off and be out of here by tomorrow."

Sobbing, she turned and fled. Blackie stood glaring after her.

"Well," Flo stuck her head around the door, "that was quite a scene."

"How much of it did you hear?"

"Everything."

"Then keep your mouth shut. I wouldn't like anyone thinkin' Blackie O'Neal had gone soft."

The middle-aged woman smiled gently. "Some think a little softness to a man is good."

He cursed under his breath. "Not in the world I live in. There's no room for softness in the saloon business." He frowned at her. "What are you doing over here anyhow?"

"Cookie fixed some barbecue and I know how you love it, so I brought you a plate."

"I'm not hungry." He picked up the newspapers off his desk and threw them on the floor.

"Uh-huh." She put the plate on his desk anyhow. "We've known each other a long time, Blackie, and I always felt like your mama. I also heard some of the commotion between you and Lacey over the paintin'. Why didn't you tell her?"

Blackie shook his head. "She wouldn't have believed that, either. And by God, I don't owe her any explanations."

"She'll ruin you in her newspaper. Newspapers are powerful. She could end up having you run out of town."

"I can't help that."

"Yes, you could. All you'd have to do is tell her the truth, all the things she don't know about you."

He sat down at his desk. "She'd laugh. She'd think I was a fool, that I was soft."

She paused in the doorway. "If you don't do something, she'll smear you so bad, you'll have to leave town. It ain't like you to give up and yell 'calf rope.'"

"I ain't givin' up. I got a few tricks up my sleeve, too, and maybe I'll use them. Now get the hell out of here!" Blackie made an angry gesture.

"If you destroy her, you may go down, too."

"I've about had enough of that high-and-mighty judgmental dame. When it comes to a fight, nobody can get more down and dirty than Blackie O'Neal. Ain't I proved that in a dozen Texas towns?"

Flo's lined face softened. "Like I said, Blackie, you ought to tell her the truth. I think she might listen."

"Naw, she ain't gonna change her mind." He shook his head. "She wouldn't believe me, no matter what I said, so I ain't gonna lower myself by tryin'."

"You're a proud man, Blackie, maybe too proud."

"It's a tough world, Flo, and only the toughest survive. I ought to know, considering my upbringin'. She's got education and money and a good family."

"Sometimes there's other things that count for more."

"Go on back over to the cafe, Flo. I've had a bellyful of Miss Lacey Durango's sanctimonious ways. Now I'm really gonna figure out a way to run her out of town."

Flo shrugged and started out the door, then paused. "Blackie, if you do that, you'll hate yourself."

He grinned at her. "But I'll have won, won't I?"

"That's for you to decide. Maybe you'll win the battle and lose the war."

"Winnin' is important, it always has been. That's the way the world works, Flo."

"You're gonna be the saddest winner the West ever saw," she cautioned and then she left.

Blackie sighed and looked at the plate of food she'd brought. Flo knew him too well; she was the closest thing to a mother he'd ever had. Now she was going to get married and he'd be alone with a friendly bartender, a piano player, and a handful of whores . . . if they'd stop gettin' married or going to work next door as waitresses. "When I get that land and build the biggest saloon in the Territory, I'll be satisfied. I'll be rich and never have to worry about bein' hungry again." He didn't want to think about his past as a barefoot, white trash kid who never got enough to eat and had to deal with his Pa's drunken customers who kicked and hit him if he got in their way.

At his feet, Lively whimpered and sniffed at the meat on the desk, bringing Blackie out of his memories.

"Here, you go, boy, we'll share this and then let's figure out what we're gonna do to run that cat-lovin' prim old maid out of town before she smears me."

Somewhere in the back of his mind, Flo's words echoed but he stilled them as he and the dog shared the food and he began to plan his strategy. He would be rid of that self-righteous, straitlaced reformer once and for all.

He went out front to where Moose tended bar. "I'm goin' out for awhile, Moose. I may even stay out overnight, enjoy the stars. Can you put me together some steaks or something I could cook over a campfire?"

"Sure, boss." He gave Blackie a questioning look. Maybe Moose had heard all the exchanges from the office, but he started putting a basket together.

"Oh, one more thing. Throw in a bottle of our best whiskey."

Moose's eyebrows went up. "Whiskey?"

The look annoyed Blackie. "I said whiskey, didn't I?"

"Well, it's just that you don't usually—"

"Just get me some supplies, all right? I hate bein' interrogated over everything."

Moose shrugged and nodded. Blackie went back to his living quarters, got some things, added a couple of blankets. Yes, he just might sit out under the stars all night, enjoy the landscape and his hobby, broil himself a steak. Maybe he could clear his head and get some thinking done.

Lacey was so angry, she could hardly sleep that night. The next morning, bright and early, she went to the sheriff. "I'm ready to file charges against Blackie O'Neal for stealing my papers and robbing the honesty boxes."

The old man blinked. "Them's mighty serious charges, Miss Durango. Can you prove it?"

"I found lots of copies in the trash behind his place."

His eyes grew wide. "A lady like you was digging in the garbage behind a saloon? That don't sound like you, Miss Durango."

"That has nothing to do with the subject." She almost screamed it at him. "I found the papers. That's evidence."

"Well maybe so." He sat down on the edge of his desk. "That don't seem like much. You find the money or did he admit to the deed?"

"My word, of course not. He's trying to run me out of town, that's what. Everyone knows it."

"And everyone knows you been tryin' to run him out, too." He grinned at her. "People's takin' bets on who's gonna win this fight."

That thought annoyed her. "This is a battle between right-thinking people and riffraff," she sniffed. "And another thing, he's copied the church's stained glass window in a painting that's hanging in his saloon office."

The sheriff scratched his head. "Wal, it might be in bad taste, Miss, but I'm not sure if it's illegal."

"But it is illegal to steal papers," she said, her voice rising. "Now I want to file charges."

"Miss Durango, let me give you a little advice. Make sure you got good proof before you smear a man's name."

"Smear a man's name? Why, this rascal hasn't got any reputation to begin with. He's a lowdown saloon bum."

"That don't make me no never-mind," he said. "You bring me some proof and I'll let you file charges."

"Proof! I know I'm right. Until I can satisfy you with enough facts, I'll wage war on him in my paper."

"Be careful, Miss Durango. You know what the Bible says about a mote in the eye."

"Oh, don't lecture me. You men are all alike, and you stick together!" She marched out of his office, returned to the newspaper and wrote a very hot editorial and handed it to Isaac. "Here, print this."

Isaac read it, hesitated.

"What?"

"Miss Lacey, we've known each other a long time, yes?"

"I know, Isaac, so?"

"What you've written amounts to a smear. I come from the old country so nobody knows better than I do that a newspaper is a powerful force. That's the reason dictators always try to squash them, silence them. Newspapers should always tell the unbiased truth, not try to slant the news to fit someone's agenda."

"Are you lecturing me about the newspaper business?"

Her voice rose as she paced up and down her office. "The newspapers were in his trash, and the painting is hanging in his office. I want the good people of this town to rise up and run him out of town. Then we'll have a perfect town."

"Are you sure there's not something else at stake here?" She paused and avoided his gaze. "I—I don't know what you mean."

"Everyone knows about the dispute over that lot. They'll think you're taking a cheap shot, that you're just out to get him."

Was she? Of course not. "I'm doing the right thing."

"Are you now? Sometimes being self-righteous causes people to get overzealous. Maybe you expect too much from people, Miss Lacey, nobody's perfect."

"Well, maybe they ought to be better than most of them are. I reckon if you set people a high bar, they'll reach a little higher."

"Or maybe give up all together, figuring no one can ever reach the perfection you expect, yes?"

She didn't want to hear this. It was the same advice Aunt Cimarron had given her. "Isaac, you've given me your advice and I've listened to it. Now print the editorial. I'm going to win this battle."

He sighed. "Don't say I didn't warn you."

The paper went out as a special edition. As word spread, everyone was lining up to buy a copy. She watched through the window as people picked up copies and stood on the street reading it. Some frowned and shook their heads. Some smiled and nodded. Some of her Temperance Association ladies came in to congratulate her, but several men dropped by her office and asked her if she had proof. She answered haughtily, "Everyone knows he's a rascal, and anyway, the end justifies the means."

Isaac sighed and watched the men leave. "Miss Lacey, every villain who ever lived used that for an excuse: that the end justifies the means."

"In this case, it does." She smiled to herself at how angry Blackie would be over the paper.

That afternoon while Isaac was at the post office, Chief Thunder entered her office hesitantly. "Miss Lacey?"

"Well, Joe, you've got a lot of nerve coming in here. You ought to be ashamed of yourself, copying that stained glass window for that whiskey-swilling scoundrel."

"Uh, Miss Lacey," Chief Thunder stubbed his toe against the floor. "There's something you should know; I didn't paint that picture."

"Don't lie to me trying to save his worthless skin," she snapped. "It's in poor taste, if not blasphemous, to copy the church's window to hang in a sleazy saloon."

Chief Thunder licked his lips and shifted from one foot to the other. "I didn't figure you'd listen to reason."

"Reason? I am a very reasonable person, but I know what I saw." she snapped. "Who sent you? Blackie O'Neal?"

"No ma'am," he shook his head. "And I'd just as soon he didn't know I was here—he'd get mad at me. But maybe you should talk to Reverend Lovejoy."

Reverend Lovejoy. She hadn't thought about the consequences of letting the whole world know that the prairie scene had been copied to hang in the Black Garter's office. "You're right. I do need to prepare him if he hasn't already seen the paper."

"You do that," Chief Thunder said. "Now I got to go, it's time for the afternoon train, and I got a whole new crate of buttons to sell. You know, Blackie offered to teach me about gambling. Maybe I should take him up on it."

Lacey shook her head. "Can't see there's any future for Indians in gambling.

He grinned. "Be a chance to get even with whites for stealing our land, now wouldn't it?"

"Reckon so," she agreed.

He left, and Lacey grabbed a parasol. She wondered where Blackie was and if he had read the paper yet. Last night she had seen Blackie passing by, driving a buggy, all alone. Good, maybe he was getting out of town. However, she remembered now that she had seen him driving out of town alone a number of times and had wondered about it. She'd even suspected he was rendezvousing with young Mable Lovejoy. She brushed the curiosity from her mind and went out the door, headed for the church.

Reverend Lovejoy was alone in his study when she arrived. He was reading the special issue of the *Pretty Prairie Crusader.* He looked up and motioned her in. She couldn't read the expression on his gentle pink face.

"Reverend Lovejoy, I hoped to speak to you before you saw the paper. I know it must come as a shock to you."

"It certainly does," he nodded. "This is a very strong and condemning editorial, young lady."

"Perhaps you didn't read it all," Lacey defended herself. "The scoundrel's done the unthinkable, he's got a painting of the stained glass window hanging in that terrible saloon's office."

He leaned back in his chair and surveyed her. "I already knew that," he said softly.

"You knew that and didn't take action?"

"I thought it was very generous of him."

"What?"

The preacher chewed his lip. "Miss Lacey, there is so much I'd like to tell you, but I'm under oath to keep silent. Anyway, I'm not sure you'd believe me."

"Of course I would, sir, but he does have the painting—"

"I think you're overdue for a long talk with Blackie."

"There's nothing to talk about. He's an unmitigated scoundrel who'd stop at nothing to run me out of town."

"And you him?"

She flushed. "It's the principle of the thing."

"Uh-huh. I am always suspicious of people who insist

it's 'the principle of the thing.' Let me only say this: the Lord works in mysterious ways his wonders to perform."

"How does that pertain to Blackie O'Neal?"

"Perhaps you're condemning him prematurely."

She shook her head. "You surprise me, Reverend. Black is black and white is white, and there's nothing in between."

"On the contrary, there's much in the world that is various shades of gray. Now good day to you, young lady, I've work to do. It's Saturday you know, and I'm leaving on tomorrow morning's train for Sweetwater to put on a revival. I've got to leave some notes for the assistant pastor."

She was being coolly dismissed, which only added to Lacey's puzzlement. She'd thought Reverend Lovejoy would have been pleased with her editorial. Or maybe it was humiliating to find out the stained glass window had been copied to hang in a sinful dive like the Black Garter.

She nodded and went outside into the late afternoon. Reverend Lovejoy had said she needed to talk to Blackie. She'd been wanting to confront that scoundrel again because she hadn't managed to tell him off last night. She had seen the gambler driving out of town alone late last night. There was no telling where he was going. Yes, she was going to confront him all right and force him to admit all his skullduggery.

Lacey went to the stable and ran into Dixie just about to mount up. "Well, what are you doing here?"

The blonde, in a gaudy purple dress, scowled at her. "I might ask you the same thing. I'm leavin' town."

"Leaving town? Does Blackie know?"

"You uppity bitch. He fired me because of you."

"What? And don't call me a bitch."

The girl pushed her, snarling. "I ought to pull all your hair out, that's what."

"Be careful, Dixie," Lacey warned, "I'm a Texas gal and I can hold my own in a fight."

"You fancy, uptown skirt. I had a thing goin' with Blackie 'til you came along and ruined everything. I ought to mop up this stable with you." She pushed Lacey again.

Now Lacey Durango was a lady, but she was also a Texan. "Be careful, Dixie, you're kicking a hornets' nest."

"Aw, you ladies don't know how to fight." And she pushed Lacey hard.

At that point, Lacey forgot she was a lady and charged, tangling her fingers in Dixie's bleached yellow hair. The two of them went down scratching and clawing.

The stableboy ran up. "You two stop that now!" He tried to pull them apart, but they were fighting and rolling around in the straw on the stable floor.

"You fancy old maid!" Dixie shouted, "I'm glad I took the papers, you deserve to be run out of this town."

"Don't try to defend that no-account gambler," Lacey shouted back and got a good grip on Dixie's hair and gave it a hard yank.

The stableboy struggled and finally pulled them apart. "You," he said to Dixie. "You'd better get out of town."

Dixie's hair hung in untidy strands around her neck and her gaudy dress was torn. "I'm going. You're stupid, Miss Iron Corset, you can't see anything, but I seen it all from the first. You're too stupid even to realize he gave the money for that damned window. I'm glad I took the papers, you hear me? I'd do it again." She swung up on the horse.

"I don't believe that for a minute. That scoundrel never set foot in that church."

"You're very narrow-minded, you prig, and a rotten judge of men. I could have told you Eugene was a rat. He was upstairs at the Black Garter almost every night."

"What? You're a liar and you're just trying to protect that worthless gambler."

"You're too blind to see what a great guy Blackie really is, and he's too blind to see he can't move up in class. We belonged together, but because of you, I've lost out. So long, you stupid bitch." She rode away from the stable.

Lacey stood blinking after her. "I—I'm sorry for the scene," she apologized to the boy. "I need a horse for the afternoon."

"You sure you want to go ridin', Miss Durango? You look like you've been dragged through a knothole backwards."

"Oh, my!" Lacey grinned sheepishly, tried to straighten her dusty, rumpled clothes and pull the wisps of hair back into her coiffeur. It had always seemed so important to be perfect, now other things had more priority. "I've got something to straighten out."

The stablehand brought out a bay horse and shook his head as he handed over the reins. "You surprised me, Miss Durango. I didn't think ladies ever got into fights."

"She started it," Lacey reminded him. "Lady or not, no Texas gal is going to let herself be pushed around."

"If you don't mind me saying so, Miss Durango, it's a little late for a lady to ride very far out of town."

"I won't be long," she said, and then it occurred to her that if Blackie were very angry, she'd better have some insurance. "However, if I'm not back by around dark, maybe you'd better tell my assistant to organize a search party." She laughed, but the stablehand didn't laugh.

"It's Saturday night, Miss Durango, lots of saddle tramps in the area on a Saturday night. Some of them pretty rough and rotten."

A good description of Blackie O'Neal, she thought. The nerve of him, getting that trashy Dixie to try to provide him with an alibi. Lacey hadn't believed her for a minute. "I'll be all right."

"Just where are you goin', Miss?"

"I'm really not sure; north, I reckon, toward the Double Bar ranch. I'll be fine." She wasn't really sure of that cheery statement herself as she mounted up and rode out of town, following the tracks of Blackie O'Neal's buggy.

Chapter Twenty

It was very late in the afternoon as Lacey rode out of town, following the buggy tracks. It appeared Blackie might be headed for the Double Bar ranch, or maybe on to Guthrie. *Now what was that scoundrel up to?*

It occurred to Lacey now that she had neglected to tell Isaac or anyone except the young stableboy where she was going and he might not be too reliable. Not that it mattered. Once she had her final set-to with Blackie O'Neal, she hoped to be home before dark.

The prairie was an endless sea of grass that rolled with the wind like waves on a green ocean. Here and there the land dipped and rose again in small hills. An ache came to her heart and she remembered life on a ranch and was homesick for that life. She would be welcome back at her uncle's Triple D ranch, but after what had happened with Homer, she was too humiliated to face anyone in that community again. Homer. She had thought he was perfect, but he hadn't been. Of course, he had long since married and Lacey was still single. "That girl was willing to settle for less than perfection," Lacey muttered, "and I wasn't." Poor thing, to get stuck with the flawed Homer. Somewhere out there was the perfect man. Maybe someday Lacey would find him, and he wouldn't be a whiskey-swilling, no-account rascal.

That made her think of the charming Blackie. In her mind, she could see his handsome, grinning face. He'd be a poor excuse for a husband with all his faults. "Pity the poor girl who gets him."

She was on the Double Bar ranch now. She saw the sign on the big gate, and the buggy tracks went through that gate. *Now where was Blackie going?* As she remembered from the July Fourth picnic, the ranch house lay off to the left, but the buggy tracks went off to the right. The scenery began to look familiar, and she realized that she was following the trail the riders had taken that day. Up ahead lay a spectacular view. The sun was setting on the rim of the rolling hills.

"My word." She took a deep breath as she remembered why the stained glass window and the painting had looked so familiar. "I've seen that sunset before, that evening right near here. Joe must have come out here to paint it."

Up ahead, she saw the buggy and reined in. Blackie's horse was unhitched and tied where it could munch grass peacefully. Nearby, the buckskin that Blackie had ridden that holiday also grazed. But it was Blackie who surprised her so much, she was speechless. He didn't seem aware of her as he stood before an easel set up under the trees. On the easel was a half-finished painting and he held a brush.

He seemed so completely engrossed in his painting and now when he heard her cry of surprise, he turned quickly, then tried to throw a canvas over his work. "What the hell are you doing out here?"

She dismounted and tied her horse to a shrub. "I might ask you the same thing. You stealing that buckskin horse?"

"Hell, no, I bought it. I seemed to be the only one who understood that outlaw. Anyway I've got permission from the owners to be here."

"That's not what I meant." She sauntered over, pulled away the covering from the painting, even through he tried to block her action. "That's really good. Who—?"

"If you go back to town and tell them, I'll cut your tongue out, sister."

She blinked in disbelief. "Don't tell me you paint?"

He made a half-hearted, embarrassed gesture. "It's just a way to capture a memory. I know it's not very good."

She stared at the painting. The colors seemed to come off the canvas at her, the vivid oranges, scarlets, and blues of the sky, the serene greens and browns of the prairie. In the scene, the buckskin ran at full gallop. On the buckskin's back was a girl, dark hair flying as she rode, a smile on her lips. And the girl . . . no, it couldn't be. For a moment, she was speechless. "It's good," she admitted. "Very good. I had no idea—"

"Why, because I'm just a scoundrel who runs a saloon? I'm just a stupid, uneducated bum who couldn't possibly enjoy a good book or take pleasure in paintin'?"

"Don't be so defensive, I didn't say that."

He tossed his brush aside. "Yeah, but you thought it. Sister, don't you go back to town and tell them. I won't have folks laughin' at me."

She was touched. She had had no idea he was so sensitive or had any feelings for the finer things in life. "The tough Blackie O'Neal is afraid of being laughed at?"

"Ain't everybody?" He was angry, defensive.

Somehow, humiliating him in front of the townsfolk and cowboys did seem now like hitting below the belt. "Don't worry, I won't tell."

It was evident from his face that he didn't believe her. "You'll just store this up to use against me later, right?"

"If I said no, you still wouldn't believe me?"

"Miss Durango," his voice was cold, "we are each tryin' to run the other out of town and I find it impossible to believe you'd pass up good ammunition like this."

She didn't answer because she was staring at his painting and the scene of the whole landscape before them. Yes, she had seen it before. "It's the stained glass window and the painting in your office."

"What about it?" He snapped, lighting a cigar.

And now she knew what Reverend Lovejoy and Chief Thunder had been trying to tell her. "It's your painting that was copied for the window, not the other way around."

"So what?" He smoked, not looking at her.

She felt tears come to her eyes and was more puzzled than ever by Blackie. Who could have guessed that the tough gambler had a soft, sensitive side? There was a long, awkward moment of silence during which she reevaluated this man and was ashamed of herself. "Look, we're having a beautiful sunset."

They both watched in awe as the sun sank, splashing scarlet with golden tendrils across the lavender sky.

"Beautiful," she whispered.

"I've been tryin' to capture it," he shook his head, "but I can't quite."

"No, you've got it," she assured him. "The work is very, very good."

"That means a lot, comin' from my biggest critic."

"I—I may have been too harsh on you."

He didn't answer.

She realized it would be dark in a few minutes. "Are you headed back now?"

He shook his head. "Actually, I was going to build a fire and cook a steak, maybe sit out and watch the stars. Nothin' prettier than a prairie sky on a summer night."

She looked at his painting and knew that the girl riding with dark hair blowing, a smile on her lips, was her. Tears came to her eyes. "Why—?"

"Yeah, it's you," he muttered grudgingly, "the way I imagined you'd ride across my ranch on the buckskin."

"Ranch? You own a ranch?"

"You think my only interest is saloons? I got dreams, too."

Lacey didn't answer, still staring at the painting. She knew she ought to be headed back before she was caught on the road after dark, but instead, she suddenly wanted to stay and talk to this man—not argue, not condemn, just talk to him. *Lacey, are you loco?*, her mind said. R*emember he's a scoundrel and he's feeding you a load of bull—right now.* Oh, of course he was, trying to soften her. Yet she couldn't bring herself to swing up in the saddle and ride back to town. She hesitated.

He seemed to sense her hesitation. "Hey," he said, "I got plenty of steak. You wanna stay?"

She paused, uncertain. "I really shouldn't."

"You worried about your reputation, spendin' time alone with a saloon bum?" He sounded very defensive.

"No," she answered quickly, "it's just that if I don't leave right now, I'll be riding back in the dark, and you never know how many saddle bums there are along the road."

"That's true." He went to his buggy and got out a picnic basket.

She watched him, remembering what Dixie had said about Eugene and wondered if she should believe the whore? "Uh, If I stay, can I do something to help?"

He smiled at her. Smiled gently, not a leer, not a grin. "You can gather up some sticks for a fire." He said as he unloaded his basket. "Look, Moose even added some fresh-baked bread and chocolate cake."

"Oh, and grapes. I *love* grapes." She was suddenly hungry and in a very good mood as she began to gather wood.

He paused and looked her over. "Sis, what happened to you? You look like the dogs have had you under the porch."

"Oh, dear." She had forgotten her set-to with Dixie. "I reckon I look a mess, don't I? I was in a fight." She tried to brush her hair back.

"A fight? You? Perfect ladies don't do that."

She shook her head. "I'm not perfect, I think I just found that out. Anyway, I tangled with Dixie."

"Dixie?" He paused, studying her. "For a lady, you look like you gave as good as you got."

"I may be a lady, but I'm a Texan," she said proudly, "nobody walks on me."

"Me, neither." He grinned at her.

Careful, Lacey, she warned herself as her heart lurched at his grin. *He's a Rebel rascal, but maybe not as bad as you used to think. After all, the war is long over. What difference does it make which side his family supported?* She hurried to his campsite with her handful of sticks. As she helped build the fire, their hands touched and they both paused and looked into each other's eyes. For a long moment, neither seemed to know what to do, then Blackie cleared his throat awkwardly. "I'll put the steaks on if you'll get a blanket out of the buggy to sit on so you won't get your dress any dirtier."

She laughed in spite of herself. "I'm afraid it's already a mess. Dixie saw to that." She went to the buggy, got the blanket. She stiffened when she saw what else was there. "I presume you want this bottle of whiskey, too?"

"Why not? I know you figure I'll guzzle the whole bottle. I wouldn't want to disappoint you."

The humiliation came back with a rush. As she picked up the blanket and the bottle, the tears began to overflow.

He looked up, evidently alarmed. "What the hell did I say wrong?"

"Nothing." She gulped and tried to stop sobbing

but in vain. "That's—that's what he said, 'that he didn't want to disappoint me'."

Blackie looked baffled as he took the bottle from her hand, motioned her to put the blanket next to the fire. "Who are we talkin' about?"

"Homer!" she wailed.

Blackie looked as uncomfortable as a whore at a church revival. "Is Homer the galoot you almost married?"

She could only sob and nod. "I—I thought he was the most perfect man—"

"Sister," Blackie said, disgusted, "there ain't no such thing as a perfect man—or the perfect woman, for that matter."

"I—I've got to be perfect so my grandfather will love me," she wailed, "but I can't seem to be perfect enough."

Blackie shook his head. "Bein' perfect don't have nothin' to do with love. You take folks like you find 'em. Both Grandpa and this Homer sound like losers."

"It—it was a huge wedding," she sobbed, "and everyone in two counties was there. I—I was humiliated in front of hundreds of people."

His brow furrowed as he put the steaks on the fire. "So what did the perfect Homer do, not show up?"

"W—worse." She sobbed and shook her head. "Oh, I—I hate it when I cry, it makes my nose run."

"Oh, here," he handed her his handkerchief. "Even perfect people get runny noses."

She blew her nose with a big honking sound. "I—I don't think I can tell you."

"Maybe you need a drink to steady your nerves," Blackie suggested and pulled the cork from the bottle. "Sorry, I don't have a glass."

She wanted to turn it down, but the memories were

so overpowering, she couldn't stand to remember them. "Well, maybe just a sip," she sobbed.

It was dark now, the camp fire throwing cheery warm shadows across the grass as she flopped down on the blanket. She steeled herself and took a drink. That brought back the rest of that humiliating memory and she sobbed some more.

"Great God Almighty," Blackie said. "Get a grip on yourself, sister."

She took a big drink and choked on it. The whiskey felt warm all the way down. "He—he was perfect, I thought. Handsome, educated, from a fine family."

"Everything I'm not," Blackie said and frowned.

"Well, you're handsome," she said. "You want a drink?"

"I don't usually—well, why not?" He grabbed the bottle and took a sip, returned it. "How do you like your steak?"

"Just wound it and run it past me." She smiled at him. She wasn't used to the whiskey, and it was making her feel very good and happy.

He grinned. "That's the way I like mine too; if you stick a fork in it, it should moo."

"Homer liked his well-done." She began to sob again.

"Oh, for God's sake, Homer sounds like a loser."

She shook her head and for a minute, she had a difficult time focusing her eyes. "He was perfect, the kind of man I wanted, but he said he wasn't and therefore, he couldn't marry me because it wouldn't work."

"Sounds like Homer knew you pretty well, sister."

She drew herself up proudly. "He could have told me before. Instead, he waited until we're down front at the altar before a huge crowd. I had a beautiful white dress, everything had been carefully planned. We looked around for the groom and then—and then—" She began to cry again.

"He didn't show up?"

"Worse than that. He staggered in, drunker than a boiled owl. He couldn't even focus his eyes, but he took my hand. He kept swaying on his feet as the preacher talked until I was afraid Homer would faint."

Blackie stared at her. "So what happened then?"

She began to wail again. "He just stood there, drunk and swaying on his feet, and when the preacher said 'do you take this woman?' Homer said, 'I believe I won't!' and then threw up all over the minister's shoes and fainted dead away while the crowd roared with laughter."

Blackie looked at her a long moment. "And?"

"Isn't that enough? Turned down by a drunk in front of hundreds of people at my perfect, perfect wedding?" She took another drink.

"I'd go easy on that whiskey, sister, since you don't drink—"

"You think I've never been drunk?" she challenged. "Well, I have. That night, the crowd came to the house anyway for refreshments and I was so upset that I got pie-eyed. I danced in the fountain out in front of the hacienda wearing nothing but my lace corset cover and my drawers."

Blackie laughed softly. "Must have been quite a sight."

She nodded somberly, trying to focus her eyes. "They tell me it was before Uncle Trace lifted me up and carried me up to my room. The perfect end to a perfectly humiliating day. To tell the truth, I don't remember most of it."

He turned the steaks over. They sizzled, and the aroma drifting from the fire made her mouth water.

"So, sister, you've been crusading against liquor and men ever since?"

She nodded and took another drink. "Licks that touch lipor will never touch mine," she said somberly, if not entirely soberly.

"Is that a fact?" He seemed to be suppressing a smile as he leaned over very slowly and tangled his fingers in her dark hair. In almost a haze, she saw his handsome, rugged face, his intense dark eyes as he pulled her toward him. She knew she should object and get up, mount her horse, and leave, but the fire was pleasant, the blanket soft, and the whiskey very, very tasty. Then Blackie kissed her.

And Lacey kissed him back. He seemed almost startled as she reached for him. His lips were warm and sensual as she kissed him deeply, thoroughly, in a way she had only read about in romantic novels. "Oh, Blackie."

"I've wanted to do this since the first time I met you," he confessed against her lips. He took her in his embrace, his tongue caressing hers until her mouth relaxed in surrender and the kiss deepened. His hand went to her bodice, unbuttoning the top buttons.

"I don't think . . . " she began and then his big hand covered her breast and she stopped thinking altogether. All she wanted him to do was caress her as she had never been caressed, kiss her as she had never been kissed, certainly not by the very proper Homer.

She felt the warmth of Blackie's lips on her throat where the pulse pounded, and he kissed his way down her throat until they reached the rise of her breasts. Lacey gasped for air. "I—I think the steaks are burning."

"So we'll eat them burnt." He growled and his lips made little feathery caresses across her breasts.

"Blackie don't . . . Blackie . . . Blackie . . . "

"Yes?"

"Oh, Blackie, don't stop . . . "

"I don't intend to." He nuzzled between her breasts and she felt his hand stroking her leg, pushing her skirt up until she felt his fingers caressing her thigh and moving upward.

Blackie had never felt as aroused as he did at this moment with this beauty in his arms. So what if she was a Yankee sympathizer? The war was long over. As he had suspected, behind all that denial was a passionate woman only waiting for the right man—not a perfect man, but the right one. She was far out of his league, he knew, so unattainable, so above the realm of a poor, self-educated gambler from the Big Thicket. And yet, here she was in his arms, and he didn't even want to think why. He only knew that the beauty was sprawled on a blanket, letting him caress and kiss her.

This was loco, he knew, because the prim miss had set out to destroy him. His pulse pounded hard in his ears as he kissed her again. Yes, he was going to seduce the proper and perfect miss, and when word got around, she'd be so humiliated, she'd pack up and leave town. He'd get revenge, the prize lot, and the pleasure of enjoying that lovely body.

"Blackie, I never—"

"I know, sweet," he whispered, "but I'll teach you."

He was as good as his promise; teasing, thrilling, enticing her until she was clinging to him, matching kiss for kiss. Her uncertain hands explored the hard planes of his body, his big hands caressed her soft velvet skin until he touched her most private place, and she gasped and pulled him toward her. "Please, Blackie, please . . . "

It was all he was waiting for. He was an expert at pleasing women, and now he would add Lacey Durango to his conquered list. Swiftly, he ripped aside her delicate lace pantalets and took off his own trousers. Her eyes were dark with intense passion as he came into her. She gasped only once. He broke through her virginity and, forgetting that he was out for revenge and seduction, he only knew that he had never known passion like this in all the years he had made love to women. He and Lacey came together like two fires igniting and feeding on each other, a perfect rhythm as if their bodies were meant to be together as one. There was a building crescendo of blazing passion as they reached a pinnacle, and then there was a long moment of breathless ecstasy like a little death. When he returned to consciousness, perspiring and gasping for air, she was in his arms, kissing his face again and again. *Oh, Great God Almighty, what have I done?*

Meanwhile, back in town, Isaac looked at the wall clock again and paced some more. There was nothing to do but go to the sheriff, and he did.

"Sheriff, Miss Lacey is missing."

The old man yawned. "Maybe she's gone for a visit."

Isaac shook his head. "She doesn't do unexpected things like disappear without telling anyone where she's going. She keeps a pretty rigid schedule, nothing unpredictable about her. Besides, it's Saturday night, there's lots of trail trash coming into town, yes?"

"Hmm. You might be right." The sheriff's chair came down on all fours. "Maybe we'd better ask around."

They went outside into the warm summer night and there were many people on the street. When Isaac and the sheriff began their search, no one had seen Lacey Durango. As word spread through the crowd, the stablehand approached hesitantly. "I don't know if this is important, but Miss Durango rented a horse and rode out of town right after she'd had a fistfight with that wh—" he looked around at the listening ladies, "that girl from the Black Garter, Dixie."

"A fistfight?" Isaac and the others looked at each other. "That doesn't sound like Miss Lacey," Isaac shook his head. "She's always a perfect lady. Are you sure?"

The boy nodded. "Yep, and boy howdy, she gave as good as she got. Real feisty! Then she rode out of town alone.

Not sure where she was goin', but she said she was headed north, maybe to the Double Bar Ranch."

The sheriff took off his hat and scratched his head. "Now why would she do that?"

"And why ain't she back?" someone else asked.

A murmur ran through the crowd, only louder this time.

"Boys," said the sheriff, "I think we'd better get a posse together and see what we can find."

The ladies, not to be left at home with such exciting goings-on stepped in. They had been emboldened by their victory over the town's names.

Ethel Wilson said, "I think the ladies had better get in their buggies and go along."

"Now, Ethel," scolded the banker, "I don't believe—"

"Oh shut up, Julius," she snapped, "the ladies want to know what's happened, too. Maybe she's been carried off by some virile Injun brave or some handsome outlaw."

"You think?" Vanetta Wren's face lit up.

A collective sigh went through the bunch of ladies. A tryst with a big warrior or desperado would certainly be more exciting than what most of the ladies were getting in their own beds every night. Of course, none said that.

Chief Thunder had just joined the crowd. "Talk about discrimination, I resent the suggestion that the Indian brave would have to carry a lady off to get one."

The sheriff pushed his Stetson back on his silver hair. "Some outlaw might have taken her and . . . " he paused and looked at the women. "Uh, might have had his way with her."

Prim little Miss Blanton, the old maid milliner, sighed wistfully. The other women smiled as they pictured just what a handsome, virile desperado might do to a captive lady.

Cookie and Flo walked out to see what was going on and listened a minute. He shook his head. "This shore ain't like Miss Lacey. She's so perfect and punctual, you can set a watch by her schedule."

"Then something terrible might really have happened to her," Moose nodded as he joined them.

"Where's Blackie?" asked the blacksmith. "He can handle a gun if there's trouble."

"Uh," Moose scratched his tattoo. "He—he's gone outa town. Not sure when he'll be back."

"If there's gonna be gunplay," the little barber said, "maybe the ladies should not go along."

"Gunplay? Who do you men think you are, Wild Bill Hickok? Anyways, we're a-going," Mrs. Anderson bounced her baby on her ample hip. "Just in case you galoots pass some road house and think about stoppin' for a drink."

The men groaned aloud. Evidently, they were not as convinced that Lacey was in any real danger, but wanted some excitement. "You'll slow us down."

"What's slowing you down," said Ethel Wilson, "is all this jawing. You men can get horses and the ladies can get buggies and we'll all head up toward the ranch to see what we can find."

The sheriff sighed and shrugged. "Wal, fellas, you heard the ladies. I reckon the whole town intends to go along on this adventure. Everyone get ready and we'll meet in front of the barber shop in fifteen minutes. Cookie and Flo, you check the south road in case Miss Durango circled back. Moose, you go to the telegraph at the railroad, see if there's' any messages. You other men, arm yourselves and bring lanterns. No tellin' what we're liable to find with all the trail trash around on Saturday night."

Chapter Twenty-one

Blackie made love to Lacey a second time. When she discovered he still owned the nude painting, she had to imitate the pose, complete with fruit. Blackie suddenly discovered he liked grapes very much. Then in a suddenly awkward silence in the darkness lit only by stars and the camp fire, they ate burnt steak.

My word, what on earth have I done? Lacey was still more than a little dizzy from the whiskey and unsure of her feelings for this rascal, who was now staring at her in puzzlement as if seeing her for the very first time.

He grinned. "Want to go for a swim in the creek?"

"Why not?" She staggered to her feet, feeling confused and more than a little woozy. Nothing was perfect, but for the first time, it didn't seem to matter and he'd already seen her naked. She hesitated only briefly before wading out into the water. The stream was surprisingly warm, but then, it was almost August.

He stood, poised naked on the creek bank. In the glow of the camp fire, she could see his lithe body plainly. "Here I come, ready or not."

He dived in and splashed her. She was having fun for the first time in a long time and she laughed gaily and splashed back. After a moment, he pulled her to him in a wet, slippery embrace and they kissed hungrily.

This was outrageous. Had she lost her mind, frolicking in a creek at night with a naked gambler? She didn't want to think about that, or tomorrow, either. "I think I need another drink," she mumbled and staggered to the bank.

"Sister, I think you've had enough already." He warned from the water.

She threw back her head and laughed as she grabbed the bottle. "You're the one who brought the whiskey," she reminded him and stumbled back into the water. She might have fallen had he not grabbed her. He kissed her again, deeply, hungrily. She held onto the bottle as she slipped her arms around his neck and kissed him again and again.

There was a noise, a sudden jingle. In a fog, she slowly raised her head and looked just beyond the shadows thrown by the camp fire. For a long moment, all she could do was freeze like a startled rabbit in a sudden lantern light. "Oh, my God."

At her gasp of alarm, Blackie turned and looked, too. Staring back at them in shock was the sheriff and a dozen mounted men who had reined in under the trees. Even as they all stared at each other in horrified shock, more and more riders were coming in. She even saw buggies in the background.

The sheriff found his voice first. "Uh, Miss Durango?"

She realized most of the local citizens were arriving. Her first reaction was simply to submerge and she did. She'd rather drown than face the curious stares of the whole town. Maybe when she came up for air, it would have all been something she imagined and the landscape would be empty. However, when she came up, gasping like a doomed fish, the staring crowd was even larger.

The stunned people blinked at the pair in the water.

"Miss Lacey, are you all right?" Isaac called as people came closer with their lanterns.

"Uh, yes." She didn't know what to do. She was still drunk and naked in the creek and in the arms of her bare-bottomed enemy.

"Nekkid. She's nekkid as the day she was borned!" The buzz ran through the crowd.

"And that gambler's nekkid, too, except for that diamond ring."

"Where? Where?" asked a dozen eager ladies including Miss Vanetta Wren and Miss Blanton.

Among the crowd, titters and whispers became laughter and shouting as word passed to the newcomers just arriving on the scene.

Lacey didn't know what to do. She just wanted to die. There she was, naked as a jay bird, in the arms of the town's biggest scoundrel with a bottle of whiskey in her hand. *Whiskey.* And she, president of the Ladies' Temperance Association. She let go of the bottle and a groan went up from the male riders as it sank out of sight.

Blackie recovered first. He waded to the bank, stark naked, grabbing for his clothes.

"Don't look, Ethel!" warned the banker, "he's nekkid!"

"And all man." Ethel sighed.

That almost started a stampede as ladies came out of their buggies to get a better view. Blackie slipped on his trousers and shirt, then grabbed up a blanket and went to the water's edge. "Come on out, Lacey."

She shook her head, still dizzy. "No, I—I'm just going to stay here and drown myself."

He waded out into the creek. "Come on, this ain't the first time a lady's been caught in an embarrassin' situation. You'll survive."

He was right, she knew. She tried not to cry as she stood up and he wrapped the blanket around her and led her to the bank.

More titters and snorts of laughter from the crowd. "My, what a hypocrite!"

"Ain't she the one who's been leadin' a crusade against demon rum and look at her, so drunk, she's cross-eyed."

Isaac pushed his way through the crowd. "Shut up,

everyone. Here, Miss Lacey, let me help you." He took her hand gently and led her across the grass.

Behind her, Blackie said, "Take my buggy, Isaac, I'll ride her horse in."

Isaac turned and there was hatred in his eyes. "You. You had to bring her down, didn't you? Well, I hope you're happy, Mister."

Blackie didn't answer. When Lacey looked back at him, she couldn't read his face, but she felt she had been played for a fool. He had humiliated and seduced her in front of half the town. She would never be able to show her face in Pretty Prairie again.

"Folks," the sheriff addressed the crowd, "show's over. Everybody go home."

All the people stared a long moment, then they began to break up and ride away.

Imagine that," Lacey heard an outraged lady say. "Here she was settin' herself up as a perfect paragon of virtue, and she's no better than the rest of us, and not as good as some."

Lacey managed not to sob as Isaac helped her up into the buggy, still wrapped in the blanket. He harnessed the horse and hooked it to the buggy. With a sigh, he bent and gathered up her scattered clothes, threw them up into the buggy. Then he climbed up on the seat beside her.

Most of the crowd was gone by now. Blackie had gotten dressed and mounted her horse. He rode up beside the buggy. "Lacey, I'm sorry. I had no idea—"

Now she couldn't hold back the tears. "I think you planned this, to seduce me and humiliate me in front of the whole town. You're a rotten, rotten bastard."

He started to speak, then shrugged and rode out. She was sick, drunk, and sad.

"Miss Lacey," Isaac began.

"Don't talk to me, there's nothing to say," she gulped,

"I thought I was going to be the perfect role model of a perfect town and I'm as big a hypocrite as he is."

"There isn't anybody perfect, but I don't think any less of you. In fact, I'd be right proud if—"

"You're just saying that to be nice," she sobbed as they pulled away. "Blackie O'Neal's made a fool of me and he's won, hasn't he?" She looked at Isaac. "The town will forgive him, even wink about it, since he's a man, but I'm ruined."

Isaac sighed and slapped the horse with the reins. "Only if you think you are."

"My grandfather was right," she sobbed, "I'm not any where close to perfection. Homer saw right through me, too. Letting myself be seduced by a worthless rascal of a gambler. What on earth was I thinking?" She couldn't control her tears as they drove along back to town.

"Don't be so hard on yourself," Isaac said gently. "They'll forget about this in time, and I don't think any less of you."

"No, they won't." She shook her head and pulled her blanket closer. "Not with me writing all those editorials about liquor and Blackie's sleazy reputation, and then I end up drunk and in his arms. He got his revenge."

"Miss Lacey . . . " Isaac sighed again and said nothing for the rest of the ride home. The town was dark when they drew up on Main Street.

"Isaac, go around to the back so I can slip inside."

"The town's dark, Miss Lacey, even the saloon is closed."

"And to think I thought I could close it permanently and run him out of town. He must be sitting in his saloon right now with his girls, laughing about what a spectacle he made of me." She wept some more.

"Much as I dislike the man for what he did, maybe he didn't intend—"

"I don't believe that for a moment, or that his intentions were anywhere near honorable. I'm an idiot and a fool, a drunken fool!"

Isaac didn't argue with that. He drove her around to the back of the newspaper office and gathered up her things. She went inside, brushed past Precious and the kittens and ran upstairs, still sobbing.

"Go to bed, Miss Lacey," Isaac yelled up the stairs, "things will look better tomorrow. Can I get you anything before I leave?"

"No," she called back, "but will you come in tomorrow in case anyone comes to the door? I can't bear to face jeering people."

"Tomorrow's Sunday. We're always closed then."

"They might come peer in the windows."

He sighed. "All right. I'll come in. Good night."

She listened for the closing of the door downstairs and then she lay on her bed, trying to think. Her head was pounding from the whiskey and she groaned when she remembered the only other time she'd had a drink—when she'd danced in her underclothes in the fountain in front of her Uncle's hacienda and had made a fool of herself. "That was bad, but nothing compared to what happened tonight." In her mind, she saw Blackie's grinning face and hated him. How she hated him. He had done this deliberately to destroy her and he had succeeded. She was a fool and a hypocrite. She closed her eyes and tried to sleep, but her head was pounding like the drum in one of her protest parades.

When she awakened, it was almost daylight and her head hurt so bad, it felt as if she'd been stomped on by a horse. *What on earth?* Then she remembered and groaned aloud. In answer, Precious and two of the yellow kittens jumped up on her bed and stared down at her. Lacey looked up into Precious' yellow eyes. "And to think I called you a slut. I reckon you're not the only fool for a fascinating rogue."

"Meow."

Maybe some coffee would help. There was a small kerosene stove in her room. She stumbled to her feet and went to get a kettle of water. Her head felt as big as a washtub. She made some coffee and put out some food for the cats. Just what was she going to do? Lacey leaned back in her rocker and thought awhile as she drank her coffee. That rotten gambler. This was all his fault. She went to her upstairs window and looked out. Sunday morning. The street was deserted although soon some of the citizens would be going to church.

About that time, Blackie O'Neal opened the saloon doors and stood there a long moment looking toward the newspaper office. As usual, he had a tall, cold drink in his hand. "And it's not even breakfast time," she muttered. "Well, I hope you're happy. You've proved to everyone I'm not perfect, or anywhere near it. The town will forgive you, but not me."

She couldn't read Blackie's expression and since she was behind the lace curtain, he surely could not see her. He kept looking toward her office and the big diamond on his hand winked in the morning light. Her heart lurched at the sight of him. That no-account rascal. She didn't ever want to face him again.

She thought a long time about what she was going to do, then she got up, brushed her hair, pulled it back, and got dressed. Then she began to pack. Downstairs, she heard Isaac come in. "Miss Lacey, are you all right?"

"I'm all right," she called, "I'll be down in a minute."

She had a small desk upstairs and now she sat down and began to write. It was ironic, she thought, that even though he had humiliated her and won the battle, she loved Blackie O'Neal. He wasn't the perfect man she had always dreamed of. He was flawed, not perfect at all. But then, neither was she, no matter how hard she tried.

Her head was clearing. She gathered up her editorial and her luggage, and went downstairs. "Find me my cat case, would you, Isaac?"

He turned and looked at her. "You going somewhere, yes?"

She nodded. "Back to the Triple D ranch to make a fresh start. I'll need the carrying case for Precious and the kittens."

"I wish you wouldn't go, Miss Lacey. "You can weather this. You're only human, after all."

She felt tears come to her eyes and blinked them away. "You still want to own a newspaper? I'll sell you this one really cheap."

"You know I would, but I hate these circumstances—"

"I know. Draw up all the necessary papers and mail them to me." She looked at the big clock on the wall. "The southbound train comes through about ten o'clock. If I go down the alley, I can get to the train station without anyone seeing me."

The little man chewed his lip. "I think you're making too big a thing of this. So you slipped—lots of people do."

"But I set myself up as a paragon of virtue with all my high-and-mighty editorials about righteousness. I know you warned me, but I was too hardheaded to listen."

"Well, you're young," he said and patted her arm. "Maybe tolerance is something that just comes with age, yes? Nobody's perfect. I still think as much of you as ever. In fact . . . "

"That's nice of you to say, but I don't believe you." She bit her lip and sighed. "Anyway, now there's a complication. You see, I've realized I'm in love with Blackie O'Neal, and he cares nothing for me. He just wanted revenge."

Isaac winced and took a deep breath. "Maybe not. I don't see how any man could not love you. I know I—"

"No," she shook her head. "He's won. I couldn't bear to stay in this town and see him every day and know that he didn't love me. He was just making a fool of me. Now go find my cat case while I finish up this last editorial."

Isaac gave her a questioning look, started to say something, shrugged, and went to rummage around in the storeroom. Then he began gathering up the squirming kittens. "At least let me drive you to the station, Miss Lacey."

"All right, I'd appreciate that. Bring the buggy around to the back door. I'm embarrassed to face people. I'll write up a bill of sale for the newspaper."

While he was gone, she finished her editorial, reread it, wrote up a bill of sale. Then she put her face in her hands and wept because she'd been such a fool.

Isaac returned and came in the back door. "You've got less than thirty minutes 'til train time," he warned.

She handed him the bill of sale. "That amount okay?"

His eyes widened as he looked at it. "Miss Lacey, that's not near enough money for a thriving paper like the *Crusader.*"

"It's enough to pay my uncle back and a little something to tide me over until I make a fresh start. Maybe I'll go back east or out west and work for another paper. Oh, about the lot Blackie and I have been at odds over—"

"Yes?"

"It's valuable and it'll probably be tied up in court a while longer, but I can't bear to see a saloon on it. I've written up a quick document saying that, if I win the legal battle, I'm giving it to the town to build a public library."

Isaac whistled under his breath. "That's a mighty generous gift."

She shrugged. "I might have left it to Blackie, if he were doing anything with it but build a saloon. I haven't changed my mind about liquor. Here, read this final editorial and see what you think."

He took it from her hand and began to read. Finally he raised his head. "Miss Lacey, this will bring tears to everyone's eyes and cause them to take a good look in the mirror. Reverend Lovejoy could preach a sermon on this."

"It's my final contribution to this town," Lacey said. She glanced at the clock. "Let's go or I'll miss that train."

Isaac took her luggage and the cage of meowing cats, and they went out back to the buggy. He drove her to the station, got her ticket, and led her to a bench on the platform, setting the luggage down alongside the mewing cats. The station was deserted, except for the ticket man in the office.

That was good, she thought with a sigh of relief. She'd just as soon a bunch of people didn't see her sitting here forlornly on the platform waiting for the southbound train to Texas.

"Well, Miss Lacey, I reckon this is good-bye." He seemed to be blinking rapidly to avoid tears.

"Don't, Isaac, I can't bear it." She stood up and hugged him. "You stay in touch now, you hear? My aunt will forward my mail, wherever I end up."

"Sure. About Blackie—"

"Don't tell him I've gone or where," she admonished. "He'd enjoy my defeat too much, and he'll find out soon enough that I've left."

"Maybe I'm stepping out of line to tell you this, but you shouldn't leave without telling him how you feel."

She attempted to smile to keep from crying. "And have him laugh triumphantly in my face? I reckon I'm only one of dozens of women who've been seduced by that charming rascal. I imagine him and his girls talked about the big joke when he got home last night."

"Well, good-bye again. You've got only a few minutes until the train comes through."

"Take good care of the paper," she tried to smile. "Tell Cookie I'm sorry I left without saying good-bye, but he'll understand that I may not come to his wedding. Speaking of which, you should think about getting married, Isaac. That little Miss Wren is educated enough for you."

"Sure." He nodded and leaned over suddenly, kissed her cheek. There were tears in his eyes as he walked away, blinking rapidly. He had never had the nerve to tell the beauty that he himself was in love with her, because he knew he didn't have a chance, and Lacey had no clue to his feelings. Well, maybe, yes, there might someday be a girl in this town who would appreciate him, even though he wasn't perfect.

Isaac climbed up in the buggy and looked one last time toward the train platform. She sat holding her cat cage and looking weary and defeated. At that moment, he wanted to kill Blackie O'Neal, but of course he couldn't because Lacey was in love with the man. With a sigh, he snapped the reins and returned to the newspaper office. He had a little work to do, and then he'd take the buggy back to the stable.

Lacey's last editorial still lay on her desk. He walked over, picked it up, read it, then read it again. His eyes blurred and his hand shook. She was a different person now than she had been when she'd first come to town, much more human and understanding.

Blackie had had a miserable night, pacing the floor of his room. What on earth had he done? One of the whores, Sal, passed his office and stuck her head in the door, laughing. "Hey, Blackie, I hear you brought Miss High-and-Mighty down. How does it feel to win?"

"Get the hell out of here!" He roared and threw a book at her.

She looked shocked, then shut the door and went on.

He had won but at what cost? Nobody expected any better from him. After all, he was just a sleazy gambler running a second-rate saloon. Flo and Moose had been right, he had won, but there was no pleasure in his victory. He sat with his dog, remembering the ecstasy he'd experienced in Lacey's arms. There had been many,

many women in his life, but none had ever affected him like this. He hadn't meant to humiliate and shame her, but she'd never believe him, nor would the town. He went into the deserted front of the saloon and got his usual drink. Stepping out the door, he stood there, watching her office. He wished he had the nerve to go tell her how sorry he was. In a fight, there was nobody braver than he was, but now he didn't have the guts to face the girl he had disgraced. There was only one thing for him to do.

He went and banged on Moose's door. He banged, and banged again. After a long moment, Moose opened the door, rumpled and very sleepy. "Boss, what's wrong? Place on fire?"

Blackie shook his head. "You still want'a buy this saloon?"

Moose's eyebrows went up and he looked toward a clock. "You woke me up early on a Sunday morning to ask me that? Couldn't it wait? Let's talk at noon."

Blackie shook his head and pushed his way into the room. "Let's get the paperwork done now so I can start gatherin' up my stuff. I expect to be gone by tonight or tomorrow mornin'."

"What?"

"You heard me; I'm leaving town!"

Chapter Twenty-two

"Boss, have you gone loco?" Moose stumbled around, finally found his pants and put them on.

"Don't try to talk me out of it," Blackie said. "Now let's do some some business. You're about to get the buy of a lifetime."

Isaac glanced up at the clock. Another fifteen minutes and Lacey would be gone. Maybe someday he'd journey to Texas and plead his case, but it wouldn't do any good. He'd seen the look on her face when she mentioned Blackie's name. The gambler wasn't nearly good enough for her and certainly didn't give a damn about her, but that's the way love was. Love wasn't perfect. Just like the people involved, it was flawed and unlikely and some-times just plain crazy, but no one could tell his or her own heart what to do.

About that time, the bell on the front door jingled and Blackie O'Neal entered, followed by that big brown hound.

Isaac glared at him. "What is it you want? The paper isn't open for business on Sunday morning."

He had a drink in one hand and he hesitated, looking sheepish. "Uh, I need to talk to Miss Durango."

Isaac resisted the urge to shout at the man, throw something at him. "Isn't it enough that you made a complete fool of her last night in front of half the town? You came over to rub it in, yes?"

Blackie hesitated. "I—I just need to talk to her, that's all. Would you call her down, please?"

"She told me last night she never wanted to see you again." Isaac glanced up at the clock. He only had to stall the gambler a little more than ten minutes and she would be safely on the train and gone forever out of Blackie's reach.

Isaac looked again at her last editorial which he was just getting ready to set in type. "You've won, isn't that enough? Why don't you just stay in your saloon and savor your victory?"

Blackie shook his head and Isaac had never seen such misery in a face. "Believe me, I never meant to embarrass her like that. I came to apologize and run a full page ad."

"What?"

Blackie nodded. "I can't stand to stay in town, see her every day and not have her, and I know after last night, she hates me. I've just sold the saloon to Moose, so the Black Garter is no more."

"This is ironic," Isaac said, "so much more than you know."

"I'm probably a fool, but I never meant to hurt her or humiliate her. That's why, tonight or tomorrow, I'll get out of town. And I want to run a full page ad explainin' to the citizens and see if I can save her reputation." He laid a handwritten sheet on the counter. "Now will you call her down?"

Isaac took the sheet slowly. It had obviously taken a lot of time and thought. There were words marked out, new sentences scribbled in. *Blackie would be leaving town tonight or tomorrow.* Lacey would be gone in another ten minutes. He had a sudden heady feeling that was almost godlike. Should he speak or remain silent? Certainly he loved her himself and Blackie O'Neal was not nearly good enough for his darling.

"How much for the ad?" Blackie reached in his pocket. Isaac told him as he started to read the ad:

To The Good People of Pretty Prairie. This is to apologize for compromising the honor of a very wonderful lady. I take full responsibility for getting her drunk and seducing this most innocent and beautiful girl. I wanted revenge for her waging war against my saloon, and maybe she was right. Maybe a fine town like Pretty Prairie doesn't need a place like the Black Garter which draws in the worst riffraff in the West. I set out to destroy her, and I did, but I take no pleasure in it. I am closing the saloon and leaving town. Soon it will be remodeled into an elegant hotel and tea room under a new owner. I hope my confession as a rotten blackguard will cause the town to reexamine their feelings and their own morals. None of us is perfect, including all the townsfolk. If people can only learn to be loving and forgiving, it will be a much better world to live in. I will never forgive myself for the trouble I have caused Lacey Durango, nor do I expect the town's forgiveness. I can only pray that you will forgive her this one small slip and keep her as the upstanding and wonderful member of this community she really is. Signed, Blackie O'Neal.

Isaac blinked to clear the mist in his eyes. "This is a mighty humble apology for a swaggering rogue like you."

"Maybe," Blackie admitted, "but lovin' Lacey has changed me. I'd like to ask her forgiveness before I leave town. Oh," he said, and pulled out some legal papers. "I'm givin' up my claim to that choice lot, and signin' it over to her. Maybe she can build a bigger newspaper on it."

Isaac glanced at the clock again. Less than ten minutes to get her out of Blackie's life forever. He thought about it a long moment, weighing his decision. Isaac cleared his throat. "I think there's something you'd better read." He handed Blackie Lacey's editorial.

"What—?" Blackie asked and then he began to read aloud:

> To The Fine People of Pretty Prairie: I owe you an apology for presenting myself as a perfect example and trying to force everyone else to live up to my impossible standards. You have all certainly heard by now of my fall from grace and many of you will be shocked that such a paragon of virtue should turn out to have feet of clay. I cannot tell you how sorry I am that I set myself up to be a perfect example and failed you. Perhaps there is a lesson in this for all of us to love people, faults and all, because no one is perfect. I will be resigning my post as editor of the *Crusader* and hope that eventually you can all find it in your hearts to forgive me for my misguided attempts at perfection and trying to dictate to other people. Best Always, Lacey Van Schuyler Durango.

There was a long moment of silence.

"Great God Almighty," Blackie whispered and blinked rapidly as if to clear his vision. "You've just got to let her know I'm here. I'll never forgive myself if I catch that train this afternoon and I haven't had a chance to apologize for what a rascal I've been."

Isaac looked at him and then up at the clock. Somewhere in the distance, he seemed to hear the whistle of the incoming train. He made his decision then because he also loved Lacey, and he realized these two flawed people loved each other and belonged together. "She's not here, she's catching the morning southbound train."

"What?"

"I've got a buggy out back," Isaac said. "Take it. With any luck, you can beat the train. I'll pick it up at the station later."

"Thanks, Isaac." He reached across the counter and patted the man's arm and then he looked into Isaac's eyes and saw the truth for the first time. "You love her, too."

Tears came to the little man's eyes. "She never saw it. If you tell her, I'll say you lied. Now get the hell out of here before you miss your train."

Blackie ran for the back door. He paused one second in the doorway. "Tell Moose to send my clothes and stuff, especially my paintin's and books—and ship the chestnut and the buckskin to my ranch."

"Your ranch?"

Blackie nodded. "You think all I ever wanted was to run a saloon? My biggest dream is to be a Texas rancher."

And then he was out the door and into the buggy, with Lively beside him on the seat. The whistle echoed from a mile away and Lively began to bark with excitement as Blackie snapped the reins at the startled horse and took off down the alley at a gallop. He passed a few people who turned and looked at him, but he offered no explanation, he only kept that buggy moving.

Up ahead lay the station. Even as he neared it, he saw Chief Thunder on the platform, making ready to sell buttons, and Reverend Lovejoy just getting out of his buggy with his little carpet bag.

Behind him, the train whistled again. Blackie glanced back over his shoulder. In the distance, he could see the big black locomotive billowing smoke as it slowed, coming into town. Blackie increased his speed and raced into the station, jumping down. He was panting and breathless as he ran up on the platform. Lacey Durango sat there, her shoulders bowed, looking at the ground with the cat cage on her lap. "Lacey!"

"What are you doing here?" She jumped up and put her cats on the bench. "Come to have one last laugh?"

"Lacey, there's too much to tell you, and I don't have much time. I only have to know one thing, do you care about me? Do you love me?"

"You lowdown skunk!" She looked at him in disbelief. What kind of grandstand stunt was this? There was hardly anyone to witness his making a fool of her so she could not understand his reasoning. The platform was deserted except for Chief Thunder setting up his Custer button display and Reverend Lovejoy arriving to make the journey to Sweetwater for the revival. "Why are you doing this? Haven't you caused me enough pain?"

"Damn it, I didn't ask you that, I only want to know if you love me?"

"This is outrageous. Go back to your saloon and your women." In the distance, she could see the train coming. If she could only withstand his charms five minutes more, she'd be safely away from this man who had broken her heart and brought her down.

"Well, I reckon I've got my answer then." He turned, shoulders slumped, to walk away. He paused once and glanced back. "I just wanted you to know, Lacey, that I love you. Now laugh if you want to." He started slowly toward the buggy, followed by his dog.

She stared at him, almost uncomprehending, and she had never seen such a beaten man. The train was roaring toward the station. In a few minutes she would be out of this town and away from this man, this flawed, imperfect man, forever. But she loved him. "Oh, Blackie, don't go!" The tears started and she couldn't hold them back. "I love you. I always will!"

For a split second, it seemed he almost could not believe her words. Then he whirled and ran toward her. Taking her in his arms, he kissed her and kissed her again as she clung to him. "Lacey, I'm not perfect. I'm as flawed as any man who ever lived, but I love you enough to try to improve."

"No one could ask for more," she wept, "if you don't mind an uppity girl whose pompousness is her worst fault."

He kissed her again, kissing her with a fire and passion

that made Lacey's knees weak. As the big black engine roared into the station, she returned his kiss with all the ardor that she had kept banked so long, waiting for the right man. Even Homer hadn't been the right man, she knew that now. He hadn't been a strong enough personality to deal with her.

The train was in the station now, blowing steam with the conductor stepping off, yelling "Pretty Prairie, Pretty Prairie. Five minutes, folks, we'll be here five minutes."

Blackie took her small face between his two big hands. "Will you marry me?"

With all the noise and confusion of the puffing train, perhaps she had misunderstood him. "What?"

He shouted at her. "Will you marry me?"

Maybe they were all wrong for each other, but her heart could not be denied. "Oh, yes, Blackie, oh, yes!"

He kissed her again. "I've got a ranch over near Amarillo I always planned to live on eventually. It's near the town of Muleshoe."

She wrinkled her nose. "Muleshoe? I think it might need to be renamed."

He groaned aloud and kissed the tip of her nose. "I'm sure you'll get that done."

"Does it have a newspaper?"

He shook his head. "I don't know. I don't think so."

"Pleasant View," she mused, "and how does the *Pleasant View News* sound?"

"First things first," Blackie grinned. "Let's get married and get on this train together." He turned and called to the preacher who was about to get on the train. "Reverend Lovejoy, can you marry us?"

"Here and now?"

"Certainly," Lacey said. "Oh, I don't have a ring, and there's no flowers."

Near them, Chief Thunder was selling buttons to eager tourists.

"Hey, Joe," Blackie yelled, "Come over and be a witness, and find the lady some flowers."

"Couldn't this wait?" The Indian said, "I've got some prime suckers, I mean, customers here."

"You can be best man," Blackie yelled.

"Done!" Chief Thunder hopped off the platform and began to pick the wild flowers growing along the tracks.

"I think we need two witnesses," Lacey said.

"I'll get one," Blackie grinned and ran over and grabbed the grizzled ticket agent out of the station. "Come on, we need you. And by the way, sell me a ticket."

"To where?"

Blackie looked toward Lacey and she smiled back, her heart too full to speak. "We're going to Dallas, then transferring to Amarillo. Final destination, Muleshoe, soon to be Pleasant View, if the little lady has anything to say about it, and I'm sure she has plenty."

"Hey," yelled the old conductor, "this train is ready to leave. You two going?"

"Give us a minute," Blackie ordered.

Curious passengers were gathering in the train's open windows, gaping at the small drama about to take place on the station platform.

"Honey," Blackie said, "I'm sorry I can't give you the perfect wedding."

"This is the perfect wedding," she answered, "even without the fancy dress and cake, because I'm marrying you."

He grinned at her. "Well, I ain't the perfect husband, I know, but I promise I'll love you 'til the day I die."

Chief Thunder wiped his eyes. "That's the sweetest thing I ever heard."

"All aboard!" yelled the conductor.

The Reverend Lovejoy looked pleased but rattled. "Dearly beloved—"

"Sorry, sir," Blackie said, "I don't think we've got time for all that."

"Okay, we'll do a hurry-up version. I hope the young lady doesn't mind."

She stood there holding an armful of bright wild flowers with a bored hound dog as her attendant and Chief Thunder and the ticket seller as witnesses, plus the gaping people on the train. She was almost too happy to speak. "I don't mind, as long as it's legal."

"Oh, it'll be legal, all right," the reverend assured her as he pushed his gold-rimmed glasses back up his thin nose. "Lacey Durango, do you take this man to be your husband, as long as you both shall live?"

"I sure do."

Cheers from the train.

"And do you, Blackie—don't you have a real name, son?"

Blackie hesitated. "Uh, Oscar. Oscar O'Neal."

Everyone on the train groaned.

"Well, Great God Almighty, I can't help it, why do you think I go by 'Blackie'?"

"All aboard!" shouted the conductor.

"Do you, Oscar O'Neal, take this woman to be your lawfully wedded wife as long as you both shall live?"

"I sure do. As long as I got a biscuit, she's got half!" A Texan couldn't make a deeper commitment than that.

The people on the train cheered and whistled.

"Good," said the preacher. "Is there a ring?"

"I never thought I would take this off, but for you, honey . . . " He took the diamond ring from his pinkie finger and slipped it on her left hand.

"A perfect fit." She looked down at it and then back up into his handsome, dear face.

"You may kiss the bride. I'll take care of the paper work later." the preacher said.

Blackie took her in his arms and kissed her. Boy, did Blackie kiss her until her knees went weak. The passengers on the train cheered.

"Last call!" The conductor stepped up on the coach as the engine began to puff and shudder. "Last call!"

"Thanks, Reverend." Blackie shoved a handful of bills in the man's hand.

"Oh, I can't accept—"

"Then give it to the church," Blackie said.

"But you've already been so generous in paying for the fancy new stained glass window."

Lacey blinked. "Then it was you who donated the window? And I was naive enough to think Eugene—"

Blackie shrugged. "I never meant for anyone to know. Anyway maybe it will make the Man Upstairs a little more forgivin' of my sins. Come on, the train is leavin'."

Indeed it was. The Reverend Lovejoy hopped aboard. Blackie swung Lacey up on the very back of the train as it pulled out, then grabbed up the luggage while Chief Thunder ran to put the cat cage aboard.

"Meow!" mewed the cats, "Meow!"

Blackie raced to jump up on the moving train and turned to yell at his dog, "Come on Lively, come on!"

For once, the lazy hound really came to life and ran to jump on the train's rear platform beside Lacey and Blackie.

"Hey," yelled the station ticket man, "I think there's a rule about pets—"

"Too late!" Blackie yelled back, "we're on our way! Hey, Joe, tell Flo and Cookie we'll be back for the weddin'. I promised to give the bride away."

"The *whole* Durango family will be back," Lacey yelled and Joe nodded and waved good-bye.

The newly married pair stood on the open platform at the back of the train as it pulled out, waving to Chief Thunder and the curious people who had gathered to watch. The dog pushed up next to her and barked.

"Mew!" complained the kittens.

"Meow!" said Precious.

"Honey," Blackie put his arm around Lacey, "those

cats will love it at the ranch." He pulled her to him and kissed her again. "Well, Mrs. O'Neal, it's a long way to Dallas, and I just paid for a private car."

"You think we can turn the cats loose in there?"

"I don't reckon Lively will mind." He took her arm and the cat cage, then they went back inside the coach. "I reckon there's a big, comfortable bed and a porter who'll bring room service."

She smiled up at him, her heart so full she could hardly speak. His diamond ring sparkled on her hand. In her other hand, she still clutched the bouquet of wild-flowers. "A perfect wedding because I married you. Mrs. Blackie O'Neal," she whispered. "Got a good sound to it."

"Doesn't it, though?" They walked to the door of the private car. He put down the cats and swung her up in his arms. "Reckon I'd better carry you over the thresh-old for good luck."

He carried her in, then went back for the yowling cats. Lively had followed them in and, lying down on the car-pet, promptly drifted off to sleep.

Blackie lay her on the bed and leaned over to kiss her. Then he closed and locked the door to the private car, and let the cats out of their cage. The train picked up speed, chugging away, the landscape rushing past. "I came close to missing this train."

"How'd you know——?"

He hesitated. "Isaac is a better man than you know. He told me where to find you. I think we'd better name our first son after him."

"Well, it's a good Biblical name."

Then he lay down beside her and kissed her again while she thought aloud. "Does that ranch house have a white picket fence?"

"It will have just as soon as I can put it up," he said.

There was a knock at the door. "Porter with a little refreshment, sir."

Blackie got up and started toward the door.

Behind him, she bristled. "Now, Blackie, you know how I feel about your constant drinking—"

"Oh, hush, honey." He grinned at her as he opened the door. The porter set the tray of sandwiches, delicate cream puffs, chocolates, and two tall, cold drinks on the table. He tipped the man and watched him leave, then he locked the door and turned back to her. "Here, my love, have a drink."

"But—"

He put the drink in her hand. "I love you, but you've got to stop bein' so judgmental. Taste it."

"What?"

"I said taste my favorite drink."

"You know how I feel about whiskey."

"Me, too."

"What?" She tasted the drink. Tasted it again. "Why, that's just—"

"Sweet iced tea," he nodded with a smile and picked up his glass. "The mother's milk of the South. Have a cookie and a sandwich."

She was thirsty and she gulped the drink. "You rascal, you let me think all these weeks—"

"You jumped to conclusions. By the way, save that cream puff for later. *I'm* your dessert."

She giggled like a school girl. They set the glasses down, and he reached for her.

The train was moving fast now, clickety-clack along the rails. The hound and the cats had settled down for a nap. Blackie kissed her again. "I'm glad it's a long way to Dallas," he murmured as he began to unbutton her dress.

"Me too, she said, "I think we're about to have a perfect journey."

"You think?" He kissed along her throat.

"I promise," she whispered, her eyes closed as she returned his kiss. "This will be the best trip ever."

And on that long, long train ride down to Texas, Lacey Van Schuyler Durango O'Neal made good that promise.

To My Readers

Yes, a lady reporter for the *Dallas Morning News* and the *Fort Worth Gazette,* Nanitta Daisey, really did ride a train's cowcatcher into my hometown during the Land Rush, hop off, and stake a claim. Edmond, Oklahoma, is in the process of building a monument to her on the outskirts of town. Pretty Prairie is of course, a fictitious town, but Guthrie and Purcell are not. Guthrie would become the territorial capital, but lost out to Oklahoma City as the state capital. Oklahoma became a state in 1907.

As far as the Land Runs: there would be five altogether. The April 1889 Run was just the first. It is ironic that the lawyer who first discovered that the almost two million acres in central Indian Territory were not assigned to any tribe was a Washington D.C.-based Cherokee, Elias C. Boudinot. This immediately started a clamor from white citizens, aided by powerful railroad interests, to open up the Unassigned Lands for settlement. Then they went after the Indian lands. The excuse was that some of the tribes had sided with the South during the Civil War and so deserved to lose their lands even though many of the Indians had fought for the Union cause. I've already written about the Civil War in Indian Territory in my last book, *To Tame a Rebel.*

There were probably at least three times the number of white hopefuls as there was free land. Claimed by cheaters, known as "sooners," who sneaked in early rather than waiting for the opening gun, many parcels of land were tied up in court for years. Finally, the government resorted to lotteries rather than runs to give away some of it. The final huge piece was sold to the highest bidder. If you would like to read more about the Land Run, I suggest this research book: *The Oklahoma Land Rush of 1889*, by Stan Hoig, published by the Oklahoma Historical Society. There have also been several movies about the land runs, including *Far and Away*, starring Tom Cruise, and at least one novel by a best-selling author: *Cimarron* by Edna Ferber. This novel also became a movie.

Some of you are going to be surprised to find out there's a swampy, almost impassable forest in southeastern Texas known as the Big Thicket. This still wild, primitive area is about forty miles long and twenty miles wide, just northwest of Beaumont, near the Louisiana line. If you go there, ask about the ghost light that hovers in the darkness near Bragg Road. There are a number of books about the Big Thicket. I suggest *Big Thicket Legacy* by Campbell and Lynn Loughmiller, and *Tales From the Big Thicket*, edited by Francis E. Abernethy, both books published by University of Texas Press, Austin, Texas.

Captain Arthur MacArthur was sent with his troops from Fort Leavenworth, Kansas, and headquartered in Guthrie to keep the peace during the 1889 Run. He had won a Medal of Honor during the Civil War and would become the father of General Douglas MacArthur, also a Medal of Honor winner. According to *The Medal, the Story of the Medal of Honor* by Frank Donovan, publisher, Dodd-Mead Co., these two are the only father and son winners of our nation's highest award for bravery.

The Potawatomi tribe is our country's ninth largest tribe with headquarters in Shawnee Potawatomie County, Oklahoma. The combined lands of the Iowa-Sac-Fox-Potawatomi-Shawnee tribes would be given away to white settlers in the September, 1891, land run. According to Muriel H. Wright's book, *A Guide to The Indian Tribes of Oklahoma,* published by University of Oklahoma Press, the name "Potawatomi" comes from the Chippewa and means: "people of the place of the fire." They are closely related to the Chippewa and Ottawa and were originally located near the Great Lakes. Today, the Citizen's Band of Potawatomi live in Oklahoma while a smaller group, the Prairie Band, live in Kansas. Because of their tribal casinos, the Potawatomi are fairly successful.

Where did I get the idea to have Joe Toadfrog (Chief Thunder) selling buttons? Geronimo, the fierce Apache leader, was relocated to Fort Sill, Oklahoma. He became a celebrity, riding in parades with notables such as President Teddy Roosevelt. The savvy Apache created a good income for himself by selling buttons off his coat to naive tourists.

If you have read my previous books, you know they all connect in some manner. Lacey and her twin sister, Lark, are the children of Summer Van Schuyler and the Cheyenne warrior, Iron Knife. You met this couple in both *Cheyenne Captive* and *Cheyenne Splendor.* You met the Durango ranching family in *Cheyenne Princess* and *To Tame A Texan.* For those of you who have missed some of my long saga, you may wish to visit Kensington's web site: www.kensingtonbooks.com.

So what story will I tell next? Lark's story is another lighthearted romantic romp about two Texans. This tale will begin in the wild, so-called whiskey towns along the Oklahoma Territory/Indian Territory border, and then move to Texas. Even most native Oklahomans don't know about the "whiskey towns," but let me assure you, they were the toughest, most lawless towns in the whole West. Renegades sold illegal liquor to the Indians. The roughest white outlaws hung out along this border.

Lark Van Schuyler Durango is the exact opposite of

her prim, prissy twin sister, Lacey. Lark is a Texas tomboy who can shoot, ride, and rope as well as any cowpuncher. She's gotten herself inadvertently mixed up in a bank robbery because of a handsome Texas cowboy, Larado, and she's now on the run, as is he. Desperate, she answers a newspaper ad for a mail order bride for the new sheriff of Rusty Spur, Texas, figuring that as the wife of a respectable lawman, she'll be safe. If all else fails, she'll pass herself off as her twin sister, Lacey.

Enter the tall, virile sheriff of Rusty Spur—Lawrence Witherspoon. At least that's what he's calling himself now. Reckon you can guess who he really is: Larado. Uh-oh. Dark and charming, the mixed-blood Comanche Larado is passing himself off as his law-abiding twin brother. Except he has no brother.

In the old West, they called this a "Mexican standoff." Neither Lark nor Larado can tell on the other without implicating themselves. What a humorous mess this mail-order marriage is going to be. Mix in Snake Hudson and Dixie from the story you just read, a funny little donkey named Magnolia, and three bumbling, bank-robbing brothers, Lem, Clem, and Slim, who would make the Three Stooges look brilliant, and you've got the ingredients for my next lighthearted Texas romance. Join me in a few months as I tell Lark's story. Title and date of publication still to be announced.

I'm always happy to hear from readers. Write me at: Box 162, Edmond, OK 73083-0162. If you'd like a reply and an autographed bookmark, please include a stamped, self-addressed #10 envelope. Foreign readers should obtain postal vouchers at your post office that I can exchange for stamps since I cannot use your foreign postage. Yes, for those of you with computers and Internet access, I do have a web site: www.nettrends.com/georginagentry.

Long As I Got a Biscuit . . .
Georgina Gentry

Discover the Romances of
Hannah Howell